~ ∞ ~

*for my high school self*

*and all who supported me despite the fact*
*I almost certainly ignored them while writing it*

~ ∞ ~

# Books by S.K. Kelley

**Sidetracked**
(Part 1)

**Borderline**
(Part 2)

**Afterglow**
(Part 3)

**COMING SOON**

**Resignation**
(Part 4)

Follow S.K. Kelley on Bluesky or Twitter @skkelleywrites
or visit skkelleyauthor.square.site for updates!

# sidetracked

## part 1

s.k. kelley

Adapted Edition: February 2024

Library of Congress Control Number: 2021914162
ISBN: 978-1-955240-01-7
(digital ebook): 978-1-955240-13-0
Published by Bleeding Heart Books
skkelleyauthor.square.site

Sidetracked is a four-part new adult contemporary fantasy psychological drama series with slice of life, romance, and thriller elements

**A CONTENT WARNING IS AVAILABLE IN THE BACK OF THE BOOK ON PAGE 537**

# one

Rose yawns, the sound loud and exaggerated. I look up from my notebook as she stretches in her oversized beanbag chair and raises her textbook far above her head.

"Jayde," she groans as her hands return to her lap. "I seriously can't take this anymore. Why did we leave the party, again?"

"I already told you. Finals are next week, and I'm pretty sure you still have a C in pharmacology."

Her eyes narrow. "Oh, come on. I need to stretch my legs for a minute. Let's go downstairs and order pizza or something. Also, Netflix just got the new season of Night Hospital, and I am dying to watch it."

*I can't imagine we'll get any work done, but—*

I sigh. "Fine. We can move downstairs."

Books in hand, I follow her to the living room. She drops her textbook on the couch and takes her phone from her pocket while I organize my things and set them on the other side.

Taking a break doesn't sound too bad. At least I don't have to feel guilty about it since I'm not in danger of failing.

My eyes wander to the window beside the door. Rose's dark

coupe is parked out front, and the parking lot stretches beyond. The sky is a clear blue. This morning's Memorial Day barbecue wore me out, but it is a lovely day.

She said something similar this morning—about what a perfect day it is and how we shouldn't waste it inside—before suggesting we attend a classmate's house party.

The party was fine.

I enjoyed eating copious amounts of watermelon and listening to music, but the party was hosted in a stranger's backyard in a questionable part of town, and I only knew a few people there. Plus, I watched Rose break up with her...*boyfriend? Friend with benefits?* Both his name and previous label elude me. Either way, it was awkward, and I do not regret making a deal to leave early.

Stepping closer to the window, I draw the blinds the rest of the way open. Warmth pours into the room through the glass. The pizza won't be here for a while, but it's still early. I can finish my assignment later.

"I think I'll head out for a minute. For a walk."

"A minute?" Rose asks. "If you're not back when the pizza shows up, I'm not waiting for you."

"Uh-huh..." I laugh as I search the bookcase for the hair tie I'm certain I left there a couple days ago.

"I'm serious this time," she says, not sounding very serious.

*Found it.*

While I comb my fingers through my hair, Rose asks if I'm okay with pepperoni and sausage. She knows I am, but she always asks. Then I pull my long hair into a bun and step out onto the concrete landing. The sun shines directly into my eyes. I shield my face with one hand.

"I'll be home in twenty minutes."

She calls back agreeably, so I close the door and make my way down the steps. I circle behind the house and through the expanse of short grass between the crescent-shaped complex of small, angular cottages and Windsor Park Natural Area until I reach a split in the trees—the start of a trail I've walked dozens of times before.

The shade is comfortable, a respite from the heat. The shadows of the leafy canopy mottle the trail with an ever-changing pattern as the branches shift in the slight breeze. Civilization isn't far away, but bird songs and rustling leaves mask the sound of the city beyond the trees.

I savor the earthy scent of nature. The packed dirt trail beneath my feet. The still-green grass, dotted with spring flowers. The cedars among the oaks and willows. A light rain might improve the experience, but we shouldn't see rain for months. Spring ends in a few weeks, and summers in Riverview are near bone-dry.

*Plus, California is in the middle of a drought.*

This is nice, though. I needed some time alone after spending half the day at that party.

When I reach the nature pond in the center of the park, I stop beside a bench and watch the ducks swim. Someone on the far side tosses breadcrumbs into the green water, sending the ducks into a frenzy as they rush to be the first to eat.

*They're so cute. I should have brought bread.*

My phone vibrates in my pocket. A text from Rose.

**Rose:** Pizza is otw! Hurry back.

**Me:** Okay, heading back now!

I start down a second trail that loops back to the cottages. I keep a decent pace, but I took my time on the walk in, and this trail is longer than the first. The sky slowly darkens overhead. The shadows grow long. The air cools several degrees.

Half-jogging, I manage to make it home before dark.

Rose greets me, standing in the doorway. "You're late," she says. "Pizza showed up ten minutes ago."

I stop to catch my breath at the bottom of the stairs. When I look up again, her hands are planted on her hips, but she's grinning.

"I thought you weren't gonna wait for me."

"And I thought you were only gonna take twenty minutes."

"Sorry. I got distracted by the ducks."

She rolls her eyes. "Of course you did."

With a laugh, I join her on the landing, and she tells me about a private conversation she overheard at the party. She's halfway through a sentence when she glances aside and points past me.

"Hey, behind you."

I glance over my shoulder.

*Oh. The sky.*

The horizon is awash with color. Vivid, painterly pinks and oranges melt into the deep violet and navy of the sky far above my head. The color shifts, darkening as the sun dips further behind the hills in the distance. Something about watching the sunset always makes me feel more grounded.

"Neat," Rose says, enunciating the *t*.

We watch the horizon a moment longer. Then I mention the pizza, and we turn toward the door. My hand touches the doorknob when I hear a soft rustling off to my right. It's not uncommon for small animals to hang around in the evening, considering the nature park a hundred feet away, but I drop my hand and turn to look out of curiosity.

"Did you hear that?" I ask.

A flowering shrub along the wall of the neighboring cottage shifts as something moves within. A pair of round eyes sit near the ground, the owner of which is hidden deep inside the bush. They vanish for a moment. Then flash green in the low evening light.

The reflective eyes of a cat.

*Weird*. I've never seen a cat around here before.

"Do the neighbors have a secret cat or something?" I ask.

"Not that I know of," Rose says. "A girl a few doors down the other side has an ESA, but they're not allowed outside, and the landlord is strict as hell about the pet policy." After a pause, she laughs. "Whoever owns it isn't doing a great job of keeping it a secret, though."

I frown. "Do you think it's a stray?"

"It's a cat, Jayde. Come on, let's go inside."

She walks past me and into the house. The eyes in the bush blink again, but I leave it alone and follow Rose inside.

# two

Maybe if I bothered to make friends in class, I'd have study buddies too. I could have asked to tag along with Rose and her friend—they would have happily agreed, I'm sure—but they're studying for a nursing class. We'd only distract each other. But it's fine.

*That's another chapter done.*

Even if studying alone is boring, I'm more productive this way.

I close my laptop and glance out the window behind the desk. Yet again, it's a perfect, warm, blue sky day. Finals are important, but I've done enough for now. I need to do something else.

*My birthday is tomorrow, so maybe...*

Well, I still don't know what I'm doing about that either.

As my gaze falls from the clear sky, a white cat slinks out of the trees behind the neighboring cottage. It paces further out into the short grass, sits in the sun, and curls a fluffy tail over its paws.

If this is the same cat we saw the other day, I don't think it's a stray. The cat's long, white fur is smooth and immaculate, free from any dirt or mats. Rose was right, though—if a neighbor is trying to hide it, they're doing an awful job.

The cat stares up in my general direction with unblinking eyes, like it can see me through the window.

Are white cats good omens? Does seeing one mean I'll have a decent birthday? *I can hope, right?*

The cat looks away.

I lose interest and head downstairs, where I eat a cold toaster pastry and peek around the cupboards. It seems we're running low on snacks. And bread.

We'll need snacks—and bread—to survive finals week.

I guess that's something to do. Grocery shopping isn't the most exciting, but Computer Science is even less fun. A quick trip to Bargain Shop is an excuse to take a break and get out of the house, anyway.

After a stop in the half-bath washroom to put on mascara, I stuff a cloth grocery bag into my purse and head out.

*The cat is still here.*

Only, now, it sits on the curb halfway between my cottage and the one it first crawled out from behind. The cat's ears twitch, and it glances over to watch me with shockingly blue eyes as I walk down the concrete steps.

I don't see a collar.

Does it not belong to my neighbor? Did it escape from somewhere else? Is it lost? Should I help, or do…something?

I look around to ensure I'm alone. Then I crouch low to the ground and smile at the cat, which continues watching me with some reservation. I hold out a hand and call it over.

The cat regards me with classic feline indifference and does not move.

"Here, kitty kitty," I say with a more exaggerated sweet lilt.

The cat stares at me. It acknowledges my presence with a slow blink of sapphire eyes but remains sitting a couple feet away.

If I stay too long, I risk missing the bus, but I really want to pet this cat. I try again, this time clicking my tongue and rubbing my fingers together to coax it toward me.

I wait a few seconds. Twenty seconds.

The cat is clearly not enticed by my attempts to gain its trust.

"No?" I ask, withdrawing my hand. "Nothing?"

The cat's whiskers twitch, and it turns to look at the trees.

*Yeah, I think that's a no.*

Our eyes meet again, but the cat stands and saunters away, dipping into the hedge bordering my neighbor's cottage.

With a sigh, I pick myself up off the ground and hurry toward the bus stop. I beat the bus there, but I find myself second-guessing if the white cat was a good omen.

* * * * *

Of course, the cookies I want are out of stock.

I spot a few packages at the top of the shelving unit with the rest of the overstock, but I can't quite reach them. I'm too short. Stepping onto the bottom shelf might give me the boost I need. With my luck, though, I'd get caught and embarrass myself. Or fall and die.

*Ugh...* I want those cookies.

I'm about to step up onto the edge when my thoughts are interrupted by a smooth, masculine voice.

"Excuse me," it says. "Do you need any help?"

My hand freezes, still outstretched toward the overstock shelf. Then I drop my arm and turn to acknowledge the person who addressed me, only to freeze a second time.

The voice belongs to the most attractive man I have ever met.

He's tall. Wavy, straw-blond hair falls over the tops of his ears, framing a chiseled, clean-shaven face. Casual, well-fitted clothing compliments his lean, athletic build, and he holds himself with a certain confidence most could only dream of achieving. He is beautiful in all regards, like a flawless, marble statue or a male model from a fashion magazine, but his eyes are the most striking. A vibrant blue, bright and dazzling.

Now that I've looked into them, I can't seem to look away.

He smiles, and the soft, pleasant expression leaves me speechless for some god-awful reason. I manage to force a smile in return, confident only that I look like an idiot.

This guy is hot—lightyears out of my league. *Lightyears.* Hell, he's probably out of Rose's league. *So why is he talking to me?*

He studies me for a few seconds. Then he clears his throat and, with a graceful sweep of his hand, redirects my attention aside.

"What were you after?" he asks.

*What was I doing?*

I tear my eyes from his face. Various brands of packaged snack cookies fill the metal shelving from top to bottom—save for the empty space where the cookies I want should be.

*Ah. Right.*

"The M&M cookies," I mumble. "The soft ones. Um… I think I saw a few near the top."

"Just one?"

I nod, but this might be more embarrassing than trying to scale the grocery store shelving would have been.

The man retrieves a package, easily reaching the overstock shelf, and offers it to me. I stare at the bright red plastic in his hand—which is also beautiful in a way.

*Jayde. Stop thinking this instant.*

I fake a cough and accept the cookies, careful to avoid any and all physical contact with him. I escape unscathed and drop the box into my shopping basket.

Then, in a desperate attempt to be less awkward, I glance up from my hands and make eye contact again. It doesn't help. He's just as gorgeous as he was thirty seconds ago. And I'm just as hopeless.

"Thank you," I say, dragging out the last syllable.

*What am I doing? Trying to prolong the conversation? Why? What do I hope to gain from any of this?*

But he smiles, and it's worth it.

"You're welcome," he says. "The name's Ice. Ice Monroe."

"Ice? Seriously?"

*Oh, no!*

The words slipped out before I could stop them. I sound like a total ass. I wouldn't blame him if he hated me, but he *laughs*.

"Yes, seriously," he says, still smiling. "My name is rather unusual, but I've learned to live with it. I suppose it fits me well enough."

"In what way?" I ask.

I'm not curious at all. I do not care what his name is or how well it suits him or why he thinks it does. His voice is smooth and sweet, drawing me in despite the mundane topic. I just want him to keep talking.

"Something about my eyes." His tone is mild until he clears his throat. "In any case, now that you know who I am, who might you be?"

I blink up at him—at this beautiful man who has no business speaking with me—and faint memories of elementary school lectures on stranger danger come to mind. Grainy video clips of older men smiling and acting friendly to lure naive children away from the safety of the playground. But I am not in elementary school, nor am I a naive child with no knowledge of the world and its dangers.

I am an adult person. I can make my own decisions. And Ice strikes me as normal and safe.

*Unnaturally hot, sure, but totally normal and safe.*

Besides, Rose would kill me if she found out I gave up the chance to talk to a guy like this. I'm usually the cautious type. The nervous type. The type to chicken out and run away rather than risk an awkward encounter, but she told me that over-thinking things only makes matters worse. She says I need to ease up. Relax. Dive in and take initiative.

Now is as good a time as any to take her advice seriously.

*What's the worst that can happen?*

I tuck a stray lock of hair behind my ear and feign confidence. "My name is Jayde."

"Jayde," he echoes. "A lovely name. Like the gemstone?"

He smiles, and the unexpected compliment gives me a rush

of real confidence.

Unfortunately, I do not know what to do with confidence.

I just start *talking*. I thank him and ramble on about *my* eyes being green and how my name *is* like the gemstone, only spelled with a *Y* before the *D*. It's stupid, pointless information, and I'm only making myself out to be more awkward by saying it, but I can't stop.

"People get it wrong all the time," I say, "so it's kind of annoying having it spelled differently, you know?"

My brain does me a favor by losing its train of thought there. I'm smiling, and he doesn't appear particularly fazed by my babbling, but anxiety flutters in my chest as I stare into his patient blue eyes.

"Understandable," he agrees. "I'm sure you can imagine the reactions some have when they first hear my name."

*Ha... Like my reaction?*

I avert my eyes.

"I'm curious," he says. "How old are you?"

"Me?"

I laugh, trying to calm my nerves as our eyes meet again. The question is innocent enough—he probably wants to make sure I'm not sixteen or whatever—but, of course, he had to ask.

"Believe it or not, it's my birthday tomorrow. I'll be turning nineteen."

His smile hitches up on one side. "What are the odds? Well, happy birthday, I suppose."

*Ugh...*

I suck it up and thank him.

He tells me he's twenty-two. His birthday was in April.

That's younger than I thought, but he's still a few years older than me. It's not weird for a nineteen-year-old to talk to a twenty-two-year-old, is it? *For god's sake, Jayde...* You talk to people that age all the time at RCC. What exactly are you expecting to get out of this conversation? *Ugh.*

Ice slips a phone from his back pocket. My heart jumps into my throat. *Is he losing interest? What should I do?* I panic and blurt out the first thing that comes to mind:

"So, what are you doing here today?"

His eyes, still focused on his phone screen, grow wide. Then he looks up in a slow, deliberate fashion. As our eyes meet, his smile stretches, crinkling the corners of his eyes like I said something especially funny.

"I'm shopping," he says. "What are you doing here?"

*Oh my god.*

My shoulders tense. I tear my eyes from his face to stare at my hands. *Did I seriously ask what he was doing in a grocery store?* I am holding a shopping basket myself. It's been right there—the handle in the crook of my left arm—this entire time.

Well, I guess that makes two horrifically embarrassing things I've done in front of the hottest guy I've ever met. Could today get any worse?

He laughs it off. "Actually, I was hoping I could get your phone number."

*Haha... Seems I spoke too soon.*

There's no point in trying to hide what a mess I am. For now, all I can do is avoid eye contact and hope for the best.

"Oh. Sure," I mumble.

*He's messing with me. He can't be serious.*

I try to get a read on him out of the corner of my eye. To my surprise, both his thoughtful expression and casual posture as he fiddles with his phone seem sincere enough. He types something out—my name, I assume—and looks up with a half-smile.

"What's the number?"

*Well, I guess this is happening.*

I manage to recite my phone number without mixing up the digits. He repeats it aloud, and I nod to confirm he has it right.

"Thanks." He flashes a brilliant smile. "Perhaps I'll call you sometime."

"Oh, ah—" A shiver runs up my spine, and I go off again. "You can call whenever you like. You can text too—but you don't have to, you know? I'm pretty busy with finals and everything. So it's cool either way."

I am an idiot. A deer in the headlights. If Ice were an oncoming car, I would be roadkill. At least the store isn't crowded. I'd hate for anyone else to be subjected to this train wreck.

*Could I have left a worse first impression?*

But he chuckles, still not bothered. And I finally shut up.

"I'll see you around," he says.

I blink. "Okay. See you."

He dips his head and turns to leave. I muster what little courage remains within me and call after him to thank him once again for the help.

"Anytime, Jayde," he says. "Enjoy your cookies."

He doesn't pause or glance over his shoulder, but he does

raise a hand to wave casually as he continues down the aisle. I watch his back until he turns a corner and disappears from view.

My grip tightens on the handle of the shopping basket, and my eyes wander down, landing on the brightly colored package of M&M cookies on top.

*Ice Monroe, huh?*

* * * * *

Helping me was a nice gesture and all, but I don't understand why he didn't just accept my thanks and move on with his day. Why stick around to talk for so long? Why ask for my number? I was so hopelessly awkward, but he didn't acknowledge it once.

What if he only stopped to talk because he felt sorry for me? I don't want anyone's pity—let alone pity from someone like that. Or maybe he was teasing me. Maybe he asked for my phone number, so he can prank me tomorrow.

*Oh, no…*

I hope he doesn't call—on my birthday or any other day. After all, if he does, and it's not a prank, how would I ever make up for how weird I acted earlier?

I pat my cheeks. They're still warm to the touch, and I've been safe at home for over an hour.

Rose will be back soon.

I almost don't want to tell her, but, on the off chance he does call and isn't trolling me, she will never believe we met at the *grocery store* if I don't mention it now. Maybe I just won't give her his name. Ice is easily the fakest sounding name I've ever heard.

I stop pacing to pull the blinds over the window aside. Rose's parking space is still empty. The sidewalk is empty. The white cat wasn't around when I got home either.

*Was it a good omen or not?*

Do I even believe in anything like omens or fate? If I did, I'd have to accept that I'm cursed, so…

*It's probably better if I don't.*

When Rose returns, she immediately groans and flops onto the couch. It's quite dramatic, but she does look drained as she gazes up at the ceiling with narrowed eyes. I guess she actually studied.

"I have the worst memory when it comes to anatomy," she says. "There are too many things stuffed inside the human body."

I offer to go over flashcards with her later. She accepts with a begrudging sigh and asks if I want help studying for any of my finals, but I'm fine. I only have three in-class exams this term, and I've studied more than enough already. I'm not worried.

She sighs and flips her ponytail over one shoulder. "Anyway, how was your afternoon?"

My heart skips a beat.

"Oh. Uh. I went shopping."

"What'd you buy?" she asks, her curiosity calling her into the kitchen.

"Not much. Snacks, mostly. And more milk."

She spots the open package of M&M cookies on the counter. I stress-ate a few when I got home and forgot to put them away. Apparently.

“Nice,” she says, helping herself to a cookie.

“And I met a guy.”

She turns, the cookie sticking out of her mouth as she judges me. Eyes wide. Skeptical. Surprised. Impressed. Then she removes the cookie, a bite missing, and smirks.

“A guy?” she echoes. “Do tell.”

I briefly summarize the encounter from *excuse me* to reciting my phone number with intentional vagueness. Then I describe his appearance. His blue eyes and perfect smile. But I underplay how goddamn tense and weird I was, and I do not mention his name.

“And you’re sure you weren’t hallucinating?” she asks, one eyebrow raised.

I laugh. “He was real, but I don’t know what to think. I have this weird feeling he was teasing me or something. He just smiled whenever I said something stupid, and I said a lot of stupid things, so…”

“Hm… How tall would you say he was?”

I hold my hand a ways above my head. He was nearly a foot taller than me, so at least six feet.

She blinks before grinning, the expression playful but ruthless. “Well, Jayde, if he does call, and you aren’t interested, feel free to give him my number.”

*I never said I wasn’t interested!*

But I don’t argue. She’s only teasing, trying to reassure me in her own way.

“Really? Normally you’d be dying to set me up with him.”

She nods. “I mean, it is sad that I’m your only real friend. So, of course, I fully support your pursuit of hot grocery store man.”

"Hot grocery store man?" I ask, fighting laughter.

"You didn't catch his name, right? So that's his name now." She drapes herself over the arm of the couch and presses the back of her hand to her forehead. "Dear Hot Grocery Store Man, why didn't you give Jayde your phone number, so I could hook you up myself?"

I toss a throw blanket over her head. "I don't need a boyfriend. Is it so wrong that I want to relax this summer?"

She flails around until she ends up on the other side of the couch and pops out from underneath the thin blanket.

"You worked so hard this year," she reasons, though her frown is fake. "You can date and still relax—hell, it might even help. But don't forget I'm leaving on Friday. My family reunion is on the Fourth, and I want to help Sara as much as I can, so I'm not exactly sure when I'll come back."

"I know. We've gone over it a million times already."

"What will you do if he does call?" she asks.

"Answer the phone."

"Ugh!" She drags her hands down her face. "I mean, would you go out with him if he asked?"

I sigh. "Rose. I asked him why he was at the grocery store. He may have asked for my number, but he is not going to call me."

A slow, incredulous smile splits her face. Then she drops her head into her hands like she's about to weep. Her shoulders shake. Stifled laughter escapes her throat.

"Oh my god," she wheezes. "That is so adorably stupid, Jayde. Any guy would be lucky to have you."

# three

Finals are over.

I step out of the car, and I'm home, and I'm free. Rose walks ahead with a skip in her step. She tosses her purse over the back of the couch as I follow her inside, leaving the door open.

Turning, she smiles and clasps her hands together. "So, how's it feel to be done with your first year of college?"

"It's community college, Rose. We're not going to Stanford or anything."

She laughs. "Not everyone is as dedicated as you. School is a real challenge for some of us, you know?"

"Oh? How did you do on your anatomy final?"

"Fine," she says pointedly. "Glad it's over."

I sigh. "What will I do with myself while you're gone?"

"Let's see…" She feigns thoughtfulness, pursing her lips as she takes a few slow, backward steps toward her bedroom door. Then she stops, snaps her fingers, and flashes an impish grin. "Oh, I know! Maybe that guy will finally call."

"What?" I ask in alarm.

She's made no mention of Ice—or Hot Grocery Store Man, I guess—since my birthday. Of course, he hasn't called, though.

My mother didn't even call on my birthday, and I'm still a little upset. *About both things.*

"Hey, you never know," she says. "Maybe you could get a boyfriend to keep you company."

*Ugh...*

She laughs at whatever face I pulled, and I close the front door—slamming it by accident. Ice is a lost cause. *Assuming Ice is his real name.*

"I don't need a boyfriend. I'm fine."

"Whatever you say, Jay. Don't forget—anything is possible."

I laugh. I don't know why.

She grins again and shuts herself into her room.

My bag's strap slips a few inches down my arm. I fix it with a sigh and head upstairs to my bedroom. I drop my backpack just inside. Then I sit on the edge of my bed and look around.

The calendar on the door. The collage of photos framing the mirror behind my dresser. An open textbook on my desk. The blue sky visible through the partially drawn blinds.

It's quiet. I don't have homework or anything to study, so I'm not sure what to do. Summer vacation is already throwing off my routine. No class. No assignments. No best friend for half of it.

*Oh, Rose...*

She knows I wanted him to call, but she also knows I haven't seriously dated since high school. A summer fling sounds sweet and fun in theory, but I've never understood her obsession with dating—casual or otherwise.

My current relationship status shouldn't matter to her, anyway.

She's leaving tomorrow. She'll be in Arizona with her family, so she won't be around to hook me up with anyone, and there's only so much she can do over the phone.

Two months is a long time, though. I've never lived alone. It's only temporary, and I know it'll be fine, but the concept is rather daunting. It sounds a little lonely. A little quiet. And I'll have to take care of everything on my own.

*Oh, the responsibility!*

It's kind of funny, but thinking of Rose's family reminds me of my family, and… *The birthday cards, and…* I fall back onto my bed and stare at the white, plaster ceiling.

Part of me wants to accept her offer to tag along and spend the summer in Arizona, but I meant what I said. Someone has to stay and look after the house. Besides, it's been far too long since I've had time to myself to relax without the stress of a busy college term and everything that comes with it.

I'm not like Rose. She's a textbook extrovert, always on the go, flitting from one group of friends to the next without losing momentum. She loves people and parties. She's social and upbeat, like a light that brightens everyone around her.

I like people, and I like spending time with people too, but not *that* much. It's hard to believe she was shy and soft-spoken in middle school. Unlike her, I never grew out of that awkward stage. Social interaction is still trying, and I don't understand the appeal of parties, alcohol, or hook-up culture.

She has fun, though. I guess that's all that matters.

I look up from my phone—I'm not sure when it ended up in my hand. My gaze lands on a weird spackling of plaster on the ceiling that vaguely resembles a face with googly eyes.

*How have I never noticed that before?*

Glancing away, I roll onto my stomach.

I'm tempted to try looking Ice up again despite my previous lack of luck, but I scroll down my FaceSpace newsfeed instead. I don't pay much attention to the names, but it seems like every other post is either a meme or something about summer break. The FaceSpace crowd seems to have it all figured out, but what should I do?

I'm stuck at the unfortunate age where I'm too old for the usual teen hangouts but still too young to visit real clubs or attend many of the local summer events. I can't drive, I don't have a lot of money, and most of my friends—or Rose's friends—are either traveling or working over the summer. I'd rather not hang out with them without Rose as a buffer, anyway.

There's always Music@ThePark. If I go, it'll get me out of the house once a week, but it doesn't start until the end of the month.

*Hm…* I could look for a summer job. Is CoffeeStar hiring?

I open the internet browser, but a series of knocks interrupt my search before it begins. I sit up to address the violation of privacy as the culprit opens the door.

Rose stands in the doorway, one hand on the doorjamb and the other on her hip. "What's up with that sad look? I haven't left yet."

"Oh? No, I'm fine."

She reacts with exaggerated skepticism, frowning and quirking an eyebrow.

I laugh. "When are you leaving, again?"

"Like nine in the morning?" She shrugs, and then grins, leaning further into my room. "Anyway, I was thinking we should order pizza and have a sleepover downstairs."

"That's kind of weird, but okay."

Her arms fall to her sides, and she steps back, her expression mellowing. "I'll be gone for a while, you know? I thought it'd be fun to spend some time together before I go—just you and me. Like old times."

"No, it does sound fun. I'll find something to watch if you order pizza."

She flashes a thumbs-up and a classic Rose grin, and we walk to the living room together.

With the couch pushed against the wall to free up space, and sleeping bags laid out on the floor in front of the TV, our pretend sleepover reminds me of the ones we had often during middle school. The setup is rather authentic—complete with delivery pizza, microwave kettle corn, and a lineup of cheesy horror movies and even cheesier romcoms in the queue.

I didn't even realize I missed doing lame stuff like this.

We sit on the floor in fuzzy pajamas and more or less ignore the movie, opting to play card games instead. We talk and laugh about everything and anything. Memories from high school. Complaints about finals and classes at RCC. It's fun.

Then Rose changes the subject. She starts talking about the guy she went to the Memorial Day barbecue with. They weren't really dating, I guess, but she still broke things off with him. She laments how hard it is to find decent guys in Riverview. There are plenty of hot guys, I guess, but they never give anyone the time of day.

"Well, who's your dream guy?" I ask.

She looks up from the cards in her hand. "Like my favorite celebrity?"

I laugh. "No. I already know that. Just describe your ideal guy—like the perfect boyfriend."

"Oh! I see what you mean," she says, returning her attention to the game to play a card. "My ideal guy would be tall, hot, and athletic. Good teeth. Fashionable. Clean. Bonus points if he's blond—I look good with blonds."

"Because you're blonde too?"

She smirks but says nothing.

I assess my cards and set one on the pile on the floor between us. Rose throws down another. She holds two cards while I'm forced to draw two more. Now stuck with eight cards, I'm losing miserably.

"You know, my dream guy is basically your Hot Grocery Store Man," she says mildly. When I fail to suppress my grimace, she laughs again. "Sorry, but it's true. Anyway, what kind of guy would my sweet, innocent Jayde go for? The Hot Grocery Store Man type, or…?"

We glance up from our hands at the same time.

I don't often fantasize about the opposite sex, and she knows it. But she also knows I've had this guy on my mind since I met him. Does she expect me to own up to it? Because, to be honest, Ice was intimidatingly attractive, and I'm not sure I could handle a long-term relationship.

*What type of person would I want to date, though?*

“I don’t know,” I say carefully. “I’d like a nice guy, I guess. Someone who is fun to be with but honestly cares about me too. I want to mean something to him, you know?”

“You’re no fun,” she pouts. “You know what I meant.”

“Hot Grocery Store Man is hot and all, but looks are a bonus.”

She rolls her eyes and drops her second-to-last card on top of the pile. “Uno!”

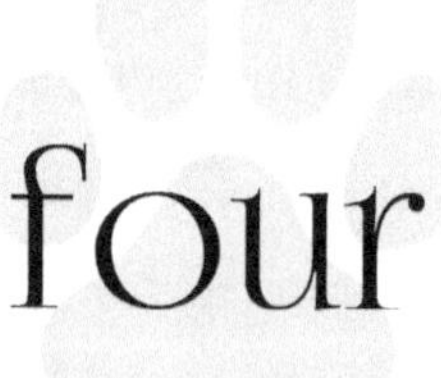

# four

Rose wakes me up in a panic over being "late."

I remove the blanket she tossed on my head and watch as she stumbles into her bedroom. The door smacks against the rubber doorstop and bounces back but doesn't close completely.

"Kyle called two hours ago, wondering where I was," she says from inside. "I'm surprised he's not knocking on the door right now."

"Did you tell him we stayed up late?"

I check my phone. It's 10:13AM.

She groans. "I did, but it's a fifteen-hour drive even if we don't stop. And we'll have to stop. Ugh! I should have agreed to take his car. Mom will lose it if we have to stay the night in a creepy motel in the middle of nowhere again."

The living room is littered with pillows and blankets and food packaging. I pick up an empty popcorn bag and stuff a few random bits of trash into it.

"It's fine. It won't kill me to clean without you."

She pops her head out of the doorway to thank me with an apologetic smile before she shuts herself inside her room. The living room isn't a complete disaster, anyway. If I don't put it off, it'll only take a few minutes to get everything where it belongs.

*Of course, I was right.*

As I fold the last throw blanket, Rose darts out of her room with a large suitcase and duffel bag. She leaves her luggage near the door and spins to face me. I set the blanket on the back of the couch.

Then her hands land on her hips, and she frowns. "Well, I hope you manage to have some fun without me."

"I'm sure I'll have an awful time," I say.

She drops the fake frown, closes the distance between us, and wraps her arms around me. A wave of blonde hair tickles my nose. I laugh and pat her on the shoulder.

"Nah, you'll be fine," she says as she breaks away. "Don't let me forget to pick up a couple souvenirs while I'm gone, though."

I must have two dozen random knick-knacks and touristy t-shirts by now—at least one for every vacation she's gone on in the past four or five years. They decorate my desk and dresser, and several made it onto a shelf by the staircase. I love them, but I'm running out of places to put them.

"Something from the Grand Canyon this time?" she asks.

"Sounds good. I don't think I have anything from there yet."

With a laugh, she pulls the front door open. "I'll get a nice, tacky sweatshirt. One with a big, ugly picture on it."

She'll run out of tourist traps to buy souvenirs from eventually, won't she?

"Anyway, I'll see you later." She hefts the duffel bag into her arms. Our eyes meet, and she grins before starting down the steps. "Well, I won't see you for a couple months, but y'know

—same difference. I'll call you when I get there. And maybe earlier, when I cross the border."

"Have fun, and drive safe."

She shoves her bags into the trunk. We both wave, she climbs in her car, and I step back inside. The front door closes behind me.

It's already quiet.

Despite being considered a cottage, the house is rather large for one person. Returning the couch to its original position in the middle of the room doesn't help. I eat the rest of the leftover pizza, finish tidying up, and head upstairs, where I sit on the edge of my bed.

*What is everyone up to?*

FaceSpace is boring. More uninspired posts about summer break. A few students worried about their final grades. I comment on something Robbie shared earlier this morning.

With a yawn, I roll onto my side to get more comfortable.

Staying awake until three in the morning and sleeping on the floor wasn't our best plan. I post about the sleepover, tagging Rose to say I miss her already. Then I rest my head on my pillow and close my eyes.

* * * * *

I took a nap—by accident.

After I woke up, I showered. I went for a short walk. Cleaned the kitchen. Rose commented on my post from a rest stop. I won't hear from her for a while, so… I've been wasting time, trying to distract myself from the empty house and my newfound lack of immediate responsibilities.

My latest idea was to sit outside and update my résumé on my phone. Not much has changed besides the number of college credits I've earned. I reword a few sentences, cycle through a handful of different fonts, and pause to yawn.

*Dragging the chair out here was more exciting than this.*

I lock my phone and stand from the uncomfortable, plastic folding chair. My fingers brush the doorknob—I'm ready to go inside—but the sight of green stops me.

Moving closer to the edge of the landing, I scan the nearest and sparsest row of trees. The forest is quiet. The expanse of grass in front of Windsor Park is empty, though it shifts in the gentle breeze. It's due for another trim before fire season sets in.

*Hm...*

I haven't seen the fluffy white cat in a while. It was cute, with eyes as blue as the summer sky. Did the owner find it? Is it safe, hidden away inside of one of my neighbors' cottages?

I lean against the porch railing.

*Speaking of things I haven't seen...*

Hot Grocery Store Man.

Ice Monroe.

He hasn't called, and it's like he doesn't exist at all on social media.

Maybe I imagined the whole thing. *No, he was definitely real, but that doesn't mean his intentions were.* Maybe he was humoring me—or teasing me—by asking for my phone number. Maybe he spent the entire time laughing to himself and never planned to call in the first place.

I bet Ice isn't even his real name.

Yeah, that's probably it.

Oh, well. I knew that Hot Grocery Store Man—a real-life example of Rose's perfect boyfriend—was too good to be true. He was just another hot guy who wouldn't give a girl like me the time of day.

With a sigh, I rest my chin in my hands.

*Maybe Rose was right. Maybe I should have asked for his phone number.*

What? No.

I meant what I said. The last thing I need is a boyfriend. I want to relax and recover from the school year. Though, it might not be so bad if it only lasted for the summer…

*Ugh.*

Stop thinking about him. If he planned to call, he surely would have by now.

My phone rings.

The default ringtone tells me the call isn't from Rose, and a glance at the screen confirms the caller isn't in my contact list. But it is a local number.

My stupid heart skips a beat.

*You're kidding.*

*It's spam, right? Or a wrong number?*

I accept the call and raise the phone to my ear.

"Hello?" I ask.

The other line is quiet a second too long. I don't breathe.

"Hello," a familiar voice replies. "It's Ice Monroe. Remember me from Bargain Shop?"

I stand up straight, holding the phone tight. *No freaking way.* I guess he wasn't playing me *or* turned off by my impressive lack of social grace, but I'm not in the clear yet.

*Act casual, Jayde.*

"Oh, hey!" Nice. That totally didn't sound forced. *Ugh.* "I was starting to think you'd never call."

He laughs. "My apologies. I've been quite busy, but things are calming down now."

"Oh? Same here. I guess."

"Are you free tomorrow?"

I stare at nothing in particular for so long my eyes lose focus. The colors and shapes of the parking lot, trees, and sky blur together into a mess of grey and black and green and blue. Then I shake my head and return to the chair.

"Yeah," I say slowly. "I'm not doing anything tomorrow."

"Wonderful. I'm free too." His voice is crisp and clear through the phone. "We should do something in town."

I glance in the direction of the phone at my ear. "Like what?"

"It's been a while since I've had frozen yogurt," he says. "There's still a shop at Century Plaza, right?"

"Yes?"

I bite my tongue. I haven't visited Century Plaza Mall in months, so I honestly don't know, but there sure as hell better be a frozen yogurt shop on the premises.

"Care to join me?" he asks.

"Sure." I wince. "I mean— Yes. That sounds amazing."

Frozen yogurt at the mall should be a casual affair, but it's for the best. I'm hopeless. Anything more involved might kill me.

"I can meet you around one-o'clock," he says. "If that works for you?"

"Mm-hm." I force myself to give my fingers a break and relax my death grip on the phone.

"Perfect. I'll see you tomorrow, Jayde."

"Okay, Ice. Thanks."

The call ends there, freeing me to breathe and properly appreciate how strange saying his name was. I mean, *Ice? Come on.* Though, I guess it's better than Hot Grocery Store Man.

Still reeling, I add his phone number to my contacts—as Ice Monroe—and set an obnoxious custom ringtone. Next time he calls, I'll know it's him right away.

*Oh.*

My face is hot, and not only from the sun.

*Did he just ask me out?*

Why? After how we met, why on earth would he want to talk a second time—let alone ask me out on a date? Well… *I guess it doesn't matter.* He must see something worthwhile in me.

I stare at Rose's name in my contact list. I want to message her. To let her know that Hot Grocery Store Man called despite my full belief he never would. To let her know I scored a date with him. I want her to cheer me on, but it still seems too good to be true.

I'll wait until after the date. Just to be safe.

# five

I step off the bus near Century Plaza Mall a few minutes after 1PM. Ice is already there, sitting at a bench outside the main doors, so I speed walk to meet him. He stands and greets me with a smile.

I force a smile in return. "Hi! Sorry I'm late."

"It's no problem."

*Ugh.*

My memory wasn't exaggerating—Ice Monroe is exactly as gorgeous as he was when I first met him. Tousled hair. Casual, high-end clothing. Confident posture. His appearance strikes me as simple yet deliberate, and I bet he spent a lot of time perfecting the look.

He's definitely more Rose's type than mine, but there is nothing wrong with being a tall, hot, athletic blond as long as you're not a conceited prick on top of it. So far, Ice checks out as okay.

He glances past me, toward the road. "You take public transit?"

*Ah... He noticed.*

Of course he noticed. The bus stop is right on the other end of the parking lot, but I hope he doesn't find it strange—or pathetic, considering I'm nineteen.

"Yeah, I don't drive," I admit. "The bus system here is fine, so I never saw any reason to get a car. Not to mention the cost of gas and insurance, and the impact on the environment…"

*You're yammering on about nothing again. Shut up, Jayde.*

He laughs easily. "If you said something earlier, I would have given you a ride."

"Well, now you know. Thanks, though!"

I glance away. I could have told the truth, but he doesn't need to hear a sob story about how none of the adults in my life cared enough to bother teaching me. That is *not* first date material.

Fortunately, he doesn't press the matter and instead suggests we head inside.

I agree, a little too eagerly, and we walk through the large front doors together. If he thinks I'm weird, he doesn't mention it. He just asks about my day, and I'm thankful for that.

Another stroke of luck—One Scoop, Two Scoops still exists! He laughs at the lame joke I tell about being worried it wouldn't be there.

When we step inside the shop, I glance around, desperate to look anywhere but at him. A few customers sit at small, round tables and eat frozen yogurt from brightly colored paper bowls. The environment is low energy and quiet, with more tables empty than occupied. It calms my nerves, and I manage to suppress the warmth in my cheeks.

Ice picks up two paper bowls at the start of the self-service froyo bar. He hands one to me, and I carefully accept it.

"What's your favorite flavor?" he asks.

"Out of these? Um…" I scan the labels on the frozen yogurt dispenser. "Lemon meringue, I guess."

He serves himself, choosing lemon meringue, and I fill my bowl with strawberry cheesecake after he says it's his favorite.

*This is cliché, but I guess it's fun.*

Moving along to the toppings bar, there are more options than I remember. I cover my frozen yogurt with strawberry slices on one half and a variety of candies on the other. Then I watch as Ice meticulously places one peach ring and three brownie chunks in his bowl. He offers my cup a mildly judgmental glance before flashing a smile.

He obviously finds the abomination my frozen yogurt bowl became funny—which is fair, if a little embarrassing—but he says nothing.

We walk to the cashier counter, I hand Ice my bowl, and he sets both on the register scale. Our total comes out to just over ten dollars, no thanks to my blatant overuse of toppings, I'm sure.

The flicker of guilt I felt fades when he slips a fifty-dollar bill from his jacket pocket.

*Hm…* He's either rich or showing off.

I had him pegged as a fellow college student, but what student walks around with fifty-dollar bills in their jacket pockets? *Why is he wearing a jacket, anyway?* It's like ninety degrees outside. Yet, there he is, standing beside me, rocking what looks to be a genuine leather jacket.

*What the hell?*

I must have spaced out for a minute because I'm already

standing in front of a small table across the shop. Ice hands over my yogurt cup—complete with a plastic spoon stuck into the center—and pulls out a chair for me.

*Wow. Chivalry isn't dead.*

I thank him and sit. The chair makes an awful screeching noise as I scoot closer to the table.

He takes the chair across from me while trying to fold what's left of his fifty dollars with one hand. I have no idea why it's so entertaining to watch, but it is. As he finishes, I stare at the pile of toppings in my paper cup.

When was the last time I did something like this?

Robbie took me out to get ice cream often when I was a kid, and Rose and I came here a few times last year, but it's not the same. Robbie is my brother. Rose is my best friend. Today, here with Ice, I'm on a real date—a date no one else had to arrange for me. A date I honestly wanted to go on.

"If you don't hurry, it'll melt," he says, his voice playful.

Glancing up, I force a smile. He's already eating. Two of the three small brownie chunks are missing from his cup.

"Do you like it?" I ask.

He shrugs. "It's not my favorite, but it's alright."

I struggle to find a spoonful of strawberry cheesecake yogurt without any toppings mixed in. Cold, sweet, fruity. The flavor is good, but I definitely went overboard with the extras.

When I mention it, he laughs.

Glancing away self-consciously, I realize for the umpteenth time that I am on a *date*. I haven't gone on one since the first week of winter term, not long before I swore off dating to focus on school. I'm a little rusty—not that I was fantastic at dating to begin with. But I dug a nice blouse out of my dresser and put my hair up for this.

I am trying.

But I still have no idea what to talk about.

"Are you a student?" he asks.

*Fortunately, one of us is decent at conversation.*

"Yeah, I've been studying at RCC." I ramble for a while—about my undecided major, a few classes I took last term, *something else that really doesn't matter*—before I finally shut up. Then I meet his gaze and ask the same question.

"I'm out at Stanford," he says. "Majoring in psychology and communication. Minoring in business management."

*I knew it!* He is a university student. Double majoring at Stanford, though? And he said it as though it weren't the least bit impressive. *Damn.*

"Are you here visiting family?"

He smiles. "Good guess. This is my first day back in town. I'm here until September."

*I knew it...*

If he's only visiting for summer break, I was right. Even if he's not playing me for laughs, he's still too good to be true.

*Hold up—*

Wasn't a casual summer relationship my original plan in the event he called? If I suddenly started expecting anything more halfway through our first date, I really am an idiot.

"Your birthday wasn't long ago, right?" he asks. "Did you do anything for it?"

The question catches me by surprise—ironic, considering I met him the day before my birthday—and I'm not sure how to answer. I specifically mentioned my birthday when we met, but he didn't call me. Even if it's dumb, and he already said he'd been busy, I'm still a little miffed about it.

"Not really," I say. "I sat at home with my roommate. We watched TV and ate Chinese food. Nothing fancy."

"Oh. I see."

He purses his lips and glances away.

This date is the highlight of my summer thus far, but I can't even tell if it's going well. With a sigh, I pick one of the gummy candies out of my frozen yogurt.

It's hard as a rock.

I watch through the shop's floor-to-ceiling windows as people make their way through the mall. Mindlessly, I stir the contents of my paper cup. After many rotations, my dessert turns an unattractive, pale brown.

The sludge looks weird—like, well, *sludge*—but it still tastes decent. I can only hope the date turns out the same way.

*Weird. But decent.*

Ice clears his throat. "Do you have many friends around here?"

"No." I suppress a laugh. "My roommate, Rose, is my only real friend. Sure, I know a lot of her friends, but most of them are too intense for me—if you know what I mean?"

*Ugh. Do I even know what I mean?*

He says something under his breath, but I don't catch it. *Should I ask him to repeat himself?* He meets my gaze and smiles softly before I decide either way.

"I see," he says at normal volume. "I don't have many close friends either."

*That's a surprise!* But I can't bring myself to comment on it.

"Any big plans this summer?" he asks.

This time, I don't bother stifling my laughter. "No. Rose is out of town until August, and I don't have family around here. I'm kind of winging it on my own this summer."

"I assume you won't mind if we talk more, then?"

My cheeks warm as I search his face. I still can't shake the nagging anxiety that he's messing with me somehow, but he watches me with focused eyes and a pleasant smile.

"Of course not," I assure him.

God knows why he wants to hang out with me, but *alright*. I'm not about to complain.

Objectively speaking, there's little risk in pursuing him. He's a college student visiting home for the summer. He'll only be around for a few months. It's not like I have anything better to do with my time, and, whether it goes anywhere or not, Rose will get a kick out of hearing about it.

We continue discussing school even as we finish our frozen yogurt. It's a safe, casual topic, but it ensures the conversation ends on a positive—or at least neutral—note by the time we grow bored with sitting around.

As we leave the shop and step back out into the mall, he offers to give me a ride home.

Images of a tense, awkward car ride cycle through my mind. Sitting in the passenger seat while he drives. Not knowing where to look or what to say. Not being able to control my breathing in an enclosed space.

I respectfully decline.

He glances away. I worry I offended him somehow, but he soon meets my gaze again and flashes a lazy grin.

"Next time, perhaps?" he asks.

"Oh, um…" I laugh nervously. "It's nothing personal. There's just a few things I wanted to do here before I go home."

"Fair enough," he agrees with a shrug. "I would offer to stay, but I'm tied up elsewhere."

"Of course. That's totally fine."

We linger near the entrance to the frozen yogurt shop. Quiet. Not doing anything besides watching people walk by. I want to express my gratitude, but I don't know what to say or how to say it. I suck at this sort of thing. So I shift my weight, biding my time.

Finally, I look up from my hands, and I smile.

"Thanks," I say. "For actually calling me."

He meets my gaze with a curious half-smile. "Did you think I wouldn't?"

"Do you want an honest answer?" I ask, tearing my eyes away to stare at nothing in particular across the building.

"I'll ask next time we talk," he says with a laugh. "But I need to head out now, so I'll call you later."

"Oh. Okay?"

"Thanks for coming," he says. "This was nice."

I nod and insist it wasn't a problem, but I have *no clue* what's going on inside his head. His smile is warm and kind, but his eyes are unreadable—deep in thought or…murky, somehow. The way he gauges my reactions so intently. It's confusing.

He seriously wants to hang out with me again?

He honestly had a good time?

*How?*

But I smile in return as we exchange pleasantries, and I wave before he turns to leave.

Once he's out of sight, I wander in the opposite direction and settle at an empty table in the food court. I prop my chin in my hands. I listen to the muddled conversations of the people around me.

I don't have anything else to do here. I don't have any plans or errands to run. Even if I wanted to shop, the only cash I have on hand is the forty dollars Robbie sent for my birthday. Money that would be better put toward groceries. I don't have the luxury of spending it however I want—unlike *some people*.

*Still...*

What was I thinking? The possibility of an awkward car ride wasn't a good reason to turn down Ice's offer. I should have taken him up on it, but it's too late to change my mind.

Instead, I have to take the bus home, and it doesn't stop here for another twenty minutes.

*Maybe next time*, he said.

Maybe next time I won't be such a baby.

* * * * *

Why am I still so nervous to tell Rose about my date?

Is it just because I decided against telling her in advance?

She would be ecstatic to learn that Hot Grocery Store Man called, but I half-expected him to stand me up. Now that I know he's legit and wants to hang out more, it shouldn't be a big deal.

But I'm sure she'll overreact—in a good way, but… It's embarrassing. And the timing was too convenient. Nothing for a week, and then he calls *the day* she left town?

What if she doesn't believe me? I should have taken pictures of our frozen yogurt cups as proof.

*Ugh. I'm seriously overthinking it.*

I sprawl out on my bed. Then I open my phone's messenger app and spend a few minutes figuring out what to say. After several revisions, I give up and tap send.

**Me:** You will never guess what I did today.

That's a little dramatic, but it's fine.

A few minutes pass, during which I do absolutely nothing but stare at the window. Then she reads the message, and her response is quick.

**Rose:** burnt down the house already? lol

**Me:** lmao no. Hot Grocery Store Man called, and we went out for froyo.

**Me:** I just got home.

**Rose:** Σ(°ロ°)

**Rose:** A date??? You're serious?

**Me:** Yeah, his name is Ice. He's super cool, and he goes to Stanford.

**Rose:** Whaaaat? No

**Rose:** Jayyyy.. That's not fair. Why'd he have to call while im not there?? (T⌓T)

My phone rings while I'm typing. I suppress my laughter, and I answer.

"You're kidding," she cries into the phone. "He seriously called right after I left? What the hell, Jay?"

If it weren't so funny, I'd feel bad for her.

"It was like a few hours after you left, but, yeah… I didn't say anything because I kind of thought he was still trolling me."

"With a name like Ice, I don't blame you," she mutters before gasping. "But how did the date go? You said he's cool, but is he your perfect, sweet dream-boy cool, or did he try to make out with you right away?"

"At least one of those things did not happen."

She laughs. "I'm joking; I'm joking. He paid for you, though, right?"

"That he did."

"Oh, good. Is he still hot?"

"Um— Yes?"

"Good, good." A pause. "I want to meet him."

*That's hard to do when you're nearly a thousand miles away.*

"I don't think it's anything serious," I tell her.

"Oh, never mind. Just give me the tea already. How'd it go?"

She laughs as I recount the state of my frozen yogurt. The toppings. How Ice raised an eyebrow at it. The leather jacket, and the fifty-dollar bill.

"A leather jacket in June?" she asks. "I'm so jealous! Forgoing comfort for aesthetic like that is a serious power move, Jayde. Please send me a picture of this man. I trust you completely, but I need to see him with my own eyes."

*What does that even mean?*

"Ha… I don't know…"

She laughs again. "It's fine. Just have fun, don't do anything I wouldn't do, and keep me in the loop."

"Of course."

"And please, please let me know if you need moral support. I fully intend on living vicariously through you during these trying times."

"Thanks, Rose."

# six

Ice called at noon exactly to invite me out on another date—this time, to Riverside Park. I love Riverside Park, and I have nothing better to do, so I agreed. He knows I rely on public transit to get around now, so, of course, he also insisted on picking me up. Lacking a good excuse, I agreed to that too.

I want to see him. I'll take what I can get.

An unfamiliar car pulls into the parking space outside—a flash of silver through the window. I jump up from the couch and double-check my appearance using my phone's front-facing camera. Everything appears to be in order, but I adjust my head-band and fuss with my hair anyway.

Then, after taking a deep breath, I grab my purse and step out onto the empty landing. *Why am I so nervous?* I make a scene out of locking the front door before I finally turn around.

*Oh, nice!*

Ice drives an expensive, silver sports car—a Porsche, I think—with a streamlined profile and dark windows. He stands beside the car, leaning against the passenger side. His expression is soft and confident, but I catch a mischievous glint in his eyes as I approach.

*Fine, I admit it*; he might be a touch full of himself. But I can't blame anyone for feeling a little confident, or even cocky, when they have the cash for such a nice car. I guess he wasn't showing off with the fifty-dollar bill the other day. It's probably normal for someone of his caliber.

Hot, suave, academic, *and* rich?

*Yeah, you are way out of my league. What are you doing here?*

He opens the passenger door—another act of cliché chivalry. I nod in acknowledgment and climb inside.

The car's tinted windows and black leather interior leave the space rather dark, but the seats are comfortable, and the electronic dashboard is lit up with an assortment of colorful digital displays. There's even a GPS built into the rear-view mirror.

I lean across the center console to peek at the dials behind the steering wheel. The numbers on the speedometer go up well over one hundred.

*How cool—and scary!*

I stop ogling the car and buckle my seatbelt as Ice slides into the driver's seat. He closes the door, and our eyes meet.

"So, what were you saying the other day?" he asks.

This flashy sports car only adds to my confusion over why he wants to talk to me, but I am not about to point out our obvious class differences. Surely, he doesn't need that much spelled out for him. *And I don't want to admit I originally thought he was pranking me.*

"It's nothing." I laugh, wishing I could avoid the question entirely. "I just don't get asked out often."

"Oh?"

He flashes a crooked smile—like it's any surprise I'm not the most popular girl in town. Then he checks the rear-view mirror, and the car comes to life. The engine is impressively quiet. A low purr that hardly shakes the vehicle.

As his gaze turns to the view outside the windshield, I glance away.

He oozes self-confidence and easy composure while I flounder hopelessly no matter how I try. It's not fair, and the fact he doesn't seem to notice or care how awkward I act around him is only *more* frustrating.

I watch the Oakwood Cottages sign pass by as the car pulls out of the parking lot.

*Why is it so quiet? Should I say something?*

Ice devotes his full attention to driving, so he doesn't talk either. The radio isn't even turned on. The silence is uncomfortable, and being stuck in midday traffic on the drive through town isn't helping. I fiddle with the Arizona keychain attached to my purse's zipper to distract myself.

*Don't be nervous. Just say something!*

"The weather's nice," I say.

*God...* At least I didn't ask what he's doing here.

He smiles. "Yes. I prefer this type of weather."

It's sunny and hot, as it has been the last few weeks, but he's wearing dark jeans and a fitted, button-up shirt—nice and casual but unsuited for the weather. It may be comfortable in the car, and the mall, but how can he tolerate wearing long sleeves outside of an air-conditioned space?

Meanwhile, I'm in shorts and a tank top, and I'm practically sweating at the thought of stepping outside for more than five minutes.

*Whatever.*

I glance out the windshield.

One minute of silence.

Two minutes.

He asks about my day. I say it's been alright.

And…it's quiet again.

Even as Ice parks in a shaded space near the start of the paved walking path that leads to Riverside Park proper, neither of us speak. The car engine falls silent, and he removes the key from the ignition. After checking his smartwatch, he looks at me and smiles.

"Shall we take a walk?" he asks.

"Yeah, let's go."

Once we leave the car and start down the path, Ice returns to being talkative. It must be a driving thing—a focus thing. Either way, I follow along with the idle conversation without asking, satisfied enough that the tense atmosphere is gone.

* * * * *

We haven't been out long, twenty minutes at most, but I'm already suffering. The sun beats down on my exposed skin. Bare shoulders. Chest. Arms.

I can't believe Ice isn't dying from heatstroke. In fact, he does not seem bothered by the heat at all. Not wanting to look pathetic in comparison, I suck it up and smile through the discomfort.

We've almost come to the point where the walking loop leaves the park again when he suggests we sit in the shade.

*Thank god.*

I point out the closest tree, a large oak off the path to our right. He approves and flashes a brilliant smile that makes tolerating the heat worth it.

He sits first. I pull my hair over one shoulder and sit cross-legged in the grass beside him—though I play it safe and leave a foot of space between us. The air is easily fifteen degrees cooler in the shade, but several blades of grass tickle my thighs and remind me how much I hate sitting in the grass while wearing shorts.

I scratch the itch.

Ice stares up into the leafy canopy while combing his fingers through his hair from his hairline to the nape of his neck. His red, button-up shirt fits like it's tailored to his body.

*Hell, I wouldn't be surprised if it were.*

He must know exactly how hot he is. He probably uses it to his advantage all the time. A guy like Ice could get pretty much anything—or anyone—he wanted.

So, why is he hanging out with me?

When he meets my gaze, I'm hit by a fresh wave of insecurity. *Is my eyeliner too heavy? Was wearing a headband too much? Should I have put my hair up instead? Is my shirt crooked?* My shirt is fine, but I'm still paranoid. I smooth the fabric, bite my lip, and stare down at the grass.

"You don't get asked out much, huh?" he asks.

I laugh.

My first impulse is to explain how I've been prioritizing my education over romantic relationships, but I catch myself before I say anything that might negatively affect the likelihood of getting asked out a third time.

"Kinda goes along with not having friends," I say instead.

"What is that like?"

He's serious. Why am I not surprised?

"It's like having a lot of time to yourself." *In my case, to study, so I get my money's worth out of school.* "I'm an introvert, though, so it's fine."

His mouth hitches up on one side. "Do you think I'm not an introvert?"

The genuine interest in his voice surprises me more than the revelation he doesn't consider himself an extrovert.

"It's not that," I insist. "You just seem very comfortable—like all the time."

"I may not be timid, but I am undoubtedly an introvert," he says with a laugh.

I shake my head and wave my hands in front of my chest. "Oh, no, it's not that I'm timid—"

"No?" He quirks an eyebrow. "I make you nervous, then?"

*He sees right through me.*

I glance away, my smile growing uneasy. "No offense, but you are kind of intimidating."

"No offense taken."

I'm not the best at casual conversation, but I've never acted as desperately awkward as I have in the short time since I met Ice. Functioning like a normal human being has always been easy enough. The social anxiety was manageable—negligible even.

*But, now...*

I doubt I've ever felt so utterly inadequate compared to another person in my life. I wish I were prettier. Less boring. More impressive.

My thigh still itches. I ignore it and pick at the grass beside my leg, pulling up blades and dropping them again.

"Do you enjoy spending time with me?" he asks.

*I should ask you that question. Not the other way around.*

"This is better than what I could be doing," I say.

He laughs again. "That's good to know."

I do enjoy talking to him. He's well-spoken and engaging, but it doesn't matter exactly what he says. His voice has an alluring quality. It's smooth and confident—like auditory honey.

Not to mention he's total eye candy.

*It's too bad he has to leave at the end of the summer.*

I watch him in my peripheral vision, careful to avoid staring.

Once again, he gazes into the tree canopy. With intense eyes and a soft frown, he looks peaceful and introspective. Splotches of shade dance over his face as the leaves shift in the breeze, and his eyes close like he's savoring the fresh air.

Ice Monroe is a truly beautiful person.

"Do you ever consider the fragility of this world?" he asks.

*Consider...the fragility of this world?*

The question came out of nowhere. I haven't the slightest idea what he means. I'm sure it's something deep and philosophical—after all, he is a psychology major—but I can't seem to conjure an adequately intelligent response.

"Not really," I admit.

He looks to me and flashes a smile. "Try it sometime."

"I will…consider it."

*Whatever that means!*

He laughs. Then he stands in one fluid, graceful motion. After he smooths out his shirt, he extends a hand to help me up. I meet his eyes, take in his cool expression, and hesitate.

*Is hanging out with him a good idea?* If our relationship turns into anything more than a series of fun, meaningless dates, won't it hurt when he leaves?

His smile softens.

*Guess I'll cross that bridge when I get to it.*

His grip is warm and strong. The muscles work in his arm as he pulls me to my feet, but it didn't seem to take any real effort on his part. *Whoa*. Awareness of his presence overwhelms me—the faint scent of cinnamon.

*We're too close.*

My gaze flicks from his chest to his face. Our eyes meet, and mild confusion creeps into his, and my breath catches.

*Oh. I still have ahold of his hand.*

Breaking eye contact, I pull away and let out a weak laugh.

He opens his mouth to speak, but pauses as something distracts him. His expression shifts. Smile faltering. Eyes narrowing.

He glances over his shoulder.

I follow his gaze and spot someone in the distance—a young woman. She stands motionless on the raised curb, as her white sundress sways in the gentle breeze. Pale in the sunlight, with feathery, dark hair, she reminds me of a ghost from so far away.

My skin prickles. *How long has she been there?*

Ice catches my attention to offer a terse smile. “Sorry, but I’m afraid I have to cut this outing short.”

“O–okay?”

*What else can I say?*

I glance from his face to the girl near the parking lot and back again. He watches her with neutral eyes and a hint of tension in his jaw. Whoever she is, he is not pleased to see her.

“Call me soon,” he says, turning away. “I hope you will.”

I do nothing to stop him as he walks through the grass toward the girl. As he approaches her, she steps off the curb and plants her hands on her hips.

My chest tightens. I grasp the shoulder strap of my purse, and I turn around—a complete one-eighty. *I do not want to watch him talk to her. Or see him leave with her.*

I mess with my hair, passing long strands through my hands. My headband gets in the way, so I stash it in my purse.

Without another glance in the direction of the parking lot, I ignore the heat and wander out onto the busy playground. A single swing is free. I claim it and watch the children. There are a dozen or so running around and climbing the play equipment.

I lose track of time, swinging and watching the kids play, but I eventually dig my heels into the wood chips beneath my feet and bring my slow swing to a stop.

I hoped getting away would distract me, but it didn’t. Even if it’s none of my business, it’s annoying. He left in the middle of our date. He apologized, *I guess*, but he offered no real explanation, and he *abandoned me* at the park without a ride home.

Well, abandoned is a little dramatic. I’m not stranded or

anything. I can take the bus home no problem. But what if I hadn't brought my purse or left it in his car or something?

*Ugh...*

He told me to call him later, though, so it's probably nothing.

*Probably.*

Even if it is nothing—even if I tell myself it's not a big deal—nothing changes. The pit in my stomach doesn't go away. I'm no less confused and no less upset.

*Who was she?*

# seven

Yesterday sucked.

I want to text Ice—to demand an explanation—but what would I say? I don't want to come across as paranoid. Or annoying. Or…*clingy.* It's presumptuous to let it bother me at all, isn't it? We went on two casual dates, but we're not *dating*. Nothing is official, let alone exclusive.

I have no right to be jealous.

*Maybe taking a walk will clear my head.*

This early in the day during the middle of the week, I don't expect to see many people out on the Windsor Park trails. I come across a woman with a cute dog, an older man speed-walking by himself, and a couple feeding the ducks at the pond.

I watch the birds for a while, once again wishing I'd brought bread with me. I feel better, though, so I leave the way I came. Not five minutes later, someone rounds a corner on the trail ahead.

Her dark hair is pulled back in a stubby ponytail, and she wears coordinated, name-brand activewear instead of a white dress, but it's definitely the same girl—or woman, rather—that Ice ran off with at Riverside yesterday.

And she's heading my way.

While I am surprised to see her, I expect her to not recognize me and run past without paying me any attention.

Instead, her leisurely jog slows to a walk as we near each other. She drapes the cord of her earbuds around her neck, opens her eyes, and makes deliberate eye contact with me.

Entirely bothered, I stop walking.

Her large almond eyes are the same shade as Ice's, the bright, saturated blue a stark contrast to her black hair and medium-toned skin. She's dainty and gorgeous and didn't break a sweat jogging in the morning's rising heat.

She offers me a small smile. "Good morning."

Her voice is soft and disarming. It suits her appearance, and she sounds kind. Even so, I find myself profoundly threatened. My guard shoots up, my attention locked on her doll-like face.

"Good morning?" I echo.

"I know you don't know me, but I need to ask." She glances away, but her eyes quickly dart back to meet mine. "What did Ice want with you yesterday?"

*Want with me? Uhh—*

Her expression remains level. My skin prickles.

We ran into each other by chance, or so I want to believe, but she doesn't appear the least bit surprised. She even stopped to talk, and for what? Just to ask a weird question about Ice?

I should ignore her and go home, but I'm intrigued. And very concerned.

"We were just hanging out—and talking."

She nods. "What were you talking about?"

"What does it matter?" I ask. "Who are you, anyway?"

*Ugh...* Is it awful to be so defensive?

Ice ditched me at the park to talk to her, and I assume they left together—because I sure didn't see him again. Yet she appeared out of nowhere to question me like I'm in the wrong?

She sighs and raises a hand to her forehead. "You can relax. Ice is family. I'm his sister."

*Oh.* I was expecting something else completely, but— They're siblings? *Great.* She's probably going to tell him how rude I was. I would if I were her.

*God, I'm so stupid.*

"Sorry," I stammer, forcing a laugh and nervous smile. "But, um, we weren't talking about anything in particular yesterday, y'know? It was small talk, mostly."

She glances away. "He's been kind to you, right? He hasn't said anything weird, has he?"

"Weird?"

"Such as…" As she trails off, she purses her lips.

The whole *consider the fragility of the world* bit caught me off guard, but he hasn't said any other strange things. Though, we've only hung out twice, and most of our conversations have consisted of little more than basic icebreakers. Just the kind of things you talk about with someone you don't know very well. Nothing deep or notably unusual—at least nothing I can put my finger on.

"Never mind," she says, looking rather embarrassed.

"It's fine. I mean…" I laugh again despite myself. "It is kind of weird that he wants to spend time with me at all, isn't it?"

She smiles. "I see. I'm sorry for bothering you."

"And I'm sorry for being so rude."

*I wish I could have a do-over of the last few minutes...*

"No harm done," she says. "I'll be on my way, then."

*Is that all?*

"Yeah," I agree slowly. "I'm heading home now, anyway."

She pops her earbuds back in and continues onward, but she meets my gaze as she passes me on the trail. Her expression is mild and curious.

"It's Jayde Palmer, right?"

A cool shiver runs down my spine.

"Well, it was nice to meet you," she says.

My eyes track her as she walks by, but I can't bring myself to follow, stop her, or say anything as her pace increases to a slow jog. She disappears into the forest while I'm frozen in place in the middle of the empty trail.

*How does she know my last name?*

* * * * *

I've worried for hours, debating whether I should tell Ice I ran into his sister—assuming she is who she said she is—or pretend it never happened. He asked me to call, and I want to, but I have no idea how to approach the subject.

What would I say?

*Hey, Ice! I randomly met your sister in the woods behind my house, and she somehow knew my last name. I haven't even told you my last name yet. Isn't that totally weird?*

Yeah... *No.*

I cave and send a text instead.

> **Me:** Hey! I ran into your sister… The girl from the park yesterday? Anyway, she asked about you, so I thought you should know.

The "read" indicator appears beneath my message, and he starts typing. I bite my lip, more nervous than I should be as I watch the three dots on the screen.

> **Ice:** Interesting.

Is that it?

No. He's still typing.

> **Ice:** I'm in the mood for a movie.
>
> **Ice:** Care to join me?

*Wow. Way to change the subject…*

I type out a response, resolved to accept his invitation despite its evasive nature, but he sends a third text before I finish.

> **Ice:** Call me. Now, please.

*Weird, but alright…*

He answers on the first ring. "So, you met my sister?"

Is he upset? I honestly can't tell.

"I guess so," I reply, more confused than I was this morning. "We only spoke for a minute, but— Is she really your sister?"

"I'd imagine so, if she said she is. Now then, about the movie; will you come?"

*Right…* I'd rather get the weirdness involving his sister over with, but he obviously doesn't want to talk about it right now.

That's fine. It's whatever. I'm sure he'll tell me what her problem is when he's ready.

"What movie?" I ask, struggling to mask my rising frustration. "When?"

"A surprise. Tomorrow afternoon. If you're free, I can pick you up at two-thirty."

I sigh. "Sure. I'm free, as usual."

"Don't worry," he says with a sigh of his own. "We can discuss my sister after the movie."

*When you put it that way, it sounds like I don't have a choice.*

"I'll see you then," I agree.

"I look forward to it, Jayde."

The call ends rather abruptly, and I stare at my phone until the screen fades to black. I am definitely interested in going on another date with Ice, but would it kill him to answer a simple question when it's asked?

# eight

The movie was okay, and Ice kept his word. He didn't mention his sister a single time, either before or during the film.

Even as I follow him outside, he's relatively quiet. We leave his car in the parking lot and walk down a random street a couple blocks from the theater. The hot air and blue sky do little to offset a sense of nagging anxiety from creeping in as we walk.

*Thanks, stupid horror movie!*

"So… Where are we going exactly?"

"There's a park about a quarter mile down this road," he says. "It's next to the river."

I never knew there was a park around here—down a narrow, unpaved road behind the movie theater—but *okay*. I let it go and continue walking at his side, periodically glancing at the aging houses and gnarled trees on our right.

Hoping to brush off the creepy vibe, I spark a safe, casual conversation. We talk about nothing for a few minutes. Then I ask if he liked the movie.

"I'm the one who invited you out," he says. "I should ask you."

Unsure how to respond, I play dumb and scratch my cheek.

His smile turns wry. "Well, did you like the movie?"

"It was okay," I say slowly.

The movie was more psychological and confusing than scary. It was fine—it wasn't awful or gory or anything—but I don't know how to explain how I feel about it. Horror movies aren't my thing in the first place. I only watch them with Rose when neither of us can sleep, and we're both bored out of our minds.

"Did you like it, though?" I ask.

He doesn't answer, but he stops walking to watch me. I have no idea what he's thinking, let alone what he might be searching for in my expression, but he looks vaguely amused.

*By my question? Or what?*

I stop and stare back at him.

"No," he says, cracking a smile.

He tucks his thumbs in his belt loops and continues down the road. My heart skips a beat, and I run the last couple steps to catch up with him.

"No?" I ask.

"I hated it," he says, but he laughs easily. "It was a god-awful movie—tacky and cliché, with weak characters and even weaker writing. I absolutely hated it. All one hundred and seven minutes of it."

"Really?"

"Yes. It was terrible. That's why I wanted to see it."

I feel myself frown. "You wanted to watch a movie you knew you would hate? That doesn't make sense, you know?"

"Of course, I know."

Doesn't it defeat the purpose of watching a movie in theater if you know you're going to hate it? Not to mention it's a waste of ten dollars.

*Though, I'm sure that's not a problem for him.*

He flashes a surprisingly hesitant half-smile. "Despite disliking the film, the experience was enjoyable."

*Yeah. This is getting strange.*

I glance away.

I think he did too.

The park Ice mentioned is so small and unassuming, I would have walked past it had he not pointed it out. It's more like a neatly mowed patch of grass on the riverbank than an actual park. There isn't even a picnic table—only an old, wrought-iron bench in the shade of a willow tree—but it's cute.

I sit at one end of the bench while Ice remains standing, and I look out over the water to distract myself from the fleeting disappointment. This section of river is wide and deep. The water is a dark teal, the surface still like glass, and trees line the steep bank on the far side.

This is a beautiful spot, but why take me here when we could have gone literally anywhere else after the movie? The setup was creepy and weird. I'd rather hang out somewhere like Riverside or just sit in his air-conditioned car.

"I assume you want to talk about yesterday," he says.

*To be honest, I forgot.*

But I nod. "There are some nature trails behind my house—you know, all those trees? Well, it's actually a park. Windsor Park? Anyway, I ran into her on my way home from a walk, and she stopped to…chat?"

"Behind your house?" he asks with a sigh. "Well, let's hear it. What did she have to say?"

"Not much," I admit. A fish breaks the river's surface to catch a bug, sending a series of ripples across the water. "But she knew my last name somehow."

"Imagine that."

His tone bothers me.

When I look up, he's staring out over the water. His lips form a soft frown, but I still can't tell what he's thinking or feeling. He's always been fairly difficult to read—I noticed it the first time we met—but it's just now becoming a real source of frustration.

"She is your sister, though, right?"

"Yes. Her name is Night."

*Oh, good.*

"Weird names," I say, hoping to lighten the mood.

A candid grimace flashes across his face. I laugh it off, but he glances away again. *Talking about her makes him uncomfortable?* That's fine. Family can be complicated. I get that.

If it's a problem, I can change the subject—

But he reaffirms eye contact and cracks a smile. "Speaking of weird, she has a twin named Smoke."

"Twins, huh?" I smile. "That's neat. Ice, Night, and Smoke…"

"We have eccentric parents."

"You're staying with them over the summer, right?"

"Yes." He glances aside, crosses his arms, and leans against the side of the bench as though thinking. "I'm staying with the twins at our parents' house, here in town. Though, we may as well be housesitting for them since they're out of the country, on yet another humanitarian mission. For some years now, they've made an unfortunate habit of putting us in charge of their domestic affairs when they're gone."

"Unfortunate? That sounds amazing to me."

"I suppose it's not awful. Our parents are good people, working hard to make a difference where they can." His expression softens, and he meets my gaze again. "Now that I think of it, I should take you by the house sometime. I could give you a tour and introduce the twins properly."

"A tour of your house?" My cheeks grow warm, but I want to meet them. "Yeah, I'd like that."

He flashes a dazzling smile. "Feel free to take me up on that offer any time."

* * * * *

The moment Ice told me about his family, I was dying to visit the house and learn more. I didn't even wait until he dropped me off at home to make plans—we discussed it on the walk back to his car.

The twins are two years younger than Ice, and their parents are passionate philanthropists and CEOs of a large tech corporation. They're influential and dedicated to helping others and improving the lives of disadvantaged people around the world. And, according to Ice, the entire family, himself excluded, is rather atypical and nonconformist.

*How will the Monroe family home reflect that lifestyle?*

I spent the last day and a half wondering, so I'm both excited and a little nervous to find out.

As I sit in Ice's car on the drive through town, I imagine a huge, modern house on a hill overlooking the city with a glass wall facing a roundabout driveway and an in-ground swimming pool or tennis court or some other extravagant fixture in the backyard. The type of house a movie star might live in.

This over-the-top image sticks in my brain until the car comes to a stop in front of a wrought-iron gate blocking the road ahead. There's a manned guardhouse off to the left and decorative wood signage above.

WELCOME TO WESTBROOKE

ACCESS LIMITED TO RESIDENTS AND INVITED GUESTS

Ice inputs a string of numbers onto an electronic keypad, the gate slides open, and we continue into an upper-class suburban neighborhood full of large, gorgeous homes and perfectly green, manicured lawns. My idealized vision of a solo mansion on a hill is shattered, but a private gated community makes sense.

"It's this one," he says.

My focus follows his pointed finger through the windshield to a white and blue single-story house with a red Japanese maple and an oblong patch of grass bordered by river rocks in the front yard. It's by no means the largest or most grandiose home in the neighborhood, but it's lovely all the same.

As though what he already told me wasn't enough, finding out his family lives in this house in this community makes Ice's fifty-dollar bill, Stanford education, and fancy Porsche add up.

The Monroes are *loaded.* A real American Dream family.

"Well, this is home," he says as the car pulls into the house's attached two-car garage.

"It's amazing."

His lip quirks as our eyes meet. "This is merely the garage."

I laugh, but if he thinks I'll be impressed, he's probably right.

Stepping out of the car, I look around. The garage is bright and surprisingly clean, with a row of square windows along the back wall, and a standing freezer, workbench, and two metal cabinets off to one side.

I make my way around the car to meet up with Ice, who flashes a smile before leading me to the door.

When he opens it, I peek inside.

The hallway's sage green walls and short, cream carpet are an interesting contrast to the house's blue-accented exterior. A few framed portraits dot the walls, and a clean, fruity scent hangs in the cool air.

Ice walks in ahead of me. I follow, and the tour begins.

He waves toward the first door on my left—a restroom with a utility room across from it. Then he offers a knowing look as we pass the next door. An ovular sign hangs on it, the swirly letters that spell *NIGHT* painstakingly painted to resemble a star-speckled galaxy. It's simultaneously cute and tacky, and I can only assume it was made many years ago.

"Night's bedroom, of course," he says.

Ice's room is on the right, after which the hallway opens into a larger space, brightly lit but separate from the rest of the house. The room features a flat-screen TV on a short, glass TV stand in front of two loveseats. Muffled rock music filters in through a door beside a row of short bookcases, and a wide mirror hangs on the same wall between the small couches.

Ice refers to this room as the den.

To my right, a sliding glass door leads out onto a wooden patio and the backyard. More short, green grass and two garden beds full of greenery. To my left, a wide arch cut into the wall opens the room up to the main living space.

We leave the den and enter the great room. The open floor plan is split between a formal living room, dining area, and kitchen. One half has the same cream carpet as the hallway and den, while the other half has glossy hardwood flooring. The space is meticulously clean and flooded with natural light as the large windows have their heavy curtains drawn open.

In the carpeted half of the room, two matching armchairs and a large, leather couch are situated around a glass coffee table. Night sits at one end of the couch, holding a worn paperback novel. She's been staring, more or less expressionlessly, in my direction since Ice and I first entered the room.

I wave. She offers a hesitant smile and returns her attention to the book. Ice ignores her, gestures to a door behind the couch, and carries on with the tour as though she doesn't exist.

"That door leads to the master suite…"

Short, white bookcases border a modern, gas fireplace and line the wall separating the great room and den. No TV here. A large mirror hangs above the hearth, and open shelving around the room is decorated with framed photographs and multicultural trinkets—souvenirs I assume they collected from around the world. A lit wax warmer rests on one of the shelves, surely the source of the fruity smell that fills the house.

More framed photos and several large pieces of bright, abstract artwork dot the walls between the shelves. The family portraits appear professional and formal for the most part, but they lend the room a personal, homey touch.

*Oh, wow!*

How did I miss the front door when I came in? It's navy blue, inlaid with intricate stained-glass panels, and set between two tall, thin windows of a similar design. The colorful, abstract glasswork looks custom. Gorgeous.

I suddenly feel lame for renting a cookie-cutter cottage. It's sad, considering I used to think living in a cottage cluster was the coolest thing even if the small homes look like basic, modern townhouses.

Ice talks about the other half of the room for a while. The breakfast nook with cushioned booth seats in front of a large bay window. A glass dining table with tall, dark chairs. The kitchen looks like it was ripped straight out of a home decor magazine, complete with marble countertops, stainless steel appliances, a skylight in the center of the ceiling, and pans hanging beneath the wall cabinets.

Ice concludes his tour here. He touches me, his hand resting on my arm, and smiles with bright eyes.

I'm still convinced he's showing off just to impress me—for all I know, the house isn't always this put together—but it worked. I have never been inside such a nice house. I've only seen them on TV and in photos.

"What do you think?" he asks.

"It's amazing," I say—for the second time.

He laughs. "We try."

I laugh too, but I shy away from his warm touch. He drops his hand and glances aside, his expression mellow.

"Well," I say meekly, "everything makes a lot of sense now."

"What do you mean?"

"Oh. I just didn't realize you were so…affluent."

I worried he might take offense to being called rich. *Affluent* was the softest alternative I could come up with, but it still sounds a little harsh. There's nothing wrong with having money, but…

"Affluent?" He laughs easily. "I suppose we are reasonably well off."

*Reasonably?* You're kidding, right?

I tuck a few strands of stray hair behind my ear and muster up a smile. "Sorry if that was weird."

He shrugs. "It's alright. I find it charming."

Charming can't possibly be the best compliment I've received, but my fluttering heart disagrees. As I glance away, I catch Night rolling her eyes—though, I may have imagined it.

Either way, Ice turns his attention on her. He clears his throat, but she ignores him and continues reading.

"It's come to my attention that you've already met," he says. "Even so—Jayde, this is my younger sister, Night."

She looks up from her book and slowly, painfully slowly, sets it on the coffee table in front of the couch.

Ice's amiable expression grows forced. "Night, this is Jayde."

I sense some…unpleasant familial tension brewing. Not that they've been trying to hide it. I'm unfortunately well-acquainted with this atmosphere, though, so I pretend I don't notice anything amiss, slap a smile on my face, and wave again.

"It's nice to meet you. Officially. I'm sorry I was so rude the other day."

"Hello," she says. "Again."

Worried, I turn to Ice.

He glances up from the smartwatch peeking out from beneath his sleeve to offer me an unexpectedly terse smile. "I have a feeling you two will get along."

*Really? Why?*

I say nothing. Night doesn't comment either. Instead, she meets my gaze and flashes a more genuine smile as she stands from the couch.

"I'll fetch Smoke," she says. "I'm sure you want to introduce him as well."

Ice smothers a grimace, but he nods, and Night leaves the great room. She knocks on a door in the den, and the muffled music stops. A moment of dead, awkward silence later, she returns with another person in tow—a thin, dark-haired young man.

Smoke Monroe.

While Night keeps her shoulder-length hair neat and polished, her brother's is choppy and left more or less unstyled past the long, side-swept bangs that partially obscure his right eye. His clothing is dark and loose, his eyeliner is heavy, and he has a lip piercing.

He looks like the type of person I would have been afraid of in middle school, but there's something cool about it as an adult.

Ice sighs, looking more disinterested than Smoke does.

"I'll leave you three to chat. I left my phone in the garage."

The moment he's out of sight, having retreated down the hallway, Night pats her twin on the back.

"Jayde, this is my brother, Smoke."

His lips form a thin smile as he looks to me, and our eyes meet. He says, "Hey," and his casual voice clashes with his appearance in a way I didn't expect.

I return the greeting. Then feel my own smile falter.

*What is it…?*

Night and Smoke are twins, but their resemblance is almost uncanny. Not only are they similar in height and build, but they share near-identical facial features. Their eyes are *the exact* same shape. The same vibrant blue color.

They exchange a glance, smile at each other, and look to me at the same time with eerily similar expressions.

"This might sound strange," Night says, "but we're actually identical twins."

She laughs at whatever stupid face I pulled.

"Smoke is transgender," she explains. "He was assigned female at birth—like me, since we're twins—but we both knew from a young age that he wasn't a girl. Without going into too much detail, he came out in middle school and has presented as male ever since."

I glance between the two to compare and contrast their features again. Smoke is slightly taller than his sister, and his face and build are more masculine. And, of course, his voice is deeper. Still, I never would have guessed if Night hadn't told me. He looks like any other guy, so I would have chalked it up to coincidence since they are twins.

If anything, he's the perfect male version of her.

He watches me with some apprehension, though. And Night's smile, while still kind, is expectant and careful.

*I wonder...* How many times has he gone through this type of introduction? I've never met a transgender person before—*as far as I know*—so I don't want to sound rude by mistake.

"That's kind of cool," I say finally.

"I think so too," Night agrees, appearing satisfied with my response. "We're identical twins, but Smoke is the opposite gender. I doubt many get to say that."

He shrugs impassively when she grins at him, but he does seem more comfortable now that it's out of the way.

"Well, it's nice to meet you," I say.

"Same." Glancing from his sister to me, he cracks a lazy half-smile. "So, I hear you're hanging around Ice."

I scratch my cheek. "Yeah. We've gone out a few times."

"Isn't that something?"

Night swipes him on the arm. A playful gesture. She laughs easily, but her smile appears the tiniest bit strained, and he raises his hands in feigned submission before rolling his eyes.

"Whatever," he relents. "I get it. You seem alright, anyway."

*Um... Thanks?*

Night tells me a bit more about him—his penchant for video gaming and art. The indie music he listens to. Then he gets a notification on his phone, frowns, and excuses himself.

A door closes in the den. The muffled music resumes playing. Then Ice dips out of the hallway and reenters the great room.

*Convenient timing, I suppose.*

"He's not very social," Night says under her breath.

*Do I even want to know?*

I don't ask.

Ice stops by my side, his attention locked on his sister rather than on me. With his thumbs tucked in his jean pockets, he looks mildly bored.

She stares back at him, though, smiling again. "I'm glad you decided to introduce your new friend properly."

*Friend, huh?*

"You may see her around more often," he replies.

Night's gaze lands on me, her eyes cool, and her expression soft and pleasant. Then she smiles more broadly at Ice.

"I think you're right," she says. "I think we will get along. Can she stay for dinner?"

# nine

Ice and I sit at the dining table, and I chat with Night while she cooks. We talk about my day. About the horror movie I watched with Ice yesterday. About the weather. A lot of small talk. This and that. But she's sociable and comes up with a new topic every time I run out of words.

All the while, Smoke is hiding out in his bedroom, his muffled music faintly audible despite the distance, my conversation, and the skillet sizzling on the stove. When I ask, they confirm this sort of thing is normal for him. He's busy or wary of new people or…*something*—they don't say—but it has nothing to do with me. He'll come out when dinner is done.

"He only leaves his room to eat," Ice says, the sarcasm so thin I nearly miss it.

Night huffs, wiping a hand on her apron. "You're one to talk."

"Ha." He looks to me, his smile dry. "You didn't have to stay, you know."

"It's not like I had plans."

I hold my glass of water with both hands. I wasn't expecting to stay, and I wasn't expecting this atmosphere. It's not tense, exactly, but the way Ice and Night interact is…peculiar. Her easy banter. His brisk responses. The way he glances at me to gauge my reaction after every remark either one makes.

*Kind of weird.*

At the same time, I'm strangely comfortable here. Even with their parents gone, it feels the way a real home should—like I want to be here, sitting at this dining table, more than I want to be at home.

"You go to RCC?" Night asks. When I nod, she returns to chopping vegetables. "Me too. I feel like I've seen you around."

"Oh? Did we have a class together?"

I feel like I would remember if we sat in the same room on a regular basis for weeks. She is beautiful, and both her appearance and style are quite striking, but—

She shakes her head. "No. Just around campus, you know?"

"Have you really?" Ice asks, propping his chin in his hands.

"Just around campus," she says again. "I take most of my classes online, so I don't spend much time there."

Maybe that's why she knew my last name? Maybe she heard it from another student? One of Rose's friends? Or Rose herself? Does she know Rose? I could ask, but I'd hate to make things awkward. *Or more awkward than they already are.*

"What's your major?" I ask instead.

"Sustainability Science and Business Administration."

"You're double-majoring too?"

*They're both unbelievable.*

"Sort of," she says slowly, "but I'm in a transfer program, and I'm pacing myself. It's easier to take care of things at home if we're less busy. I never know when we'll get called down to

Fresno for one reason or another. I'm not sure what Ice has told you, but our parents' company, MonroeWorks Global, is based there—in Fresno. The assistants can handle themselves more often than not, but you never know, so it's best to keep our schedules open while our parents are overseas." She trails off and laughs. "Sorry. I don't mean to sound like I'm complaining."

"It's fine," I say, genuinely invested. "It must be rough if your parents are gone a lot."

I get it, though. My parents bounced as soon as Rose suggested we get an apartment together.

Night shrugs, but she glances away. "It can be difficult, but their overseas work is important. They're supervising relief efforts in the Middle East right now—though I'm not sure when they'll be back. November or December at the latest, I hope."

"This is an especially long trip," Ice says, seemingly bored. "They rarely leave for more than a few months at a time."

"What does their company do?"

"Alternative energy."

"*Green* energy," she clarifies. "Ocean turbines, solar panels, and the like. We fund research and development for sustainable technology like saltwater filtration systems and biodegradable plastics too."

*How cool!*

"And you both work there?"

"Not exactly," she says with a laugh. "If anything, I act as a figurehead of sorts while they're away. I have the Monroe name, and other companies like to have at least one of us present for major negotiations, so I go wherever they need me. Most times, though, I just smile and nod while my dad's assistant does the talking."

I turn to Ice, and he sighs. "I'm not interested in corporate matters, but I help out where I can. When I have time."

Night tips a cutting board full of chopped vegetables over a sizzling frying pan. She's making stir-fry. It smells dreamy—like ginger and soy sauce.

"What do you do for fun?" she asks.

"Uh—" *I don't do much of anything.* "I've been so busy with school, you know? I took eighteen credits last term. I was lucky if I managed to get out and take a walk a few times a week."

This piques her interest. "You like nature, then?"

"Yeah, of course."

"Not as much as you do, I'm sure," Ice says with a dry laugh.

We both ignore him, and she asks if I live near Windsor Park Natural Area.

I answer, but she already knew. No matter how much I want to believe otherwise—especially now that we've properly met, and I want to like her—I know we didn't run into each other on the trail by chance. I think she only asked to be polite.

"Is it almost done?" Ice asks.

*He doesn't want to talk about it either?*

"Yes. Almost done." She looks over the kitchen—the steaming skillet, the rice cooker on the corner counter, me and Ice at the dining table. Then she sighs and retrieves a phone from her pocket. "I'll call Smoke in."

"Perfect," Ice says with an easy laugh.

She shifts her weight as she types, narrowed eyes trained on the screen. *Wait…* She texts Smoke to call him to dinner? *They're in the same house!* Once finished, she puts her phone away, washes her hands, and continues cooking.

Several seconds pass. The music on the other side of the house falls silent, and Smoke walks out into the great room.

With a crooked smile and raised eyebrows, he holds up his phone. "You called?"

Ice stifles a laugh. Smoke glances at me and snickers before sitting at the end of the glass table. Night sighs again.

"Dinner's just about ready," she says, pouring the contents of the skillet into a wide bowl.

While she finishes getting everything together, Smoke props his elbows on the table and watches me with a passive curiosity. He doesn't say anything, and neither does anyone else, so I speak up.

"So, what do you do?" I ask.

He smiles. "I vlog. And play video games."

"Vlog? Like YouTube?"

He nods, and I ask what his channel is about.

"Video games. And trans stuff. Whatever I want, basically." He shrugs. "I hit two hundred thousand subs a few weeks back."

"Oh, wow!" And he makes it sound like that's nothing.

Night sets a few serving bowls on the table. We're definitely having some kind of Asian-inspired meal. Shredded cabbage salad with almonds and mandarin orange slices. Fluffy, white steamed rice. Stir-fried chicken and vegetables that smell strongly of a sweet and spicy sauce.

I didn't eat much for lunch, so I'm hungrier than I thought.

"You go to RCC, right?" Smoke asks, sitting up straight. "Now that I think about it, I feel like I've seen you before."

"Right?" Night exclaims. "We have, haven't we?"

He looks between the two of us. "Yeah, I think we have."

"Small world, I suppose," Ice says, frowning softly as he glances at the glass tabletop.

"It's not a big school," I reason. "I hang out in the library or student center with Rose all the time in between classes."

Night sets the table with porcelain plates, polished silverware, and embroidered cloth napkins. The plates are a matching set—not exactly fine china, but the intricate, floral border appears to be hand-painted. They're nice. Like the crystal water glasses.

"Rose?" she asks. "I may have taken a speech class with her. During winter term, I believe."

I laugh, not surprised she would remember Rose. "She's my best friend. You probably saw me while I was with her."

"I'm sure that's it." She joins us at the table and looks at each of us, smiling warmly. "Please, enjoy the meal."

The awkwardness lifted after we dished out our food and got to eating, and dinner with the Monroes went wonderfully. The food was delicious—Night is an amazing cook. Ice relaxed. Smoke was surprisingly talkative. I felt good. It was fun. Almost makes me not want to go home to my empty, quiet house.

But I obviously can't stay.

Smoke was quick to return to his bedroom as Night cleared the table after dinner, so only Ice, Night, and I remain in the great room. He helps his sister in the kitchen while I examine a row of framed family photos near the front door.

The Monroe patriarch, August, is a tall, white man with a strong jaw and dark hair. His wife, Sarai, and the twins appear to be of Southeast Asian descent with straight, black hair, tawny skin, and delicate features. Ice is tall like August, but he's as white as they come and has wavy, blonde hair.

*Is he a child from a previous relationship like Robbie?*

I don't want to make assumptions, but he does not resemble the rest of his family in any way but one, as all five share the same bright blue eyes.

*I'm probably overthinking it.* Lots of people have blue eyes.

"Ready to go?" Ice asks.

My face warms—certainly my subconscious calling me out for being nosy—and I turn away from the photos. Ice shrugs into a leather jacket as though it isn't nearly one hundred degrees outside.

"Leaving already?" Night asks, drying her hands on her apron as she joins us near the door.

Ice gives her a look. "It's after seven."

"Is that late?" But she shrugs and offers me a smile. "Well, it was fun, Jayde. I haven't had the chance to entertain new guests in some time, so thanks for indulging me."

"Oh, no; thank you! You're a wonderful host," I say, sounding more animated than intended.

She grins, turning to Ice. "And thank you for bringing her by."

"Of course," he says mildly.

After another moment of small talk, Night must have run out of ways to stall my departure because she finally says, "Have a good night, Jayde. You're welcome back any time."

She returns to the couch and her book, and Ice shuffles us out of the great room and into the hallway. We don't speak again until we leave through the door we first came in.

"She has a tendency to be overbearing," he says. "You weren't uncomfortable, I hope."

"Uncomfortable? No—" *I'm not sure that drawn-out no was convincing.* I clear my throat and laugh. "Your family dynamic is a little…different, I guess—"

"Different?" he echoes with a short laugh.

"I don't mean anything by it," I insist, waving my free hand about. "I had a good time. Honestly."

"That's a relief," he says, his tone lighthearted but rather dry.

The silver car's doors click as they unlock. Ice opens the passenger door for me, and I climb in.

Staring at my purse in my lap, I wonder—

Well, I'm even more curious about the Monroe family than I was before. About the decor in their house. The parents' company. Their blue eyes. The terse glances Night and Ice shared before dinner. Maybe it was a little uncomfortable at times, but only because it felt *familiar*.

That's why I won't ask. We still know next to nothing about each other, so…

"Thanks for inviting me," I say.

He smiles. "My pleasure."

As we chat during the slow drive through the neighborhood, I watch the gorgeous houses, this time trying to imagine how luxurious they must be on the inside if they're larger and grander than the Monroe's. Short, green grass. Expensive cars. Exotic trees. Charming lawn ornaments.

Does Ice know many of his neighbors? Does Westbrooke hold community barbecues like upper-class neighborhoods on television sitcoms? Will I ever have the chance to attend an event like that? *Assuming they exist.*

We leave through the electronic gate. Ice stops talking as he focuses on the busier roads in town, and the world outside returns to the mundane, so I check my phone.

It's after 7:30PM. I have a few texts from Rose, but I'll talk to her when I get home. I need to reflect. To brag and…*decompress?*

Today was different. Good. But stranger than expected.

How much do I want to tell her? I still have a hard time believing this isn't some elaborate prank—that Ice actually wants to hang out with me. Or date me. Or whatever this is.

*Do I care at this point?*

The car pulls into the parking lot.

Oakwood Cottages is a nice place—more than I could afford without Rose and my dad's help. Cottage clusters are novel and cool in theory, but each "cottage" is essentially a detached townhouse in a bare-bones complex. No dishwasher. No gym. No pool. The only permanent outdoor decorations we're allowed to have are potted plants, but the buildings are modern with central cooling and heating, and there's a card-operated laundromat on site, I guess.

*Why am I complaining about this now? I loved Oakwood more than my childhood home this morning.*

"Here you are," Ice says as he parks outside my cottage.

To my surprise, he steps out too, leaving his car idling in the parking space. He walks with me up the short concrete steps, onto the small landing, and to the front door.

My heart decides now is a good time to make itself known within my chest—or try to escape it; I can't be sure.

*Why am I suddenly so nervous?*

He must be so hot in that black leather jacket. Uncomfortable hot—not *hot* hot. Not that he's not hot—

*What? Why am I like this?*

I force eye contact. "Thanks for the ride. And everything."

"Again, Jayde, it's no real inconvenience," he says, cracking a humored smile. "After all, a short drive through town is nothing for someone in my position."

Reminded of my earlier "affluent" comment, I fail to choke back a laugh. It miraculously eases my nerves, even if it is embarrassing.

His expression softens. "I have to ask, though: What do you think of my family?"

A lot runs through my mind. Too much to verbalize.

"They seem cooler than mine," is what I say.

"How is yours?" he asks.

"My family?" I echo, ignoring the pit in my stomach.

"You mentioned growing up in Riverview, but you've said very little about them. I'm simply curious."

"Oh, um—"

*Do I have to answer?*

He introduced me to his family despite the unfortunate manner in which I first met Night, and I witnessed the weird tension between them firsthand. I don't understand it, but I experienced it.

Sure, I can't introduce him to my family, and I wouldn't want to even if I could—with the exception of Robbie…maybe—but would it be unfair to not say anything?

Because there is a lot I *could* say.

My dad helps pay my rent because he feels guilty for leaving. My mom ignored my phone call last Christmas. Robbie left home as soon as he turned 18. My parents' choice to "keep it together for the kids" did more harm than good. The damage was already done by the time they finally wizened up and got a divorce, and they both decided to move "closer to family" after I'd already enrolled at RCC, so I was left in Riverview alone.

I don't need to explain any of that, do I?

*Nope.*

"My brother moved to L.A. for college a couple years ago," I say. "And my parents are…fine. Family problems called them both out of town last year, so…"

"You have no family in Riverview?" he asks. He doesn't sound surprised, exactly, but it also doesn't seem like he was expecting it.

"Nope." I force a smile. "It's just me now. Well, me and Rose, I guess. But it's fine. She's like family too. I don't miss the drama, anyway."

"You're not close with them?"

I shake my head, my smile faltering. "Not exactly. But it's—"

"—fine, right?" He chuckles. "I see. I'm well aware how complicated family matters can be."

I let out my breath. After what I saw today, I'm not surprised he can relate in some way.

"Yeah, it's not always easy," I mutter, dropping the act.

"I understand."

*Does he?*

I don't say anything. I just search his eyes—for what, I don't know—and he watches me, also quiet.

What is he thinking? Why is he still here, standing on my porch? Why hasn't he said goodnight and walked back to his car?

Why am I still standing here? Why haven't I gone inside? Should I say something? Do something? Invite him in? *Stop staring at his mouth?*

Why is this so awkward?

Why do I wish he'd hold my hand?

Or hug me?

Or kiss me?

Or *something?*

*Oh, no…*

As I reaffirm eye contact, his soft smile falters for an instant, and he averts his gaze. He laughs, runs a hand through his hair, and tucks both hands into his jacket pockets. When he meets my eyes again, his expression is muted but still kind.

*Oh.*

"Thanks for coming, Jayde," he says. "I'll talk to you later."

"Yeah. Okay. Thanks."

He dips his head and turns to leave.

I don't move. I watch him walk down the steps, and I wave when he glances back before he gets into his car. The engine purrs as the car backs out of the parking space. Then I tear my eyes away, dig through my purse, and stare at the front door.

The tiny peephole watches me. *Judging me.*

*Wow.*

I don't know what the heck I was expecting to happen, but I'm honestly disappointed that he didn't kiss me.

*Yikes.*

I take a deep breath and head inside.

Leaving my purse on the bookcase, I drift to the couch and fall upon it. I hide my face in my hands, my chest still in turmoil, my stomach still holding onto a small, heavy pit.

I told Rose I'd call when I got home, but I don't know what I'd say. I know I'm awkward, but I didn't think Ice had an awkward bone in his body. I was convinced he could play off just about anything. Be cool in any situation. But interacting with his siblings threw him off, and then standing on my porch…

*That was the worst.*

It's not his fault. Surely, he didn't realize asking about my family would kill the mood. For most people, it wouldn't. Maybe it's weird for a nineteen-year-old girl to be estranged from her parents?

*Ugh...* Here's to hoping he never asks about them again.

I drag myself off the couch and head upstairs. I need to wash my face. I should take a shower too—maybe in the morning?

*Maybe I should call Rose now.*

I wasn't expecting to stay for dinner, so I was out longer than planned. I'd better get it over with before she gets worried.

With a sigh, I set my phone on the shelf above the bathroom sink, start the call, and turn speakerphone on. The phone rings while I hunt for a bottle of makeup remover.

*Click*. "Hey, girl! It's getting late. You home?"

Her voice echoes loudly in the small bathroom.

"Yeah, I'm home," I say.

"How'd it go? Did you have fun?"

"Um, yeah. I stayed for dinner. It wasn't the original plan, but it was nice."

"Dinner?" she asks. "Did he cook for you?"

"No," I say, focused on not jabbing myself in the eye with a cotton pad.

"Did you get takeout? Pizza? I would kill for pizza right now."

"No. His sister cooked. She's the one who invited me to stay in the first place."

"Oh." She almost sounds disappointed, but she soon laughs. "You met his family, though? Does he have any hot brothers? Maybe you can hook me up when I get home."

"Rose, no!" I very nearly jab myself in the eye with a cotton pad, but I laugh. "He has a brother, but I'm pretty sure he's gay."

Smoke mentioned a boyfriend rather casually during dinner, but I didn't ask, so I can only assume he meant a *boyfriend* boyfriend. Either way, he is not Rose's tall, athletic, blond type.

"Dang," she says, still cackling.

I ignore her. "You might know Ice's sister, actually. She goes to RCC."

"Oh? I know a lot of people at RCC. What's her name?"

"Night Monroe."

"Ah…" She mutters under her breath, but I can't make the words out over the phone. "We might have had a class together. Fall term? Winter term, maybe? Not sure, sorry."

“It’s alright. She wasn’t sure either.”

“Hey, your new boyfriend’s last name is Monroe too, right?”

“He’s technically not my boyfriend,” I say, “but yes.”

“Ice and Night… They have some weird names, huh?”

*That’s exactly what I said.*

“Anyway, are you having fun in Arizona?”

I drop the soiled cotton pads into the wastebasket and turn on the cold water to wet a washcloth.

“Not as much fun as you,” she says. A pause. “Hey, am I on speaker?”

“You’ve been on speaker the whole time.”

“Oh. Okay.”

I finish rinsing my face and stare at my reflection in the mirror. I look tired, but I regret not putting my hair up considering I bothered wearing makeup.

Rose clears her throat. “Well, we should definitely order pizza when I get back.”

“Sounds good. I can’t wait.”

# ten

I probably put too much effort into my appearance, but I've been nervous since our phone call yesterday. Ice invited me out to dinner—a fancy dinner.

He has something important to tell me, and I'm meant to dress well, but I have no idea what it's about. He refused to share any hints over text or during the equally vague phone call, so I'm at a complete loss…

What could he possibly want to say? Where are we going? How important is *important?* Is it something bad?

*Is it a love confession? Ha!*

I'll find out soon enough, but, right now, I'm more concerned with my state of dress. Am I overcompensating by wearing jewelry, or am I still not dressed up enough? Did I paint my nails the right color? Should I have bothered painting them at all?

*It's almost six.*

I've been pacing, checking my phone more than I should. If I don't calm down, I'll just embarrass myself when he shows up. *Well, no—* I'm sure I'll embarrass myself tonight regardless, but stressing out won't help.

I should…distract myself.

Maybe I could put my hair up? A ponytail? Or a bun?

*Hm...* A bun will work as long as it isn't too messy.

Styling my hair into a decent half-up, half-down look wastes a good five minutes, after which I continue staring in the mirror. Large, anxious green eyes stare back, so I practice looking like I'm not terrified while applying a third coat of mascara.

My winged eyeliner isn't perfect. My attempt at smoky eyeshadow is timid at best.

I am wearing lipstick. *I never wear lipstick!*

But I glance down at my dress again and worry I haven't done enough. What kind of formal events has Ice attended in the past? What does *dress well* mean to the eldest son of a wealthy business family? Dressy casual? Semi-formal? Black tie?

*God, I hope not.*

A knock on the front door startles me.

I suppress the urge to pretend I'm not home and instead scramble into action, grabbing my purse off the couch on my way to the door. I take a deep breath—*do not touch your face; do not smear lipstick everywhere*—and I pull the door open.

For an instant, I swear I've seen God himself. Light shining from above. An angelic choir singing.

Then I blink, clear my mind, and hope I wasn't drooling.

Ice is not in a suit and tie, like I had feared, but I immediately realize I'm underdressed. He wears a grey dress shirt and red tie, with the hem of his shirt tucked into dark, pressed slacks. He looks considerably more put-together than usual, which is saying something, and he smells vaguely of cinnamon even from this distance.

*His sleeves have cufflinks.*

*I'm wearing a poly cotton summer dress.*

As we scrutinize each other, he regards me with unabashed amusement.

"I did mention to dress nicely, didn't I?"

"This is nice for me," I say, attempting a curtsy to show off my dress' flared skirt.

He laughs, covering his mouth with a raised hand. My informal appearance obviously doesn't bother him *that much* if he finds it comical, but it's still a little humiliating.

I smooth my dress and ask if I should grab an overcoat—since I own a decent one—but he waves it off.

"It's nothing of consequence," he assures me with an easy smile.

As we walk to his car, he rolls his sleeves up to his elbows, loosens his tie, and unbuttons his collar, transforming his outfit from semi-formal to dressy casual. I feel better, but not by much. I guess I should have worn one of my old homecoming dresses.

Ice smiles and opens the passenger door for me. The car smells good—like whatever spicy body spray he's wearing. I fiddle with the thin, silver bracelet on my wrist.

*Semi-formal dress. Something to tell me.*

What kind of date is this?

"You look nervous."

"Ah…" I glance up from my hands, my face warm. "I was just wondering where we're going."

He casts a shifty glance with an equally shifty smile as he turns the key in the ignition. "Don't worry; it's my treat."

*I never assumed for a second it wouldn't be his treat.*

"What a relief," I say. "I doubt I could afford whatever you have in mind, anyway."

His smile doesn't falter even as his focus shifts to driving.

Judging by the route displayed on the silent GPS, we're heading downtown. There are dozens of fancy restaurants there, but I've only eaten at one—an Indian restaurant for a graduation party with a group of Rose's friends. We were messing around and having a good time, so we didn't take the upscale atmosphere serious.

That was nothing like a date.

Ice clears his throat. "You must be curious to hear what I have to say."

"Curious would be putting it lightly," I mutter.

I did *not* mean to say that out loud.

My heart races as I watch for a negative reaction on his part, but he simply laughs. The same as earlier, he covers his mouth with one hand. He doesn't normally do that, and I can't remember him ever taking a hand off the steering wheel while driving before. He's also talking more than usual.

Is he nervous too?

*Oh, god...*

With both hands safely planted on the steering wheel, his gaze flicks to the rear-view mirror. His eyes are contemplative, and he doesn't quite smile or frown.

"There's something I haven't told you about me yet," he says.

I ignore the annoying urge to scratch my arm and keep my attention locked on his face. He watches me out of the corner of his eye, gauging my expression between glances at the road ahead.

"Something about you?" I ask. "Well, what is it?"

His mouth hitches up on one side. "It's a secret."

*Seriously? He's gonna play it like that?*

Okay. I'm intrigued.

"A secret? Are you gonna tell me or not?"

"In time," he says, averting his eyes. "For now, I need to park."

*Oh.* We're already at the restaurant?

I watch the people on the sidewalk through the passenger window until we turn into a parking garage. Ice drives up to the third level and parks in a corner space. The car falls silent as he removes the key from the ignition. He unbuckles his seatbelt, but he doesn't open his door, so I don't move either.

After a beat of silence, he looks to me and smiles.

"It's a secret of the most sensitive nature," he says.

I frown as concern sets in, crushing my previously lighthearted curiosity. "So, it's like a real, serious secret, then?"

"Oh, yes." He nods, his smile unwavering. "I'm not meant to speak of it freely, but I'll make an exception for you—if you swear you won't tell anyone else."

"Sure," I say, the word more like a question than an agreement.

"Very good."

He steps out of the car.

I fumble to unbuckle my seatbelt. I never had issues with it before, but *my hand trembles.* As the button finally clicks beneath my thumb and frees me, the passenger door opens. I hold the strap of my purse to still my hand and look up at Ice, who stands just outside the car. He watches me with a smile and a touch of caution in his eyes.

"What's your secret?" my voice asks.

"I'm not human."

"What?"

I search his face for the punchline. But there isn't one.

Amusement creeps into his expression, though he's clearly not teasing me. His warm, humored smile holds no mischievous darkness. He just finds my startled reaction funny.

*This is not funny.*

I don't move.

He sighs and shakes his head. "Now then, Jayde, shall we head inside?"

He holds a hand out toward me, and I scrutinize his face again, but I still sense no malice. His smile is easygoing and mild, and his eyes are kind. He looks…as human as anyone else—as human as he always has.

Slowly, I release my grip on my purse's strap.

*I should see this date through, right?*

My fingers brush his outstretched palm, and his warm hand closes around mine. *For an instant, I wish I never agreed to come.* But I let him help me out of the car. And I take his arm when he offers it for me to hold.

As we walk, he prompts a normal and completely unrelated conversation as though he never said anything strange in the first place.

We already have a reservation at the restaurant. It's a formal, sit-down establishment with burgundy decor and moody lighting.

Service is fast even considering the reservation, as a uniformed waiter ushers us to a small table immediately after greeting us at the front door. Our meal arrives quickly too, and it's delicious, but the seconds manage to drag on like hours.

This date is going far worse than I anticipated.

Ice…*isn't human?*

I pick at my fancy pasta and drink fancy iced tea out of a fancy crystal glass and contribute to our idle conversation. He eats and smiles and chats so easily, and I'm too confused to do anything but follow along. His words echo in my mind, but I have no idea how to bring it up.

He said the secret is sensitive, but why would he mention it so casually and then drag me inside without any explanation? *Just to torture me?*

Ice finishes eating first. A fork clinks softly against the porcelain plate as he sets it down. I'm almost done too.

*Say something—*

"Um…" I look up from my plate. My resolve wavers, but I might burst if I don't speak up. "You were saying—back at the car…"

He shrugs. "What of it?"

*Is he playing dumb?*

*Are you kidding me?*

I glance around the restaurant. We're in a secluded corner, and, as far as I can tell, there isn't anyone within earshot as long as I speak quietly. On the off chance it's not a joke or weird, edgy metaphor I'm not cultured enough to get…

"I don't understand what you mean," I whisper.

He canvasses the restaurant himself before watching me for a quiet moment. It drives me up the wall, but at least I know he intends to say *something*.

"It's simple," he says. "I'm not human like you are, kid."

*Kid?* Yeah, no. I don't like that. And he said he's not human aloud like it's nothing a second time.

"Not human?" I ask delicately.

"Not at all." He smiles, but the expression is soft and strange. "I'm…something different."

For once, he seems uncomfortable—his eyes periodically dart around the room, and his usual air of confidence is muted—but I never expected this. We've been hanging out for a while. I met his family. They're normal—for the most part. I refuse to believe he isn't human. What else could he be?

Surely, it's some kind of joke. *Still—*

"Okay, fine," I say with a sigh. "If you're not…*human*, what are you?"

He covers his mouth and laughs like what I said is funny. I don't find this situation funny at all, but I'm obviously missing something. He stops laughing, checks his watch, and then rests his elbows on the table, holding his chin in his hands with an unwavering smile.

"I'd love to explain in more detail, but not here. It's a secret, remember? I only mentioned it because I wanted you to think about it before we talk."

*Talk?*

"Where?" I ask.

"Home," he says. "Will you join me?"

# eleven

I accept the invitation.

As we finish eating, Ice Monroe—Hot Grocery Store Man, the mythical perfect guy who apparently isn't human—wastes no time in whisking me out of the fancy restaurant and into his car.

I follow willingly, of course, but the drive from downtown to Westbrooke is tense and silent. I hug my purse and stare out the passenger window. I steal glances at him often, but he focuses only on driving and says little even as he parks on the curb outside his house.

We walk inside.

Through the house, and down the hallway.

*If he's serious…*

Finally, Ice leads me into his bedroom. With a deep breath, and a quick glance at Night's room across the hall, I close the door behind me.

"Have a seat," he says. "This will take some time to explain."

He gestures toward his bed, which is neatly made up with a coordinated grey bedding set. I slip out of my heels and sit on the edge. The softness of the mattress throws me off.

What is it? *A pillow-top? Memory foam?*

I scan the rest of the room, looking at anything and everything to avoid making eye contact.

The bedroom is clean, meticulously organized, and furnished almost entirely in shades of grey and black—though the walls are still a sage green. An end table with a lamp, metal water bottle, and digital alarm clock on top. A short, black bookcase full of hardcover novels—a lot of classics and creative non-fiction, from the look of it.

My host stands in the middle of the room in front of a desk with next to nothing on it.

A full-length mirror hangs on the closet door to my left. My reflection sports a terse frown and wary eyes. For some reason, I want to let my hair down, but I can't bear staring at myself for very long.

So I return my attention to Ice.

He's still quiet, though he watches me carefully.

I worry I'll start sweating if he doesn't get on with it, so I make direct eye contact, but he breaks it immediately. As he glances at the ceiling, he runs a hand through his hair.

Finally, he refocuses on me, though his cool expression betrays a twinge of discomfort. *Not a good sign.*

"Yes. As I said in the car, I am not human." Despite his uneasy appearance, his voice remains level and calm. "I'm an immortal."

"Immortal," I echo, soaking up the word.

"Let's see…" He paces, making a full circle. Then he brings a fist down in his open palm and meets my gaze again. "Immortals and humans are similar, except—"

"Can you die?" I ask.

He falls quiet. His eyes are wide, his brows somehow furrowed at the same time. Then he sighs heavily.

"Of course, I can die. Don't be absurd."

*Why is that even more confusing?*

But I keep my mouth shut, and his frown softens.

"However," he continues, watching me rather defensively, "one could argue it's more difficult for an immortal to die than it might be for a human under similar circumstances."

I hesitate to ensure he's finished before I admit that I don't understand.

"The name is a misnomer. Don't ask what genius chose it—or why—because I couldn't tell you, but it is what it is," he says with a tolerant shrug. *If this is a joke, he's taking it way too far.* "In any case, the main difference between humans and immortals is our ability to assume feline form."

He winced halfway through his last sentence, and I take solace in the fact he also finds this conversation overwhelmingly uncomfortable. *Still...*

"You can do *what?*"

He smooths the front of his shirt. "As an immortal, I have the ability to transform into a cat at will."

When I don't reply, he grimaces.

"I can turn into a cat," he says. "You know: fur, ears, tail?"

*Obviously, I know what a cat is, but this is...*

He groans, raises his hands to chest level, and flicks his wrists in a scratching motion. "*Meow?*"

I force myself to nod, if only to make him stop before I die of secondhand embarrassment, but I avoid meeting his eyes directly even as he relaxes and drops his hands to his hips.

“Cat,” he repeats dryly. “In short, immortals are shape-shifters.”

“Shapeshifters… Is that right?”

I glance at my lap—at the fabric of my dress balled up in my fists. *Is Ice crazy?* Is this some kind of game to him? Is the elaborate prank he’s been working toward for weeks finally coming to a head?

*Or is he telling the truth?*

I’m not sure after that sad display. He seems like the type who cares how others see him—that’s the impression I get, anyway—so why would he damage my perception of him like this?

Seriously, though? *A shapeshifter?*

“Tell me you’re kidding,” I say, my mouth dry.

Our eyes meet, but he merely shrugs.

“What could I possibly gain by lying to you?” he asks. “I’m dead serious.”

I stand from the bed and cross my arms over my chest.

He is several inches taller than me, and my half-assed attempt at intimidation only appears to amuse him. As my eyes narrow, his smirk grows more pronounced.

It’s a challenge.

I take the bait.

“I don’t believe you.”

“Oh, come on.” He groans, his frustration only feigned in part. “Surely, you’ve noticed the cat hair around the house. It doesn’t make sense considering we don’t own any cats, does it?”

He beams down at me.

"Or perhaps you're not so observant?"

I bite my tongue at the accusation because it's true; I never saw any mysterious cat hair. *Not that I went over the carpet with a magnifying glass or anything!* I don't want to admit it, though—in case it is as obvious as he thinks. Instead, I force a smile.

"Alright. Fine. If you can turn into a cat, prove it."

His smile grows uneasy.

"I dare you."

He clears his throat, his eyes narrow. "Very well. I accept, but only because you remain so unconvinced."

I take a step back as his smile fades. He crosses his arms, parodying my belligerent stance. Our eyes meet, but, rather than looking either uncomfortable or smug, he now appears bored out of his mind. He lets out a deep, disinterested sigh, and then he's gone.

No, he's not *gone.*

This is impossible.

*People cannot turn into cats!*

I blink and rub my eyes, but I'm still met with an unobstructed view of the window behind the desk. Ice is no longer standing there. I stare at the strip of clear blue sky and the top of a tall privacy fence on the far side of the backyard for a few seconds. When I finally glance down, a white cat stands on the cream carpet in front of the leather desk chair.

The cat jumps up onto the desk and turns back to reveal striking, electric-blue eyes. The eyes are feline with slit pupils in the well-lit bedroom, but they're unmistakably Ice's.

"Done," his voice says. "Are you satisfied?"

"You can talk?" I squeak.

"Of course, I can talk. Why wouldn't I be able to talk?"

The cat's mouth doesn't open to speak, but it's somehow still obvious where the voice came from. I can't quite comprehend it. Any of it. The fancy dinner. Shapeshifters. Talking cats.

*Something bothers me, though...*

I study Ice's feline form more carefully as he sits on the desk. One ear flicks, and he curls his fluffy tail over his paws.

My hands fall to my sides.

*Something else...*

Oh.

*Oh...*

"I recognize you," I cry, pointing at him. He glances away, but I don't back down. "You were there—outside my house—the day I met you at Bargain Shop."

*Well...*

Surely, there are a lot of fluffy white cats with bright blue eyes in Riverview. *Am I being presumptuous again? Jumping to conclusions?*

"I mean… That was you, wasn't it?"

His gaze returns to my face. Feline eyes blink slowly.

"You are correct," he says. "I was there."

My mind buzzes with concerns—*many, many concerns of varying severity*—but I offer a solemn nod and return to sitting on the edge of his unreasonably soft bed.

"But why?" I ask. "How long have you been watching me?"

He maintains unblinking eye contact, though he shifts his weight and flicks his ear again. This seemingly dismissive gesture only makes me more frustrated.

"Answer me, Ice."

The fear of betrayal stings, but I want to give him the benefit of the doubt. I don't want to believe he's been screwing with me this whole time. After all, he's been nothing but kind and patient since we met. Even after sharing his secret and being called out, he doesn't seem angry.

"I suppose you deserve an explanation," he agrees. "The why is simple; I was bored and felt like being there. As for how long? I believe I first saw you only a week or so before I decided to meet you in person."

*Decided? Ha...*

"I—"

How am I supposed to respond? He denied nothing. He openly confessed to stalking me and made no excuses for himself. He even admitted, albeit in a roundabout way, that he orchestrated our initial meeting.

*I don't... How am I supposed to feel?*

He sighs, his fluffy shoulders dipping. "If it's any consolation, I never intended on sharing this secret with you when we first met. As you can see, I've since changed my mind, though humans aren't meant to know of our existence."

*What is he trying to prove by saying that?*

I'm still struggling to put the pieces together. A few things make more sense; others make less. I don't know where to begin. I'm confused. A little nervous. A little hurt.

To make matters worse, Ice's expressions and posture are more difficult to read as a cat. His large feline eyes are narrowed, and his ears are angled ever so slightly backward, but I don't know the first thing about feline body language or if immortals have the same habits as normal cats.

I am totally lost.

"Are you angry with me?" he asks.

*Am I—?*

"Somehow…" *I honestly want to be angry. I have every right to be pissed off about the whole thing, but—* My hands fall into my lap. "No. I'm not angry."

His ears perk up. "Is that so?"

"Angry isn't the word I'd use. I'm just…annoyed that you hid it from me. I guess."

"Hid what from you, exactly?" he asks. "The fact I stalked you or that I'm not human?"

"Both," I say, my aforementioned annoyance slipping through.

He laughs and returns to human form, sitting on the edge of his desk. Then he drops to the floor, smooths a crease in his shirt, and meets my gaze. Looking him over again, I freeze, as he's now sporting a t-shirt and jeans instead of the semi-formal ensemble he wore before…*shapeshifting?*

*Is that the right word?*

"How did you do that?" I ask.

"Do what?"

His eyes are wide like I caught him off guard, so I point at his shirt. He glances down, clearly puzzled, and his face remains blank as he looks up again.

"My clothing, you mean?" he asks, also pointing to his shirt.

I nod.

There's a short pause, after which he cracks. He hides his face in his hands and throws his head back, howling in laughter as though my confusion is completely unfounded.

I frown, watching with antsy patience.

As he recovers from his fit of hysteria, he wipes an imaginary tear from his eye and smiles. "I apologize if I startled you. This is second nature for me."

I listen, feeling like my brain might turn to mush as he speaks, but it seems as though he can turn into a cat *and* change his clothes in the process? It's some kind of immortal power. *Okay...* That's fine. I'll just pretend it makes sense.

"Can all immortals do that?"

Without allowing time for him to answer, I ask if Night and Smoke are immortals too. He looks offended that I cut him off again, but he simply sighs.

"Yes," he says. "Of course, the twins—and our parents—are immortals as well. That said, the answer to your first question is a resounding *no*."

"Are you special or something?"

He glances around the room for a moment, scratching his jaw and shifting his weight. Then he shrugs. "Not particularly."

"Oh."

*He must think I'm terribly stupid.*

"That's alright," he says with a smile, "but it is getting late. You should go home."

The frustration that has worn at me all evening finally overflows, and I stand from the bed. "No way. I want to know more about you—and about immortals too."

"I shouldn't say any more tonight. Now that I've told you this much, you need to decide whether you want to involve yourself further or if you'd rather return to living your life as it was before. You are human, after all, so you can't have it both ways."

*That's ridiculous!*

"Of course, I—"

"I am not simply referring to myself, Jayde," he says, a flash of warning in his eyes. I bite my tongue. "Choosing to involve yourself with immortals is a matter of legality and social status. We could both end up in serious trouble if we're not careful. This secret isn't something you can take lightly."

*Legality? Social status? Serious trouble?*

It does sound complicated, but how could he possibly think I wouldn't want to hear more? His secret is life-changing. Even if I refuse to get involved, or whatever, it's not like I can forget there's an entire race of shapeshifters living alongside humans.

"I don't get it," I admit. "You won't explain anything now?"

He smiles apologetically. "I'm sure you have questions, but there is a certain protocol I must follow, and these things take time. Do you understand?"

*If there's no other option...*

"Fine," I agree. "When can you tell me more?"

"That's the spirit." He flashes a grin, sounding a bit too cheery and self-assured. "I'll drop by your place in a few days —Thursday, perhaps—and we can discuss the matter in more detail then."

"Okay. That's fine. I guess."

Begrudgingly, I slip my feet back into my heels.

"Night knows you're here," he says. "She can take you home. I'd offer myself, but I have a lot to consider as well."

*Do you?*

What does he mean? What does getting further involved with immortals entail, exactly? What would it change?

Even as he leads me out into the hallway, I can't understand why he shared this part of himself with me. He's only in Riverview for the summer. He's leaving in September, and immortals are a secret. Humans aren't supposed to know, and, if he hadn't brought it up, I never would have. I never would have found out about shapeshifters or his feline form—or the stalking. Surely, he realized I might recognize him. I could have cut him off right there and demanded to go home.

*Why risk telling me?*

He waves goodbye, closes himself in his bedroom, and leaves me alone with my thoughts in the empty hallway.

*Does he even like me?* We've gone on several dates, and now *this*, but I still can't tell. *How annoying.*

When I go to knock on Night's bedroom door, I hesitate with my hand hovering inches away. But the door opens anyway. Her expression is soft and not unkind, but she looks uneasy.

I force a smile, trying to suppress my own nervous energy.

"Ice said you could take me home. Is that okay?"

She nods, a beaded keychain held in one hand. "Let's go."

Wordlessly, I follow her to the front of the house.

We walk down the stone path from the front door to the curb, where her blue sedan is parked. I take the passenger seat. The car starts, and she's driving, and neither of us say anything. Her lips form a soft frown, and her focused eyes scan the road ahead.

Should I ask about immortals?

*Would she tell me anything?*

I don't want to go behind Ice's back. I'm sure he has a good reason to wait before he answers more questions—something about protocol or rules or whatever—but Night is also an immortal. *It's tempting.*

After a few minutes, a soft sigh from the driver's seat breaks the silence.

"He told you, didn't he?"

"Aah—" I hold my hands close to my chest, averting my gaze for an instant. "About immortals? Yeah, he did."

Her grip on the steering wheel tightens, but her face remains passive. "What do you think about it all? Knowing we're different from you?"

"Are you guys really that different?"

She sighs again. "He hasn't explained a thing, has he?"

"What do you mean?"

"Sorry." She shakes her head. "I told Ice he shouldn't drag you into our world, but he hates taking my advice. As usual. I shouldn't be surprised."

"Is it bad that I know?"

"Bad?" Her eyes remain fixed on the road for some time before she casts a cryptic glance in my direction. "I don't know if I'd go so far as to say it's bad, but don't you think it would be better if you didn't? Wouldn't life be easier if you didn't have this secret you must now keep from everyone you know? Your family? Your friends?"

The dark flash in her eyes sends a shiver down my spine even though I don't understand the meaning behind it.

"Maybe," I agree, messing with my bracelet. "Maybe it would be easier, but I can't forget what I've already heard."

"What happens next is up to you—both you and Ice," she says. Her frown is pensive. Disappointed. "Your decision is your own, Jayde. No one can stop you, but at least try to give it more thought than he did."

# twelve

After a day and a half, I'm on the verge of tearing my hair out.

Immortals aren't simply humans who happen to turn into cats. I'm not stupid. There's more to the mystery, but no amount of prodding gets me any closer to a real answer. Night added me as a friend on FaceSpace, but she hasn't responded to a single message I sent her, and Ice carefully evaded every question I asked over the phone yesterday. He hasn't even replied to my most recent text—and it had nothing to do with his secret.

They both expect me to make up my mind without knowing the first thing about what I'm getting myself into.

It's not fair, but I can't dig up any information on my own either. An internet search on "immortals" brings up nothing but literature and mythology regarding literal, undying immortals. It's a dead end.

*Still, I guess it can't hurt to try again?*

It's not like I have anything better to do, so I head upstairs and sit at my desk.

With some determined and creative Googling, I find a series of lengthy forum threads on cryptozoology, government conspiracy theories, and the paranormal. It's all fascinating, sure, but I spent three, long hours scouring the weird part of the internet, and I failed to uncover a single mention of immortals or human-feline shapeshifters in the correct context.

*Hm…*

Is there a reason I can't find anything online?

Switching tactics, I open FaceSpace.

I study Night's profile and scroll down her timeline going back several weeks, but neither her *About Me* nor any of her posts even vaguely hint at the existence of immortals. No subtle mention of cats. No pictures of cats. Nothing suspicious at all. It's the same as scrolling down any other young woman's FaceSpace page. She shares pictures of her daily outfits, headbows she made herself, and artistic shots of flowers, interspersed by reflective statements and posts about going out with friends—usually accompanied by fun group selfies.

I pause on a candid photo of Smoke from a couple months ago with the caption "*it went outside and SMILED*". The resulting comment thread between the twins and two of Night's friends makes me laugh, but it's hardly revealing.

Immortals are a well-kept secret, but there must be *something*.

Out of ideas, I expand Night's friend list. *Wow.* She has over five hundred friends, but we have zero mutuals.

Scrolling slowly, I scrutinize the physical features of a few dozen people before it occurs to me that none of them have brown eyes. I keep scrolling, focused on the eyes in profile photos, and the trend continues.

I guess brown eyes aren't *that* common, but for none of her friends to have them? *No grey or hazel either…* Around half her friends have blue or pale violet eyes. Some have warm, golden eyes—a color similar to light brown but *not* brown or hazel. And others have green eyes. There are a few slight variations, but they all appear to have one of those four eye colors.

It's not much, but I assume most, if not all, of her friends are immortals. It makes sense since they're such a big secret. There's less risk of spilling it that way. But, after an hour spent creeping on FaceSpace, I've learned only one thing for certain:

Immortals are incredibly attractive.

*Awesome.*

Even if my eye color theory isn't a coincidence, it's nothing groundbreaking. Though, if I'm right, there must be hundreds or thousands of immortals in Riverview alone. *Seems like they're not rare, after all.*

I rub my tired eyes, close my laptop, and realize the sky outside is growing dark. I haven't moved from my desk since lunch.

I stretch my limbs and embark on a house-wide search for my phone, which I eventually find downstairs, on the bookcase next to the TV. There's one missed call from Rose. From like three hours ago.

*Ugh...* I was so in the zone, I didn't hear the phone ring.

**Me:** Hey! Sorry, I was distracted. You still up?

As I stare at the screen, a pit grows in my stomach.

She knows about my fancy dinner date with Ice, but I lied when she asked how it went. She thinks we ate dinner at an uncomfortably upscale restaurant and hung out at his house for a few minutes before he dropped me off at home. She thinks I had a pleasant but slightly underwhelming time.

I can't tell her he literally isn't human. God forbid I break *the rules* and have an assassin sent after me—or whatever happens when you disclose the world's most important secret without express permission.

*I'm losing control of my life.*

My phone rings, startling me. Of course, it's Rose.

*Well, here goes nothing...*

"Hey," I say, trying to sound normal and failing.

"You sound like shit."

"Oh, I'm sure. How are you?"

I tap speakerphone, set my phone on the arm of the couch, and get more comfortable. Once I'm warmly nestled between the couch cushions and a throw blanket, I feel a bit better.

"I'm fine," she says, "but you've been busy, haven't you? Have you seen your hot boyfriend since the hot dinner date?"

I groan. "Not yet—and he is not my boyfriend."

"So you say."

"Do we have to talk about him?"

"Oh, come on," she whines, but I can imagine the stupid smile on her face. "It's not like you have anything else fun going on right now, so what's up? How are things with you two?"

"Things have certainly been going," I say.

"Good? Bad? He's rich and hot, right? You described him as my dream guy."

I roll my eyes. "That's not why I like him."

"But you do like him?"

"What is this? *Twenty Questions*?"

She laughs. "I'm just saying, Jay. If this Ice character really is my dream guy, he's either screwing with you because he pegged you as a squirrelly virgin—in which case, he's not wrong—or he's looking for an easy summer armpiece. You know that, right?"

"Ugh. Can we not go there? Besides, I already told you he goes to Stanford, and it's nothing serious."

"So, you do realize it? Yet here you are, torturing yourself over a hot, rich, university guy. Why bother?"

The line goes silent as I have nothing to say in my defense. I don't know how Ice feels about me, so she's not wrong, exactly, but he wants to hang out for some reason. And he revealed his big secret. Though, it's hard to explain without mentioning things I shouldn't.

She gasps. "Did you have sex with him?"

"N–no," I stammer, my face catching fire.

She bursts out laughing, but I guess it's a valid question. If all Ice wanted out of me was sex—and it was something I had considered after he first called—he's dragging it out rather long. His intentions for our relationship are different, even if I still don't understand what those intentions are.

"Honestly, I haven't once gotten the impression he's interested in having sex with me."

"Maybe he's not my dream guy, then," she says, still cackling.

*Should I humor her…?*

I can't mention immortals, obviously, but her general dating advice can't be that bad, can it? Either way, she offered to help, and I should be happy with any advice I can get.

I sigh. "Let's assume you're right—he's only in it for the short-term. What should I do?"

"Have fun! Seriously, Jay, you should try it sometime." *Of course, she'd say that.* "On that note, you really should send me a picture of this guy. Y'know, just to confirm he's as hot as you say."

"I'm not sure I should. You might try to steal him for yourself when you get back."

"Oh, come on. There's no point in trying if he won't even sleep with you," she says, unable to keep from laughing between words.

I cover my eyes, grateful for her sake she's a thousand miles away. If we were together, I'd wring her horny neck in an instant. *Take control of the situation—*

"Anyway, Rose! Let's pretend that Ice has a secret. He's cool and friendly and stupidly hot and all, but he also has this huge, weird, potentially problematic secret. Would you still go for it?"

"Me?" she asks, falling quiet. "Well, unless his secret is that he moonlights as a serial killer, and he chose me as his next victim… Yeah. Definitely."

I wish I could tell her the secret, but this much is still useful. I mean, it's safe to assume being a shapeshifter isn't nearly as bad as being a closet serial killer.

*Though, he did admit to stalking me.*

"Okay," I agree. "Why?"

"You see, Jay, the situation you're in is perfect. He's a college student, right? And he's going back to school in the fall, right? So, you can have a fun summer fling with this guy, okay?"

"I'm following."

"Since he has to leave Riverview because of school, and you have to stay in Riverview because of school, and you both know that, there won't be a messy breakup at the end of the summer. You'll just go your separate ways. No big deal. As long as you don't get too emotionally invested in this guy, it's perfect. There are no strings attached."

*No strings attached, huh? Ugh.*

She sounds so confident and matter-of-fact, I'd be convinced if I weren't already too emotionally invested or caught up in a secret I can't escape. *Hm…* Ice didn't plan to tell me about immortals when we first met, but something changed his mind.

*What changed to make him want to tell me?*

"Honestly, I'm sure that's all he's after, anyway," she continues flippantly. I open my mouth to respond, but she cuts me off with a gasp. "Oh my god. His secret isn't that he has a girlfriend back in Stanford, is it?"

"Um… No, that's not it."

Well, he never said he doesn't have a girlfriend. *But I'd rather not consider the possibility.*

"Is he in a cult?" she asks instead.

"Uh—" *I mean, that might be closer to the truth, but—*

"Jayde, if he's trying to convince you to join his cult, please resist."

"He is not in a cult."

She lets out a deep breath—as though she was legitimately afraid I was dating a cultist—and then laughs. Something about the depth of her relief concerns me.

"Anyway… I don't think it's that bad, really, but it left me with a lot to think about. I haven't been getting a ton of sleep."

"Oh, no. This isn't like a *Fifty Shades of Grey* thing, is it?"

I laugh. "No, I don't think so."

"You gotta admit it kinda sounds like it," she muses. "Rich, hot guy, always taking you out places and paying for everything. Hm. But, anyway… Yeah, if I were you, I would totally go for it. Do your thing. Take risks. Make mistakes. Just don't fall head over heels for this guy. You're way more sensitive than I am, but I think you can handle yourself."

*Uh-huh... Don't fall head over heels,* she says.

"It'll be a good learning experience and build character, if nothing else."

"I guess I haven't scared him off yet," I say slowly.

"That's a start! Just trust your instincts, okay?"

*My instincts?* The same instincts that told me to forgive him after he openly admitted to stalking me?

*She's right, though.*

Until now, I never dated anyone I truly liked, and I never saw any of the guys I tried dating for more than a few weeks. I never did anything particularly fun or interesting with any of them either. It was always something like, "*Let's watch a game,*" or "*Let's go to a party,*" but I don't care for sports or parties.

It hasn't been like that with Ice. I don't mind going to the park or watching a movie or hanging out at his house. I know I shouldn't fall too deep, but…

"You probably won't even go official," Rose says.

She's trying to make me feel better, assuming whatever I do isn't a big deal, but the truth is more…complicated? She couldn't possibly understand there's more on my mind than my relationship with Ice, and I can't tell her.

I say nothing and examine my hands. My cheap, silver nail polish is chipped around the edges—just like my life, apparently. It does nothing to help me feel less pathetic.

"But, um…" She coughs. "When are you seeing him again?"

"Tomorrow," I mumble. "We're supposed to talk more about his secret. I think."

"It'll be fine, Jay. Don't be so nervous!"

"I'll try."

"He asked you out first, right?" She laughs, her voice warm. "He's obviously into you, so there's nothing to worry about."

But *why* has he been asking me out? Is he into me? Does he even see what we're doing as dating?

*Whatever.*

I sit up and rub my eyes. "I guess you're right, Rose. Thanks for talking to me about it."

"No problem!" She's always *so* cheery. "Let me know how it goes, okay? And please, please try to snap a picture of this guy for me. Even a creepy stalker pic is fine. I'm not kidding."

*Yeah, right.* That is not happening.

"I'll see what I can do," I say mildly.

"Awesome. I'll text you tomorrow. Don't forget to have fun!"

*Fun... Right.*

# thirteen

I don't have a choice, do I?

It doesn't matter if I agree to Ice's ultimatum or not. Immortals will still exist, and that awareness will weigh on my mind until the day I die. Even if it has no impact on us seeing each other moving forward, I can't just *forget* what he said.

Either way, I feel weird dating a person if I can't learn more about them—especially when it comes to something as important as their species.

*Is species even the right word?*

Maybe immortals are more like a variant of humans? I have no idea, but *the way he changed clothes while transforming...*

*Something to do with eye color...*

I can theorize all I want, but I won't learn more unless I accept, and I have to know. So, in truth, the decision was made the day Ice gave it to me. That's how I feel, but…

*Is it worth it?*

A matter of legality and social status? What does that mean?

Even if our relationship, whatever it is now, doesn't outlive summer, this *getting further involved with immortals* deal surely extends far beyond Ice and his family. I doubt I can weasel my way out of it if things don't work out between us.

*Even knowing that...*

If I want to satisfy my curiosity, there's only one option.

*This is a risk I have to take.*

A knock on the front door startles me, and a glance through the window confirms the presence of Ice's silver Porsche outside.

He's here. This is it. The point of no return.

I slap a hopefully not-nervous smile on my face and answer the door. "Hey, Ice!"

"Hello, Jayde."

My breath catches.

He's not wearing the typical casual yet slightly unseasonal clothing I'm used to. No dark jeans or leather jacket. Instead, he's dressed in a similar fashion as during our tense dinner date: a dress shirt, tie, and slacks. His tie is loose, his collar unbuttoned, and his hair is pushed up and out of his face, held in place with some type of hair product.

Whatever this look is, it's *hot.*

I stop gawking and invite him inside.

He glances over the decor in the living room while I worry my hands and briefly explain the cottage's layout. There's not much for him to see. Rose and I are broke college students, and he knows it, but he's obviously judging me based on the appearance of our house. He doesn't seem particularly impressed either.

*At least it's clean.*

After a moment spent examining a random Arizona-related knickknack on the bookcase beside the stairs, he turns and flashes a crooked smile.

"Quaint," he says simply.

"Yeah, sorry. It's not nearly as impressive as your parents' place."

He shrugs, and I realize his comment may have been in reference to me calling him affluent. *It is kind of funny.*

"Have you made your decision yet?" he asks.

I nod, feigning confidence. "Yes. I want to learn more about immortals."

"Perfect. Glad to hear it."

His expression shifts, now seemingly guarded as he studies something else on the same shelf—a framed photo of me and Rose at our high school graduation, maybe? It's hard to tell exactly what he's looking at.

"That said, if you ever find yourself regretting this decision, I want you to remember that I gave you a choice."

*Okayyy... There's still time to say no, Jayde.*

"Do you think I'll regret it?" I ask with a timid laugh.

"How am I meant to know what you may or may not regret?"

He moves on to study yet another object on the bookcase, his expression once again mild. It's a little frustrating.

"It's not like I can forget what you said or what I saw," I reason aloud. "Now that I know, my life won't return to normal even if I don't accept your offer. Besides, I think I should learn more about immortals if we're gonna keep hanging out like this."

"I see." He turns away from the bookcase with an easy smile. "I assumed that would be the case."

*Is he impressed? He sure doesn't seem surprised.*

I scratch my arm. "What now? Time to sign my soul away?"

"Not quite," he says, laughing. "But there is something I need you to sign. Can you stay the night?"

My face grows hot. I may have gasped audibly.

"Stay the night?" I ask. "At your house?"

What did Rose say about *Fifty Shades of Grey*?

*Oh my god. Stop thinking, brain.*

Ice hits me with a blank, blank stare.

"It's nothing inappropriate," he says, his voice painfully dry. "The paperwork has to be approved in person. I'll leave for Seattle first thing in the morning, but my visit will take some time. If you don't mind, I would prefer you stay with the twins until then."

*Oh.*

"Um, alright," I say slowly. "I guess that's fine."

*Yeah...* That's totally normal and not weird at all.

He flashes another smile. "I'll wait here while you get ready."

* * * * *

*What on earth did I get myself into?*

Sitting in Ice's car with a fat backpack on the floor between my feet, I stare at my lap and try to ignore the nagging sense that something isn't right. I've known this guy for less than a month, and I packed enough that anyone watching could assume I'm moving in with him.

He insists it's nothing—the paperwork is standard procedure and staying at his house is merely a precaution—but this sure feels like *something*. The reason he told me about immortals in the first place? The reason he's willing to go through so much trouble for someone he hardly knows and has no reason to trust with such an important secret?

Surely, it can't be nothing.

We walk into the house together, entering through the garage. I drop my backpack in the den and catch Night watching me from the breakfast nook clear across the house. Ice notices her too, and they stare at each other, generating the same cool tension I sensed during my first visit.

I desperately want to break the silence. But Ice asks me to collect the documents I brought before I can think of anything worth saying.

"I'll meet you in my room," he says on his way out of the den.

He sits across from his sister at the small breakfast table, where they speak in hushed tones. They both sound and look fairly annoyed—jaws tense and eyes narrowed. It's none of my business, though, and the risk of involving myself in their family drama fills me with dread.

I shuffle through the contents of my backpack, trying to find my wallet.

For *whatever reason*, I had to bring my ID, birth certificate, Social Security card, and a voided check. It's…strange, but I didn't argue. I figure Ice knows what he's doing. Not that it matters. I have to play along if I want to learn more about immortals.

*Found it.*

Glass clinks in the great room. The sound is gentle—like a cup tipping onto wood—but louder than their voices. I keep my eyes on my bag, suppressing the urge to peek over my shoulder.

"Have you lost your damn mind?" Night asks, her voice low

but raised enough to hear.

My skin prickles. I zip my bag, scurry down the hall, and shut myself inside Ice's bedroom, where I stay with my back pressed against the door.

*This feeling... The tightness in my chest.*

It reminds me of the way my parents acted toward each other in the months leading up to their divorce. The strange tension. The forced smiles. The uncomfortable, passive-aggressive dialogue. They tried to hide it by acting like everything was fine, but they never succeeded for long. The cracks were always there.

It's similar, but Ice and Night don't seem to resent each other like my parents did. Maybe I'm reading into it more than I should? It's probably nothing. Just her aversion to me having learned about immortals. Or...sibling rivalry.

*So, let it go.*

Stepping away from the door, I look around.

Ice's bedroom is just as tidy as it was the other day, but I soon detect an anomaly—a stack of paper on the desk. The paperwork he mentioned earlier, I assume. Inching closer, I make out *ADULT APPLICATION* printed across the first page in block letters.

I drop my documents off to one side and sit in the leather chair in front of the thick packet.

*The U.S. Department of Human-Immortal Affairs* is printed near the bottom of the page in a smaller font. I can only assume it's a government organization based on the name alone, and the small seal beneath the title all but confirms it. A circle containing a lion and an eagle on either side of a shield with some sort of greenery bordering the edges.

I stare at the stack of paper with dagger eyes, working up the courage to remove the cover page. As my fingers brush paper, the bedroom door opens.

It's Ice, and I know it, but his arrival spooks me nonetheless.

"You weren't kidding about the paperwork," I say.

"No, but you can relax. I'm responsible for the bulk of it. You have a few things to sign, but I have to write an essay."

"You're serious?"

"Essentially."

If his heated conversation with Night bothered him, he doesn't show it. He looks bored, almost. Maybe it wasn't as serious as I thought. Maybe it was harmless bickering. Maybe it didn't even have anything to do with me.

"Shall we begin?" he asks with a muted smile.

I glance at the daunting stack of paper. "Where do we start?"

He closes the distance between us, stopping right beside me, and leafs through the papers. After he removes a thick, stapled packet from the bottom, I'm left with three individual sheets, including the cover page. He then opens one of the desk drawers, takes two pens from an organizer, and offers one to me.

Our eyes meet as I accept the pen.

His smile grows somewhat uneasy. "You see? This shouldn't take you long at all."

Once he settles himself on the bed with his back against the wall and a clipboard in one hand, I return my attention to my share of the paperwork. I move the cover aside and find what appears to be a contract, rather vaguely titled *Secrecy Agreement*, underneath.

According to the agreement, I shall **NEVER** discuss immortals or other *immortal-related topics* with *non-immortals* (i.e. other humans) unless they have also signed the same document or one covering similar terms.

Fair enough, I guess.

> The U.S. Department of Human-Immortal Affairs reserves the right to access and modify the Subject's personal information without advance notice or approval. Subject or Sponsor reserve the right to an appeal.

*What does that even mean?*

I continue reading and grow increasingly concerned.

If I sign this agreement, the conditions span *the entirety of my natural life*, and breaching those conditions is severely punishable. Though, the document never clarifies what "severely punishable" means. *Yikes.*

Parts of the agreement are sketchy at best—I mean, *modifying my personal information without permission*?—but I'm dealing with a secret government document issued by a secret government organization. I'm not supposed to know about any of this, anyway, so it's only fair I sign an NDA, right?

*Right?*

The strict guidelines laid out also explain why Ice didn't want to say much the other day. I hadn't signed anything yet. He had to take my word that I wouldn't talk to anyone else. It was risky on his part, so I hope he didn't get into trouble for telling me without this paperwork on hand.

The bottom of the page has space for three sets of signatures.

It asks for today's date as well as my name, signature, and Social Security number. Below that are the same four lines, blank and meant for the applicant's sponsor.

*My sponsor?* That would be Ice, right?

The last set of lines at the very bottom of the contract have already been filled out by someone else. Both the printed name and Social Security number of this mystery individual are blacked out, and the signature is illegible. But it was signed yesterday.

"Who signed this?" I ask, glancing at Ice over my shoulder. "Who?"

He looks up from his clipboard, so I turn, hold the Secrecy Agreement up, and point to the blacked-out name. Understanding quickly replaces his passive curiosity.

"Some bureaucrat from Human-Immortal Affairs, I'm sure," he says.

"What is Human-Immortal Affairs, exactly? What do they do?"

He shrugs. "It's your standard government agency. Mediators, I suppose, between the human and immortal aspects of society. They regulate contact between the two groups, protect the secret of our existence, and oversee humans with knowledge of immortals."

"Oh, wow." I turn back to the desk. "I had no idea."

"Of course, you wouldn't. Few humans know about us. But that doesn't make for less paperwork."

*The U.S. Department of Human-Immortal Affairs...*

This is standard procedure, after all?

I skim the Secrecy Agreement once more to ensure I haven't missed anything especially unsavory before I resolve to sign it.

I scribble my name, copy my Social Security number onto the appropriate line, and stare at my handwriting.

*Is this okay?*

*Does it matter?*

I already signed. It's too late to change my mind.

With a sigh, I flip to the last page. It's a double-sided personal questionnaire—the type of form you'd fill out when applying for an apartment or a loan. Whatever it is, it asks for a lot of personal info: legal name, address, date of birth, Social Security number, income bracket, etcetera, etcetera. It's fairly straightforward, and the information is easy to provide. For the most part. I do not have my bank account number memorized, but I guess that's what the voided check is for.

Ice is still hard at work on his packet when I finish. I'm not convinced he literally has to write an essay, though his portion is clearly more involved than the two forms I filled out. He doesn't look particularly thrilled about it either, but he is nice enough to suggest I take a break when I say I'm done.

"Have Night fix something for you to eat," he says. "I'll finish up here and make copies of everything they need."

Discomfort nags at me, but I've resigned myself to go with the flow today, so I agree and stand to stretch. Ice leaves the bed, takes my place at his desk, and continues filling out the paperwork. He seems a bit irritated—by the tedious nature of completing government forms, probably.

I pause in the doorway.

"Want me to get anything for you?" I ask.

He nods slowly. "I'll have a glass of water."

# fourteen

I find Night reading in the breakfast nook, and she glances up from her paperback novel as I approach. Without taking her eyes off me, she slips a bookmark between the pages.

"Need something?" she asks, her voice soft and pleasant.

"Something to eat, if that's alright."

She studies me for a moment. Then she nods and leaves the table. I follow her into the kitchen, maintaining some distance between us. She's been kind since Ice formally introduced us, but *their argument involved me, didn't it?*

"What would you like?" she asks.

*I don't know what you have...*

"Just a snack," I say. "I'm not too picky."

With a delicate laugh, she retrieves a small plate from a cabinet above the counter. "If you're here, I assume you took Ice up on his offer."

"Yeah, I did. After watching him turn into a cat with my own eyes, I wasn't sure what else I could do."

"I can imagine."

She fans several table crackers around the edge of the plate and drifts over to the large three-door refrigerator. I watch her, keeping close to the counter at the other end of the kitchen.

"We're filling out the paperwork right now, so I hope I can learn more about immortals soon."

Her expression is pensive, but she remains quiet even as we return to the breakfast nook. She offers me the plate of crackers, grapes, and sliced cheese, and we sit across from each other.

"What kind of paperwork?" she asks.

"I'm not sure, honestly, but I guess it's from Human-Immortal Affairs."

She glances away. I make a tiny sandwich using two crackers and a slice of cheese.

"You want to know more about us?" she asks. My mouth is full, but I nod with vigor, and she rests her elbows on the table. "Well, what do you know so far?"

"I know that…you guys can turn into cats."

"That's all?"

She sounds genuinely surprised—meaning I was right. There is more to immortals than the shapeshifting ability. I nod, and she glances around. When her attention lands on me again, she smiles.

"If you've already filled out the paperwork, I see no harm in telling you," she reasons, smoothing the tablecloth with her hands.

"Really?" *That was easy.*

She glances out the window. "I bet Ice intends to keep you in the dark until the paperwork goes through, but it's not right, especially if he wants you to stay here in the meantime."

"I swear I won't tell anyone about immortals. I mean, I already signed the Secrecy Agreement, so—"

"You signed something like that?" She laughs and rolls her

eyes. "But, yes, feel free to ask me anything you'd like to know. I'll do my best to answer."

"Thank you! I have a few theories, but—" I mess with my hair, suddenly embarrassed. "I don't know anything. I mean, when Ice first told me he was an *immortal*, I asked if he could die."

"That's a fair misunderstanding," she agrees with a short laugh, "but I assume he was quick to correct you."

"He was, but he also said it's harder for immortals to die. What do you think he meant by that?"

"*Harder to die?*" she mouths, but she quickly clears her throat and nods. "He told the truth, in a roundabout way, as immortals are quite resilient, and we do recover from injury and exhaustion faster than humans."

"So, you're saying immortals aren't literally immortal, but they are…superhuman?"

She hits me with a blank stare and laughs again. "I've honestly never thought about it like that, but I suppose you have a point. Immortals tend to be stronger physically and have better reflexes because our brains process information slightly faster. It's one of the feline features that carry over into our human forms—along with little things like heightened vision and hearing."

She takes a drink from the mug in front of her, giving me time to absorb the new information. If what she says is true, immortals are *more* than human on basically every level. They're tougher, stronger, faster…

She smiles, an obvious attempt to clear the strange air between us. "We can see in the dark too. It's rather useless, but it's a neat gimmick."

“Wow. That’s…a lot, actually.”

*And Ice made it sound like the main difference between humans and immortals was the whole turning into a cat thing.*

She shakes her head but continues smiling. “Immortals are complex—like humans are in their own right. I am curious, though; you mentioned having your own theories?”

“Oh, that?” My face warms. “I hope you don’t mind, but I went through your friend list on FaceSpace the other day. I figure most of your friends are immortals, so…”

“You’re not wrong.”

“I noticed they all have the same few eye colors, so I thought those specific colors might have something to do with it. Blue, green, yellow, and purple, right?”

Her smile grows wide, her eyes alight. “Oh, I’m impressed.”

*Nice!* Maybe I wasn’t completely wasting my time the past couple days, even if I could have just waited.

“There are no real underlying differences between us, but it’s commonly accepted that there are four different types—or groups, rather—of immortals. They’re separated by eye color and named after the four elements of ancient alchemy: water, air, earth, and fire.”

*This is what I was waiting for.*

“Water immortals, like my family, have blue eyes. Air immortals have lavender eyes. Earth immortals have green eyes—though their eye color is more vivid than your own. And fire immortals have golden eyes. As I said, though, there’s not much separating the groups besides eye color and common social class.”

“If all immortals are the same, why separate them at all?”

She frowns and glances out the window. “I don’t know, but it’s been this way as long as anyone can remember.”

*Moving on…*

“How many immortals are there—in the world, I mean?”

“Oh, there are lots,” she says, perking up. “I’d say there’s only one immortal for every four or five humans, but we tend to concentrate our population in certain areas. If I recall correctly, immortals make up about half the population of Riverview.”

My jaw drops. “Seriously? Half of Riverview? You’re kidding. I’ve lived here my entire life, and I never knew.”

“I’m not surprised,” she agrees with a nod. “Secrecy is deeply stressed in our society from a young age, so we try to separate ourselves from humans as much as possible. Our existence is subtle. It works out best for everyone that way.”

“Do you know why Ice told me?”

“No. I don’t.” Glancing away, her pleasant expression falters. “I’ve asked several times, but he brushes it off or changes the subject. I haven’t managed to get a straight answer out of him in weeks.”

*Well, it was worth a shot.*

She stares at the tabletop as her manicured nails click against the smooth surface. She appears deep in thought until her eyes widen slightly, and she meets my gaze.

“You called immortals superhuman, right?” she asks. When I nod, she grins. “It flew well over my head when you first said it, but immortals do have unique abilities. Humans would consider much of it fantastical. That’s rather superhuman as well, isn’t it?”

“Unique abilities…”

"Immortals are usually born with one or more of these abilities. They range from mental or psychological quirks like telepathy and ESP to enhanced physical capabilities. There are even elemental abilities—like the ability to control fire or water. There are hundreds, if not thousands, of different abilities and variations. Some run in the family, while others are random happenstance. I've even read a few studies that aimed to rate the rarity of certain abilities. It's truly fascinating."

I already came to terms with the existence of people that can transform into talking house cats, so the addition of magic powers isn't much of a stretch. Though, I'm surprised she didn't mention the abilities earlier if she's so interested in them.

"What ability do you have?" I ask.

"Oh, I'm a psychic of sorts," she says with a sheepish smile. "It isn't a frequent occurrence by any means, but I sometimes see things—visions of the future, most often in dreams. Smoke and I share a telepathic connection with each other too."

"That's amazing."

She tells me a bit more—it seems her mother also has some psychic ability. Then, between eating the last of the grapes, I ask if Ice has any abilities besides the clothing swap thing.

Her smile fades, and she glances out the window. "I can't say. I know there's more to that little parlor trick—it's not as simple as he makes it out to be, at least—but he's never told me exactly how it works."

"Even though you're siblings?"

"Ice has his secrets." Her voice is cool as her frown deepens. "Though, I am surprised he never told you he's adopted."

"No." *That's news to me!* "But it explains a lot."

*Like how he looks nothing like the rest of his family, for one.*

"I'm sure it does," she replies dryly.

Is the Secrecy Agreement the only reason he never explained any of this earlier? I mean, immortals are *magical, superhuman beings*. Surely, he planned on telling me this eventually, right?

Well, I hope he doesn't mind I heard it from Night first.

She collects my empty plate and loads it into the dishwasher. Then she returns to the table with a glass of water.

"For Ice," she says.

*I never mentioned that he wanted water, but alright...*

I take the glass and thank her.

"And tell him—" Her eyes flick away for an instant. "Tell him that I apologize."

"For what?"

She smiles. "He'll know."

Something to do with their tense...*conversation?* It's none of my business either way, so I agree without prying.

She sits and picks up her book. "Thanks. And...good luck."

"Yeah, thanks."

*I probably need it.*

When I return to the bedroom, Ice announces that he finished his paperwork while I was gone.

I set the water glass on the desk, and he has me sign a few pages within his packet. Then he signs the bottom of my Secrecy Agreement, and everything goes into a manila folder.

Right. Before I forget...

"Night wanted to apologize for something. She asked me to

tell you."

"Is that so?" After a pause, he smiles. "Very well. I accept her apology. For now."

*Right...*

He clears his throat. "Now then, I'll run this up to the regional office first thing in the morning. Do your best to remain here while I'm away."

I hear him fall back onto his bed, and I turn from the window.

He lounges casually atop the grey bedspread. At some point while I wasn't looking, he switched out of his button-up and slacks into a t-shirt and sweatpants. Strands of hair that were once neatly pushed up now fall into his face.

He's being unintentionally gorgeous, and *we are alone in his bedroom.*

When he glances in my direction, I avert my eyes and mess with my hair. He doesn't seem uncomfortable with me here, but I'm out of my element. I may be an adult, but Rose had a point —I have never done anything like this before.

*Oh, no. I am a squirrelly virgin.*

"How long will you be gone?" I ask.

I'm not missing out on anything at home by being here, but I'm not sure how I feel about staying at someone else's house when the one who initially invited me isn't around.

He sighs. "Forty-eight hours if I'm lucky, but it's safe to assume it will take longer. I believe I mentioned it earlier, but the closest Human-Immortal Affairs regional office is in Seattle."

"That sucks."

He meets my gaze with impassive eyes and an obviously

forced smile. "I returned from my first trip to Seattle earlier today, you know."

"Oh—"

"It's nothing," he says, looking away.

*How is he functioning?*

Seattle is easily a ten-hour drive from Riverview even if you don't stop or run into any traffic, which is surely impossible on the interstate as you pass through Portland and the Puget Sound. Yet he expects me to believe he drove down from Seattle today and arrived in Riverview early enough to pick me up at four in the afternoon?

He must have left Seattle around five or six in the morning at the *latest*. Just to fill out paperwork for an hour when he got home? I would be *dead* tagging along on such a long trip as a passenger, but he honestly strikes me as more bored than tired.

"Feel free to use my bedroom while I'm away," he says.

*What?*

"Sleep in here?" I stammer.

He stares at me for a long moment before rolling his eyes.

"It's a courtesy, Jayde. I can sleep in the den tonight."

Glancing away, I wring my hands uneasily. "That's fine, I guess. I'll grab my bag."

* * * * *

The main characters, both tired, ragged, and covered in soot, turn to face each other and reach for the other's hand. Their fingers intertwine. The camera pans out. The music swells with cautious optimism. The scene fades to black. Then the end credits roll, and the movie is over.

It was a Netflix-original sci-fi drama about the apocalypse. Parts of the film were sad and foreboding—since it was a warning against the dangers of apathy and social intolerance—but it was good and emotional.

Night yawns from her spot on the second couch. "It's getting late, isn't it?"

"Is it?" Ice asks.

Warm light streams into the den through the uncovered slice of sliding glass door. It can't be any later than 7:30PM.

"Well, I'm going to get ready for bed," she says, unbothered by our incredulity as she stands from the couch. "Have a nice evening. Do try to get some sleep before you head out."

She passes the remote to Ice before walking down the hall. He backs out of the film credits, silencing the sentimental pop music, and scrolls down rows of movies and TV shows. His bright eyes flick right to left, scanning the titles as he clicks through the menu.

*Get some sleep…*

He drove down from Seattle just this morning, and he has to drive up again tomorrow. He said he plans to leave early, possibly before the sun rises.

It's still light outside. I'm not ready for sleep myself, but—

"Are you tired?" I ask.

His eyes stop scanning. Then he looks at me, and he smiles.

"No," he says. "I'm fine."

I frown. "Tomorrow sounds like it'll be a long day for you.

You're waking up super early, right? Maybe you should go to sleep soon?"

No reaction.

"Are you tired?" he asks, still sort of smiling.

I shake my head.

He glances at the TV. A pause. Then the screen goes dark—turned off—and he sets the remote on the arm of the loveseat.

"You're right," he says. "Tomorrow will be a long day."

I don't know what to say. Suddenly, now that we're alone, I feel…awkward? Being here isn't uncomfortable, exactly, but he seems more muted than usual. I wasn't expecting it.

"Will you be alright staying with the twins while I'm gone?"

"It's only a couple days," I say with an unintentionally nervous laugh. "I'll be alright."

"Call me if you need anything."

I nod, thank him, and stand from the couch.

"I'll see you in a few days," I say. "Good luck in Seattle."

He meets my gaze with a measured expression before glancing away. "Goodnight, Jayde."

* * * * *

Falling asleep in Ice's bed is turning out to be more difficult than I thought—not that I imagined it would be easy.

For a while, after shutting myself in his room, I sat at the desk. I tried to tire myself out by completing the daily quests in a mobile game, and then by scrolling down FaceSpace for a while, but I had to move to the bed eventually.

The mattress is so soft and so comfortable, and I'm warm beneath the covers, but I've been lying here for at least two hours. Strange, unsolicited images pop into my head every time I close my eyes. I just can't get past the idea of sleeping where he usually does.

It's late, but I reach for my phone and text Rose.

**Me:** He asked me to stay the night.

I half-expected her to be asleep, and I had hoped she would be, but the *read* indicator pops up beneath my text. And she types.

**Rose:** What?? Did you???

**Me:** I'm in his bed right now.

Knowing Rose, she has the completely wrong impression after reading *that*. I ignore a hot flash of embarrassment and don't give her enough time to respond before clarifying.

**Me:** I mean, he's sleeping out in the living room, but still

**Rose:** Σ(°ロ°)

**Rose:** I'll call you tomorrow!!

**Me:** Go ahead.

I roll onto my stomach and hide my face in the soft pillow. It smells like him—like cinnamon and shampoo. The image of Ice lounging on the bed with soft strands of hair falling into his face sends my heart racing.

My grip tightens on my phone as I stare into the dimly lit

room. *How am I supposed to fall asleep like this?* I can barely stand lying alone in Ice's bed when I like him so much, and his feelings toward me remain a complete mystery.

It's not fair.

*Smells good, though...*

# fifteen

I lie still. My heart beats loudly, and I stare at the wall for some time before I finally convince myself to roll over.

Of course, I'm alone in the room.

*As expected. And as I should be.*

I sit up, and my reflection greets me from the foot of the bed. My hair is a mess. *Ugh.* I push the grey comforter aside and instead admire the light filtering into the room through the thin curtains. Then I check the alarm clock on the end table.

It's 10:14AM—a little late, but excusable considering the grief I had falling asleep.

I leave the bed and find a slip of paper on the desk. It's a short note, written in neat cursive on off-white stationery.

*Please make yourself at home.*

Ice was right.

He did not wake me up before he left. Though, he probably did see me sleeping with my mouth open.

*How embarrassing...*

I groan and rub my eyes.

After dressing and brushing my hair into submission, I crack the bedroom door. The scent of bacon hangs in the air. The den is empty, so I leave the room and wander further out into the house.

Both Night and Smoke are in the great room, sitting near each other on the large couch. She's reading a book. He's on his phone. She's dressed in an earthy blouse and knee-length skirt, while he's wearing pajamas.

*Did I miss breakfast?*

Night glances up from her book and smiles.

"Good morning," she says brightly. "Did you sleep well?"

I shrug. I'd rather not talk about it.

"You hungry?" she asks, setting her book down. "I made egg toast. There's some left if you'd like me to warm it up."

"Oh, sure. Thanks."

She puts together a plate—a fat slice of bread with an egg fried in the center and a couple slices of bacon. As it's reheating in the microwave, she retrieves a bowl of chopped honeydew melon from the fridge.

"What do you like to drink?" she asks. "Tea, water, juice?"

"Water is fine. Thanks."

I stand around awkwardly while she fills a glass with water from the refrigerator tap. She hands it to me and welcomes me to sit at the breakfast nook as the microwave beeps. After adding melon to the reheated plate, she finally sets the plate, utensils, and a cloth napkin in front of me.

Looking up at her, I suddenly feel like a child. Like I just watched my mother fix me a plate after I slept in on a Saturday morning.

"Thanks again," I say lamely before picking up the fork.

She sits across from me. "It's no problem."

Her mom vibes were unexpected without being uncomfortable, and don't seem at all artificial on her part. Something about her is warm and nostalgic, but she's only a year older than me, so I feel a little guilty too.

"I'm sorry you're stuck here," she says. "Are you settling in okay, at least?"

"It's weird staying in Ice's room, but I'm okay."

"You're free to sleep in the den instead."

"It's fine." *Why am I so nervous?* "Do you know what time he left?"

She shakes her head. "He was gone when I woke up. Divulging the secret of immortals has made him very busy."

"It is a lot of trouble?"

"Ice did this to himself," she says with a smile. "Though, I doubt he expected it would be so much work."

Well, she obviously doesn't think I should feel bad for him. Maybe I won't. I don't regret learning about immortals, but this slow-burn summer romance—*or whatever it is*—would have been less complicated if he never brought it up.

"Are you the only cook in the house?" I ask, hoping to change the subject.

She blinks before laughing. A faint pink touches her cheeks.

"They both know how to cook—to some extent, anyway. But I love cooking. My mom taught me." She lowers her voice and cups a hand near her mouth. "To be honest, I can't watch Ice or Smoke in the kitchen without wanting to nag whenever they do something wrong, so it might be my fault if they're not very good at it."

For some reason, it makes me laugh.

As I finish eating, Night asks if I'd like to join her on a quick errand. A trip to a bookstore at the mall. She figures I have nothing better to do—she's right—and assumes I may not feel comfortable staying at the house alone—right again.

"A new book in my favorite series came out yesterday," she says, drying her hands on a kitchen towel. "We can get smoothies after I pick up my copy."

"Okay. Sounds good."

While she gets ready, I gather my things from Ice's bedroom. I tie my shoes. I put on mascara. And I worry I'm a burden—on Ice, and now on Night.

She has a point, though. He did this to himself.

But that doesn't make it any less confusing.

Why bother introducing me to the world of immortals if he has to leave in September? It seems like it would only inconvenience him, and it saddles me with this massive secret. Now, being here with the twins and stuck waiting for him to deliver the paperwork that will bind me to said secret forever…

The reality of it all is finally setting in.

Plus, I missed a phone call from Rose this morning and haven't returned it because I have no idea what to say—or what excuse to give her.

*Ugh.*

A soft knock on the door cuts through the turmoil, and Night pops her head in. She asks if I'm ready. I nod, tuck my wallet into my pocket, and follow after her.

"We'll be back," she says as we pass Smoke in the great room.

He's wearing a headset, but he still tells us to have fun.

As I climb into Night's blue sedan, unease washes over me —the same as when she drove me home before. But the sun is high, and her demeanor is mild and warm. What's done is done, I guess. She doesn't blame me that Ice told me about immortals.

I relax further as she offers me a smile. Then she turns the key in the ignition, and we're off.

We talk about reading; how I used to read more in high school, and she reads more now than she did a few years ago. She tells me about her favorite romantic crime thriller series. Each book ends on a huge cliffhanger, and she's waited months with bated breath for the latest installment.

"Maybe I should get into reading again," I say.

I ignore another text from Rose.

Night offers to let me borrow books from her any time I want. It sounds like she has a small library tucked away in her room.

We arrive at Century Plaza Mall and make a beeline for Barnes and Noble. The series must not be the most popular, as it's not displayed on the flashy new-release shelf near the entrance, but she speaks with the store clerk, and he retrieves a hardbound novel from beneath the counter.

"Is that everything?" he asks.

She shakes her head and joins me beside a revolving rack full of bookmarks. We wander around the store for several minutes. She points out a few series she's read before and picks up two other books she's been planning to read. She then pays for everything, and we head back into the mall.

We order drinks and find a table at the food court, where we chat more about school. I admit I don't have a "real" major—though she assures me that keeping my options open with a general education transfer degree is nothing to be ashamed of.

Her phone distracts her, so I suck it up and check the messages I've been ignoring all morning.

**Rose:** Are you asleep? lmao

**Rose:** Jayyy, I need details (T⌓T)

**Rose:** GIRL, HEY

**Me:** Sorry. I've been a little busy.

**Rose:** Busy?? Uh… details now, pls

I sigh and drink my smoothie, chewing on the silicone straw. *Rose thinks I'm up to something?* She's not wrong, entirely, but I hate to imagine what she thinks I've been doing.

**Me:** I'll call you when I get back to the house.

**Rose:** Back to his house?? Are you not going home?

**Me:** I'm hanging out with his sister.

**Me:** Ice isn't here right now. Calm down, I'll explain later.

I suck at this. Maybe I shouldn't have told her I'm staying at Ice's house in the first place.

**Rose:** Okkk please do that ( ͡• ͜ʖ ͡•)

**Me:** Don't worry. I will.

"Oh. Jayde," Night says. When I glance up, she's frowning. "Ice's timing couldn't be worse. I made plans to go to a summer solstice festival with Smoke tomorrow. I still intend to go, but it's up to you whether you'd rather stay at the house or join us."

I hesitate. "Where?"

"Riverside Park."

*I love Riverside Park.* But that reminds me.

"You remember a while back at Riverside—?"

Her expression blanks, and she winces, stifling embarrassment.

"When I interrupted your date by accident?" she asks. "Yes. Sorry. I was delivering a message from my mom—business, you know? It wasn't an emergency, but he wasn't answering his phone, so I went looking for him. After we spoke, I asked if he wanted to stay behind and wrap things up with you, but he didn't. He wasn't happy with me, and he didn't want to talk about you at all."

"I was worried when he didn't come back," I admit.

"His behavior concerned me as well," she says, averting her eyes. "That's why… I had to make sure everything was okay. Since Ice wouldn't talk to me, I felt I had no choice but to check on the situation firsthand."

She speaks slowly, her word choice careful and deliberate. To skirt around the issue of immortals? *Or Ice's stalking?* Does she know about that?

I glance around. Several people wander around the food court, but the level of activity in the mall renders all nearby conversation to a low, jumbled buzz.

"But I realize now that involving myself did little to help," she says lamely, her eyes on her brightly colored tea.

She didn't want Ice to tell me about immortals, and she still isn't happy he went through with it. But he told me. I signed the paperwork. It's done. Neither of us can change that.

I clear my throat. "Anyway, about tomorrow?"

"Right. Sorry." She smiles. "The festival is mixed company, so it's fine if you want to come. I agreed to meet a few friends there, but I can tell them about you in advance. Hopefully, it won't get…stranger than it has to be."

"It's super weird that I know, huh?" I ask, scratching my neck.

Her smile doesn't falter. "I've only met a handful who do—one in high school, and a few others through my parents' company—so… While it's certainly not commonplace, it's not unheard of either. I'm sure Ice is taking care of the details as we speak."

He's probably still driving as we speak, but she's right.

Dealing with Human-Immortal Affairs is Ice's responsibility. Until he gets back, it's out of my hands. Night is only trying to help by spending time with me. And she wants to introduce me to some friends, so I might learn even more about immortals.

"I'll go," I agree.

"Great," she says, her voice bright. "It'll be fun."

* * * * *

I thank Night for letting me tag along on her errand before we part ways. She heads down the hall, toward her bedroom, while I linger in the empty den. Judging by the muffled music coming from behind the door, Smoke is in his room too.

*I'm alone.*

Letting out my breath, I check my phone. Rose hasn't called or messaged since I told her to wait, but I need to call her before she decides I'm being held against my will.

I pull the heavy curtain over the sliding glass door aside.

*Oh, wow!* The backyard is lovely. I'm not surprised, but I'd only caught glimpses of it before.

I step out onto the sizable wood patio, half-covered by a glass canopy. There's a small patio table near the door, and a wrought-iron firepit circled by three wicker chairs on the far end. A short set of stairs lead down to the maintained, grassy yard. The yard itself isn't huge, roughly three times the size of the patio, but it appears to wrap around the side of the house and link up to the front. The garden beds are near overflowing with produce, half of the first bed full of ripening strawberries.

I sit on the edge of the patio, which is bordered by smooth river rocks below, and I call Rose before I have time to change my mind.

"Heyo," she says.

"Is now a good time?" I ask, hoping it's not.

She laughs. "As good a time as any."

"Sorry I didn't answer earlier."

"It's fine. It's fine." Then she sucks in a breath. "Sooo, let me get this straight: Your boyfriend asked you to stay the night? And you did?"

"It's not nearly as exciting as you think," I say dryly. "He slept out in the living room and had to leave super early this morning for, um…work."

*Uh…*

"Work?" she asks.

"Yeah." *Guess I'm rolling with it.* "He was called away all of a sudden. I don't really know what it's about. Anyway, I've been hanging out with his sister, and she asked me to go to some summer solstice thing tomorrow. I've been lonely at home, you know? It's nice having people to hang out with."

Two truths and a lie, I guess. Makes it a little easier. She'd never believe me if we were speaking face-to-face, though.

*Ugh. This secret might be harder to keep than I thought.*

"Aww," she coos, oblivious to my deception. "You've been lonely without me? Well, I'm glad you found someone to hang out with, even if it is your boyfriend's sister. It's about time you made more friends."

"Yeah..."

"What happened with the secret talk?" she asks.

"Oh, um, we got it figured out. It's still a secret—sorry—but I'm not so worried about it anymore."

"Glad to hear it. I knew you were working yourself up over nothing."

*Nothing...* Right.

* * * * *

Smoke is more talkative tonight, making dinner ever so slightly less awkward than it was last night. Night watches attentively as he describes a series of collabs he has planned with other YouTube creators. She praises him for doing well.

*How much money does vlogging bring in?*

I'm curious, but I don't ask, and the conversation soon shifts away from YouTube. After glancing at her phone, Night perks up and says her friends look forward to meeting me.

"They don't mind that I'm human?"

She shakes her head. "Nope!"

"We don't hang out with anyone that would if we can avoid it," Smoke says. "Those types tend to not like me either."

Night makes a face that doesn't quite agree, but she doesn't disagree either. Then, moving along, she asks if anyone wants another kebab. Smoke takes one. I still have one I haven't touched yet.

She's a great cook, but I'm distracted.

Lying to Rose has bothered me all afternoon. Lying about Ice's secret and why I'm staying at his house and where he went. I know hanging out with the twins won't suck, but I'm still lying to her, and I will never be able to stop because she can't know the truth.

*And it's not fair.*

Clearing my throat, I glance up from my plate. "Can I ask a question? About immortals?"

"Oh?" Night seems surprised, but she smiles. "Of course. Go ahead."

"Why is it a secret?"

Her smile falters. Smoke glances at her, but she remains focused on me. She doesn't seem to notice her twin's inquiring gaze and remains quiet. Watching me. Thinking.

Then she sighs. "Honestly, Jayde, I don't know. It's always been this way. There's no record of any major conflicts between immortals and humans, but our existence has always been kept quiet. Or so we've been told."

"How, though? Immortals have an entire government agency."

"A few, actually," she says, glancing away. "Human-Immortal Affairs is only one of the US agencies, and there are more internationally. I'm sure plenty of humans in the government have high enough clearance to know about immortals."

"So, only the public isn't supposed to know?"

"I suppose they think it's easier that way."

"Easier?"

She frowns. "I don't particularly know how it works."

"It's politics," Smoke says with a shrug. "There's nothing folks like us can do about it."

My first instinct is to argue with him, but I recall the Secrecy Agreement, and I change my mind.

# sixteen

Why am I so nervous?

The solstice event is neutral territory. It's open to the public, both human and immortal, so it won't be weird for either of us to be there.

*It's just...*

What if Night's friends don't like me? She said they're cool with me being human, and Smoke backed her up, but do they think it's weird that I know the secret? Will they treat me differently?

It doesn't help that Ice hasn't responded to most of my texts. I asked about his drive yesterday, and he said it was fine—he was safe at his hotel by 5PM—but he didn't answer when I asked how he was doing a few hours ago. He hasn't even read the message.

Night told me not to worry.

I am trying. But it's not so simple.

*Well...* We're at the park, and I'm still nervous.

I leave the car and walk alongside Night, crossing the packed parking lot with Smoke in tow. We pass a few food trucks near the bathroom pavilion, and we enter the park proper, where at least two dozen children run around and play on the playground. A large *RIVERVIEW SUMMER SOLSTICE FESTIVAL* banner hangs on the side of the park's main pavilion, but there aren't too many people around.

The event officially begins at 4PM. We're a little early.

Most of the vendor booths along the walking path look like they'll sell crafts of some sort, but none are open for business yet. At the pavilion, several large coolers are set up on picnic tables. A soda fountain. Local wine sampling, maybe. People are still busy preparing for the evening.

Down the hill, the pop-up bandstand looks ready for a band—microphones, lights, speakers, the works. No one is playing, but a large group gathers to the left of the stage.

I've heard of these events before—they're held every solstice and equinox—but this is my first time in attendance. I usually stick to Music@ThePark. This looks similar, but I'm not quite sure what to expect.

"Are your friends here already?" I ask Night as she surveys the vendor stalls from afar.

She nods and points down the hill, toward the stage. "They should be down there. Carmen's boyfriend is in one of the bands."

"Oh?"

"A bunch of local indie groups play this gig," Smoke says. "That's the appeal—the vendors and bands are all local."

Night smiles. "These festivals are all about celebrating the season and supporting the local community."

She offers to introduce me to her friends before the park gets crowded, so we take the nearest path leading downhill.

When I ask if the bands playing today are all fronted by *immortals*, she laughs at me for covering my mouth as I spoke. But she shrugs, not having a real answer. I guess it's another thing that doesn't matter when it comes to this event.

The exact level of separation between humans and immortals still confuses me. We live together in the same town, and there isn't any obvious distinction when it comes to the places either group frequents. Humans visit the mall. Immortals visit the mall. Humans attend RCC. Immortals attend RCC. Riverside Park and the solstice festival are the same, but the fact she explicitly described it as "mixed company" leads me to believe there are places and events not open to both.

Maybe I'll understand one day. Maybe Ice will explain more when he gets back from Seattle. *Or I can ask Night later.*

We approach the large group. Several vans and other vehicles are parked in the grass closer to the trees along the riverbank, and three pop-up canopies are set up beside them. Night leads me straight into the crowd. A few heads shift to look at us.

Then she calls a name—*Carmen!*—and a young woman with bright blue hair glances over. Her violet eyes light up when she spots us, and she breaks away from the crowd to give Night a tight hug.

"Night, Smoke; it's so good to see you guys!"

Her voice is boisterous and rougher than I expected from someone with such a soft, round face. Her eyeshadow is bright, eyeliner sharp, and lipstick dark. She has a nose piercing—a small gem that matches her hair—as well as a few piercings on her ears. Several jelly wristbands adorn one of her arms, and she wears platform boots, denim shorts, and an unbuttoned vest over a band tee.

Night returns the greeting, and the girl turns to me.

"You must be Jayde," she says. "Night told me all about you."

"Nothing bad, I hope."

Her answering smile is genuine, but she laughs harder than she probably should.

Someone taps her shoulder, and her head turns. *Ah, these two must be related.* The second girl has long, dark brown hair, kept out of her face with a headband made of silk flowers. Her makeup is understated, and her loose, linen sundress is fashion-forward and looks super comfortable.

The two women seem like opposites in taste, but they're the same height and look incredibly similar otherwise—both gorgeous and confident.

"Oh! Hey, Nat; Night's here with her new friend." Carmen turns to us with a grin. "Jayde, this is my sister, Natalie."

"Jayde? The girl Ice told about—?" She trails off and smiles. Her expression is more strained than Carmen's but not unpleasant. "Oh, sorry. It's nice to meet you."

*They totally think it's weird.*

But I return the sentiment, and I mean it. It is nice to meet more immortals. So far, they all seem like normal people—like anyone else I met before learning about them.

"Are you busy?" Night asks.

Carmen pulls a face. "I have to help Lucas with setup and breakdown, but we can hang out after. He's up at, uh…five-thirty? So any time after like six-fifteen should work. How long are you planning to stay?"

"Until eight or so."

"Is Ice still in Seattle?" Natalie asks.

Night nods. "For the second time this week."

"Haven't seen him in a couple years. How is he?"

A beat of silence.

"The same as always," Smoke says.

Carmen cackles. "Well, I should go. I'll text you when we're done."

She dips back into the mass of people and meets up with a guy of similar aesthetic to Smoke—choppy black hair, dark clothes, and several piercings and tattoos. Her boyfriend, Lucas, I assume.

*What kind of music does he play?*

The four of us remaining chat about nothing in particular for a while. Then Night suggests we check out the vendor stalls. Smoke stays behind with the growing crowd, and I follow Night and Natalie up the hill.

The solstice event is officially on. The park is more crowded, and the stalls are open. We take a cursory glance.

As Smoke and Night said, they're all local vendors, mainly small businesses. Baked goods. Fresh produce and small-batch canned fruit. Herbs. Candles. Handcrafted gemstone jewelry and leather-bound journals. Expensive but lovely things. A table selling honey products has a thin beehive with dozens of bees crawling behind glass on display.

*Neat.*

Natalie points out the flower crown vendor. She bought her

headband from them during the Spring Equinox festival in March. Night asks if I want one and picks up a headband made of silk roses, but I get embarrassed and refuse.

Moving on, we buy fresh fruit smoothies from a food truck and sit at a bench off to the side of the walking path. The two girls chat about crafting and ethical consumption and the best native flowers to plant in a pollinator garden. I contribute where I can—I also care about bees—and they both go out of their way to keep me involved in the conversation, but I remain intimidated and strangely isolated.

Natalie is the careful, delicate type, not unlike Night. It's obvious why they're friends. They both love niche fashion and nature and art. They're passionate about their interests, while I don't feel too strongly about anything in particular, and I'm...*a little jealous.*

* * * * *

Lucas' band surprised me. I expected it to be a metal band, but it's not. *Well, not exactly.* It might be a subgenre of metal, but they have a female vocalist with a crisp voice, and the instrumentals are slower and softer and more soulful with a subtle Celtic twang.

The first band was Celtic-flavored too—though more explicitly so. Will the other artists be similar? Maybe that's the point. The event's general energy is folksy and mystical, almost. Eclectic and artsy. A little witchy.

It's a different vibe than Music@ThePark, but I don't hate it.

Smoke meets up with us after the set, and we wait with Natalie while Carmen helps the band move their equipment offstage. The breakdown takes ten minutes, and she jogs over to us with her boyfriend once they're done.

"Jayde, Lucas. Lucas, Jayde," she says breathlessly. She brushes wayward strands of blue hair out of her face and grins. "I'm starving. Let's grab something to eat."

The six of us wander around the parking lot full of food trucks. While we deliberate what to eat, I learn more interesting things about Night's friends.

Lucas' band, in which he is the bassist, is for fun. A hobby. By trade, he's an apprentice piercer and tattoo artist. Carmen pushes her right sleeve up to show off a colorful celestial scene he tattooed on her upper arm a few months back. He also dated Smoke some years ago, and they're still good friends.

Carmen attends a local beauty college and took a few business classes at RCC last year. She wants to open her own hair salon.

Natalie has been working and going to RCC part-time since graduation. She doesn't know exactly what she wants to do yet, but she designs and sews clothing as a hobby. Night owns a few of her custom pieces.

When they ask me about myself, I don't know what to say.

But I talk about my education plans, anyway. I admit I have no idea where I want to transfer after I complete my associate degree. Somewhere in California to save on tuition, for sure, but I don't have a real preference. I need to look into it more.

We get our food, our group having split orders between three different food trucks, and walk down the path through the park for a while. Then Night points out an empty picnic table beneath the shade of a maple tree. There's enough room for all six of us. I sit at the end of one bench.

Night sits to my left.

Carmen plants herself directly across from me. Our eyes meet. I haven't said anything, but her interest is already piqued.

"So," she says, "I didn't ask earlier 'cause there were folks around, but how'd you get in with immortals? I know Ice told you, but that's about it."

Four faces watch me in expectant silence. Smoke doesn't seem to care in the least, but the others are focused on me. Even Night. I get the impression that, no matter what she told me, it is extremely unusual for normal humans to know about immortals.

I'm not a high-ranking government official with the security clearance to know these things. I'm nobody. I'm just a college student—and technically still a teenager.

"Ice told me about a week ago," I say. "Not gonna lie; I didn't believe him at first. Until he turned into a cat right in front of me."

Carmen laughs. "He morphed? Oh, no! I don't blame you for not believing it. Must sound crazy to someone on the outside. Anyway, you and Ice are friends, or—?"

*Friends? Ha.*

"Not sure," I admit. "We've gone on a few dates, and now this, but that's all. I'm sure it's nothing serious."

Her smile hitches up on one side. "Yeah? Gotta say, I'm surprised he'd get involved with a human at all, but I can't blame you for being interested. Haven't seen him in a while, but, from what I remember, he's damn hot."

With a glance at Lucas, she laughs and apologizes, but he rolls his eyes and takes a bite of his wrap.

The conversation shifts back to the mundane.

I follow along and contribute where I can, but I hate being the stranger among a group of close friends. Carmen is boisterous and blunt while Natalie is reserved and low-energy. Lucas watches and listens more than he speaks, even compared to Smoke, but he strikes me as a laid-back person.

I want to be friends with them—all of them. But I don't know how to approach people like this. The gap between us is so wide. They're a tight-knit group of friends and siblings who've known each other for years. They share dumb inside jokes that leave me feeling lost, and they're so comfortable with each other.

But I'm new and different and human.

*How can I bridge the gap?*

"You guys have special abilities too, right?" I ask.

The table falls quiet. Then Carmen lights up.

"For sure," she says before holding a finger to her lips. "But I like to keep mine a secret. Because it's so cool, obviously."

This time Natalie rolls her eyes. "I can shape water. I can't, um...*create* water, but I can make it do things."

She takes a sticker-covered bottle out of her small, canvas backpack and pours a splash of water onto the table. Her finger brushes the surface, and it rises off the table as a tiny orb. It only moves a couple inches before she shakes her hand, and the water splashes onto the painted wood.

*I'm sorry, but that's actual magic.*

I glance around—though, I don't notice any bystanders watching. "Is it okay to do that in public?"

"Not really," she says mildly.

Night and Carmen nod in partially feigned solemn agreement while Natalie mops up the tiny puddle with a paper napkin. It was cool, but I'm not sure why I thought immortal abilities were the best thing to bring up at a crowded park.

"Well, please don't do anything that might get you in trouble."

Natalie laughs and brushes her long hair over one shoulder. "It's a secret, sure, but it's only a problem if you get caught. A drop of water is nothing."

*Are all immortals so dismissive about it?*

"Sooo," Carmen says. She folds her arms over the table as she watches me with a deep curiosity. "What's it like being human?"

I blink. "It's like, um— Well, what's it like not being human?"

"Fair point," she says with a laugh. "I guess it's basically the same thing, right? You've probably talked to tons of us without even realizing it. A lot of profs at RCC are immortals, you know."

"No way!"

I can't remember any of their faces well enough. A couple of my instructors may have had lavender or amber eyes. The golden honey color stuck out to me even in the photographs I saw while scrolling through Night's friend list. My writing instructor in fall term had the same eyes, I think.

*He was very handsome...*

Rose and I had the class together, and she went on about him the entire term. Was he really an immortal, though? Are any of Rose's friends immortals? Were any of her hook-ups immortals?

*So weird!*

I'll check her FaceSpace later.

*Wait— Maybe I should check mine.*

I resist the urge to grab my phone, choosing to laugh at another joke instead. Even if they still think it's strange that I know about immortals, I'm glad I came.

# seventeen

Hanging out with the twins and meeting a few of their friends was a nice change of pace compared to the sitting alone at home I would have done otherwise, but I am more than ready to hear what Ice has to say after his trip to Seattle. In his last message, sent about an hour ago, he mentioned passing through Redding.

It's late—after 10PM—but he should be here any time now.

Night and I have sat across from each other at the glass dining table ever since Ice sent that message. She's been visibly antsy for a while, putting me on edge as well. And he never answered when I asked how things went.

"He's pulling up now," she says.

She turns to the bay window, and I follow her gaze.

A silver car stops in front of the house. The headlights shut off, but the red taillights stay on as it idles on the curb.

Night sighs. "I wonder if he'll be hungry."

"Has he said anything to you about what he did up there?"

"No," she says with a short laugh. "I wouldn't be surprised if you know more than I do."

*And I know nothing.*

We sit at the table for a few minutes in relative silence. The car is still idling outside. Then the red glow goes out, and I hear a car door slam shut.

Night doesn't move from the table, but I do.

As Ice steps through the front door, I'm there to greet him. He glosses me over, mild disinterest flashing across his face. *Ah— I forgot I was wearing pajamas.* Desperate to mask my embarrassment, I glance away long enough to catch my breath. *What was I thinking, changing before he got here?*

"Good evening, Jayde," he says, offering me a dim smile.

He takes a seat at the dining table and glances at Night, who is already putting together a plate of leftovers. He's giving off especially weird vibes tonight, so I play it safe and leave an empty chair between us when I sit.

"You might consider taking a plane next time," Night says, her voice soft and teasing.

"I prefer driving."

If he's worn out from the drive, he doesn't look it. I study him a moment longer, searching for the fatigue Night must have picked up on. His expression reads as passive and indifferent—mildly annoyed, maybe—but not particularly tired. No shadows beneath his eyes. No significant change in the way he carries himself.

Though, I suppose she knows him better than I do.

"So… How did it go?" I ask.

Besides turning in the paperwork we filled out, I have no clue what else he may have done in Washington. He was gone for three days, but no amount of asking on my part convinced him to tell me what he was up to.

"It was interesting," he says. "It seems they don't receive

many of those applications, so it was reviewed quickly."

I frown. "Didn't I just fill out some standard paperwork? Is it that rare for humans to learn about immortals?"

"Not exactly." He shrugs and glances away. "While I was in Seattle, I took the liberty of enrolling you in an experimental program. Human-Immortal Affairs put it together years ago, and it's very exclusive."

*What?*

"I assumed you wouldn't mind."

*WHAT?*

"Um."

*I don't know what to say!*

"An experimental program?" I ask, my voice sharp.

He gives me *a look* before glancing away again.

I worry my hands in my lap. *This is worse than when he told me he wasn't human.*

Night casts a suspicious glare in his direction as she sets the reheated plate of dinner leftovers in front of him, but he doesn't pay her any mind. I'm not sure he even noticed.

"It's nothing bad," she says, her expression softening as our eyes meet. "I'm sure Ice will explain when he's feeling better."

She sets a gentle hand on his shoulder. Irritation flashes across his features, revealing his exhaustion for an instant, but he relents and picks up the fork she presented him with.

"Oh, yes," he agrees dryly. "I'm bound by contract to tell you all about it, but we'll cross that line tomorrow."

*Oh, um...*

"I can wait," I say. "It's fine."

"Good."

Night, who doesn't quite appear placated, removes her hand from his shoulder and sits across from him. The silent look they exchange sends a chill down my spine, and I immediately know I want no part in whatever conversation they're about to have.

I excuse myself from the table and retreat to Ice's bedroom. I stand in the dark with my back to the door, and I stare at the bare wall across from me.

*An experimental program?*

This is not fine.

* * * * *

I wake up to my 9AM alarm.

After swiping the screen to silence my phone, I sit up and look over the room as I have every morning. Today, something is out of place. A ball of white fluff at the foot of the bed. I'm confused until I realize it's breathing.

The ball of fluff is a cat.

"Ice?" I ask sharply.

*Oh my god, Jayde. It's not like you slept with him.*

A head pops out of the white fur and rotates to blink vibrantly blue eyes at me.

"Yes… I apologize." Ice uncurls his feline body and arches his back, stretching. "I haven't slept in several days."

I wave my hands disarmingly. "Oh, no. It's fine. You surprised me; that's all."

"I see."

My face is still warm. I adjust my camisole and detangle my hair with my fingers, hoping I'm at least semi-presentable. My appearance doesn't seem to make any difference to him—I'm not sure it ever has—but the possibility of looking like a hot mess in front of him still stresses me out.

When I check again, he's sitting at the foot of the bed in human form, dressed in a t-shirt and jeans. He stares into the mirror on his closet door, idly messing with his hair.

His eyes flick to my reflection. "Would you prefer we talk now or later?"

"Ah..." *As much as I want an explanation now...* "Later is fine. I think I want to take a shower first, you know?"

"Works for me."

He looks away to continue fixing his hair. He's acting normal, as though nothing unusual happened last night. Like he was never snappy. Like he didn't drop the bombshell of having signed me up for some experimental program behind my back.

*He can be rather odd.*

I collect my toiletry bag and a change of clothes and slink out of the room.

Showering tends to reduce anxiety, but no luck today.

Today, I am brooding.

I asked how things were going multiple times while he was out of state. He had so many opportunities to say something. Anything. So I cannot believe he'd sign me up for some secret, experimental government program without asking.

I brush my hair and stare at my reflection in the foggy mirror.

*What are you doing here?*

Ice invited me to stay, but why? He didn't even plan to tell me about immortals when we first met. Why would he change his mind—especially if I'm supposed to be nothing more than a stupid summer fling?

*God...* Does he even feel that way about me?

We've known each other for about a month, but—with the two glaring exceptions of Ice's awkward immortals reveal and *this* most recent and concerning development—all we've done is go on a few relatively safe dates. I've gone out to dinner or to the park or to the movies with plenty of *just friends* before, and it's not like he's ever made a move on me or anything.

*Ugh!*

I really like him, but… I keep picturing the flash of disinterest in his eyes when I met him at the door last night. Was he just tired from the drive?

My reflection stares at me, lost and confused. I force a smile and plug my hair dryer into the outlet beside the sink.

I shouldn't worry, right?

Ice will tell me why he wants to hang out. And why he told me about immortals. *And why he signed me up for an experimental program without my knowledge...*

Well, even if he doesn't today, I will find out eventually.

Hair dry, and heart injected with as much determination as I can muster, I slap my cheeks and head out into the hallway.

Ice's bedroom door is cracked, so I push it open and find him seated at his desk. As I step inside, he spins the chair to face me. His expression holds an interesting combination of sincerity and playfulness. If one thing is clear, he feels better than he did last night.

I close the door without taking my eyes off him.

He gestures toward his bed. "Please, sit."

I drop everything in my arms onto my open backpack before taking a seat on the edge of the bed.

From this angle, I spot two things in his lap. The first appears to be a white envelope, but the second is carefully hidden both by the envelope and one hand. I catch only a glimpse of silver.

*I see.* If he intends to play coy, I may as well join in and hope it makes me feel a tiny bit better about the situation.

I pull my hair over one shoulder and fold my hands in my lap. "About what you said last night—"

"Of course," he agrees with a nod. "The forms you signed were the Secrecy Agreement—a standard NDA—and an application for admittance into the Human-Immortal Affairs aware human registry. The same day, I completed my sponsor application."

"Okay, and you're considered my sponsor because you're the one who told me about immortals?"

"That's correct."

*Sounds straightforward enough, but—*

"What does that really mean?"

He glances away. "How should I put this…? As your immortal sponsor, I am responsible for you and your place within immortal society. As such, I was granted some level of legal standing over you when it comes to related affairs."

I feel like I saw something similar mentioned on a page in Ice's paperwork. Maybe I should have actually read them before signing them. Or asked about it then instead of waiting until now.

*Oh, well.*

"And you used that standing to enroll me in some experimental program?" I ask, just to be sure.

"I thought you may find it interesting," he reasons, rubbing his jaw. "This program has been around for decades. It's harmless enough, and any human admitted into the registry is eligible to apply."

"Okay… But what is it?"

With a sigh, he leans back in his chair. "It's not so uncommon for humans to learn of immortals for one reason or another, but the transition can be a struggle due to the vast differences between the two groups."

I open my mouth to speak, but he cuts me off by raising his hand.

"Don't worry," he says. "I'm perfectly aware that Night took it upon herself to enlighten you on *those* matters already, so I won't bother explaining the difference between us further."

I flash an apologetic smile. He waves it off and moves on.

"In any case, the program's goal is to streamline the process of integrating aware humans into a predominantly immortal-operated society. We have a distinct culture, and humans typically exist outside of it, so it's…" He glances away. "Well, it can be *difficult* for many immortals to accept humans into the fold."

*Immortals* are *prejudiced against humans?* I'm not surprised, but it leaves me with more questions than answers.

"How is this program supposed to help me?"

He smiles and hands the envelope to me. It's a standard, white mailing envelope with my full name, *Jayde Nicole Palmer*, written on the back in bold pen.

"I believe it's your new ID," he says.

"New ID?"

He shrugs. "It may also be an acceptance letter."

The single sheet of paper inside the envelope indeed has a new California ID card with my name and photo attached at the bottom. I expected it to be different somehow, but I don't notice anything new or unfamiliar about it.

The top half of the page is a typed letter.

*Dear Jayde Palmer and Sponsor...*

Clearing my throat, I read aloud, "We are pleased to announce that your request for admittance into the U.S. Department of Human-Immortal Affairs Aware Human Registry was accepted. Your personal information has been successfully updated in our database. In addition, after careful review, your application for enrollment in the Human Immortal Program was approved..."

I trail off and continue reading in my head, but there's not much else. Nothing revealing, anyway. A vague thanks from the Human Advocacy Unit. A sentence referencing my updated ID. A messy signature below a printed name at the bottom of the page.

*Victor Morano...*

Who is that?

*Whatever; it doesn't matter.*

I peel the card away from the paper and scrutinize both sides for anything to differentiate it from my old one. With the exception of the updated issue and expiration dates, it appears identical.

Confused, I voice my concern.

Ice thinks for a moment, nods, and fishes a wallet out of his pocket. I watch for him to slip up on hiding the thing in his lap, but he doesn't even as he removes a card from his wallet and offers it to me.

Giving up, I accept the card—a California driver's license.

"Take a look," he says.

I examine it carefully, but the only real difference between his license and my ID—besides the obvious—is that he's over twenty-one. His card has the horizontal layout while mine is still vertical. And his photo is flattering.

*Born April 13th. He's six-foot-two.*

I return the card.

"There is no visible difference between our cards and anyone else's," he explains. "The real difference is concealed within the barcode on the back."

I flip my ID over and run my fingers across the barcode.

"Normally, it contains the same information that's written on the front in an electronic format. However, for immortals—and humans like yourself—the barcodes store additional encrypted information, accessible only by certain devices. Any other way of setting them apart could raise suspicion if the wrong person were to notice."

"I guess slapping an '*immortal*' label on the card would be too obvious?"

"That's the idea." With a laugh, he sets his wallet on the desk behind him. "Now then, enough suspense. This is what you're really here for, right?"

I force a smile and tuck my new ID into my pocket while he reveals the object he spent the whole conversation hiding. It's a small, thin, rectangular package, neatly wrapped in silvery paper and topped with a tiny, blue bow.

"A gift—courtesy of The U.S. Department of Human-Immortal Affairs, Research Division."

*Research Division?*

He hands it to me, and I hesitate before taking it.

The box is surprisingly light, and the metallic paper reflects the sunlight coming in through the window. The ribbon and bow are similar in color to his eyes—the eyes of a water immortal. Was that intentional? Is he the one who wrapped it?

I glance up to meet his gaze.

"What is it?" I ask.

He smiles. "Open it and find out."

I remove the bow and tear the thin wrapping paper to reveal the plain, black jewelry gift box underneath. Whatever is inside, it's from Human-Immortal Affairs. It's not from Ice.

*Calm down.*

With a deep breath, I remove the lid.

Inside the box, nestled in cottony padding, is a necklace. A pendant featuring a blue, diamond-shaped gemstone. The stone itself is taller than it is wide, rather flat, and mounted on a silver base with four tiny prongs holding it in place at each corner. The delicate chain twists as I lift the necklace out of its box, and the light from the window reveals the gem's translucent and reflective properties. I've never seen anything quite like it—in cut, color, or anything else. It's beautiful. Mesmerizing, almost.

*This is for me?*

"What is it?" I ask again.

"The River Sapphire" he says. "It's a synthetic gemstone. A scientific marvel, I suppose. Theoretically, it should enable you to morph."

"Morph? You mean turn into a cat? Like you?" I look up, surprised to find my own curiosity reflected in his eyes.

"Theoretically," he agrees with a short laugh.

"That's amazing! How does it work?"

His smile wavers. "The River Sapphire is an untested trial item developed for you specifically. They've made similar gemstones in the past for others, but it was explained to me that the utilization varies for the individual."

"Oh."

The creator doesn't even know how it works?

*Great.* Wish me luck.

"You could start by trying it on," he suggests.

He's clearly as intrigued by the prospect of me turning into a cat as I am. It's something I never thought could be possible—even after learning about immortals.

*What fur color will I have?*

*Will my eyes still be green?*

Not wanting to disappoint, I stand in front of the full-length mirror on the closet door. I look both nervous and excited, and Ice watches my reflection from the desk chair. Then, with my eyes closed, I fasten the necklace around my neck. I wait a moment, but Ice says nothing, and I don't feel any different, so I open my eyes to check.

Of course, my body remains unchanged in the mirror.

The intensely blue River Sapphire rests at the top of my sternum, a gentle weight just below my collarbone. The pendant isn't gaudy or obnoxious, and the color complements my eyes, but it failed to accomplish its intended purpose.

Ice's reflection appears rather disappointed as well, so I turn and crack a smile. "Do you think it has a transformation phrase —like in a cartoon?"

"Cute." He chuckles, but his expression mellows. He rubs his jaw and glances away. "Unfortunately, I don't know much about it. I spoke with one of the scientists who made the gemstone before I left, but I wasn't offered many specific details."

"Well, I like the necklace even if it doesn't work. Thanks for giving this to me."

He sighs. "As I said, it's not from *me*."

"It is from you," I insist, if only because I think it might cheer him up. "You're the one who signed me up for the program—or whatever—right?"

"I suppose. In that case, you're welcome." He offers me a faint smile before standing. "Take good care of it, will you? Those gemstones aren't easy to obtain."

"Of course."

I'm disappointed too, but is it so terrible that I can't morph the instant I put it on? The River Sapphire is part of an experimental program, right? It's an untested product, and he said the gemstones work differently for everyone, anyway. Surely, they don't always activate right away.

*Right?*

We watch each other in silence for a while.

He glances away first.

"It suits you," he says.

It's a compliment. He's trying to be nice, but the clear hint of disinterest in his voice bothers me—the same as last night.

I sigh and turn back to the mirror.

As I mess with my hair, Ice says nothing and remains standing in front of his desk. I watch his reflection. His muted expression. After another moment of hesitation, he leaves the room.

*Yeah... The River Sapphire is lovely.*

# eighteen

Night asks about the necklace over lunch.

When I tell her what Ice told me, her surprise lasts only an instant. Then she glances at him, her eyes cool and sharp. He says nothing about it—instead commenting on his omelet—and she drops the subject entirely.

After that, I answer Ice's basic questions regarding how things went while he was gone. I talk about the solstice festival and meeting Night's friends and how nice it was to not pay to do laundry. Honestly, staying here wasn't nearly as awkward as I expected, and my admission seems to come as a relief to everyone at the table.

As before, Ice divulges next to nothing about his time spent in Seattle—not that I can bring myself to ask. Then, for better or worse, lunch concludes uneventfully.

Smoke thanks his sister for the food. She smiles at him, and he retreats to his bedroom. Ice remains seated as I stand to join Night in tidying the kitchen. She seems grateful for the help, but her smile is forced and shallow.

Is she mad? *At Ice?*

He watches us from the table, his expression mild.

What did they talk about last night? Did they get into a fight?

To be fair, an argument may have been justified. He ignored both of us while he was gone, and he exercised his authoritative power as my sponsor to sign me up for an experimental program. I thought I was in over my head before, but I have absolutely no idea what's going on now. And I can't do anything about it.

When I'm done helping Night, I excuse myself and leave the great room. I shut myself in Ice's bedroom. Grabbing my phone from the end table, I sit on the edge of the bed and check my notifications.

Night is obviously upset with Ice's recent behavior. I wouldn't feel bad if she's chewing him out for what he did right now.

*That's not very nice.*

I sigh and continue scrolling down my FaceSpace feed.

Night shared a selfie we took with Carmen during the solstice festival the other day. I don't know why, but I asked if it was okay, since I'm human and all.

The question surprised her, and she laughed. She said, "*The internet doesn't care about things like that,*" and I guess she's right because the post received only positive attention. No angry reacts or "*Who's your new friend?*" or anything.

Even so, I don't think Ice exaggerated the division between humans and immortals.

Rose has 487 friends on FaceSpace. Only a dozen or so aren't human. If most of her friends live in Riverview, where immortals make up half the population, that's nothing. Even more revealing, out of my own 94 friends, Night is the only one with those bright immortal eyes.

*Why is that?*

Do Night's friends honestly not care that I'm human, or are the reactions positive only because mentioning such things online is forbidden? Does she have friends who were unhappy to see her hanging out with me?

*And now, with the River Sapphire...*

A sound startles me. A knock at the door.

"Um—" I lock my phone. "Come in?"

The door opens.

It's Ice. He doesn't step inside, but he does offer me a smile. Warm. Apologetic. And I'm suddenly more conflicted than before.

"You want a ride home?" he asks.

"Yes," I say, flooding with relief. "Thank you."

"Of course." He laughs lightly and turns to leave. "Whenever you're ready, then."

* * * * *

My hands rest on the backpack in my lap. We've been in the car for a few minutes, and neither of us have said anything to the other. It's awkward. Part of me is so incredibly frustrated with him. Part of me just wants to spend more time with him.

*We need to talk, though, so...*

Maybe I should invite him inside?

I could offer him something to drink. *Do we have anything besides water? Maybe a few Crystal Light packets.* Doesn't matter. We could sit and talk without Night around. He acts a little off when they're together—subdued and wry. If we're alone, maybe he'll explain more about the program he signed me up for. *The…Human Immortal Program?*

At the very least, I can ask about Seattle.

*If he'll talk to me at all.*

Maybe he's still tired from all the running around, but his attitude bothers me. Dismissive and uninterested. I don't like it.

*I feel…weird.*

I touch the River Sapphire. *Surely, this means something.*

He wouldn't have gotten it if he weren't serious about… being my sponsor, or whatever, right? I'm sure he thought I'd want to join the Human Immortal Program. I'm sure that's why he signed me up for it—to save himself another trip. But I still wish he would have asked first.

*Ugh…*

The car pulls into the Oakwood Cottages parking lot, and Ice takes Rose's usual space in front of my building. The engine quiets. I hear him sigh, and I glance up from my lap.

"I'll walk you to the door," he says.

"Oh. Okay."

I fumble to unbuckle my seatbelt with my bag in the way. Ice opens the passenger door the moment I touch the handle. He offers to take my bag while I climb out of the car, and we walk to the front door together.

I unlock it, but I don't open it yet.

Ice returns my backpack, and he smiles, finally looking as tired as he should. "My time at the Seattle regional office was… hectic. It sounds like Night kept you comfortable and busy while I was away, but I appreciate your patience these last few days."

*Maybe he is willing to talk.*

"It's been a lot," I admit. "But it was alright. I had fun hanging out with the twins."

"Glad to hear it."

*Okay, this is your last chance, Jayde!*

"Hey, ah—" I pull the front door open. "Wanna come inside for a minute?"

His expression recovers some of its previous warmth. "Yes. In fact, there's something I wanted to discuss with you."

*There is?*

"Okay. Come in."

Ice has been inside before, but I'm more anxious this time. Instead of the looming mystery of immortals, it's the mystery of the Human Immortal Program. I want to trust that he has my best interest at heart, but dang—I still can't believe he didn't ask. *Even if his trip was hectic.*

"Can I get you anything to drink?" I drop my bag on the couch on my way to the kitchen. "Do you want some, um—" *Again, what do I have?* "—water?"

"Water is fine."

He takes a seat at the small dining table while I fill a mug with ice and tap water. After handing over the mug, I sit in the chair across from him.

"What did you want to talk about?"

"You asked how I was doing while I was in Seattle." He pauses to take a drink. "I wasn't trying to be unreasonable by not answering. Truth is, I'm not meant to discuss it in detail."

"They told you that?"

He nods. "There's only so much I can say about my dealings at the regional office, but I told you everything they told me about the necklace. Sadly, there isn't much to know."

"I guess I shouldn't be surprised. And you said the program is experimental? Not dangerous, though?"

"Not dangerous," he assures me with a smile.

"Oh, good."

"That said, I am curious: Have you told anyone about me?"

Anxiety pricks at me—concern that my past-self messed up somehow—but Ice's demeanor remains casual and unbothered. *I hope I'm overreacting.*

"In what context?" I ask, trying to ignore the nagging tightness in my chest.

He thinks about it for a moment, quiet, his hand still on the handle of the mug. Then his eyes meet mine. "Any."

*That's not very reassuring!*

"Only my roommate," I say slowly.

"Ah. Rose, right?"

"Yeah, why?"

He smiles, the heaviness lifting. "As I said, I'm merely curious. I trust you said nothing of immortals to your friend, of course, but I have one request moving forward: Do try to keep my name out of the ears of other humans."

*Um...*

"It's nothing personal," he continues, his tone bordering on flippant, "but it's better if they don't know. Between the secret of immortals and the rather sensitive nature of my parents' company's interests, their knowledge poses a potential security risk."

"I—"

*Breaking the rules is severely punishable.*

Okay, he has a point.

After all, I still don't understand what is and isn't considered an immortal-related topic, so I don't know what I can and can't talk about with other humans—Rose, my family, anyone. What if my innocently vague comments about his secret were against the rules?

His presentation was a little intense, but maybe I should be more careful.

So I nod. "I understand."

"As for your friend, I'll let it slide," he says, his smile wry. "As long as you don't reveal immortals or provide further identifying details that could connect her to my parents or MonroeWorks Global, feel free to discuss me at your leisure."

*It's probably too late for that second part, but okay.*

"What should I tell anyone else if they ask?"

"Use your imagination," he says with a shrug. "Give them a fake name. I'm sure you can come up with something to placate any inquisitive minds."

He seriously trusts me to do that? *Well...* I guess there is some benefit to not having friends or a close relationship with either of my parents.

"I will try," I agree.

His expression softens. "Thank you."

We sit quietly for a few minutes. Ice drinks his water. I tap my fingernails on the table.

I want to know what he did in Seattle. I want to know where the Human-Immortal Affairs office is. What it looks like. Who he talked to and what they said. *But he was sworn to secrecy. There's no point in asking, is there?*

"You said Night took you to that solstice festival?" When I nod, he smiles. "Did she bother you much while I was away?"

"Oh, no. I had fun. She wanted to buy a flower crown for me, but I didn't want her to spend any more money."

"You were concerned about money?" He laughs easily, but his expression quickly mellows, and his hands return to the frosty mug. "Though, that does sound like Night. I don't understand the appeal of such events, but she enjoys cute things."

"I met a few of her friends too. She seems popular."

He glances away. "She has many friends, yes."

I frown.

More lengthy silence. Ice's hand on the handle of the mug. The hum of the fridge behind me. Night's cryptic warning, and her concern that I learned of immortals.

"Is she mad because of me?" I ask.

"Because of you?" He studies my face for a couple seconds, and then he makes a small sound—something between a laugh and a sigh. "No."

I tip my head. "But she is mad at you?"

"She is. I ignored you both during my trip to Seattle. I was rather busy and did not have access to my phone for most of it, but I suppose her anger is not…completely unjustified."

"Yeah, I wish you had—I dunno—asked before you signed me up for some random experimental program."

"I see." He cracks a smile, his sharp eyes meeting mine again. "You're upset with me too."

"I guess I was a little upset at first, but I'm more curious now. If the River Sapphire can help me fit in with immortals, maybe things will be easier for me in the future?"

"That's the idea, isn't it? Your understanding nature is most refreshing."

I watch him carefully. "You're just trying to help me, right?"

"Of course." His eyes flick to the mug in his hand. "Human-Immortal Affairs has an entire department dedicated to supporting aware and sponsored humans like yourself. A representative I spoke with suggested the Human Immortal Program might benefit you, so I agreed to enroll you."

"I still wish you had asked first."

He shrugs. "Phones weren't allowed beyond the front lobby. Your admittance to the program was a last-minute decision made inside. I suppose I could have told you after the decision was made, but I thought you'd prefer to discuss it face-to-face."

Is this a *better to ask forgiveness than beg permission* thing? *Ugh...*

"Do you wish I hadn't enrolled you?" he asks.

"No," I say quickly. "It's not like that. It surprised me, but I appreciate the thought."

He takes a drink, and then smiles another faint smile. "That's all I wanted to say, so I should go."

"Oh, okay. Well, thanks for talking to me."

"Of course." His smile warms, though it still doesn't seem to touch his eyes. "Thanks for the drink."

# nineteen

Every so often, a gentle weight against my skin reminds me of the River Sapphire's presence. Light from the window reflects off a few facets and casts tiny, white speckles onto the ceiling.

Borderline magical properties aside, I've never owned such a quality piece of jewelry. *A one-of-a-kind necklace...*

I adjust the pendant to center it on my chest, take a selfie in the mirror behind my dresser, and send the photo to Rose without context. Her response comes a few minutes later, while I'm sitting on the edge of my bed and scrolling down FaceSpace.

**Rose:** hello, what is that? (◉ v ◉)

*Ah...* What did Ice tell me about discretion *not even two hours ago*? Was sending a picture of the necklace a bad idea?

It's not like I can hide it from her forever. I'm meant to wear it, and Rose lives with me. *I'm sure it's fine as long as I don't tell her exactly what it is.*

**Me:** It was a present, I guess.

**Rose:** You guess? From Ice, right?

**Me:** Yep!

**Rose:** Wowww.. is it sapphire?

**Me:** I think so? Not entirely sure.

Lab-created sapphire, maybe, but who knows?

My phone rings. It's Rose, of course.

*What if she has questions?*

I can't tell the truth, so my only choice is to weave an even more complex lie. But she's coming back soon. *We live together.* How am I supposed to keep all of these stupid secrets forever? First immortals, and now the Human Immortal Program…

And what if the River Sapphire lets me turn into a cat in the future like it's supposed to? How the heck will I hide that?

I take a deep breath. I pull myself together. I sit on the edge of the bed that isn't nearly as soft as Ice's, and I answer the phone.

"Hey, you're not busy?" I ask.

"Nope," she says, chipper as usual. "So, how'd it go? I see you're home, and you have a prize, so it couldn't have been bad, right?"

I laugh. "I guess? I mean, it was alright, but it was weird."

"Weird?"

"Well… I did spend the entire time with his sister because he was out of town. Isn't that weird?"

"Sure, but what's up with the necklace all of a sudden?"

"Oh." *Um…* "It's probably an apology for inviting me to his house before suddenly leaving me with the twins for three days."

A pause. Then laughter. So much laughter. Too much laughter, honestly. *I nailed it.*

"What a man," she wheezes. "Doesn't he know you're not a jewelry kind of girl?"

"I think it's cute—the necklace, I mean."

"The necklace!" She cackles, the sound tickling my eardrum

through the phone. "Oh my god, Jayde. When did you get so damn funny?"

*It's called misdirection, Rose.*

She laughs so hard she loses the ability to speak, and I can no longer restrain my own laughter until she finally calms down.

Feeling more relaxed than I have in days, I fall back onto my bed and stare at the ceiling. "You know… I really like him."

"I can tell." Her voice is warm and genuine. "Hey, I saw the picture his sister tagged you in the other day. Night, right? You looked like you were having fun. I'm glad. Before you started hanging out with them, I was worried you'd be bored and lonely or whatever. So it's good to know that's not the case."

"Rose…"

She laughs again. "It was dumb of me to worry, wasn't it? I should have known you could take care of yourself."

"Well, I appreciate the concern. Honestly. But how are things going in Arizona?"

Talking to her makes everything feel…normal.

* * * * *

*This is so frustrating!*

My hair is damp. Beads of water drip onto the sink's edge as I glare at my reflection.

I put the necklace on the moment I stepped out of the shower, and I fiddled with it for a while, but nothing happened. No matter what I try, the pendant does nothing but sit below my collarbone and taunt me with its cool weight.

I groan, finish getting dressed, and leave the bathroom.

With a glance at the empty downstairs beyond the banister, I dip into my bedroom. I find my phone face-down on the bed, so I sit and scroll through the notifications on my lock screen. There are a couple emails. An article from a news app. And…

**FaceSpace**
An event you might be interested in…

I click the banner, and FaceSpace opens to an event page—an image of a pop-up bandstand.

*Right.*

The first Music@ThePark is tomorrow. Do I still want to go?

I could ask Ice if he's interested. After all, he doesn't seem to have an issue with me, so my personal insecurities are the only thing stopping me from talking to him.

*Ugh.*

We haven't spoken much since he dropped me off. A text here and there, but—

*Jayde, it hasn't even been two days.*

*What are you so worried about?*

I am definitely overthinking this one.

With a sigh, I tag myself as interested in the event. Then I text Ice to ask if he's busy tomorrow and tuck my phone in my pocket.

* * * * *

I'm awake.

*Why am I awake?*

It's dark—clearly still late at night—but my phone is ringing. The dimmed screen illuminates part of my bedroom, and, as the haze of sleep clears from my mind, I recognize the ringtone.

*Okay, I'm up!*

I snatch my phone off the bedside table and tap to answer. My throat is hoarse, but I manage to say, "Hello," without croaking.

"Did I wake you?" Ice's crisp voice asks on the other end.

"No, um—" I move the phone from my ear to check the time. *It's 1:38AM.* "Alright, maybe you did."

He laughs. "My apologies. But I wanted to ask if you'd like to go to Riverside with me tomorrow?"

"For Music@ThePark?"

"That's correct."

*Hm...* He didn't respond to the text I sent before I fell asleep, so I assumed he already had plans, but…

"Sure. I wanted to go anyway."

"Wonderful." He sounds…relieved, almost. "I'll pick you up tomorrow afternoon. Around four?"

"Sounds good. Thanks."

"Goodnight, Jayde."

"Goodnight."

The call ends. I return my phone to the table and roll onto my other side.

*Hopefully, I remember this conversation when I wake up.*

# twenty

My phone goes off on the edge of the sink. A text.

> **Ice Monroe**
> I'm outside. Whenever you're ready.

*Aaaaaa—*

I drop my phone into my purse and brush my hair with more vigor. Maybe I should put it up? It's super hot out, so a bun might be more comfortable. Wearing my hair up would be cuter with my dress, anyway, and will expose more of my back.

*Hmm...*

A more elaborate style would take too long, so...

*Messy bun, it is.*

I throw my hair up into a bun that isn't awful and stab several bobby pins into the mess to hold it in place. A dusting of hairspray I'm lucky Rose didn't take to Arizona with her later, and I'm as ready as I'll ever be.

My phone is in my purse.

My purse is on my person.

*Alright, here I go.*

Ice's silver Porsche idles in Rose's usual parking space as I approach. The doors click unlocked, and I open the passenger side. Ice watches me, one arm resting on the steering wheel. Night sits in the back seat behind him—a surprise that doesn't bother me.

She smiles. "I hope you don't mind I asked to tag along."

I thought this was supposed to be a date, but maybe I should stop making any assumptions.

"No, it's fine," I assure her. Once buckled in the passenger seat, I turn to Ice. "So, how have you been?"

"I'm doing well," he says with a pleasant smile.

"Oh, good!"

I was a little worried, but he looks to be in a better mood than he was a few days ago. He seems relaxed. His attention on me, and his expression mild and kind.

"You got some sleep, then?"

"Yes," he says with a laugh. "I am well-rested."

Night laughs in the backseat, but it is a relief. I guess he was just tired from his concurrent trips to Seattle after all. *Though, he was awake at like 2AM last night...*

"Any luck with that necklace?" he asks, his tone casual as he checks the rear-view mirror.

"No. I've been working on it, but it hasn't done anything yet."

"That's too bad."

He shifts the car into reverse, ending our conversation as his focus turns to driving. I fiddle with the keychain on my purse. *I wore a cute dress and put my hair up, and he didn't say anything about it.*

"Is it like a real gemstone?" Night asks.

"Um—" I stop fidgeting and raise a hand to touch the pendant. I've worn it all day, but the stone is strangely cool beneath my fingers. "I think so."

She glances away, one hand on her jaw. "The River Sapphire. I understand it was created in a laboratory, but I wonder if the chemical composition is the same as natural sapphire."

*Rose asked if it was sapphire too...*

I take the necklace off. The gemstone doesn't look like glass. It's not completely transparent, and there are several imperfections within—the tiny specks almost imperceptible—but surely glass can have imperfections too? I don't know how to tell.

"You wanna see it?" I ask.

Her eyes widen with curiosity. "May I?"

"Sure."

I pass the necklace to her, and she holds it carefully, like it's something precious and fragile. After a thorough examination, she looks up at the rear-view mirror.

"Do you know what this is made of?" she asks.

Ice takes a deep breath, his attention still on the road ahead. "No. They explained little about the gemstone creation process. It was made in a lab, as you said, but that's all I know."

"How are they attuned to the individual?"

"Your guess as to how the necklace works is as good as mine, Night. All they told me is that it should."

*Oh, well...* Whether it worked or not, I appreciate her attempt at weeding out more information.

"Hm..." She studies the gemstone again, turning it over and holding it up to the window for a moment. Then she sighs and returns it. "It's a lovely pendant, Jayde. I hope you're able to figure it out."

"Thanks. Me too."

* * * * *

I don't often catch myself people watching. I tend to keep my head down and avoid attracting attention while in public.

Today is a bit different. Once again, I'm a human in a group of immortals, but I'm more relaxed than I was during my last park outing, and I find my eyes drawn toward random strangers.

As I engage in idle conversation with Ice and Night while we sit at a picnic table beneath the shade of a tree, I sort the people who pass by close enough to reveal their eye color.

*Blue. Gold. Gold. Violet. Grey. Hazel. Blue. Gold. Brown. Green. Blue. Gold. Brown. Green. Pale blue.*

After a while, I don't really need to see their eyes anymore. I can tell if any given person is human or immortal based on the way they walk. The way they carry themselves. Their…presence.

Humans have very little presence. They bumble around from one place to the next, engrossed in whatever they're doing in the moment, without giving their surroundings much consideration.

But an immortal's movements are deliberate. They scan their environment as they walk, though it's hard to notice if I don't pay close attention. They act so relaxed, carrying on conversations or checking their phone, without losing any of that passive awareness.

Plus, the vast majority of immortals are unreasonably attractive. Keeping conventional beauty standards in mind, there's a decent chance any given hot person is an immortal.

*Not fair.*

Maybe the difference between humans and immortals goes beyond magic abilities and shapeshifting. They seem more present in the world—more aware of it. Humans just…*exist here.*

Now that I know, can I learn to emulate it?

A pair of violet-eyed teenagers giggle to each other as they walk by. One catches me watching. Our eyes meet for an instant. Mild curiosity crosses her face only to be replaced by disinterest.

I glance away.

Quite a few immortals have looked at me that way—like they're surprised to find a human perceiving them and hanging out with other immortals.

Was it the same during the solstice festival, or is it new?

Are they looking because I'm sitting so close to Ice? Because our eyes meet, and I laugh at his easy banter with Night? Because we talk to each other and look like a couple?

*Does that bother them?*

Music@ThePark has a reputation as a couple's event, which makes sense, as it's something cheap and fun to do on a Wednesday evening. Food. Music. Tons of places to sneak away from the crowd. An obvious choice for a date, especially for young people. Of course, plenty of friend groups, families, and singles attend too, but… I don't know.

Maybe that's why being here with both Ice and Night is so surreal. My first impression was that they didn't get along, but everything seems fine today. They speak normally, and they smile and laugh, and I haven't sensed any tension between them.

So, that's both unexpected and a huge relief.

But am I right? Does me being here with Ice set off alarm bells in the heads of passing immortals? Just because I'm human? *Ugh.* If only *someone* would be honest with me about how strange my situation is instead of pretending it's perfectly normal.

Now that I think about it, Ice has the same cool awareness. I've been distracted by people watching and holding a conversation about carnival food at the same time, but I catch his gaze flicking away from the table for an instant—like he's taking note of the people around. His expression shifts slightly in the middle of a sentence, though his casual tone remains unaffected.

He must see them looking our way. Does it bother him too?

*Oh, no…*

Is he embarrassed to be seen with me?

He never glanced around so much before—unless I missed it every other time we went out. Maybe I was too flustered to notice? Unless something has changed? Are things different now that I know about immortals? Now that I have the River Sapphire?

*Does it mean anything at all?*

"Oh, Jayde," Night says brightly, drawing me out of my head. "Carmen is here somewhere if you want to find her and say hi."

I wouldn't mind seeing her. She was unfazed by my humanity last time, and I have a feeling she'd think the River Sapphire is neat. Even if she didn't send me a friend request after Night tagged us both in her photo, and I was too nervous to send one myself…

I glance to Ice, who awaits my response with a notably neutral expression.

*Right. I'm here to hang out with him.*

"Maybe for a minute," I say.

"It's been a while since my friends last saw you," she says. Ice meets her gaze, and she smiles. "If you don't mind tagging along for a minute."

"Of course," he agrees.

Night leads the way across the park, and I walk a few steps behind her with Ice. His thumbs are tucked in his belt loops. He's not wearing the leather jacket today—just a fitted t-shirt, dark jeans, and boots. He seems kind of bored, but he watches the path ahead with the same focus he displays while driving.

*Would it be weird to tell him that he looks good?*

He glances down at me before I decide.

"You've been quiet," he says.

"Aren't I always quiet?" I ask, caught off guard.

He laughs. "I suppose so, but you seem especially distracted today."

"I've been thinking about…" *Uh—* I glance away and spot Carmen's bright blue hair mixed in with a nearby crowd. *Oh, good, a distraction!* "Oh, look, we're here."

To my surprise and relief, he drops it as Night flags Carmen down. She acknowledges us, pats the person she was talking to on the back, and slips away from the group. She hugs Night before regarding me and Ice with heightened interest now that we're all standing together.

"Ice Monroe," she says.

"Carmen Choi." His voice is smooth and personable. "I believe you've already met Jayde."

His hand rests on my back—an unexpected, soft touch—and

I feel like I might burst into flames. Struggling, I manage to say it's nice to see her again.

Her violet eyes flick between us. "So, how'd you guys meet?"

Ice offers a watered-down and half-accurate version of our "chance" meeting at Bargain Shop, and my eyes wander. A few pairs of gemstone-colored eyes watch us from the group Carmen left across the walking path. I look away before I have the chance to meet anyone's gaze by accident.

"Uh-huh," Carmen says, clearly unconvinced by something Ice said while I wasn't paying attention. "Anyway, I'll leave you to it. Night, you wanna hang out here for a while?"

She hesitates, looking to me before she smiles. "I suppose so. I wasn't expected to tag along in the first place. You two can handle yourselves, right?"

I nod, still unfortunately aware of my affected breathing as Ice's hand falls away from my back.

"Of course," he says.

Her smile widens, a flash of genuine brightness, and she says I can message her if I need anything. Then she dips her head, steps away, and leaves hand-in-hand with Carmen. They slip seamlessly into the large group, which appears to consist entirely of immortals. One of the girls gives Night a bear hug.

Ice lets out a breath beside me. "You said something earlier," he says. "Do you still want a snow cone?"

I don't remember mentioning a snow cone, but I'm down. As we head toward the parking lot full of food trucks, the heat of the sun replaces the warmth where his hand once rested on my back.

# twenty-one

"What should we do now?" I ask.

Ice looks around.

We've been standing in the grass near the large pavilion for several minutes. Music plays at the bandstand downhill. The park is full of people, both human and immortal. Families with kids. Small groups of teenagers hanging out in the shade. Couples walking down the path holding hands.

I glance at Ice's hand, but I don't reach for it.

Being with him doesn't feel the same as being with the other guys I dated. I don't want to think they were pushy or rude, really, but… I've always been shy and passive. That's what I'm like when I'm out of my element, but I was never afraid to hold someone's hand if they wanted to.

Maybe because I knew it was meaningless? Because, even if I liked the guy a little, it was stupid and silly, and we wouldn't be together for long?

*Why don't I feel the same now?*

Why do I hope this relationship is different?

Why does a simple touch that probably doesn't mean anything set me on fire? Why am I too nervous to reach for his hand? *Just because I don't know what he wants?*

I hold my empty snow cone cup with both hands, wishing it did more to cool me off.

"I don't mind staying here," he says. "Though, I wouldn't mind getting away from the crowd either."

"So, you don't know?" I ask with a laugh.

He smiles, but his attention diverts to a group of young men walking by, and he frowns again. "This is more Night's scene than mine. She enjoys this sort of busy atmosphere."

"You don't?"

He watches me with a mild frown. Then he raises a hand and points off into the distance, indicating a vast crowd of people near the top of the hill on the other side of the walking path.

"She's there—near the oak, with her friends," he says. "You can go if you'd like."

*Huh?*

Scanning the crowd, I eventually spot Night's flower crown and Carmen's blue hair over a hundred yards away, not far from where we left them nearly an hour ago. But I look back to Ice.

"I'd rather stay with you."

He cocks his head, his lips forming a curious smile. "You know, I'm running out of interesting things to say to you."

"Huh?" I tip my head too.

Then he laughs. "It's nothing. Come with me."

His hand brushes my arm as he turns away, and my heart skips at the intentional touch. After sucking in a quick recovery breath, I follow a couple seconds behind. I weave through the mass of people gathered near the pavilion, careful not to bump into anyone, and eventually pop out on the other side face-to-face with him.

Flashing a half-smile, he points toward the far end of the park. In the direction of the river. Then up.

"Let's go up there," he says.

"The bridge?" A concrete staircase off the main footpath leads up the hill and connects to the sidewalk. We could easily get to the bridge from here. It would only take a few minutes, but—"Why?"

He shrugs. "To get away."

"Ah…" *Being here bothers him? Why?* "Sure. We can go."

I drop my snow cone cup in the nearest trash can, and we walk through the short grass—the path of least resistance—toward the stairs.

Ice talks about the work he does for MonroeWorks Global. He sorts digital documents. Applications. Inquiries. Media requests. Some dabbling in HR, forwarding employee concerns to other departments. Things like that. But he doesn't seem to care for the work, and it sounds like more of a favor to his parents or something he does in his spare time rather than an actual position he holds within the company.

"You're not working this summer?" he asks.

"I mean, I could," I say. *And I probably should.* "I worked at the CoffeeStar by RHS last summer, so I guess I could do that again, but I don't know."

"How do you pay rent?"

*Ha*... "My dad feels bad for bailing on me, I guess. He's doing well for himself now, so he agreed to pay my half of the rent until I graduate. Financial aid helps too."

"I see. Though, I doubt you'll worry about that much longer."

"What do you mean?"

He smiles. "The Human Immortal Program doesn't come without proper compensation, Jayde. That necklace won't be their last gift to you."

"Could you be any more vague?"

His eyes widen like my comment surprised him, and he laughs. Eyes closed and mouth shielded by one curled hand, it's the same strange, honest laugh I've seen from him only a couple times before. When he looks to me again, his smile carries slightly less cryptic energy.

"I would hate to ruin the surprise," he says without a hint of apology.

We continue from the paved sidewalk onto the bridge walkway. Some of the aging wood slats shift ever so slightly beneath my feet. I avoid looking down and slide my hand along the metal guardrail to my left.

Ice stops walking as we reach the bridge's mid-point. He rests his elbows on top of the guardrail and gazes out over the water.

I stop too.

The water is a cool teal with a gentle current. People gather on the bank along the park side, concentrated in sandy areas. Several lounge on beach towels. Some are swimming, and I hear periodic hoots from children splashing in the shallows.

The live band is audible from here too, but the sound of the river and the busy road behind me leave the music muffled. I can't make out the lyrics. Only bass and drums. A general mellow vibe.

Ice's eyes are closed when I look back. His hair shifts in the slight breeze. He is beautiful, an image of comfortable peace.

*I want to touch him,* but I don't move.

"Do you even like Music@ThePark?" I ask.

His eyes open and flick toward me. "I don't dislike it. Why?"

"I only come to get out of the house and hang out with friends. It's not important to me. We can go somewhere else if you want."

"It's alright." He returns his attention to the sky. "Night used to drag me to these events all the time, so I'm used to it. Though, this is better than listening to her friends."

*Is it?* He honestly prefers doing absolutely nothing with me over hanging out with Night's friends? *That's…surprising.*

He's not even watching me, but I avert my gaze.

"Still—" A hawk dips down toward the water. Diving in, it resurfaces with a small fish in its talons. "Oh, look!"

My hand reaches for Ice's arm. The other points toward the bird as it flies off with the fish. My fingers brush his skin, he makes a soft sound, and the muscles in his arm tense beneath my hand.

Our eyes meet. His expression is rather blank, carrying a vague air of surprise, and my face flushes hotly in response. I release his arm and clasp both hands near my chest.

"Sorry," I stammer. "Um— Did you see the hawk?"

He looks at the sky. At me. At his arm where I touched him. And then he laughs. His hand does not cover his mouth. In fact, he tucks his thumbs in his pockets.

*Ugh. Why am I like this?*

"I saw it," he says.

"Pretty cool, huh?" Unfortunately, I don't have pockets to hide my hands in, so I tug on my bracelet instead. "You don't see them in town often…"

"Mm…"

We're both quiet for a moment, during which I stare only at the round, pink beads around my wrist and the slatted wood at my feet. Then Ice takes a breath.

"You ready to head back down?" he asks.

When I look up, he's smiling again, seemingly unaffected. But I don't believe it, and something about his expression leaves me with a lingering sense of guilt.

Even so, I force a smile, and we walk back to the park.

Thanks to Ice's sharp eyes, we quickly meet up with Night. She's still with Carmen, though they're browsing a table full of band merch down the hill from the rest of their friend group. Night grins when she spots us and immediately asks me if Carmen should buy a rubber wristband or a t-shirt.

Both include overt feline imagery, leading me to suspect Ten Toe Beans might be an immortal band—as though the name didn't give it away.

After checking his smartwatch, Ice excuses himself and turns onto a path leading up the hill, toward the restrooms. I watch for a second, but Carmen's exclamation over a keychain shaped like a stylized cat paw print distracts me.

Night laughs. "Have you even heard of this band before?"

"Does it matter?" she asks with pursed lips. "Few artists are this bold, and I can't ignore the irony."

I glance over the merchandise arranged on the table and have to agree it's a lot of fun.

"You could get all three?"

Carmen beams at me, her arched brows betraying a touch of mischief, and she takes my questionable advice without hesitation, much to the satisfaction of the golden-eyed woman minding the table. After paying, she pulls the neon orange t-shirt over her tank top without removing the tag. The color clashes with her blue hair, but she pulls it off.

"What's next?" Night asks.

"Well…" I glance up the hill. "Should we wait for Ice?"

Both shake their heads.

"He can catch up with us later," Night says brightly. "Or give one of us a call if he gets lost."

Carmen snickers and starts up the path away from the stage. Night offers me a more reassuring smile, and we both follow. We end up sitting at a bench in partial shade. They discuss the band for a moment, and then Carmen leans forward to catch my attention.

Her smile is shrewd and humored. "So, you and Ice, huh? I thought Night was kidding, but *oof*."

*Oof? I guess I can't argue, but…*

"Kidding about what?"

She laughs instead of answering.

"Ice is trying," Night says, though her eyes are averted. "He's just…struggling a little."

"Struggling with what?" I ask, no longer playing dumb.

"Accepting reality. The sponsorship process was more complex and involved than he thought, and he has to live with that now."

"Oh." *I see.*

Carmen's eyes widen. "Oh, right!" She flashes a conspiratorial smile, cups a hand near her mouth, and lowers her voice. "You were officially sponsored, right? Night said Ice picked up one of those necklaces for you. Is that it?"

She points at my neck. As I nod, I feel more comfortable.

"It's called the River Sapphire. But it doesn't work."

"Yet," Night says.

"Oh. Well, it's cool anyway."

"Thanks."

The bench falls quiet. I listen to the band playing at the bottom of the hill—assertive female vocals over acoustic guitar—and watch people walk by on the path only a few feet away.

I keep picturing the look on Ice's face when I touched him. Blank surprise. Mild discomfort. It clearly bothered him, yet he set his hand on the small of my back hardly twenty minutes before. He laughed and said it was fine on our way back to the park, but…

I know guys are confusing, but are they always *this* confusing?

"Jayde," Night says, perking up. "I asked Carmen earlier, but she can't, so maybe you can spend the night?"

"Spend the night?" I echo.

She smiles, the expression warm. "Like a sleepover. We can listen to music, and I can do your nails and makeup if you want. It'll be fun."

"Sure," I agree, unsure why I'm so intimidated by the offer. "I mean, it's not like I have anything better to do at home."

Carmen throws her head back in a dramatic groan. "Now I really wish I didn't make those appointments in the morning."

Night's smile grows apologetic as Carmen rants on about how she's falling behind on verifiable intern hours for her cosmetology program. She mentioned beauty college before, but I didn't realize it was so intensive. Working up to five days a week without pay?

*At least she knows what she wants to do.*

"I'll invite you next time," Night assures her.

She pouts, her disappointment largely feigned. "At least send me pictures. I would kill to do Jayde's hair and makeup." Flashing a wicked smile, she raises a hand and holds it just below her ear. "An asymmetrical bob would be perfect."

"On Jayde?" Night asks, her eyes wide.

I gasp and hold my hands to my fat, messy bun as I laugh. "I really like my hair, you know."

Carmen shrugs. "Hey, I know growing your hair out that long takes serious dedication, but it makes you look like you're fifteen."

"Do I seriously look like I'm fifteen?"

Night laughs, shaking her head. "Of course not."

"You're so small and cute." Carmen sighs, her hands pressed to her cheeks. Then she stops kicking her legs, sits up straight, and looks to me with a vacant expression. "How old are you, anyway?"

"Nineteen," I answer, my voice echoing her uncertainty.

She lets out a deep breath. "Oh, wow, I guess that makes sense since you just finished your first year at RCC, right? Dumb question, sorry."

"No, it's fine!"

*Do I seriously look so young with long hair?*

"Actually—" She hops up from the bench and turns to face me. "—can I see your hair for a minute?"

*The hairspray has probably eased up by now, so...*

"As long as you don't pull out scissors," I say.

She laughs and hovers nearby as I undergo the arduous process of locating and removing all eight bobby pins from my hair. I take out the first hair tie. Carmen stops me there, so I let the slightly crispy ponytail fall. She asks for permission before she combs her fingers through the hair trapped by the ponytail.

"It is very nice," she says, her voice wistful. "But give me a minute; I've been dying to fix that bun."

"Oh, ah—"

Fluffy, blue hair falls over her face as she leans to one side to look me in the eye. "If you don't mind?"

"Go ahead." I feel my cheeks warm, so I glance away. "I don't know much about putting my hair up, to be honest."

I half expect her to say, "I can tell," but she doesn't. She beams and lets my hair out of the ponytail. Standing behind me and the bench, she begins to braid my hair.

"Not many people have hair this long," she says. She compares the length to her sister's hair, but I guess mine is thicker.

I forgot how relaxing it is to have someone else mess with my hair. Maybe I should go to a salon. Rose usually trims my split ends every few months, but we've both been so busy with school. And now she's out of town.

*Ah, I don't know...*

*Where the heck did Ice go?*

It takes Carmen less than five minutes to braid my hair and fix it into a surprisingly loose bun, and she only had to use a few extra bobby pins from the stash in her wallet. After asking permission again, she takes a few pictures with her phone.

Night and I scoot over to make room for her, and Carmen sits beside me. She jumps right into showing off the photos. She's quite proud of her work, and she should be. The bun is perfect—neat and round, formed from a swirl of teased braid at the back of my head. It's still heavy, but there's not much to be done about that.

"Thanks," I say. "It looks way better now."

She grins. "No, thank you. It's always fun working with super long hair. I will definitely be at your next sleepover."

"Might be sooner than later," Night says. She fluffs up her own hair and adjusts the large bow atop her head. "I need a haircut. I may go quite short this time."

Carmen gasps. "A pixie?" When Night nods, Carmen reaches over me to grab both of her hands. "Yes, girl, finally!"

They laugh, but I'm distracted as I spot Ice approaching. Our eyes meet, and he raises a hand in acknowledgment. He looks more relaxed and comfortable, full of effortless immortal awareness.

"What do you think?" Night asks, glancing at Ice as he stops beside the bench. "Should I get a pixie cut?"

He considers it briefly before shrugging with his hands. Instead of answering her question, he asks me how late I want to stay. It's still fairly early—just after 7PM—and the concert usually wraps up around nine.

*Should we stay for the whole thing?*

I don't know, but I do mention Night's sleepover invitation. He isn't fazed. When he asks if we'll need to stop by my house on the way, she interjects to say I can borrow anything I need from her.

"Ugh! The more you talk about it, the more bummed I get."

"Oh? You can't come?" He flashes an easy smile. "You and Jayde are also friends, then?"

"Well, duh," she says, patting the bun atop my head. "Any cute friend of Night is a friend of mine. But what about you, Ice? I know you're her sponsor or whatever, but are you guys a thing?"

*Carmen! A thing?*

I force the flustered dismay off my face and turn to watch Ice, surely more expectant than she is. His expression hasn't shifted at all—well, it may have mellowed slightly, but it's hard to tell.

"A thing?" His eyes flick between us. Then he glances aside with a fleeting frown before refocusing Carmen with renewed confidence. "I suppose you could say it's something like that."

A pang of uncertainty rattles me.

Carmen groans to my left. When I glance over, her lavender eyes are narrowed in suspicion.

"Fine," she says. "Keep your secrets."

Ice smiles. "Now then, ladies, what shall we do next?"

# twenty-two

Night stuck with us after Carmen took off with her boyfriend, and the three of us hung out for another hour before deciding it's time to go. It's almost 9PM. The last band is wrapping up their set, and I'm getting a little hungry.

As we walk down the path toward the parking lot, Night suggests we stop at a restaurant on the way to their house.

"You girls get along better than I expected."

"Does it bother you?" she asks.

When I look to Ice, he flashes a smile and shakes his head. "Of course not. It's merely an observation."

"I wasn't sure we would get along at first," I admit. "Because of how we met, you know?"

"Ah— Yes, well…" She shields her face with one hand, her smile forced. "It turns out I was wrong, and I'm lucky you're quite forgiving."

I laugh. "I still feel bad for getting so defensive. For a second there, I thought you were his girlfriend."

"Ha." It sounds like a laugh, but her eyes betray surprise. "You thought that?"

"Oh, um—"

My face goes hot.

As she watches me with muted curiosity, I suddenly wish I hadn't mentioned it. The conversation we had that day was beyond uncomfortable. It was not my greatest moment—rivaling the first impression I left Ice with. *Ugh…*

"What are we doing for dinner? Any preferences, Jayde?"

I clasp my hands around my purse's strap, both thankful that Ice changed the subject and absolutely unsure what I want to eat. But I go with the first thing that comes to mind.

"Crêpes, maybe?"

"A diner, then?" Night asks with a smile. "I know the perfect place, and it's on the way home."

We eat at a family-owned diner, pick up a to-go meal for Smoke, and head toward Westbrooke.

In the backseat, Night gushes over the gel polish kit Carmen gifted her last Christmas. She hasn't had the chance to use it on anyone besides herself—and Carmen, once. I've never had gel nails before, and that only excites her more.

Ice parks his car in the garage and, while we're gathered in the hallway, excuses himself to take a shower. He shuts himself in the bathroom, so I follow Night to meet up with Smoke, who is sitting at the dining table in the great room.

"Why didn't you come with us?" I ask.

I take a seat as Night hands her twin the clear plastic takeout box. He opens the container and looks over the chocolate crêpes inside before meeting my gaze.

"Night can third wheel if she wants, but I'm not interested."

"Oh, come on." She waves off his comment with a mild laugh.

"It wasn't like that at all. I spent most of the evening with Carmen. I saw Hannah and Dawn, and— Oh, that reminds me…"

She trails off, and Smoke tips his head as though still listening. After a moment, they both glance at me.

Then he shrugs and takes a bite of crêpe. "Besides Carmen and Lucas, I hardly talk to anyone from high school anymore. Most of my friends are online. You know that."

She smothers a grimace. "I suppose neither of us knew them well back then."

*That twin telepathy thing is something else.*

"You had fun, though?" he asks.

She nods.

I also nod even though I have mixed feelings. Between Ice's reaction to being touched and his noncommittal answer when asked if we were dating, the evening was…a lot to take in. I need time to process.

Maybe this sleepover is a good idea.

We speak with Smoke a few minutes longer before returning to the hallway, where Night collects several things from the small linen closet. I help her carry the pile of bedding, and she opens her bedroom door for us.

Despite having stayed at the Monroe house before, I never saw Night's room for more than a few seconds. For whatever reason, I just never went in there.

The walls are a soft blue gradient. The color compliments the other pastels and neutrals in the room, though I can barely make out the wall through the photos, framed paintings, and grade school art projects hanging on it. The rest of the decor is equally cutesy, and a variety of niche collections on the desk and floating shelves make the room feel deliberately cluttered.

Her bed is a twin-size mattress set with an elegant wrought-iron frame and muted violet bedding. An impressive collection of bows and other hair accessories hang from the curled headboard, and fairy lights strung on the wall cast a soothing, warm glow over the area.

There's an open closet to the left, obscured by a curtain. A compact, white desk is set up further in the corner, with a stained-glass lamp on top and a cushioned desk stool pushed underneath.

The centerpiece of the room is the fancy dressing table against the far wall. It has a large built-in mirror, and the drawers are embellished with colorful glass knobs that resemble cut crystals. At least a dozen silk flower crowns border the oblong mirror frame.

Night closes the door and sets the guest bedding near the foot of her bed. I leave the pillow I offered to carry on top and drop everything else I brought beside it.

"Sorry it's a mess," she says.

*A mess?* There's nothing on the floor or atop any surface that doesn't look like it belongs there. But what do I know?

"It's fine," I assure her. "I like it."

With a smile, she pulls the sheet over the closet aside and reveals a collection of feminine dresses, blouses, and coats hanging above a chest of drawers. Tall bookcases are set up behind the clothing on either side of the dresser, and I count a good two dozen pairs of boots and shoes neatly arranged on the floor.

"Do you want shorts, pants, or a nightdress?" she asks before gesturing over the drawer she opened while I was busy admiring her closet.

She owns several nightdresses and pajama sets made from fine cotton or silk. Some simple, some lacy, others a little sexy—which surprises me for some reason. They're obviously nice pajamas, and the idea of wearing them intimidates me.

*Especially when the sound of the shower running on the other side of the wall reminds me that Ice is here.*

In the end, I settle on a pair of silky green sleep shorts and a cream camisole. They're simple and comfortable, but definitely a step up from sleeping in cheap cotton gym shorts and whatever undershirt I wore that day.

Night picks out an off-white nightdress with short sleeves and lacy trim. Then wastes no time in setting up a nail station atop her dressing table. I take the desk stool while she fishes a folding chair from her closet for herself.

"What color do you want?" she asks.

She sets a box of assorted nail polish bottles on the table. There are a few neutrals and a handful of brighter colors, but the majority are pastels, earth tones, and various shades of blue and green.

"Blue," I say.

"Blue, huh?" She smiles and points to her eye. "Like this?"

My face goes hot, and, although water immortal blue was my first thought, I point to the River Sapphire.

"Um… Maybe more like this?"

"Alright," she agrees with a delicate laugh.

She picks up a shimmery sapphire polish and gets to work.

We talk idly about this or that, but the unfamiliar environment of her room has me rather distracted. I keep glancing at two of the framed photos on her dressing table. They only catch my attention because both include a younger version of Ice.

The first is a photo of Night, Smoke, and Ice as young teens, with their house, and its distinctive stained-glass door, in the background. The twins, holding hands, wear white and red school uniforms. Night's hair is long and done up in curled pigtails, while Smoke's is cropped short. Both are beaming. Ice wears a different uniform—a white dress shirt, blue tie, and unbuttoned navy blazer with khaki slacks. Compared to the twins, his expression is muted.

The other picture must be a few years older than the first. It depicts Ice, Night, and her mother in front of a car. Sarai Monroe, a lean, confident woman with kind eyes and short, dark hair, stands between the children with her hands on their shoulders. Night, who looks to be nine or ten, grins. She's holding up a sheet of paper. Ice smiles as well, but he looks tired. His posture is stiff, and his hair is short and messy.

I ask about the first photo, and Night says it was taken the year the twins went into eighth grade and Ice started high school. All three went to Wisteria Private Academy—Riverview's K-12 school for immortals. Carmen mentioned it last week, but Night explains that it's their version of public school.

*Further deepening the rift between humans and immortals.*

I don't ask about the second photo.

* * * * *

"It's too bad Carmen couldn't join us." Night returns her

makeup case to its place in a drawer and picks up her phone. "At least she can live vicariously through us online."

We take a few photos of our finished nails and makeup in the dressing table mirror. She touches them up on her phone before uploading them.

A notification sound pings in my lap, and I check my phone. After confirming the tag in Night's FaceSpace post, I scroll through the handful of photos. The ones she chose are cute and a little silly, and she tagged Carmen in the comments.

I back out of the post and scroll further down my newsfeed for lack of anything better to do until another notification pops up. I tap the banner to find a comment on Night's post.

**Carmen Choi**
I AM SO JEALOUS!! YOU'RE BOTH SO HOT
(T⌓T)

She laughs. "I suppose she thinks I did a good job."

"Well, she's not wrong."

*A third notification.* I accept Carmen's friend request and check out her profile. It looks like she hangs out with friends a lot. Half of her posts involve parties and lunch dates and the like, but she shares a lot about music, fashion, and her cosmetology training too.

I like a set of pictures she uploaded earlier today—of herself, Night, and a handful of other girls. The last photo is of me, with my hair in a neat, braided bun.

"Are you hungry?" Night asks, tossing her phone onto the bed. "We can grab a snack before we clean up."

I nod. She smiles and says she'll meet me in the kitchen, so I head out alone.

The den is dark. The usual music in Smoke's bedroom is quiet. A light is on in the great room, though, and I find Ice sitting at the dining table. He glances up from an iPad as I cross from the carpet to the hardwood.

For an instant, his eyes are wide, and I can't tell what he's looking at. *The makeup? The low-cut, silk pajamas?* Before I can figure it out, he stifles a laugh and sets his tablet face-down beside a short glass of clear, caramel liquid. *Alcohol?*

"What?" I ask, hoping the foundation masks the color in my warm cheeks. "Do I look bad?"

He shakes his head and flashes a smile. "No, no. You look fine. Though, I have to say I think I prefer your hair down."

*Down? I guess I'm never putting my hair up again.*

If there weren't five million bobby pins holding this bun in place, I'd let it down right now. Instead, I center the flower crown on my head and step closer.

"What are you doing out here?" I ask.

"Oh, you know—" He glances aside and takes a drink. "Work."

For his parents' company? *While drinking?*

A soft laugh sounds from somewhere near the den—Night.

"You're actually working?" she asks, her voice approaching.

He rolls his eyes and sets his glass down, but his mild, pleasant expression remains otherwise unaffected.

"Believe it or not," he says.

Night joins me near the dining table and places a gentle hand on my shoulder. "So, what do you think of my handiwork?

She looks good, right?"

"Hm?"

He rests his chin in his hands and checks me out a second time. I smooth the camisole and force a smile, but I can't stop from scratching my arm.

"She looks fine," he says again.

Night sighs. Her hand falls away from my shoulder. Then she walks past me, past the dining table, and into the kitchen.

"Fine is not a compliment, Ice."

His expression remains vaguely humored as she digs through the snack cabinet with her back to us and continues to berate him for being inconsiderate. She says he needs to think before he talks and work on his conversational skills.

"Is it a problem that I said you look fine?" he asks, glancing to me with a touch of frustration in his eyes.

I look between him and Night, who is still quite offended, and I laugh. I cover my mouth, but I can't stop myself. This is such a dumb thing to argue about. It's the type of pointless bickering siblings should engage in.

"It's fine," I insist. "You guys are so funny."

Ice watches me with wide eyes. "Funny?"

"There's nothing funny about it," Night says under her breath, upending an entire bag of peanut butter pretzels into a serving bowl. "He's rude. He's always so rude."

I sit at the table, and a smile comes easily. "I'm glad I met you guys. This summer would have been so boring if I hadn't."

Night, finally reassured that Ice didn't offend me somehow, sits across the table from me. She sets the bowl of pretzels down and glances between me and Ice, who is still rather amused.

"See," he says. "I told you it's fine."

She smiles, her eyes dangerously narrow. "I swear, if you say *fine* one more time—"

"Being here makes me miss my brother," I admit.

"Your brother?" she asks. "I didn't know you had one."

"Yeah, Robbie. He goes to UCLA, so I don't see him often anymore, but we were close as kids. I almost miss arguing about stupid stuff like that."

Her expression softens, and she glances toward Ice. His playful smirk fades as their eyes meet. Then she looks at me with a more wistful smile.

"I can't imagine being separated from Smoke. I know it's not quite the same, but… The thought sometimes makes me not want to grow up."

Ice raises his glass to his lips. "Why separate at all? I'm sure he'd be satisfied living in the basement of your future home for eternity."

"Oh? I planned on saving my future basement for you," she says. He chokes on his drink, and she laughs. "I'm kidding! You're doing alright for yourself in Palo Alto, and now you've sponsored Jayde. Really moving up in the world, huh?"

Rubbing his jaw, he clears his throat. "I suppose so. Though—" Our eyes meet, and he frowns. "—it's late. I should turn in for the night."

"Weren't you working?" I ask.

"It's nothing that can't wait until morning."

He sets his empty glass on the nearest counter before

walking past the table. I turn to say, "goodnight," and he stops. He glances over his shoulder and smiles.

"Goodnight, Jayde."

Then he leaves. His bedroom door closes in the hallway, and Night sighs before turning to me.

"Sorry," she says with an apologetic smile, "but bringing up his personal life is the fastest way to scare him off—just a friendly piece of advice."

"You wanted him to leave?"

She laughs. "You didn't just now?"

I frown. My blue nails sparkle, appearing a shade brighter beneath the white light cast by the chandelier overhead.

"He thinks I look better with my hair down."

"He said that?"

She sounds surprised. When I glance up, her head is tipped to one side, her expression curious but neutral. *He didn't say those words exactly, but...* I nod anyway.

"Hm." She glances aside and pushes her chair out. "You want some water while we're in here?"

"Oh. Sure."

I watch as she works in the kitchen, setting Ice's glass in the sink before filling two new glasses with filtered water from the fridge tap. After a while spent sitting at the dining table, she suggests we wash our faces in the bathroom.

It's a shame to wash it off right after she applied it, but even I know I shouldn't sleep wearing a full face of makeup. So we stand around in the bathroom with the overhead fan buzzing, and we eat pretzels while wiping our faces with reusable cotton pads soaked in makeup remover.

“About Ice,” she says slowly. “I know you like him, so I’m sorry about what he said earlier.”

I shrug. “Fine isn’t the best compliment, but—”

“Not that. That was just him being an idiot. I mean what he said to Carmen at the park.”

“Which thing—? Oh.” *That thing.* “It’s, um… It’s not your fault, but has he ever said anything to you about whether he thinks we’re dating?”

She turns the water on and rinses her cotton pad. I hand her the one I used and start picking bobby pins out of my hair.

“We’ve discussed it,” she says, her voice dry. “Or, rather, I’ve asked. A few times. He doesn’t often let people get close to him, so it made me curious, but he, ah… Well, he never wants to talk about you for long.”

“It’s a good sign that he wants to hang out, though, right?”

She smiles. “Things like Music@ThePark tend to bore him, but he suddenly wanted to go after I mentioned you were interested.”

“Really?”

“Yeah.” She laughs delicately. “So, whether he wants to admit it or not, I’m sure it’s fine as long as you’re both having fun.”

# twenty-three

We wake up to Night's new age piano ringtone. I feel the vibration on the dressing table through the floor as the phone rings.

She hefts herself out of bed to answer it. I sit up and rub my eyes, a bit surprised by how well-rested I feel considering I slept on a mat on the floor.

"Today?" She checks her phone screen and grimaces. "In two hours? Talk about short notice. Well, what is this about?"

She sorts through the dresses hanging in her closet while I fold the blanket she let me borrow.

"Oh, I see," she says with a sigh, lifting a navy dress off the rod. "And it has to be me? They can't meet with you and Douglas or… Perhaps Ice could…?"

"Everything okay?"

She offers me an apologetic smile and returns her focus to the phone at her ear. "No, of course. I can meet you at one-thirty. Okay. Thanks, Erica."

The phone call ends, and she sighs heavily.

"Work?" I ask.

"Yes. I'm the MonroeWorks heiress, and duty calls," she

says, her humored smile a little tired. "We'll have to reschedule lunch, though. This meeting won't be brief."

"We can always do something after instead."

"Tea might be nice," she agrees. "But what will you do until I'm done? Go home? Stay here?"

I pile the guest bedding near the foot of her bed and grab my purse. "I can hang out at the mall for a few hours."

"Ask Ice to go with you," she says, collecting more clothes.

*Maybe I will.*

After borrowing one of Night's less intricate outfits, I take a quick shower and get dressed in the bathroom while she changes in her bedroom. I comb and dry my hair and still make it out to the den before her.

Ice is sat on one of the loveseats with the iPad from last night in his lap. He glances up as I step out of the hallway.

"You sure slept in."

I laugh and pull my hair over one shoulder. "It was a late night. Anyway, Night got called into a meeting, so I was wondering if you want to hang out with me for a few hours instead?"

He looks at his iPad. Then at me again.

"And do what?" he asks.

"I was thinking of going to the mall. I have some money I've been saving since my birthday, so—"

He flashes a smile. "You want to go shopping?"

"Oh. Maybe?"

He sets his tablet on the arm of the couch and crosses the room, his fingers brushing my arm as he walks by. My breath catches. I turn to keep an eye on him, and he glances over his shoulder.

"Come with me," he says.

I follow Ice into his room. He stops at the desk, opens the top drawer, and removes a plain, white mailing envelope.

"I'm afraid I'm too busy to join you, but I'm more than happy to help."

He opens the envelope, revealing the thick stack of crisp, green bills stuffed inside. As he runs a thumb over the top edge, he meets my gaze. His smile is crooked, but he somehow doesn't look smug at all.

He then offers me several large bills folded together.

I protest, hoping to protect what little dignity I have left after the past few weeks, but he shushes me and plants the cash in my hand. I stare at the mess of twenties and fifties and *hundreds* in alarm. *This is easily a thousand dollars! How much is just sitting in that envelope?*

"Are you sure?" I stammer.

"This is nothing." He laughs breezily and returns the envelope of cash to his desk. "Do with it as you will."

"Um…"

*This is WAY too much to give someone out of nowhere so casually.* I have no idea what this money means to Ice or how it might relate to his feelings for me, but I give up and thank him.

Then I jump at a knock on the door frame behind me.

"Almost ready to head out?" Night asks.

"I guess."

Still holding the money, I turn to face her. She leans against the doorjamb, wearing a navy cocktail dress, dark ankle boots, sharp eyeliner, and red lipstick. The whole look is bolder and more serious than her usual aesthetic, but her smile is confident.

"What kind of meeting is this, exactly?" Ice asks.

She rolls her eyes. "Oh, shut up. I like dressing up, and I find it helps to adopt a vaguely threatening aura when dealing with young, male CEOs from kitschy start-ups."

"Is that so?"

She feigns a scowl, but he laughs. A gentle hand rests on top of my head and ruffles my hair before falling away. Then he walks past me.

"Have fun," he says.

Our eyes meet for an instant before he passes Night on his way out. After watching him walk down the hallway, she crosses her arms and turns to me again.

"He didn't do anything to upset you, right?"

"Oh, ah—" I shake my head to clear my mind. "No. Why? Do I look upset?"

She shrugs. "I don't know. But you turn around, blank-faced with a stack of cash in your hand after talking with Ice, and I get a little worried."

"I did nothing!" he calls from the den.

Of course, she doesn't appear genuinely concerned. She's teasing him, and his retort only prompted another smile.

Not that she should worry.

The money was a surprise, but I am fine.

*Still... Is it an immortal thing? A rich person thing? I don't know how any of this works...*

I force a smile and stuff the haphazardly folded bills into my purse. "It's all good. He gave it to me because he's too busy to come to the mall."

*I guess.*

"Busy. Right. Well, it's his loss. Let's go."

I avoid looking at Ice on our way through the den. He doesn't say anything either, so we make it out of the house unscathed. I carefully close the front door behind us.

"It's totally weird that he handed me a ton of cash, right?"

She laughs—sort of. "It sounds like something Ice would do. He's convinced he knows how others think, but he doesn't understand women at all. Time doesn't always equal money."

"Should I spend it?"

"Why not? He's your sponsor, right? It's silly, but you can let him treat you every once in a while."

* * * * *

I ate lunch and finished my smoothie, but I've been sitting at this table for a while. I just…don't know where to start. I counted the money before I ordered the Chinese food, and he gave me $1,270 simply because he was too busy to hang out.

*What does that mean?*

When I told Rose, she accused me of being a sugar baby. But I don't feel like a sugar baby. Sure, he pays for me every time we go out, but he's rich and knows I'm not. He's never just handed me money before, and I've certainly never done favors in exchange for cash.

Even if he likes spending money on me or whatever, it's not

like that. Our relationship is more like…

*Well, I don't know.*

He's my sponsor.

Maybe he feels responsible for me and thought this would help me out. Or maybe he just felt bad because he was too busy to come, and it was an innocent gesture—a somewhat misguided but otherwise innocent gesture *like signing me up for Human-Immortal Affairs' secret program.*

I touch the River Sapphire and sigh.

He did tell me to have fun with the money, though. Night said it was fine too, and Rose even challenged me to spend it all today.

*If it's fine, I may as well give it a go.*

An hour later, I leave a boutique having spent more than *eight hundred dollars* on designer clothing. Of course, I understand on a fundamental level that designer clothing doesn't make one person better than anyone else, but I might feel a little more comparable to immortals if I wear this sort of thing. Maybe I won't feel so inadequate when I hang out with Ice or Night and her friends.

*How pathetic…*

I step out into the mall, and a body appears in my path.

Their head turns, but neither of us move quickly enough to avoid the other. I smack right into their side and promptly trip over them. I land on my hands and knees, horrified as my brand-new clothing scatters on the floor around me.

"I am so sorry," I stammer.

Without moving from the floor, I rush to collect my things, stuffing my purse into a shopping bag to expedite the process. The person I ran into recovers his balance and kneels down to assist. As we both reach for the same article of clothing, I accidentally touch his hand and recoil in embarrassment.

"My bad," he mumbles. He grabs the crumpled fabric before offering me his free hand. "Need help up?"

I've managed to collect everything except for that blouse, so I accept his help, and he drops my hand the moment I'm upright. Holding both shopping bags in one arm, I smooth my shirt and brush my hair out of my face before thanking him.

But my voice catches in my throat.

*He's an immortal.* A young man with short, orange hair and wide amber eyes. He looks to be roughly the same age as Ice, but he's a few inches shorter and lacks Ice's lean, athletic physique. Even so, he's rather cute. *No surprise there, considering he's an immortal.* But something about the golden fire immortal eyes gets me every time.

"Sorry about that." He scratches the back of his neck. "I wasn't paying attention."

"It's fine."

He returns the final top, and I take a moment to fix my jumbled shopping bag situation. As I do, our eyes meet again. He glances away immediately and shoves his hands in his pockets.

The silence is heavy and awkward. *This is a mess.*

"I was spacing out too," I say, "so…"

He frowns, his gaze drifting toward the floor. "Still…"

"I'm alright. No harm done. See?"

He looks up again, unshadowing his eyes and the greyish bags beneath them. *Weird.* Ice didn't develop the faintest of dark circles after a full week with little rest.

*Does this guy ever sleep?*

He tips his head, brows furrowed. “Have we met? I feel like I’ve seen you before, but I’m not sure…”

I scan his features a second time. Short, messy, orange hair. A tired, round face with tired, round eyes, and a faint scar that cuts through his left eyebrow. His appearance is rather distinctive, but I don’t recognize him. Though, I’m not great at remembering faces.

When I shrug and admit as much, he sighs, and his shoulders deflate as though he expected my uncertainty. I avert my eyes, dig my purse out of the shopping bag, and shift my weight from one foot to the other.

Why is he standing around and dragging this out?

What is it with men lately?

*I give up.*

“Do you go to RCC?” I ask. He shakes his head, but… *If all immortals in Riverview went to the same high school—* “Do you know Night? Night Monroe?”

For a moment, it looks like he wants to say something, but he hesitates. His eyes flick away for an instant. Then he frowns and studies me more carefully. Maybe we have met somewhere. Maybe he’s friends with someone who goes to RCC, and he spent some time on campus, and that’s how he recognized me.

Before I get the chance to ask, he sighs and looks away once more. “Nah. Guess I was wrong. Sorry for wasting your time.”

“Oh? Alright…”

He dips his head in a quick farewell and walks past me, in the opposite direction of wherever he was headed before we collided. I glance over my shoulder and watch him slip into a secondhand bookstore a few doors down.

*Okay...*

I walk the other way.

Clear across the mall, I find a shoe store, where I spend a good half hour trying on expensive boots and staring at myself in the mirror. I eventually purchase a pair of short, lace-up leather boots and leave, but I can't stop thinking about it.

There was something off about that guy.

*He thought he recognized me?*

*He stopped to talk even though I'm obviously human?*

I try to forget. To distract myself by shopping.

I spend more money. I buy a cute bra and silk pajamas—a lacy camisole and matching shorts. Then I get myself a giant peanut butter cookie and sit at a bench outside the mall doors. I scroll down FaceSpace. I text Rose. I play a stupid idle game.

*But it's not enough.*

It was nothing. It was dumb. I tripped over someone, and he helped me up off the floor. That's it. The fact we were both socially incompetent was an unfortunate coincidence, right?

*Who was he?*

Even as Night's blue sedan pulls up to the curb, I can't get it out of my mind. So I don't let the car fall quiet.

"How'd your meeting go?"

She smiles. "It went well. We agreed to buy half of the start-up's stock and connect them with a few outside investors."

"What kind of company is it?"

"A small eco-tech group hoping to develop high-efficiency portable saltwater filtration systems. We invest in and acquire a lot of small, independent companies like that."

A beat of silence. I mess with the River Sapphire's chain.

*What caught that guy so off guard?*

He's an immortal, but he clearly wasn't paying attention to where he was going. And then he hung around like he wanted to chat despite his obvious discomfort.

*Why bother?*

"Anyway," she says with a sigh, "I'm exhausted. Is Coffee-Star alright with you?"

"Yeah, that's fine."

*That's right...*

When I asked if he knew her, he hesitated. He paused. And he looked at— *Well, my chest, I guess.* Or the River Sapphire.

Does he know what it is?

Finally, I break down and ask Night. I explain what happened and describe the man's appearance and behavior. How he reacted when I mentioned her name. When I ask if he sounds familiar, she sucks in a breath.

"Hm… That does remind me of someone I knew as a child." Her voice is neutral but careful, and her grip on the steering wheel shifts slightly. "We haven't spoken in years, but it could be James Reid."

*James Reid?*

"I asked, and he said he doesn't know you."

"Perhaps I'm mistaken, but, if it was James, he lied." She flashes an uneasy smile, but her eyes remain focused on the road ahead. "Though, I suppose I can't blame him for wanting to forget about me."

# twenty-four

Before we left CoffeeStar, I asked Night if we could stop by her house. One: I forgot both my portable phone charger and the dress I wore yesterday in her bedroom. Two: I want to ask Ice if he knows James Reid.

She parks her car on the curb outside and grabs her phone from the center console. "I'll wait here. I'm sure Ice will want to see you off, so take your time."

"Thanks."

Upon stepping into the house, I find Ice at the dining table, his phone in one hand and a half-eaten rice cake in the other. He sets the phone down before he looks up to greet me.

"So," he says, flashing an easy smile, "did you spend it all?"

"Aah—"

*That's what you're leading with?*

But I laugh. "Most of it. I bought some new clothes."

"Good for you."

"Thanks again. You really didn't have to do that for me."

"I wanted to," he says mildly. "Are you headed home now?"

"Yeah, Night will take me. I just need to grab a couple things, but there's something I wanted to ask you first."

"Oh?" He sets his rice cake on a napkin and offers me his full attention. "Did something happen while you were out?"

I shake my head. "Not really, but I tripped over some guy and threw my stuff all over the floor."

"Whoops," he says with a laugh.

"Yeah, it was…super awkward."

He seems to find the story rather amusing, which is fair, until I get to the point and mention that Night suggested the man I ran into could have been someone she knew. The instant I say the name *James Reid*, Ice's laughter stops. His expression mellows, growing more inquisitive.

"A ginger, right? He's rather pudgy; has a scar on his face?"

*Ah...*

I wouldn't say he was pudgy, but— *I mean, he did have a scar over one eye.* My teeth click together, but I nod and try to keep my expression level.

"Hm." He smiles again, but it's unpleasant. "Well, if Night thinks you saw James Reid, I'm sure that's the case. How funny."

"You know him, then?"

He shrugs, uninterested. "Haven't seen him in years, but I suppose you could say that."

Night's answer was similarly vague. *Why?*

"Who is he?"

Ice sucks a breath through his teeth and leans back in his chair, one hand on the nape of his neck. I consider sitting too—as I worry I'm in for a long story—but I second-guess myself.

I don't move.

"James is what you might call defective," he says. Blue eyes flick in my direction, but he quickly refocuses on the ceiling. "He can't morph. He's physically weak. Slow. Cowardly. No real skills or talents worth mentioning. In my eyes, he's hardly an immortal at all. James Reid is an utter waste of space."

*Wow. Um...*

He obviously doesn't think much of James. I know next to nothing about him, and I honestly can't say he left me with a stellar first impression, but he didn't have to stop and help. He can't be that bad. Besides, I assume he was born defective.

And calling anyone a waste of space is too harsh. Why does he feel so strongly about defective immortals—and this James guy in particular?

I do not ask. I do not want to know.

He sighs. The fleeting darkness fades from his eyes, and he picks up his rice cake to take a bite. "In any case, James is nothing to worry about. Nothing but a coward, as I said."

I wasn't worried before, and I'm not sure I should even bring it up now, but—

"Well, um, I could have imagined it, but he might have noticed the River Sapphire. We talked for a minute, and he thought he recognized me, so…"

"Wow." He laughs, still holding the rice cake to his lips. "How pathetic."

Clearing my throat, I step away from the table. "Right. Anyway, Night's waiting for me out front. I should grab my stuff from her room and go."

I turn to leave through the den, but I hear a chair slide against the hardwood behind me as Ice stands, so I stop. I listen. *I bite the inside of my cheek.*

"Hey, you mind if I take you home instead?" he asks.

"Oh, that's fine." I glance over my shoulder—he hasn't moved from beside the table. "My bags are still in Night's car, though."

He smiles. "I'll grab them for you. Meet me in the garage."

I nod, and he leaves through the front door.

My phone charger is exactly where I thought I left it, on the floor at the foot of the bed. I secure it in my purse, quickly change out of Night's clothes and back into mine, and check the time—6:17PM.

Then I head to the garage. The car is already unlocked, so I let myself in.

When Ice returns with my bags, he notes I have quite the haul. I deny it, embarrassed for one stupid reason or another, and he laughs. But he says nothing as he arranges the bags in the backseat. Still nothing as he sits in the driver's seat and turns the key in the ignition. The engine purrs, and a button on his key fob starts the garage door opening.

"Did you get a lot of work done today?" I ask.

"I finished what I started."

"Oh, that's good."

After what he had to say about James, I was looking forward to commiserating with Night on the way home. But I didn't want to be rude. So, here I am, staring at my lap while Ice drives quietly.

He even turned on the radio. The soft classic rock drifting from the speakers only exemplifies the uncomfortable atmosphere.

*This sucks.* Maybe I shouldn't have said anything.

I glance out the window as we near Oakwood Cottages.

Going home won't be so bad, though. I'm ready to lie down on the couch and talk with Rose. There are so many things I can't say, but I can at least tell her what I bought.

Ice parks in the usual space in front of my cottage.

"You had fun, right?" he asks.

I meet his gaze, but I can't figure out exactly what he's asking. Did I have fun at Riverside yesterday? During the sleepover with Night? Going shopping with the money he gave me?

But I smile. "Yep. Thanks for the ride."

"Good," he says with a smile of his own. "I'll call you later."

"Okay."

I take that as my cue to leave.

After piling the bags from the backseat in my arms, I make my way down the sidewalk. I set everything on the concrete landing outside the door. I glance back and wave at Ice as he pulls out of the parking space.

Then I unlock the door and head inside.

* * * * *

"One thousand, two hundred seventy dollars?" Rose gasps. "And you said he just handed you this money?"

I laugh and upend the laundry basket onto my bed. The clothes are still warm to the touch.

"Yeah, that's basically how it happened."

"Wow. I'm so jealous. Seriously."

*I'm not so sure you should be. There are some strings attached.*

"What all did you buy?" she asks. "Just clothes?"

I look over the pile on my bed. "I mean… I got a couple outfits. A nice dress. Some boots. And then lunch. Shopping for expensive clothes kind of stresses me out, to be honest."

"Even when it's not your money?" she asks with a laugh.

"That money could pay my phone bill for two years."

She laughs harder. "And you're sure this guy isn't a sugar daddy?"

"He's not," I insist, fighting laughter as I pick up the plum cocktail dress I spent nearly three hundred dollars on. I hang it and a layered muslin sundress in my closet. "Ice is just a little strange. And it's not like he doesn't have the money to spare."

"Well, obviously."

I set the phone to speaker and drop it on the bed, leaving me free to fold the rest of the clothes.

"I already told you; I don't care if he has money."

"It doesn't hurt, though, right?"

I frown. I've never been poor to the point of struggling, but someone who can give away a thousand dollars on a whim is living on a whole other level of existence. I have a hard time even comprehending such a comfortable life.

But Ice has that life, and he's sharing a piece of it with me.

"Isn't it weird, though?" I ask. "How am I supposed to feel about that kind of thing?"

"I don't know. Grateful?" After another laugh, her voice grows surprisingly mild. "Some guys only know how to show affection by throwing money and gifts at people, you know. Have you ever heard of love languages?"

"Is that a real thing?"

"No idea."

While she rambles on about love language theory and some personality test she took online during a psychology class, my phone's text tone goes off on the bed behind me. I place the last article of clothing in my dresser and close the drawer.

Rose is still going on about words of affirmation through the speaker as I open the messaging app. The text came from Ice. He usually doesn't message me first, but—

**Ice:** If you see James Reid again, do not speak with him.

**Me:** What do you mean?

I watch the read indicator appear under my message. He starts typing, but the typing icon soon vanishes, and an incoming call overtakes my phone screen instead.

*Ugh... Seriously?*

"I'm getting another call. Give me a minute."

"—A'ight."

I answer Ice's call, dropping Rose's, and hold the phone to my ear. "Hello?"

"I'm serious," he says, his voice tinged with annoyance. "Stay away from James Reid. He's bad news."

*Bad news? What? Why is this coming up again?*

"What are you even talking about?" I ask, my own frustration bubbling to the surface. "I tripped over the guy at the mall. I don't know him, and he doesn't know anything about me. It's not like we exchanged phone numbers. He doesn't even know my name."

A beat of silence. "Jayde—"

*No. This is stupid.*

"Two hours ago, you told me James was nobody. You laughed and went off like he's nothing, and now he's suddenly bad news? I don't get it. You're not making any sense."

"Yeah?" His voice remains calm. "Well, I changed my mind."

I relax my balled fist and move to look outside. At the trees across the short grass. I open the window. It's getting late, but the breeze is still warm.

"What are the chances we'd run into each other a second time, anyway?" I ask. "It's just something dumb that happened because I wasn't paying attention. Why make a big deal about it?"

"Yes, but— Ah…" He sighs. "Forget it."

I turn back to face my empty bedroom, my grip on the phone easing as confusion softens my anger. "I was trying to. You're the one who brought it up again."

The room falls quiet. The phone is quiet too, for a long, tense moment. Then Ice clears his throat.

"Right," he says. "Forget I called."

"I—"

The line goes silent, and I move the phone from my ear to check the screen.

*Oh.*

He hung up on me.

# twenty-five

After breakfast, I find an envelope on the floor in the living room. Someone must have slipped it through the crack beneath the front door while I was in the kitchen.

I glance through the window, but I don't see anyone outside, so I close the blinds and return my attention to the mystery mail. The envelope is unassuming. White paper. A clear, plastic window over the recipient address.

Whatever it is, it's for me.

Honestly, it kind of looks like junk mail, but *this is too weird.* Someone slipped it underneath my front door, for one, but it also lacks any sort of logo or name above the—

*Seattle-based return address.*

Could it be…?

I head upstairs, where I sit on my bed, tear the envelope open, and remove two sheets of paper from inside. It's a typed letter. *And I was right.* The header and ornate seal reveal the sender as The U.S. Department of Human-Immortal Affairs' Human Advocacy Unit.

Ms. Jayde Palmer,

You are receiving this notice on account of your recent admittance into The U.S. Department of Human-Immortal Affairs' *Human Immortal Program*. Please consider the following information regarding your role in the *Human Immortal Program*, and the issued Accessory Item (*River Sapphire*, model 418A-RVCA) before destroying this message.

In recent decades, our expert researchers and technicians developed and refined the production of synthetic gemstones using modified human DNA. The human DNA is synthesized with segments of the immortal genome in our state-of-the-art laboratory, and combined with precious minerals to create a synthetic gemstone with unique properties. Crafted into an Accessory Item, the gemstone may allow the human donor to assume feline form in a manner similar to that of a natural-born immortal.

Due to the experimental status of the synthetic gemstone Accessory Items and natural variations in the nervous systems of individual humans, we have yet to develop a reliable method of determining the exact means by which an Accessory Item may activate or whether an Accessory Item will perform in a desirable manner. Despite this complication, the majority of synthetic gemstone recipients in the *Human Immortal Program* have reported positive results.

To date, 418 incarnations of synthetic gemstone Accessory Items have been produced and received by human donors through the *Human Immortal Program*.

For your reading convenience, the *Program's* provisional results as reported by the 418 participants to date have been included below:

— 41% report the ability to assume feline form by wearing or removing their Accessory Item, or by otherwise interacting with their Accessory Item while wearing it.

— 19% report the ability to assume feline form at will.

- 17% report the ability to change forms while wearing their Accessory Item.
- 2% report the ability to change forms without their Accessory Item present.

— 5% reported random human-to-feline transitions and were removed from the *Program*.

— 20% reported an inability to assume feline form after possessing an Accessory Item for 3 years.

— 15% of recent participants (having received their Accessory Item within the past 3 years) have yet to report the ability to assume feline form.

The *Human Immortal Program*'s trial period concludes three years after the initial date of admittance. As such, we hope you successfully assume feline form within that time frame. Please note that, while the current trial period is limited to three years, the majority of *Program* participants reported results within ten weeks of receiving their unique Accessory Item.

In the event that you successfully assume feline form or experience unexpected difficulties related to the *Program* or your Accessory Item, we ask that your sponsor contact your assigned Human Advocacy case manager at their earliest convenience.

On behalf of everyone at The U.S. Department of Human-Immortal Affairs, we once again wish to express our deepest appreciation concerning your interest in the *Human Immortal Program*. We look forward to hearing from you in the future.

As requested, please destroy this message at your earliest convenience. Your continued discretion in matters of Secrecy and Security is vital.

Respectfully,

David H Clarke
Human Advocacy Unit
Chief Human Advocacy Officer

Dr. Richard Lacombe, Sc.D.
Synthetic Morphology Research Division
Senior Researcher, *Human Immortal Program*

The Human Immortal Program…

The lack of blacked-out names is refreshing, and it's a relief to finally receive legitimate information about the strange program Ice enrolled me in. He was most unhelpful before—though I'm not sure it was entirely his fault.

*Wait—*

If the synthetic gemstones are created using the human donor's DNA, that means Ice had to get his hands on a sample of my DNA to have one made for me.

*Doesn't it?*

When did he do that? How did he get a sample?

*Maybe I don't want to think about it.*

I refocus on the letter—the minimum sixty-percent odds of success and gemstone activation methods it mentioned. I leave my bed, set the letter on my dresser, and reach for the River Sapphire, where the pendant rests against my skin.

My reflection waits expectantly.

Nothing happens when I flick the stone. I rub it with the pad of my thumb until the friction warms it. I tap the hard surface with my painted fingernail. *Nothing.*

I unfasten the necklace and hold it in the palm of my hand. I wait, staring into the blue stone, but it's the same as always.

Nothing happens.

With a sigh, I put it on again, but I'm still human. The River Sapphire is exactly the same as when Ice first gave it to me—pretty but useless. The necklace doesn't work.

*No.*

The Human Immortal Program's trial period lasts three years. It's only been a couple weeks. There's still plenty of time, so I have to remain optimistic.

The River Sapphire will work.

# twenty-six

I sit on the couch, eating white cheddar popcorn and scrolling down title cards on Netflix, and my eyes glaze over the countless shows I've already watched with Rose. Until Night Hospital's thumbnail catches my attention.

*No way.*

The lead actor, who happens to be one of Rose's top celebrity crushes, is an immortal. His perfect cheekbones and pale, violet eyes are a dead giveaway. It's no wonder she likes him.

*How many famous people are immortals?*

Standing close to the TV, I scrutinize at least a dozen title cards and preview clips of popular shows and movies. Maybe I shouldn't be surprised, considering their uncanny penchant for being stupidly attractive, but many of the actors are immortals.

There are plenty of human actors too, but do any of them know about immortals, or are they living in ignorant bliss like the rest of human society?

I turn off the TV and head upstairs.

Sitting in bed with my laptop, I idly skim the Wikipedia pages of several immortal celebrities I recognized. It leads me down a deep, deep rabbit hole.

*There are* a ton *of famous immortals.*

Actors and actresses, musicians, talk show hosts, sports stars, politicians. Social media influencers. Tech giants. CEOs. *The Vice President of the United States?*

Based on what I've read, famous immortals and humans often work with each other. In TV and film especially, it's not unusual for humans and immortals to costar in projects, even as romantic leads. But I skim the sections detailing their personal lives, and it seems few share close relationships with humans outside of work.

*Are more intimate relationships taboo?*

The fleeting surprise when someone passing by realizes I'm the lone human in a group of immortals. The way their interest turns dismissive as they look away. The fact we have separate public schools.

Before, I thought we more or less coexisted on the same level despite humanity's obliviousness, but it's more like immortals tend to ignore humans—like they look down on us for some reason.

*So then... Why is Ice with me?*

Why would he pay me, a random human girl, any attention? Why orchestrate our first meeting at Bargain Shop and ask me out? If I'm just an easy summer armpiece like Rose thinks, why does he still act so passive when we're together?

*And why tell me about immortals?*

Summer is only so long, but our relationship isn't really going anywhere. We go on dates—but are they even dates? He smiles and laughs and pats me on the head, and I love that, but what does he see when he looks at me?

I have no idea, and, after the way he answered Carmen's question the other day, I'm hesitant to ask.

*Was Rose wrong? Was I wrong?*

I don't know. I really like Ice, but…

With a sigh, I set my laptop aside and fall back onto my bed.

*Why tell me? What is so special about me?*

Does it matter? We've barely talked since he went off about the random guy I tripped over at the mall.

First, he hung up on me. Then, last night, I got a random message asking what I bought with the money. I sent a picture of my new boots, he replied with "nice," and that was it.

Was that a fight? Is that what a fight is like?

If it was, at least he's not ignoring me. Obviously. I'm the one who didn't reply to his last message.

*Ugh… It's so annoying.*

I roll onto my side, pick up my phone, and call Rose. I can't explain a damn thing, but she answers promptly, sounding a little distracted but otherwise like her usual, cheery self. It's refreshing.

"Hey."

*Oops.* I do not sound like my usual self.

"Uh, oh," she says in a sing-song voice. "What's wrong this time, Jay?"

*Ah…* She knows I went to Music@ThePark and had a sleep-over with Night, she knows I bought a bunch of clothes with Ice's money, and she knows I went home after. But that's it. She doesn't know about James or the…*disagreement?*

“I don’t know,” I admit with a nervous laugh. “I guess that Ice has been acting a little strange lately, and I keep thinking about it.”

“Strange? What do you mean?”

“He’s been kind of distant?” I pause. “I don’t know how to explain it, Rose. Maybe he’s just tired from…work? Anyway, we haven’t talked much since he dropped me off the other day.”

“Did you guys break up?”

“I mean, we’re not exactly dating as it is, so it might be hard to actually break up.”

“Oh, no,” she says with an easy laugh. “I’m kidding. Maybe he’s on his man period.”

I laugh despite myself. “I’m starting to wonder…”

“Wonder what? You think he has more secrets?”

“More secrets?” *Like the deal with James Reid?*

“Yeah. I’m talking deep, dark shit he really doesn’t want you to know.” Humor slips into her dramatically lowered voice. “Like that he’s secretly married or gay or only dates girls to collect clippings of their hair while they sleep.”

*Oh, god, please don’t remind me.*

“Rose—”

“Maybe he is a serial killer.”

“I don’t think so,” I say dryly.

She laughs again. “Oh, come on, Jay. Do you even like this guy, or are you just in it because you’re bored? You’ve known him for, what, a month now? And it hasn’t gone anywhere yet?”

“I do like him—” I groan. “It’s complicated, okay?”

“If there is one, single thing a summer relationship should

not be, it's complicated."

"I don't think it's *that* kind of complicated, really—" I catch myself saying the exact opposite of how I feel and hesitate. "Ugh. I don't know. He just sends so many mixed signals, and I don't know how to deal with that."

"Mixed signals, huh?" she asks, intrigued. "Sound like you're the one who needs to make up your mind, then. Either get the ball rolling yourself or give up and move on."

*What?*

"Maybe you're right, but—"

She groans dramatically, and I imagine her rolling her eyes. "I know you suck at social things, but this is just sad."

"That's not fair," I protest, my face growing warm.

But she laughs. "You know what I think, Jay? You should ask him out. Or at least kiss him. You can't rely on a guy to make all the moves himself."

Dating Ice isn't even my main concern right now. Of course, I am losing my mind over the mystery surrounding his feelings, but it all boils down to the matter of immortals. The status quo I don't know how to break. But I can't tell Rose, and that makes trying to complain about it all the more frustrating.

"Maybe he doesn't think you're into him."

"Ha…" I sit up and rub my temple, my eyes wandering toward the window across the room. "He'd have to be blind."

"Don't forget that men are stupid, Jayde. They're all dumb as rocks. Especially the hot ones. They tend to think that, if a girl isn't actively throwing herself at him, she's not interested at all."

"I don't know. Ice doesn't seem like the dumb type."

*None of the immortals I've met do.*

"You never know," she reasons, stifling laughter. "Anyway, it won't kill you to ask someone out for once in your life."

"That is true, but, Rose—"

"You are totally overthinking this. You just—" She stops, distracted by a second, distant voice on her end of the phone. "Anyway, you good? I gotta go. Family stuff, you know?"

"Yeah, I'm fine. I'll talk to you later, then?"

"Of course!" Her voice is bright and warm. I can easily picture the grin on her face, and I miss her. "But you really should give him a call and set up a date yourself. Go somewhere for lunch. Bowling. Swimming out past Rock Creek? Doesn't matter. Just relax and have fun."

I sigh. "Okay. I'll give it a shot."

"Tell me how it goes. And send pics. Byeee!"

The call ends, and I stare at the screen for a moment. A long moment. Long enough for the screen to dim. Then go black.

*Oh, Rose…*

Her advice would be perfectly sound if Ice were any other guy—or any human guy, anyway—but I don't think it's so simple when it comes to immortals.

Immortals don't just *date* humans.

I could call him, though.

I could ask if he wants to hang out at…*the bowling alley? No. Where do people with money like to go on dates? Another classy restaurant? Or…pizza?*

*Everyone likes pizza, right?*

Then again, I'm honestly not in the mood to talk to him.

After scrolling down FaceSpace for several minutes, I come across an outfit-of-the-day post Night made this morning. A lacy, pale green blouse. White cotton shorts. Knee-high socks and brown Mary Janes. A bow in her hair. It's cute.

Did she go out today?

I like the post and, with nothing better to do, open FaceSpace messenger. Night's currently online, so I click her photo and stare at my phone's keyboard.

*But what to say? Mm...*

**Me:** Hey, what's up?

*That's lame.*

Frustrated, I work on reorganizing the top of my desk for the third time this summer until she responds.

**Night:** About to cook dinner. Why? Is something the matter?

**Me:** No, everything's good. How's Ice?

**Night:** He's fine. Keeping himself busy.

*See, he's fine. I'm worried about nothing.*

**Night:** Are you keeping yourself busy?

**Me:** lol, no. I'm super bored.

**Night:** Haha... I have plans to meet with Carmen and Natalie tomorrow afternoon. You're welcome to tag along.

**Me:** Sounds fun! Count me in.

**Night:** Alright. I'll pick you up around 3pm. (^ω^)b

**Me:** Okay! See you then.

I'm sure hanging out with Night and her friends will be fun, but I've been hanging out with her more than Ice lately, and I'm not sure how to feel about it.

# twenty-seven

The moment Night lets me know she's on the way, I second-guess my decision to wear one of my new designer outfits.

I don't need to impress anyone—let alone Night, who is easily the most accepting person I know—and I'm not unhappy with how I look, but I worry I stick out as…*other* when I hang out with her in public.

*Ugh. I hate feeling like this.*

My attention turns to the River Sapphire at my collarbone.

I may not compare to an immortal in appearance or have any magic powers, but can I still consider myself completely human? I haven't morphed using the government-issued accessory item yet, but has it already affected me in some way? Isn't the goal of the Human Immortal Program to change me into something that's not quite an immortal but more than simply human?

*Hm…*

When Night arrives, she's beautiful as always. A mix between a woodland pixie and a 1950s housewife. I'm glad I at least tried to look cute.

"Oh! I love your outfit," she says with a warm smile.

I scratch my arm, fighting the urge to make a self-deprecating comment. "Thanks. It's all new."

She gushes over my boots in particular. I return the favor by complimenting her appearance, and then we walk down to her car. Her smile remains bright and pleasant, but she strikes me as rather thoughtful.

"You don't mind Carmen, right?" she asks. "She can be rather intense, I know."

My hand freezes on the door handle as I laugh. "Oh, no. To be honest, she reminds me of Rose. They have the same energy. It's fun."

"Oh, good."

We get ourselves buckled in, and Night starts the car, reacting with muted embarrassment when her radio comes on far too loud. She turns the volume down with haste.

"So, what have you been up to?" she asks.

"Not much." *Just wallowing in self-pity.* "Oh— But I did get a letter from Human-Immortal Affairs in the mail. About the River Sapphire."

She takes her eyes off the road for an instant. "Oh? Did you learn anything interesting?"

"A little. I mean, it was made using my DNA."

"Your DNA, huh?" she asks with a stifled grimace, her tone dry and unimpressed. "That is interesting. I wonder how Ice pulled that one off."

"Right?"

"Sorry. And—" She sighs, adjusting her hands on the steering wheel. "I'm sorry about the other day too. I don't know if the man you saw at the mall was James or not, but I should have told you that mentioning him to Ice was a bad idea."

I stare at Night's profile as she drives. Her eyes don't leave the road ahead, but her expression is muted and uneasy, almost like she feels guilty.

*Why?*

"Anyway, I'm sorry he took it out on you."

"When he called, he made it sound like I was friends with the guy or something," I mutter. "It was weird."

She laughs, but her smile doesn't touch her eyes. "Ice? Weird? You'd be surprised, Jayde."

"Who is James, anyway?"

"As I said before, he's someone we knew as children, up until high school. James and Ice didn't always get along, so I imagine it touched a nerve to hear about him so unexpectedly."

"Is he…a bad person?"

"James?" Surprise flickers in her wide eyes, but she shakes her head. "No. He has a nervous disposition, I suppose, but he was never unkind to me. Or to anyone else, as far as I'm aware."

"Hm."

*Then what's the issue?*

She takes a deep breath and flashes an obviously forced smile. "Anyway, I hate talking about high school as much as Ice does. So, could we…"

"Oh!" I glance at my lap. "I'm sorry. I don't mean to pry."

"I know," she says, her voice brighter. "But thinking about the past isn't always fun, so I'd avoid bringing James up in the future if I were you—especially with Ice."

"Right. I'll keep it in mind."

There are things I'd rather not talk about too, so I get it. Even if their history only makes Ice's reaction slightly less uncomfortable and annoying in hindsight.

*No. I'm still frustrated.*

When we get to the mall, the Choi twins have yet to arrive. Night and I order smoothies, sit across from each other at a food court table, and talk about nothing—the weather, reality TV, how a disproportionate number of immortals are famous.

She doesn't have much input on that either.

I'm in the middle of a sentence when a hand, wrist adorned in rainbow jelly bracelets, and a third smoothie slam against the tabletop.

"Night," Carmen says, her voice loud. She glances between us and grins. "Thanks for inviting us."

Natalie stands calmly beside her sister. As our eyes meet, she brushes her sleek, dark hair over one shoulder. She smiles, the soft expression crinkling the corners of her lavender eyes.

"Thank you for coming," Night says.

"Of course." Natalie takes the chair next to mine. "It's nice to see you again, Jayde."

I return the sentiment.

Carmen cuts off her energetic conversation with Night, slides into her chair, and points across the table—at me. "Did you see it, Nat? The necklace she got from *you know who?*"

Her sister laughs. "I saw it. You showed me, remember?"

"It's pretty, right? Taylor has a purple one, doesn't he?"

*Who?* I glance between the twins.

Natalie nods. "Can't recall if I've ever actually seen it, but

Dawn's whole family is air, so it only makes sense. Since Jayde's is blue, and the Monroes are water, you know?"

"Wait—" I sit up straight, caught off guard by my own realization. "Is there someone else like me in Riverview?"

Night catches my gaze before looking to Carmen, who shrugs.

"If you're not a complete ass, you're nothing like him," she says, flashing a wry smile. "Trust me, girl. We invited him here, stressing the fact that another human was coming, but he didn't respond to our messages. He didn't even bother telling us off. And I know he read them all."

Night frowns and glances at her drink. "I figured as much. I asked Dawn about him too, but he has her blocked online."

"That's cold," Natalie says under her breath.

"You guys tried to invite him here? For me?"

"Keyword *tried*," Carmen says before glancing away, her eyes narrowed and arms crossed over her chest.

*That's too bad.*

I'd give almost anything to talk to someone who can relate to me in any way. Few humans know about immortals and even fewer are part of the Human Immortal Program.

*Just over four hundred in the United States.*

What are the odds that two of us live in the same city?

"Taylor's not so bad," Night says, her eyes averted as she takes a drink of her smoothie. "But he is the only other human immortal I know of, so I thought I'd at least try."

*Human immortal, huh?*

Carmen cackles. "Riiight."

"So—" Natalie clears her throat. "How does yours work?"

I smile. "It doesn't. The necklace doesn't work yet."

"Still?" Carmen asks, clearly disappointed. "Is there something wrong with it? Or is there, like, a charging period?"

"I don't know," I admit. Suddenly, all eyes are on me. "I heard it can take a few months before anything happens. But, um, do you know how it works for Taylor?"

The twins exchange uncertain glances and shrug, but Night, who suddenly looks worn out, nods.

"He has a necklace too," she says. "If I remember correctly, he morphs by taking it off. To remain in human form, he has to wear it all the time."

I tip my head, unable to mask my unease. "That seems kind of inconvenient, doesn't it?"

"Especially when you hate, uh…*cats*," Carmen says with a short laugh. "I bet ten bucks he wears that thing twenty-four seven. You won't be like that, will you, Jayde?"

"Oh, no. I think it'll be neat. And…I like cats."

* * * * *

"Well, that was fun," Night says warmly as we leave the mall together. "I'm glad you get along with Carmen and Natalie, but I'm sorry Taylor didn't show."

I shake my head. "It's fine, honestly. I had a good time, and it's enough to know I'm not completely alone in this thing."

"Even so, I had hoped he would want to meet you." She sighs, adjusting her grip on her purse. "Before now, he was the only human immortal in Riverview, and one of the only humans our age who knew about immortals at all. At the very least, he was the only human going to Wisteria while I was there."

*Was he lonely?*

Night stops beside her car and turns, her expression careful. "But Carmen isn't entirely wrong about him either. Taylor has a…low opinion of immortals."

"He doesn't like them at all, huh?"

"No," she says as she opens the driver's side door.

I sit in the passenger seat and buckle my seatbelt, focused on her as she mulls it over with her hands on the steering wheel.

"For as long as I've known him, Taylor has hated immortals," she says. "I don't know if he was always so disenchanted, or if he's changed any since graduation, but I hope the same doesn't happen to you."

"It won't."

She offers me a smile.

"Do you know how he learned about immortals?" I ask.

Her nails tap the steering wheel, but she shakes her head. "He was adopted by an immortal family when he was in elementary school, I believe? I can't quite remember when he transferred to Wisteria, but he was a grade above me, and we had a couple classes together in high school. He was quiet. Rather antisocial, really—if you tried to talk to him. I assume most of the information circulating about him was rumor, though."

He was adopted by immortals as a child, but he hates them all?

*What happened?*

"Not meeting you is his loss," she says with a sigh. "Even if you didn't get along well enough to be friends, I thought meeting might benefit you both…"

"It's fine!" I force a smile. "Thanks for trying, though. It means a lot."

She smiles in return, but she seems distracted. "Is it fine? To be honest, Jayde, I still wonder if you would have been better off if Ice never told you about us. Isn't it already causing trouble for you?"

*Is it?*

"Maybe a little," I admit. "But I'm glad he told me."

# twenty-eight

It surprised me when Ice called.

He laughed easily, and he spoke as though everything was fine. He asked how I've been—I said I'm doing okay. Then he asked if I like Thai food and invited me out for an early dinner.

Of course, I agreed to go.

I don't have anything better to do at home, and I probably should stop avoiding him. Nothing will change if we never talk.

Sadly, there's no expectation of dressing well this time.

I gaze longingly at the plum cocktail dress in my closet. I only bought it so I'd have something formal to wear in the future.

*But there's plenty of time for that, right?*

Tonight, the clothes I'm already wearing will work. I brush my hair and try to decide if I want to attempt eyeshadow while I apply mascara. *Nah. This is fine.* I stick a bobby pin in my hair to keep it out of my face and call it good.

When I answer the door, Ice smiles. He's wearing the black leather jacket, his hair is perfectly tousled, and he more resembles the man I met the day before my birthday. Cool. Confident. Hot.

I think he was just tired from the Seattle trips, after all.

"You look good," I say.

He laughs and runs a hand through his hair. “Ready to go?”

I nod, and we’re off.

Everything feels normal. Ice is quiet—as he usually is while driving—but he’s clearly in a good mood, so I tell him about the letter from Human-Immortal Affairs. He listens with heightened interest. I get the feeling he was serious when he claimed he didn’t know much about the River Sapphire.

“It’s good news, though,” I say with a laugh. “I was worried when it didn’t work at first, but it sounds like it’s normal. Hopefully, it will activate in a few weeks—or a couple months, I guess.”

“Makes sense. Perhaps the gemstone needs time to calibrate to your body?”

“Maybe. But, um, I do have one question… How did you get the DNA sample they used to make it?”

His expression shifts almost imperceptibly.

“Ah. You found out about that, did you?” With a mild laugh, he shakes his head. “The DNA sample came from hairs I found in the passenger seat. It was easy to tell which were yours.”

“My hair?”

*Ugh.* At least he didn’t cut it off in my sleep.

He meets my gaze for an instant, his smile mellow. “Why? Did it bother you—finding out how it was made?”

*Did it bother me?*

“Not really,” I say slowly. “I was just curious.”

“You aren’t upset with me?”

I force a smile to mask my confusion. “No? I mean, that’s like the least invasive way of collecting someone’s DNA, right?

And, in hindsight, it only makes sense the gemstone required mine."

"It seriously doesn't bother you? None of this bothers you?"

"Should it?"

"Should it?" With another laugh, he adjusts his hands on the steering wheel. "I don't know, Jayde."

The conversation is strange, but this is the most talkative he's ever been while driving outside of Westbrooke, so I'll take it. He doesn't seem upset over the way I yelled at him last week, anyway.

*I'll take it.*

Eventually, the car pulls into the parking lot of Twantok House Thai Restaurant. It's a cute building with a red and green exterior and signage in both English and Thai. I follow Ice inside. The decor is gold and orange and red and green, full of beautiful East Asian imagery. A sweet tang fills the air.

## Please Wait to be Seated

A small, older woman lights up when she sees us. She steps out from behind the hostess station with a broad smile and pats Ice on the arm. Her kind, almond eyes are dark brown. She's human, and I don't know why it surprises me so much.

"Ah, it's the Monroe boy." Her voice is warm, her accent thick. With a glance at me, her smile softens. "Where is your sister? And who is your new friend?"

Ice returns her smile and pats me on the head. "This is Jayde. It's just the two of us today, Mrs. Bunmi."

"With me," the woman says. She ushers us further into the

restaurant and stops again at a booth beside a curtained window. "Sit, please. I will bring tea."

"Thank you," Ice says before taking a seat at the table.

I sit across from him, and Mrs. Bunmi offers me a laminated menu. She announces the daily dinner special. Then, with a polite nod, she returns to the front of the restaurant.

"She's so friendly," I whisper, both surprised and awed. "Is that normal service here?"

He laughs. "I've been coming here for years, quite regularly at times, so she is rather familiar with me."

"She likes you, then?"

"Mrs. Bunmi likes most everyone she meets," he says in vague amusement. "Though, I suppose she may have a soft spot for return customers."

The menu contains several photos, and everything is written in Thai with English translations and short descriptions below. I recognize a few dishes, but I'm unfamiliar with Thai food and not sure what I'd like.

*I'm not too picky, but...*

"What are you getting?" I ask.

He shrugs. "The same thing I always get. Pad thai."

Pad thai? *Well...* I ate instant ramen at least three times in the past week, so I'm not exactly in the mood for noodles.

"I'll just have the dinner special," I decide aloud.

He flashes a bright smile. "How adventurous of you."

According to the menu, chicken satay is essentially just grilled chicken skewers served with rice and a savory peanut sauce, but sure.

*Adventurous.*

Mrs. Bunmi returns with a tray carrying glasses of ice water, a metal teapot, and two small, porcelain teacups. She sets the table and takes our orders—Ice's being *the usual*. Then, after a polite promise to return shortly, she hurries away.

I pour a cup of tea. Steam rises from the pale liquid. It smells floral, like jasmine. *Green tea, maybe?* I add a little sugar and an ice cube from my water glass.

"So, is this your favorite restaurant?"

"I suppose," he agrees, filling the second cup with tea. "For the pad thai, that is. I've been told the sauce is an old family recipe. It's quite mysterious and second only to Sarai's. It's a shame that Night can't seem to replicate it—her mother is a genius in the kitchen."

"Maybe I should have ordered that instead."

He tips his head and watches me for a quiet moment. Then he glances away and takes a sip of steaming unsweetened tea.

"I suppose I could spare a bite for you," he says.

"Maybe…" *Change the subject.* "So, why'd you want to come here? With me? Today?"

*Not like that!*

"Today is my cheat day." His voice is casual as his gaze flicks up to meet mine. "And I wanted to see you."

*Aah... Was I avoiding him for no reason?*

I force a smile and fiddle with my bracelet. "Well, I'm glad you called. To be honest, I kind of thought you were mad at me."

"Mad at you?" He smiles, his eyes wide and sparkling with curiosity. "Whatever would I be mad at you for?"

"For, um…"

I glance aside. I hoped to get an apology out of this date, but I doubt that's why he asked me out.

He's acting like nothing happened. Like he never said those nasty things about James. Like we never snapped at each other on the phone. But Night said I shouldn't bring it up again, and trying to skirt around the topic would only make things awkward.

"Never mind." *Uh... Say something else. Anything else.* "Hey, are you doing anything for the Fourth of July?"

Today is the second.

I should have asked about his plans earlier, but this is fine. *What can we do on such short notice, though?* The fireworks display at Riverside Park? Are there other events? *Something on the coast, maybe?*

A flicker of disinterest crosses his face—the ghost of a frown. "Night was invited to a party. She asked me to go with her, but I intend to decline."

"So, you're free?" I ask, but my relief falters. "Or do you not like the Fourth of July?"

"I am a full-blooded American, Jayde," he says with a dry laugh. Resting his chin on his fingers, he offers me a smile. "Why? Did you have something better than a crowded house party in mind?"

"Not exactly. It's just that I don't have any plans either, so…"

His smile widens. "Well. You're more than welcome to come over. Surely, I can work something out. Pick up some fireworks. Buy some drinks. Fruit. Convincing Night to stay home will be easy."

*Oh, thank god.*

"I'm down. That sounds fun."

By the time Mrs. Bunmi brings out our food, we have a plan worked out. He'll get everything ready tomorrow and pick me up in the evening. I'll spend the night—I insisted on sleeping in the den even after he wryly suggested I have another sleepover with Night—and then we'll do Fourth of July festivities and shoot off fireworks once it gets dark.

He laughs at a dumb joke, and my face grows hot.

"Do you still want to try the pad thai?" he asks.

I blink, glancing from his face to his plate. He twirls noodles onto the fork, stabs a piece of chicken, and offers it to me, holding his arm—and the fork—across the table.

"It's very good," he says.

"Oh, sure!"

I take the bite.

The pad thai is good. Sweet and spicy. The noodles firm, and the chicken tender. It might be better than the chicken satay—though, it turns out peanut sauce is awesome.

"Do you like it?" he asks. When I nod, he grins. "If you ever want to come again, let me know."

# twenty-nine

~ ∞ ~

*Where am I?*

*I can't see anything, but...*

*Wait.*

*Someone's there—*

~ ∞ ~

# thirty

I sit up, cold sweat beading on my forehead.

*It's dark.*

My breath comes fast and shallow. Still gasping, I reach for my neck. My fingers touch clammy skin.

*Where am I?*

I scan my surroundings. A faintly illuminated doorway to my right. A sliver of light to my left. *Oh. That's right.* I'm at Ice's house. I'm safe—on the loveseat in the den, where I fell asleep. But a hint of anxiety remains.

"A dream?"

Hearing my own voice is a relief.

I touch my cheeks with shaky hands and feel warm tears. *I'm crying? That's new.* I rub my arms, hoping to calm down further.

*What the hell did I dream about?*

I lie down facing the back of the couch and try to fall asleep again, but inky shapes swirl around my eyelids every time I close my eyes. I know it's not real. It's irrational—fear from a dream I can't even remember—but the lingering unease is enough to keep me wide awake.

*This is stupid.*

I roll over and reach for my phone on the TV stand. The screen brightness blinds me. When my vision clears, I check the time. It's just after 5AM.

*Really?*

The curtain over the sliding glass door is truly impressive. If I hadn't checked the time, I would have guessed it was well before sunrise.

I leave the couch and wander into the quiet great room. Soft light streams in through the skylight in the kitchen, but I pull open the thick curtains over the bay window to fight off more of the darkness left behind by my mystery nightmare.

*What was it?*

Outside, perfect houses with perfect lawns sit across the road. It's so early, the streetlights are still on, and the street itself is empty. Westbrooke looks like a normal upper-class neighborhood, but is it really? How many immortals live here?

*Hm...*

A prickle on the back of my neck. I scratch my wrist.

Then I glance over my shoulder, and my heart nearly stops. *Ice is standing behind me.* A shiver runs up my spine as something inexplicably dark flashes through my mind, but I can't pin the haunting afterimage down before it slips away.

*Aah— He isn't wearing a shirt.*

My cheeks flush hotly, and I avert my eyes.

"Ice." I swallow and try to fix my hair. "Good morning."

"This seems early for you," he says.

I struggle to make eye contact—and fail, so I'm stuck looking just off to the side of his face instead. Maybe it's close enough he won't notice.

"But not for you?" I ask, still messing with my hair.

*Why am I so jumpy?*

He smiles rather uncertainly. "This is normal."

Waking up at 5AM is normal for him? *How?* When does this man find time to sleep?

In my confusion, I manage to make eye contact. Though, his smile fades as he studies my face again, and he glances around the room.

"Is something wrong?" he asks.

"Oh, no." I laugh. "I had a nightmare—or whatever. I couldn't fall back asleep, so I got up and came out here. That's all."

"A nightmare?"

As I stare into his shockingly blue eyes, he watches me with a level expression. Honestly, I can't recall a single specific detail about the dream, but something about it has me on edge, and I don't want to talk about it. The thought feels wrong somehow.

He quirks an eyebrow, trying to prompt an answer.

I wish I had one to give.

"I don't remember. What are you doing up this early, anyway?"

He smiles hesitantly and gestures toward the lower half of his body. My eyes skim over his bare chest before taking in his track pants and worn sneakers.

"I'm going for a run," he says.

*How on earth did I miss that?*

"Right… Duh."

I try to keep from staring, but his body is perfect and *right* in front of me. I indulge in one last glance at his lean, muscular torso before meeting his gaze again.

"Do you run every morning?"

"Generally."

Well, it explains *a lot*, though I can't tell whether he's amused or irritated that I've been ogling him. His posture is casual and unconcerned, but his face is more or less unreadable.

I clear my throat. "I shouldn't hold you up then."

He offers another half-smile before heading out, and I watch through the bay window as he puts earbuds in and takes off down the sidewalk. He's a quick jogger and looks so at ease while running. He reminds me of a professional athlete—lithe and agile.

When he disappears from view after turning down another street, I leave the breakfast nook. I take a few steps, but I pause.

My eyes land on the brightly colored package of department store fireworks on the glass dining table. Then the small, cardboard box containing the three larger mortars Ice mentioned last night —real skyrockets.

*Something...*

*The sound of fireworks...?*

*A flash of white?*

If I could remember the dream, maybe I would understand why I'm so uncomfortable. It just feels like something is *off*. Like...I shouldn't be here, or someone might be watching me from just out of sight—from just around the corner.

*Relax, Jayde.*

It was only a dream.

* * * * *

All day, the feeling has lingered.

The sensation of being watched. A prickly, itchy sort of hyper-awareness, as though my privacy was invaded by some malevolent force during the night, and my subconscious is trying to warn me of the danger I missed out on. Even as I took a shower, it followed me, prickling down my spine.

*But no one else feels it.*

I stay at the breakfast nook after lunch. Ice and the twins move on to do other things—I didn't pay attention to what—but I don't move. I look through the bay window for a long time.

It's a beautiful, sunny day.

A few children play in the street, running or riding scooters and bicycles. They laugh and shriek loud enough I can hear their voices through the glass.

I'm not watching the children, though.

I'm not really watching anything. I'm just gazing through the window, trying to remember anything from my stupid dream. It was dark. Empty. I heard breathing—or crying, maybe. A… *sound.* And then I woke up with tears streaming down my face.

*That can't be it… That's not even scary.*

After a while—maybe ten minutes; maybe a half hour—Ice joins me at the table. He asks if I'm alright. This is the third or fourth time he's asked today.

My unease makes him uncomfortable.

"It's nothing," I say.

He stares at me, his eyebrows raised. All I can do is shake my head and smile. I may want to remember the dream for myself, but I still don't want to talk about it.

"Do only immortals live around here?" I ask, hoping to distract him.

He glances out the window. "No, I don't believe so. Why?"

"Night told me that immortals make up half the population in Riverview. She said you guys like to group together, and this is a gated community, so I wasn't sure."

"I see. She's not wrong. Plenty of immortals live here, though not exclusively by any means. The cost of living in Westbrooke is high, but there are humans who manage it."

Immortals tend to have more money than humans too?

*Why am I not surprised?*

That said, I can only imagine the cost of living here. My family would never have been able to afford it. Sure, the house I grew up in was nice in its own right, but this place is almost *too* nice—and it's not even the nicest house on the block.

"How long have you lived here?"

"In this house?" He focuses on me for a long moment before turning to the window again. "Night and Smoke grew up here—the house was built before the twins were born—but I was adopted into the family as a child. It's been about eleven years now."

*Only eleven years?* Aren't most kids adopted younger?

Well, I suppose it explains the lack of childhood photos around the house. But he has no idea that Night already told me he was adopted, does he?

"Really?" I ask, hoping my voice carries enough surprise to

convince him.

His eyes narrow, and his lips form a thin smile as he meets my gaze. "Don't tell me you thought the twins and I were related by blood." When I shrug and laugh, my embarrassment genuine, he rolls his eyes. "In any case, Westbrooke is an ideal community for children. I was fortunate to come here and live with this family."

"That's great."

I want to know more about his past. He was adopted into an upper-class family as an older child. His life before he was a Monroe could have been anything, but… I don't want to push my luck or make him more uncomfortable than I already have.

"So… When are we doing fireworks?"

"The skyrockets? After nightfall." He sits up straight, his shoulders relaxing. "The darker, the better for those. We can set the others off earlier."

"I'm excited for the big ones," I admit. "I've never seen skyrockets up close before."

"They're very loud. Very bright."

"Do you shoot them off every year?"

He flashes a crooked grin. "No. I picked them up just for you."

"Oh." I smile, feeling my face warm. "Well. Thanks."

He shoots me a cool glance with bright eyes and stands from the table. A moment of hesitation. Then he pats me once on the head and walks away.

*What on earth is that about?*

# thirty-one

Two hours to sunset.

Small, whistling fireworks already sound off elsewhere in the neighborhood. I sit on the raised patio with my feet dangling over the edge and a small plate of cubed watermelon in my lap.

The sliding glass door opens to my left.

Ice steps out onto the patio with the unopened package of department store fireworks under one arm. Night and Smoke, carrying a pitcher and stack of drinking glasses respectively, trail out after him. The three gather near the round patio table, and Smoke's mild expression shifts to a small smile as he observes the fairy lights I helped Night set up earlier.

"Festive," he says, tapping her on the shoulder.

"It's nothing special," she says. Then she pauses, glances up from the pitcher in her hand, and turns to me. "Oh, Jayde— Do you drink? I didn't think to ask."

*Alcohol?* I really don't, but…

Leaving my plate behind, I join the others around the table.

Night fills a tall, clear glass with pale pink liquid. Spherical ice cubes, quartered strawberries, and several lemon slices float inside the elegant glass pitcher.

"What is it? Spiked lemonade?"

She nods. "Would you like to try a glass?"

I have a couple years to go before I'm of legal drinking age, but the illegality of underage drinking does nothing to stop most people. I've only tried alcohol a few times, though, and I never drank much at once.

What if I have a low alcohol tolerance? *What if I throw up? Or black out?* I hate to think I might embarrass myself while under the influence, but I don't want to feel like the odd one out either.

*Aah...*

Night frowns. "It's fine if you want something else. We have cola, San Pellegrino, and ginger ale in the garage. Or I could make an Italian soda."

"No, it's fine. I'll try it."

I take a glass and turn to Ice. He's done removing the fireworks from their packaging, and they're now neatly arranged by height on the table.

I smile as he hands me a steel sparkler, but I turn away to hide my face before I taste the spiked lemonade. The drink is citrusy and syrupy, but the astringent flavor of hard liquor is not subtle. I suppress a cough.

"Do you like it?" Night asks, her eyes still carrying a touch of concern. "I made the syrup using berries from the garden."

She mixed the drink herself?

It's not bad, but alcohol is definitely an acquired taste. I'd prefer something sweeter—something less obviously alcoholic.

"It tastes like lemonade," I say.

*This is fine.*

I return to my spot on the edge of the patio and set the glass down, so I can hold the sparkler in one hand and eat watermelon at the same time. Ice sits rather close, holding his own sparkler and glass of lemonade. I watch as he takes a generous drink, but the taste of alcohol doesn't seem to faze him.

He catches me staring and smiles.

"You don't drink much, do you?" he asks.

"Not much, no."

His smile grows wry. "You're a good girl, huh? Not used to this sort of thing?"

*As always he can see right through me.*

"Is it that obvious?"

"Painfully," he says with a laugh.

The twins descend the patio stairs and walk out into the center of the grassy yard. Night holds two drinks while Smoke carries an armful of fireworks. They speak and giggle in hushed tones. Smoke's playful smile is wide, and I imagine he's not as serious as he often makes himself out to be.

"Here," Ice says.

He holds up a lit pocket lighter. I dip my sparkler into the tiny flame. Sparks shoot from the tip as it catches, and I angle it over the river rocks bordering the patio below.

The bright light is mesmerizing. Beautiful. I haven't played with sparklers in years. It's nostalgic and a little sad.

*Being with Ice's family like this…*

I take a drink, wincing again, but I persevere. Hopefully, the alcohol will help me lighten up. It's like Rose said; I need to take matters into my own hands. Be more assertive. *Make a move?*

*That's easier said than done—*

With a sharp hiss, Ice's sparkler bursts to life. We sit in relative silence as our sparklers burn, flinging white sparks in all directions. Red embers fall to the rocks and grass below, losing their glow as they fade and die.

The twins play in the yard with more energy. They move and dance about, waving their sparklers to form shapes and letters in the air. They're having a blast.

*Why can't I get in the mood?*

I glance at Ice out of the corner of my eye. He takes a slow drink from his glass, his attention focused on the tip of his sparkler. A soft frown forms on his face as he stares into the sparks with narrowed eyes that reflect the bright light.

What is he thinking about?

Me? The twins? His childhood? *Should I ask?*

As my sparkler's smoldering tip goes dark, a shrill whistle fills the backyard. The noise startles me, but it's just a firework Smoke set off. Sparks fly a couple feet into the air as the twins stand only a few strides from the screaming thing in the middle of the yard.

I take a more determined drink of lemonade.

Setting my spent sparkler aside, I study the drink more closely. The ice cubes and lemon slice. The condensation forming on the outside of the glass.

*How much do I have to drink before I feel any different?*

I have never drunk enough to get tipsy before. Just…half a lite beer I later abandoned on a kitchen counter. A shot of cheap liquor washed down with an entire can of soda. A couple homemade jello shots that barely tasted of alcohol.

*Is this a good idea?*

When the first firework falls silent, Night sets up another, and Smoke lights the fuse. The small, cardboard tube erupts into a series of hissing, blinding flashes. The light is so intense, I have to look away.

All the while, I continue nursing my drink.

The cold liquid feels strangely warm in my throat as I swallow, but the sweet strawberry with a sharp bite is growing on me. Either that or it's easier to tolerate now that I'm used to it.

Ice takes the remnants of my sparkler and mumbles something before standing. I glance up and notice the empty glass in his hand.

*Wait—*

I turn as he walks to the patio table, where he sets the spent sparklers down and pours himself a second glass. *How much is he planning to drink?* I'm not even halfway through my first cup.

As he returns to sit beside me, I ask if he knows what kind of alcohol Night used in the lemonade.

"Vodka and triple sec, I believe." He looks up from the glass in his hand. "It's not good vodka, though, and Night knows I don't care for citrus."

"Oh." *I have no idea what triple sec is.* "Do you drink a lot?"

He tips his head, his smile soft and curious. "Have you seen me drink before now?"

Only once—*I think.*

"I guess not," I admit.

We return to gazing out over the yard, watching the twins as they laugh and set off more small fireworks. I steal another glance at Ice. His smile softens as he watches them.

* * * * *

After finishing the hot dog I roasted over the small fire Smoke lit in the wrought-iron firepit, I return to the table near the stairs. I eat another piece of watermelon, and Ice hands me a full glass of pink lemonade. I accept it, and we make our way back to the edge of the patio.

*BANG!*

I scan the sky, but I don't catch the bloom of colorful sparks from whatever large firework went off in the distance.

The twins play with sparklers in the dimly lit yard, and I check my phone between drinks. Scrolling down FaceSpace, I pass a few party posts from friends. Rose spent the day at a huge family barbecue. Carmen is at a house party, but I don't recognize any of the tagged names or faces in her photos. Night uploaded a selfie, a picture of Smoke posing with a lit sparkler in each hand, and… a photo of me and Ice, sitting on the patio together—though an emoji sticker covers his face.

I didn't notice her take it, and she didn't tag me in the post. With a shifty glance in Ice's direction, I lock my phone.

"You plan to sit there all evening?" Night asks, coming toward us with a skip in her step.

Ice smiles easily. "Perhaps we will. What's it to you?"

"Poor Jayde." She laughs. "You're gonna bore her to death."

"I'm fine," I insist.

"It's far easier to enjoy the evening vicariously through you," Ice tells her.

Rolling her eyes, she continues up the steps and past us. She pours herself another glass of spiked strawberry lemonade—this is the second or third pitcher she's mixed, I think.

"We're heading out in about an hour, right?" she asks.

"That's the plan."

She ignores him and smiles at me. "Having fun?"

I grin and nod.

And I mean it. Even if we're only sitting on the patio, watching as the twins set off fireworks in the yard without us, I'm having a good time. This isn't stressful or overwhelming like some of the parties I attended with Rose in the past. The atmosphere is relaxed. Calm. And the anxiety I felt earlier in the day is gone.

Sitting here with Ice, I am having fun.

She offers me a thumbs-up before racing back into the center of the yard, where Smoke is setting up another round of mid-sized fireworks.

"I dare you to light one off with a sparkler," he says.

Ice sort of laughs and rolls his eyes. His expression is humored but mild and friendly.

"She's worried," he says, holding a conspiratorial hand near his mouth as though to block his voice from reaching the twins in the yard. "About everything, all the time. Isn't that funny?"

"It's not a bad thing, you know? She's like a mom."

"Like a mom…?" He glances away.

A flush of warmth rises from my chest to my cheeks.

"Hey, um—" *This is your moment, Jayde.* I hold up my phone. "Will you take a picture with me?"

Our eyes meet, his just wide enough to betray surprise. Maybe he doesn't like to be in pictures if he can avoid it, but, when we're not together, it almost feels like he doesn't exist at all. So, maybe having a picture would…

*That doesn't make sense. Ugh…*

"Yeah, why not," he says with a mild shrug.

*Wow. I didn't expect it to work.*

He motions for me to move closer. So I do, and he slings his arm over my shoulder. Our heads don't quite touch, but… *This is the closest we've been. And it doesn't bother me.*

I open my phone's camera and frame both of us in the screen. My arm wavers for a few seconds before I steady it enough to snap a decent photo.

He's smiling in the picture. My cheeks are flushed—*from the alcohol?*—but I look happy too. It's not so bad. Though, I wish he were more like that all the time.

Removing his arm from my shoulder, he peeks at my phone screen. And he sighs. "Just don't post it anywhere, alright?"

*I knew it.* But it is the perfect excuse to not send it to Rose.

"That's fine," I agree, my smile unaffected as I touch up the picture's lighting and contrast.

I make the photo his contact image in my phone, take another drink of spiked lemonade, and eat the last chunk of watermelon on my plate.

"Need more?" he asks.

"Ha. I can get it."

Empty plate in hand, I leave the edge of the patio—opting to hop off and walk back up the stairs to get to the table. I set my phone down as I fill the plate with watermelon chunks and pretzel sticks.

"Jayde!" Night calls from the middle of the yard, her voice muffled by the sharp crackling of the firework going off beside her. "Come here for a minute!"

"Coming!"

I leave my plate with Ice before I dash down the stairs.

# thirty-two

The alcohol kicked in by the time I emptied my second glass. My face grew warmer. My eyes tracked slower. No one stopped me when I went for a third—I guess they thought I was alright—but I haven't moved for at least twenty minutes, so I don't even know if I'm alright.

The sun is gone, the sky black and navy and dotted with faint stars. From what I understand, the plan is to head out to a cul-de-sac in some unfinished subdivision within Westbrooke. It's not far, so we'll walk. Then we'll set off the skyrockets and come back.

Or something like that. I can't remember exactly.

I scratch my neck where the River Sapphire's thin chain rests against my skin. The air is cooling slowly but surely. The breeze prickles the hairs on my arms, but my cheeks are still so warm.

Am I drunk?

*I don't think so?*

I feel…fuzzy, I guess. And I laugh at the dumbest things, including Ice's suggestion that we leave and head for the cul-de-sac soon.

But I'm fine.

He helps me stand. I laugh again as lemonade sloshes over the rim of my glass—it's nearly empty. Then I look up into his eyes.

And I wish he would kiss me.

*Huh? What?*

Oh. We're still holding hands.

Shaking my head, I pull away. I glance around, but the twins must have gone inside while I wasn't paying attention. Ice and I are alone on the patio, and I'm still giggling, holding my free hand over my mouth.

He chuckles. "You good?"

I nod, but he tries to take my glass away. I glare at him and down the last mouthful. Flashing a grin, I finally hand over the empty glass.

"Yeah… That's enough for you."

I laugh. "You drank like two times that."

"The difference being, I am perfectly fine after drinking two times that."

What is that supposed to mean?

I am fine.

Confused, I stare into his eyes.

They're pretty—so bright and blue even in the low light. After several long seconds of quiet staring, the thinly veiled amusement leaves his expression, and he rolls his eyes. I have half a mind to be offended until he smiles and shakes his head.

"Come on. Let's go."

He rests a warm hand on my shoulder and leads me into the house. But, instead of meeting up with the twins out front, we end up in his bedroom, where we drift apart. Feeling uneasy—a little sick to my stomach all of a sudden—I sit on the edge of the bed.

While he slides the closet door open, I reach down to fix my loose shoelaces.

This would be easier if I weren't hiccuping.

"Need to borrow a coat?" he asks.

I consider it carefully—if only because it's hard to imagine wearing any of Ice's clothes. I may have had a fleeting thought that I wouldn't mind trying on his leather jacket a couple weeks ago, but I don't know.

Though, I eventually agree through stifled laughter. I wasn't expecting a chill breeze, so I did not pack one of my own.

"There aren't many options," he says slowly.

I glance over. He's browsing the clothes in his closet. I've never seen it open before.

He shifts his weight every few seconds, appearing indecisive, but he soon pulls something off the rod to show me. A long, black overcoat with all sorts of neat buttons and straps on the front. It would look cool on him, but he asks if it will work for me.

*That seems like a bit much.*

My mouth accepts his offer, though, and he tosses the coat onto the bed. It lands halfway in my lap.

*Well, alright...*

I heft myself to my feet, nearly falling over in the process, and manage to shrug into the dark overcoat. On me, it is unfashionably large, the hem falling well below my knees, but the heavy material is surprisingly soft. It's warm and comfortable.

The coat smells like Ice too—or his closet, anyway. Clean. A hint of sweetness. A touch of spice.

"This is fine," I say, hiccuping between words.

I fiddle with the buttons, but I can't get my fingers to work well enough to fasten them. I had similar trouble with my shoe-laces, but this is worse. *For some reason...*

Why can't I button up a stupid coat?

*Silver, metal buttons. Black fabric.*

*Just put it in the hole.*

Ha—!

*Come on, Jayde.* Focus.

With a quiet huff and an offer to help I only hear half of, Ice crosses the room and stops in front of me. He bypasses the buttons and goes straight for the waist strap instead—which rests more on my hips than on my waist.

I find myself watching his eyes as he works. He seems intent and carefully focused on tightening the waist strap without touching me more than absolutely necessary. *How annoying.*

Once finished, he meets my gaze, but he doesn't say anything.

A loud firework goes off somewhere in the distance.

"Hey, um..." My head tips to one side. "Do you like me?"

*Huh??*

My question catches him off guard, and his eyes widen ever so slightly as his pleasant expression falters.

I can't believe I asked out loud either, but I don't panic or get so flustered I take it back. While my heart races, the alcohol works its magic, lending me the courage I need to commit and stand my ground.

Then he smiles.

"Of course I do," he says. "You're very interesting."

*Interesting?*

I lean closer. The motion throws me off balance, and I plant a hand on the nearest surface, which happens to be Ice's chest, to steady myself. He tenses at my touch, but he doesn't move or take his eyes off me, and his expression hardly shifts.

"Interesting?" I echo. "The hell does that mean?"

He laughs.

My hands close around the fabric of his t-shirt.

And I kiss him.

His lips are warm and soft. His breath smells like lemon syrup and alcohol. I've been aching for this moment for weeks.

But my eyes are still open.

I don't know why they're still open, and I wish they weren't. Because, as he draws a sharp breath, his eyes immediately grow wide. Blue and beautiful and full of alarm. He doesn't look away even as the fleeting surprise fades. He doesn't break the kiss or step back to distance himself, but he's not exactly reciprocating either.

I finally made a move.

He said he likes me, and I kissed him, but…

*Oh, god. I screwed up.*

Stumbling backward, I cover my mouth with my hands.

"I'm sorry," I gasp. "I— I don't know why I did that just now. I'm, uh…"

He averts his eyes and presses a couple fingers to his lips. Both his posture and expression are unreadable. Neutral. Blank, almost. Until he takes a deep, even breath and regains his composure.

As he meets my gaze, he clears his throat.

“It’s okay,” he says. “It was nothing, right?”

*Nothing?*

This was clearly a mistake.

He offers a smile I can only assume is meant to be reassuring, but it does not reassure me at all. I have never felt so humiliated in my life. My cheeks are on fire. My heart races. The stupid hiccups are back, and I want to cry.

He probably doesn’t even like me *like that*.

He probably hates me now.

*Ugh... I’m such an idiot!*

“We should go.” He pats my head, his touch gentle. “The twins are waiting out front.”

Ice leaves the room. I trail after him, but I stop just outside the door. I glance down the hallway, away from the den.

And, as my feet go for it, I yell, “One second— I have to pee,” and stumble into the bathroom before he has a chance to stop me.

Back pressed to the door, I pause to catch my breath, unexpectedly winded after traveling hardly six feet. Then a rush of nausea rises in my throat. I step further into the room, and my hands grip the edge of the sink.

*You will not throw up, you coward.*

I take a few deep breaths and, after pushing the sleeves of Ice’s ridiculous coat up to my elbows, splash some water on my face. I use the toilet, knock the soap dispenser over while washing my hands, and splash more water on my face.

*Okay, maybe I am a bit drunk.*

I fix my hair and creep out of the bathroom.

The hallway is empty, the den at the end lit only by the fairy lights in the backyard and a single light turned on somewhere in the great room. Dreading every moment, I make my way through the house. Through the den and empty great room, and out into the front yard.

Ice and the twins are waiting near the curb. He speaks easily with them, and Night waves me over, her voice warm as she calls my name. I can't bring myself to return her smile, but I walk out and join them.

Honestly, no matter what Ice said, I feel like I ruined the night beyond salvaging. I really did want to kiss him, *but I didn't think I'd actually do it.*

Night passes the small cardboard box containing the sky-rockets to her brother. Ice looks at me, his expression unclear in the shadow cast by the streetlights, and I immediately avert my gaze. The guys walk several paces ahead while I trail behind with Night.

This works better, anyway. I'd rather spontaneously combust than deal with Ice right now.

*Oh! She still has some lemonade.*

Before I can change my mind, I point at the half-empty glass in her hand and ask if I can have it.

"Is everything alright?" Concern flashes over her delicate features as she takes a good look at me. "Did Ice do something? Are you okay?"

I shake my head, stifling panicked laughter. "He didn't…do anything. I'm fine, but I kind of, um—" Cupping a hand over my mouth, I lower my voice. "—kissed him for some reason."

"You're serious?" she asks, eyes wide and voice hushed.

"You kissed him?"

"Yeah, and I think it freaked him out, so…"

"Are you sure you should drink more?"

My eyes drift around the dim street until I'm once again facing straight ahead. Ice glances over his shoulder, and our eyes meet by chance—for an instant. I don't know which of us looked away first.

I grimace.

"Yes," I say, my mouth dry. "I think so. Yes."

She frowns uncertainly, but she passes me the cup.

We walk for several minutes. We're quiet. Small fireworks go off throughout the neighborhood, but most households have turned in for the night, and, as we walk, we pass more homes still under construction. More empty lots with *For Sale* signs on the curb.

We're already in the unfinished subdivision? How long have we been walking?

*BANG!*

A shower of multicolored sparks blooms in my periphery from a large firework like the ones we're off to launch ourselves.

And Rose comes to mind.

It's late. She hasn't texted me since early this afternoon. I'm sure she had fun spending time with her family, though.

*What is she doing now?*

I reach for my phone—but it's not there. The pockets of my jean shorts are empty. I check my bra. I even check the large pockets of the oversized coat. Still no phone.

I stop walking. "Shoot."

The others stop when they realize I'm not moving. Night, only a couple steps ahead, turns to check on me.

"You okay?" she asks.

I point toward the dimly lit area off in the distance. "That's the cul-de-sac you guys were talking about, right?"

"Yes, that's it… But what's wrong?"

Behind her, Ice and Smoke watch us. I can't make out Ice's face in the low light from this distance, but the memory of my lips pressed against his and the scent of lemon and vodka haunts me. The nausea returns.

"I need my phone," I say. "I promised to text Rose. And record the fireworks. Um…"

Taking a few steps closer, Ice crosses his arms over his chest. "This can't wait? You need your phone now?"

"Yes!" I nod with enough vigor to spur a headache. "But I—I can get it. I'll be right back."

Night frowns, brows furrowed. She glances over her shoulder. At Ice. At the glass in my hand. At me. And her frown deepens.

"You can borrow my phone to take a video," she says. "Or, if you really need yours, I don't mind going with you."

The wave of nausea passes. I'm once again more bubbly than sick, as the prospect of having some space floods me with relief. But it's not a big deal. She's worried over nothing.

I smile. "No, it's fine! It'll only take me a minute."

Ice, still several paces ahead is not convinced. He doesn't want me to walk back to the house alone. *Will he stop me? Does he think I can't handle it?* His arms fall to his side, and his mouth opens like he wants to argue, but he sighs instead.

"I will come find you if you're gone too long," he says.

"Of course!"

Arms still crossed, his expression darkens. "I'm serious, Jayde. You have thirty minutes."

"Okay, thirty minutes," I agree, raising my free hand. "Hold off on the fireworks until I get back, okay? Can't wait to see them!"

With that, I offer the group a small wave, turn one hundred eighty degrees, and take off. I half-jog down the street, still holding the glass of spiked lemonade. The liquid sloshes, threatening to spill over the rim. Somehow, I lose very little of my drink, but I only last a minute—around a single bend in the road—before my side aches, and I slow to a walk.

I listen to my footsteps against the asphalt. I focus on my unsteady gait and try to walk between the yellow lines in the middle of the street. All the while, a nagging unease slowly rises in my chest. A mild discomfort. A sense of something…*off.*

My collarbone itches beneath the River Sapphire.

Headlights from behind illuminate the road, startling me as the light casts my form as a long, dark shadow stretching down the pavement. I pick up the pace, leaving the road and stepping onto the sidewalk instead.

The car passes where I stood and disappears around the next curve.

I glance over my shoulder—*how many times have I checked behind me?*—but there's no one there. There hasn't been anyone there. The streets are well-lit and empty. Westbrooke is a secure private neighborhood.

It's safe, right?

*Why am I so jumpy?*

The alcohol?

I scratch my neck. The gentle, previously negligible weight of the necklace's thin chain bothers me. An uncomfortable awareness of the tiny, metal links touching my skin. A new heaviness I never felt before.

*It's annoying.*

So I take the River Sapphire off.

I don't turn into a cat or anything, but the itching subsides, so I clasp the chain and stick the necklace in one of the internal pockets on Ice's dark overcoat.

Fireworks still go off every few minutes *somewhere*, but this street is empty. There aren't any families out lighting off sparklers in their driveways. There aren't any kids running around.

How late is it, anyway? 11PM? A little later? Earlier? I have no idea. I don't remember the last time I checked my phone. I don't remember glancing at the alarm clock before I left Ice's bedroom.

*Where did I leave my phone, anyway?*

Even after turning onto the familiar street Ice lives on, a sense of anxiety remains. The prickly discomfort does not mix well with the increasing fuzziness from the alcohol. It leaves me sort of dizzy and sick.

I watch my feet, struggling to walk one foot in front of the other without wavering. *Why is this so difficult?*

I don't feel any better.

With a sigh, I look up.

There's a car parked on the curb beneath a streetlight up ahead. This is an upper-class neighborhood, full of nice cars, but this one's…*not so nice*. It's grungy and beat up, so it stands out. And the parking job sucks. The car is empty, though, and the lights are on in the house beside it.

I scratch my shoulder, tickled by stray hairs affected by the breeze.

*Everything is fine, Jayde. Stop being so weird.*

Despite my valiant and reasonable attempt at rationalization, the rising paranoia only becomes more tangible the closer I get to the Monroe house. But I walk up the stone path and step onto the concrete landing anyway.

*A heavy weight on my chest. A pit in my stomach.*

I shake my head. The door is unlocked, so I walk right in. The great room is decently lit by the chandelier over the dining table, as it was when I left, but that doesn't stop the profound, cold dread from crashing over me.

My skin prickles uncomfortably. My breath catches. *It's the same as this morning.* The nausea returns full force too, bringing a headache with it. Coughing, desperate to regain control, I power through and shake it off to dispel some of the tension in my body. Then I close the door, and the search for my phone commences.

I check the kitchen counters and the coffee table in front of the couch. Moving into the den, I flip the light on and check my backpack. My phone isn't on the TV stand or any of the low bookcases. It's not in Ice's bedroom either.

I set the now-empty glass on the desk and drop myself onto the edge of Ice's soft bed. I hold my aching head in my hands.

It's hard to ignore.

*Oh, no...*

Maybe I should stay here. Maybe I drank too much.

I sit a moment longer. My eyes close. Sleep calls to me, the warmth in my chest overpowering the sense of unease.

*Just a moment longer...*

My head dips. My chin slips past the heel of my palm, jolting me awake. I shake my head again to calm my nerves. Then I fall back onto the bed and roll onto my side.

Eyes closed again, I give up.

The only sound is my breathing. The soft, rhythmic whirring of the central AC. The sliding glass door…

My eyes snap open, unable to focus on anything in particular in the low light.

Did I hear the sliding glass door?

Slowly, I sit up. I rub my eyes. I look around. The clock says it's 10:48PM. Faint light filters in from the backyard through the sheer curtains. Even more light comes in through the open doorway, from the light I left on in the den.

I don't hear anything.

The sound was probably my imagination—considering I was half-asleep and paranoid—but I leave the bed anyway. I take the empty glass from the desk, cross the room, and poke my head out the doorway.

The hall is empty. The den is empty. The house is quiet and well-lit, the same as before I nearly fell asleep.

"Hello?" I ask the house.

No one answers.

Frustrated with myself, I step into the hallway and wander through the house. I don't perform a thorough search, but there isn't anyone here unless they're hiding out in one of the bedrooms.

The house is empty. I'm clearly losing my mind.

I stand in front of the sliding glass door for a moment. The backyard is empty too, but— *Ah!* My phone is on the patio table. *That's right.* I set it down earlier, didn't I?

Maybe I won't miss the fireworks after all.

I pull the door open and step outside. I pick up my phone. The screen is so bright it hurts my eyes, so I turn the brightness down before checking my notifications.

*Mm...*

I missed a call from Rose less than an hour ago, but I shouldn't return it now. She's never seen me drink enough to get tipsy—let alone enough to turn into a stupid, wobbly mess.

*Ugh.* I even kissed Ice. *He said he likes me, but...*

I start typing a message. I don't want to talk about Ice. I just want to apologize for missing her call, but—

*A sound.* Soft footfalls in the grass behind me.

*Someone is—*

I freeze, unable to glance over my shoulder. The footsteps continue, and my heart sinks. It's not my imagination this time. I guess that hearing the sliding glass door probably wasn't either.

But who—? What do I…?

*What should I do?*

My head hurts. It's hard to think. I can't seem to—

*Ugh.*

I can't pretend I'm not alone, but I'm scared to look, and they haven't said anything yet, so I don't even know who it is. I seal my eyes shut, slap my phone down on the table, and spin to face the backyard.

"Who's there?" I call with my eyes still closed.

Please be Ice—*actually, please be Night.* Even Smoke would be fine. Ice said he would come after me if I didn't show up after thirty minutes, but I don't know how long it's been. What time was it when I left? I have no idea.

*Ugh...*

My hand clutches the empty glass so tightly I worry it might break. *Why didn't I leave it in the kitchen?*

I can't think—

*Damn it...*

The person in the backyard still hasn't said anything, remaining quiet even as they ascend the patio stairs. If they don't intend to answer my question, they'll be right in front of me before I even know who they are.

I peel my eyes open, but my mind blanks.

At first, I register only the red glow of a lit cigarette. It falls from a hand and lands on the wood, and my eyes track upward again, toward the intruder's face.

*The man in front of me—*

"James?" my slurred voice asks.

He wears a black hoodie, and his orange hair is concealed by a dark knit cap, but I recognize him in the soft light cast over the patio from the fairy lights behind me. His eyes, shadowed and rimmed by dark circles, are wide.

*Is he surprised to see me? Or—*

My breath catches as an image from my dream flashes before my eyes. *A wall, dripping crimson red. Thick, warm blood slicking my hands. So much...*

*Someone behind me.*

*No—*

The vision is wiped away as an intense wave of nausea grips my stomach. A sharp pain stabs my head. I raise a hand to my mouth, but the world spins and goes dark before I have a chance to vomit.

Suddenly, I'm weightless. And I can't see.

The glass slips from my hand and shatters. I hear the sharp sound—the crack of broken glass—followed by a heavy thud, and then...*nothing*.

# thirty-three

*Aah… My head… Like a drum…*

It's dark.

*My eyes are closed.*

I open my eyes, slowly and warily, only to discover that I'm slumped over in the backseat of a moving vehicle. A bump in the road jostles me, and a dizzying sickness rises in my throat. The faint scent of tobacco smoke? And, oh my god, my head—

Wait. When did I get into a car?

Last I remember, I was walking to the cul-de-sac. But I turned back, didn't I? I made it to the house. I almost fell asleep, but then I found my phone. I was on the patio. And then…

*And then…*

*Shattering glass. Wide, golden eyes in the low light.*

Oh.

*Oh, no…*

I sit up quickly. Far too quickly.

My stomach twists as pain splits my skull.

Everything goes black for an instant. I manage to catch myself, but cradling my head and sucking air through my teeth does little to help. I'm a mess. My chest hurts. My stomach hurts.

I can barely breathe.

"You stay back there," a sharp voice calls from the front seat. *It's James*...or the guy from the mall, anyway. "Don't move. I—I have a gun!"

*What the hell?*

I try to speak, but my voice is so rough and slurred, I hardly recognize it. I cough to clear my dry throat.

"What do you want?" I ask.

My hand comes away from my temple with a smear of dark red blood. I passed out, right? What did I hit my head on? The patio? The metal table leg?

How bad is it?

*Ugh*...

I glance out the window. It's dark. I make out a sea of shadowy trees at the edge of the road, but there aren't any signs, buildings, or streetlights.

*Where am I?*

"I want that necklace. It's blue, right? That's what I want."

"What? Why?"

Another bump in the road brings a fresh wave of nausea. I tear my eyes from the window and groan, torn between hugging my midsection and holding my pounding head.

The car screeches to a halt. The wheels grind in loose gravel, and I'm thrown forward. Hand pressed over my mouth, I fight back the nausea. Through my coughing, the engine idles. Then a seatbelt unbuckles, and the driver's side door opens. I look up through a mess of my hair as James turns in his seat to watch me.

I grit my teeth.

*Seriously, why?*

Even in the dim, yellow light cast by the dome light above, his face is etched with panic. His shadowy eyes are wide, his features taught and muscles tense. Sweat drips down his brow.

Do I look like that too? Only with blood?

*Gross.*

I ignore James and look out the windshield. The car is stopped in front of a large, dilapidated building—easily three stories tall. The lot is otherwise barren and surrounded by thick trees like the road leading up to it.

*Where the hell am I? How long was I out?*

"You have it with you, right?" he asks, pulling his knit hat off with one hand. "So just give it to me, and I'll let you go."

"What? No. What are you even talking about?"

He says something I ignore completely as I sneak a peek at the door to my right. The handle is within reach—*and the door is unlocked.* It's so dark out there, though. I don't know how well I can move, but…

James holds out a hand, palm-up, and reaches over the center console and into the backseat. I shy away, shifting closer to the door without taking my eyes off him.

"Come on," he says. "Just hand it over."

The River Sapphire?

"No—"

My hand shoots for the door handle, and I throw myself out. Course stones scrape my palms and knees as I land in gravel. Pushing the fresh, hot pain to the back of my mind, I climb to my feet and take off toward the looming building.

Feet crunch in loose gravel behind me, but I can't afford to hesitate. I wipe the budding tears from my eyes, ignore the stitch in my side, and push my legs to move faster.

*But where am I going?*

Running this way seemed like the best option in the moment —better than ending up lost in the woods in the middle of the night. But I don't know how long I spent passed out in the car before I came to. I don't even know if I'm still in Riverview.

James is definitely following me, though. I don't look back, but I hear him sputtering frustrated curses somewhere between me and the car.

Maybe getting lost in the woods is my only option.

Or… *Maybe this building has a back door.*

The oversized front doors are unlocked. I heave one open and dash through the small, well-lit vestibule. The space beyond is far darker, but all I can do is press forward. Dust motes float in the air, catching in my already parched throat. Wood scraps, cardboard, and paper litter the hardwood floor and get in my way.

*What is this place?*

I spot a staircase with light at the top to my left, but my eyes glaze right over it. I can't climb stairs. I have to go further inside. Stay on the ground floor and find another exit. A second door that leads outside. Or a window. But it's so dark. Hardly any light from the vestibule reaches here, and the room is a disaster.

*Where should I go?*

James is still coming, so I—

My toe catches the edge of something solid.

I fall.

My ankle twists as the rubber tip of my shoe remains stuck a second too long before breaking free, and I catch myself on the ground with my forearms. Heart and head pounding—each beat like an ice pick to the temple—I stare at nothing with wide eyes, my nose an inch from the plywood board that tripped me.

*I need to go.* Can't stop even to catch my breath.

Ignoring my burning ankle, ignoring my stinging palms and aching head, I scramble to my feet. I take the first step without stumbling. My ankle should be fine.

Then a hand catches the back of my coat.

I spin to face him, ready to throw hands, but James grabs ahold of my wrist, and I freeze. Clammy fingers wrap around bare skin. *Too close.*

"Don't touch me," my rough voice hisses.

I plant my free hand on his shoulder and shove as hard as I can. He shifts slightly, but my foot slips on a piece of loose debris, and I'm once again weightless. Falling backward and throwing my assailant off balance with me.

Suddenly, we're both on the floor.

My shoulder hits first. The impact knocks the air from my lungs, and James pins me to the uneven ground, holding both of my arms down.

The building falls quiet, save for our winded breathing and the blood rushing in my ears. His shoulders rise and fall, his hands shifting slightly with each breath. I can't make out his expression in the darkness. Only wide eyes, reflecting what little light there is. The faint, lingering scent of alcohol and smoke.

And, still frozen, I can't move.

"Come on," he gasps. "Where's the necklace?"

*Oh, it's...*

*Not around my neck, is it?*

The gentle weight is missing. Because the River Sapphire is tucked inside a coat pocket. I could hand it over. If he's serious about letting me go, it's the easiest way out, but… *The gemstone is irreplaceable.* Ice went through a lot of trouble to get it for me.

*But, if I don't give it to James, how will I get out of here?*

"I don't— Ah—" I shake my head and wince as pain flares between my eyes, but I keep talking. "I don't have it. I'm sorry. I don't. So, please—"

*Ugh...*

He grits his teeth. Wide eyes scour my face and then my neck, where a necklace would be.

His expression falters for an instant, but he shakes his head too. "No way. You'd never go anywhere without it, right? So where is it? Come on…"

*What does he think he knows about me?*

Why was he at Ice's house in the first place? Did he know I'd be there? There's no way this was an accident, right?

"No!" I twist about, trying to free my arms. He tells me to stop, and I scream. "I don't have the stupid necklace! I already told you. Get off of me!"

"Stop," he says again, his voice quiet.

*From the floor, I just can't manage to—*

An attempt to knee him in the groin fails—I miss by a wide

margin—and he laughs weakly. A tired, uneasy sound.

Then something heavy clatters to the floor.

James freezes, his wide eyes locked off to the side. My left. *In the direction of...* A pit grows in my riling stomach as I follow his gaze. It takes a moment to register what he saw, but light glints off whatever fell from his pocket, and my breath catches.

*He wasn't kidding.*

A black handgun. Hardly a foot away.

*Aah—*

I almost scream again, but I feel an opening—a weakness in James' hold on my arm through the heavy coat material. Drawing in a deep breath, I wrench the arm upwards. His grip slips from the oversized sleeve, and my right arm is free.

He sputters. "Hey, wait—!"

As he scrambles to stand, he drags me to my feet. The room spins from the abrupt movement, renewing the nausea and stabbing pain behind my eyes. I press my free hand to my sticky temple to hold it in.

James glances toward the gun on the floor, and then to me. His eyes like saucers, his jaw slack. Raising his hands to chest level, one still holding my wrist, he shakes his head wildly.

"I didn't mean to—"

"What the hell is wrong with you?" My voice trembles, and I keep my now-free arm close to my chest and obscured inside the sleeve. "Why do you want the River Sapphire, anyway?"

"Is that what it's called?" he asks blankly, the words slurred. He quickly covers one eye with his free hand and returns to shaking his head. "I just need it. You don't understand. I just—

Please listen to me."

*Why should I?*

Hot, angry tears fill my eyes. One spills over, rolling down my warm cheek. Another follows, and suddenly I'm crying.

James recoils, stepping back as some other, more complicated emotion overcomes him. His focus darts around the room. At my face. My free arm. The gun. His hand still tightly wrapped around my wrist. Then he shakes his head again, stammering but not saying anything meaningful.

I don't get it.

*But I don't care.*

Ice and the twins are wondering where I am. I have to get back to Westbrooke. I don't care if I messed up by kissing Ice earlier, I just…

*Ah…*

Tugging on my restrained arm, I scream at him. To let me go. To leave me alone. But he keeps shaking his head, teeth clenched, one hand balled in his short hair while the other holds my wrist.

"You don't understand," he says, his low voice trembling. "If that necklace can—"

*Shut up!*

"Let go of me, you freak!"

He meets my glare with a blank gaze. Empty, shadowed eyes. But I ignore it. Teeth bared, I hit him with everything I have. The sharp smack of my palm striking his cheek echoes in the dark room until a deep, uncomfortable silence replaces it.

Pain flares in my scraped palm, but James is frozen in place.

Like he's no longer breathing. His glassy eyes open wider than ever, not focusing on anything.

*Like he might burst into tears any moment too.*

His mouth opens wordlessly. He looks down at the floor. His shoulders rise shakily as he takes a sharp breath, and his grip on my wrist relaxes.

I free my arm with little resistance.

My eyes gloss over the gun on the floor, but I leave it. I push past James and stumble toward the front of the building.

He calls after me—*Hey, wait!*—but he doesn't move to stop me even as I take off. Even as I trip on the steps outside. Even as I wipe the tears from my face with the dusty sleeve of Ice's coat and pick myself up off the ground and keep running.

He's not following?

I run past the car with its lights on and doors still thrown open. I run down the road for a minute—or two or five; I don't know—before I make a sharp left turn to duck into the forest and disappear in the darkness of the trees.

I stop and plant my hands against the rough bark of a large evergreen. I lean into the tree, panting as a pervasive soreness sets in. My head is killing me. My lungs burn. My side aches. My palms sting. My ankle hurts. My pounding heart threatens to burst from my chest.

The lingering nausea is the least of my concern, but it's enough to bring me to my knees. I cough and cough and cough, struggling to catch my breath and regain control of my body.

*This might take a minute.*

I curl up on the ground. I breathe. I cry. I try to keep quiet and small—to blend into the forest floor. When my breath finally comes soft and easy, I reach into the coat wrapped around me, and I find the River Sapphire in an internal pocket. I stare at the dark outline of the pendant in my trembling hand.

*What would have happened if I didn't take the necklace off when I did? If I was still wearing it when I found James in the backyard?*

With shaky hands, I fasten the chain around my neck. I sit with my back to the tree trunk. The road is only a few yards away, but I haven't heard or seen any cars.

Maybe he isn't planning to follow at all.

Either way, I don't have my phone, so I can't call for help. All I can do now is try to make my way back to Ice's house. *Or at least back to civilization.*

Groaning, I climb to my feet with the tree's help and carry on, trudging through the woods that border the gravel road. After what feels like forever, the trees clear, and I pop out onto a real street.

Pavement beneath the thin soles of my Converse.

I comb my hair with my fingers, situating it to hide the wound on my temple, and continue in the direction of buildings and light pollution. I pass a few houses. A convenience store—closed. A thrift shop—also closed. It's probably like 3AM. More houses with dark windows. When I come to a larger four-way intersection, I stop to read the road signs on the light pole.

*Wait— I know this place!*

I am still in Riverview.

*Thank god...*

I'm on the outskirts of town, to the south, but Ice's house isn't too far. It'll take about an hour, maybe a little longer in this condition, but I can make it. I feel safer under the streetlights on a major road, anyway.

All that's left to do is get there.

# thirty-four

~ ∞ ~

*It's dark. It's cold. I'm floating.*

*Floating? No. I'm lying down.*

*I sit up, but my eyes open to nothing. It's pitch black. And dead silent, save for my soft breathing. There's no sign of light, or anything else— But I can see my shoulder. Hair. Hands.*

*How?*

*How can I see myself, but not—?*

*Where am I? How did I get here?*

*Confused, I look over my shoulder.*

*—No.*

*I'm not alone, but that's impossible. Why is it…*me?

~ ∞ ~

# thirty-five

I open my eyes to a white ceiling and a stab of panic.

*Where—?*

I sit up, but relief quickly washes over me. I'm in bed, in Ice's bedroom, half covered by the soft, warm comforter. Bright light streams in through the curtains. It's morning—8:46AM, according to the clock on the end table—and I'm alone.

My mouth is dry. My stomach aches. A dull throb radiates from the base of my skull…

*Last night—!*

As if on its own, my hand moves to my face, but— *How is this possible?* The nagging headache is there, but I find no tender wound at my temple. I run my fingers through my hair. No blood comes away, not even a dry flake. And my palms are smooth and soft. No scrapes. No dirt.

Last night… *I was hurt, wasn't I?*

I feel sick. A little sore. I flex my fingers, and my hands are fine. I check my hairline from ear to ear, but there's no evidence a wound was ever there. Even my reflection in the mirror beyond the foot of the bed looks fine—confused but clean and uninjured.

*Am I wrong? Was it a dream?*

I tug at the loose cuffs of the unfamiliar shirt I'm wearing. The wine-red men's dress shirt doesn't fit me at all and is unbuttoned enough to have fallen aside and exposed one of my shoulders when I sat up. *Is this Ice's? Why am I wearing it?*

I remember kissing him, but—

What the hell happened last night?

I adjust the shirt's collar, fastening two more buttons, and take another look around. My phone is on the bedside table. The River Sapphire lies beside it. I took the necklace off while walking last night, but…

*What are these blurry memories?*

Pushing the covers aside, I find I'm still wearing the same jean shorts as yesterday. A smear of darkness stains the denim on the right side.

Is that…*blood?*

*Oh.*

I hit my head. I fainted. And then… *James was there, right? A gravel road. A huge building.* We fought, and I escaped. *Lying on the cool ground in the dark. The sound of my feet crunching leaves.* But I don't remember getting back, and I definitely do not remember changing my clothes.

*Ugh...*

I never want to drink ever again.

Slowly and carefully, I leave the bed. I stand, shifting my weight. My right ankle is sore, but it doesn't feel like I twisted it. I feel okay. Mostly. I don't think I'll throw up either, but I definitely need some water.

I look to the closed bedroom door.

Whatever happened, it wasn't good. I'm sure Ice and Night have questions, but the entire evening—everything after I kissed Ice—is a blur.

*Trees. Pain. A red, blinking crosswalk light.*

James wanted the River Sapphire.

*But why?*

What would the River Sapphire mean to an immortal? Why would he want it so badly, he would…?

Frowning, I pocket the necklace. My hand hovers over the doorknob for a long moment. Then I take a deep breath, roll my aching shoulder, and pull the door open.

*Aah—*

Ice is there, sitting on the floor with his back against the opposite wall. Eyes closed and arms folded over his chest. His head is tipped to one side, and his shoulders rise and fall slowly and evenly.

He's asleep?

*Right outside the door?*

He must have been so worried when I didn't meet them at the cul-de-sac. And then to find me gone when they came looking? Leaving was a mistake. I didn't need my phone. I was embarrassed, sure, but…

Ugh.

Should I wake him up? Ask if he knows anything? What happened or how long I was gone? I made my way back somehow, so I must have been conscious. Did we talk before I fell asleep?

I scraped my hands and knees on gravel—I clearly remember

the pain in my palms—but there's nothing now. Was any of it real?

*Was it all a dream?*

Did I fall asleep in Ice's room and imagine everything else? Or did I faint on the patio for some reason? Did they move me inside after they found me passed out there? Maybe the stain on my shorts is ketchup.

I look to Ice again.

*There's only one way to find out.*

Stepping closer, I kneel in front of him and tap his arm once. His muscles tense, and his eyes snap open as he wakes.

"Jayde—"

His hands land on my shoulders, and I lose my balance and fall into a sit on the floor. He doesn't apologize. He just searches my face with sharp, focused eyes.

"What happened last night?" he asks.

I blink at him, my soft laughter nervous. "Actually, I wanted to ask you the same thing."

"You don't remember?"

I shake my head. His hands fall from my shoulders, and the fire in his eyes dies down.

"Well, I remember…something," I admit, glancing away, "but I don't know what really happened and what didn't. I thought I was hurt, but—"

"You were," he says.

"I was?"

He sighs, leans back against the wall, and runs a hand through his hair. "You had a head injury. Scrapes on your hands and knees. I cleaned you up, and Night's twin healed the wounds."

"...Huh?"

I stare at my palms.

He explains Smoke's minor healing ability, and a sense of cold, sinking dread pools in my chest as I come to understand. When I don't respond, Ice repeats his question—asking what happened after I left.

My gaze flicks up from my hand. His eyes are guarded, and his jaw is tense, like he's struggling to avoid looking too pissed off.

"You were out cold when I got back," he says, "but Night told me you mentioned James."

*James—*

My headache flares, a sharp pain behind my eyes. Gasping, I press a hand to my forehead. It's like the fuzzy memories want to break free. Like they're trapped just beneath the surface, but I can't quite reach anything more than tiny snippets.

*The scent of cigarette smoke. A tall, dark building. The wood floor littered with debris. My stinging palms. The twisting pain. A brief weightlessness. Gravity. Blood. Dripping.*

*Why is there so much blood? There wasn't nearly that much—*

The image shatters as skin brushes my chin, and Ice gently tilts my head up with curled fingers. I meet his gaze reluctantly, my eyes filling with tears I don't quite understand. Then his hand falls away.

He looks...frustrated. "Tell me, Jayde. What did James Reid do to you?"

"He—" I pause to wipe my eyes. "Well, um... I found my

phone on the table. On the patio. He was in the backyard. I didn't even notice him at first. And I guess I fainted?"

"You fainted?" he asks, wholly unimpressed.

"I guess? I mean, I hit my head when I fell, and then… I woke up in a car? In the backseat. James was driving, and—"

Ice's eyes widen—a flash of wild panic. He grabs my arm with a warm hand, and my stomach twists. *Gold eyes, wide and empty. A trembling hand wrapped around my wrist. A desperate, pleading voice.*

"What did he say to you?" Ice asks with a rough urgency.

"He didn't say anything," I stammer, my head aching as I shake it. "Not really, anyway. He just wanted the River Sapphire."

"The—"

His expression blanks. Leaning against the wall again, he nods and glances away. Then he releases my arm. His grip hadn't been tight, and my wrist doesn't hurt, but I rub the affected skin anyway.

*What the heck...*

"James wanted the necklace?" His eyes flick up to meet mine. "Did he happen to mention why?"

I frown, trying to remember. He just…kept asking for it. Over and over. *The necklace. The blue necklace. Please. I need it.* I'm not sure he explained why or said much else.

"No. He seemed kind of out of it. To be honest, I was too."

"I see."

With a heavy sigh, Ice stands. He offers a hand to help me up, and I accept. When he drops my hand, I scratch my arm.

"How do you feel?" he asks.

"Like I should have stopped after the first drink," I say with a laugh. His answering smile is clearly forced, so I drop mine. "No. I'll be fine."

"Did he hurt you?"

There's a certain uncomfortable coldness in both his words and eyes. A careful focus. A soft, quiet anger. Seething.

"He didn't really, um…" *My back hitting solid wood. Both arms pinned. The shadowed silhouette above me. Light glinting off a black handgun in the low light.* I shake my head. "No. I fell. He just scared me half to death."

"Hm. Right." His hand brushes the top of my head, but I can't bring myself to meet his gaze. "Go drink some water."

He stops messing with my hair. Then, with another sigh, he walks past me and shuts himself in his bedroom. I stare at the door for a long moment.

Then, my jaw set, I glance down at my arm.

When Ice grabbed my wrist, all that flashed through my mind was the look in James' eyes. Realization. Blank terror. Guilt. *What was he thinking?* Even if he was as messed up as I was last night, what went through his head before he threw me in the back of his car after I knocked myself out?

*What was he even doing here?*

A door opens behind me. When I turn, Night is already out of her bedroom. She closes the last step between us and wraps her arms around me. A tight, warm hug.

My eyes fill with moisture again.

"Are you okay?" She steps back, revealing wide eyes full of maternal concern. "You were so weak when you showed up, you collapsed on the front steps. We cleaned you up, and Smoke healed your injuries, but—"

"I'm okay. Hungover, I guess, and sore, but I'm okay."

She frowns. "Maybe you should drink some water."

"Ice said the same thing."

She glances from me to Ice's bedroom door. "You spoke with him already?" Then, meeting my gaze, she smiles rather uneasily. "Oh, right, let's get you that water first."

I don't argue, so she leads me into the great room, where she has me sit at the breakfast nook while she roots around in the kitchen. I stare at my palms. I can still imagine the stinging where the gravel broke skin, but it doesn't feel real without evidence.

"Hey—" My voice is hesitant. "What happened last night?"

"Honestly, we weren't too concerned when you didn't show up," she says, joining me at the table with two glasses of water. "We walked back, thinking you fell asleep or something, so Ice damn-near lost his mind when we realized you weren't here. Smoke found a broken glass and blood out on the patio, and Ice took off. I have no idea where he went—driving around looking for you, I suppose. Then, a couple hours later, the security camera detected movement in the front yard, and there you were. With blood on your face."

She falls quiet, both hands on her glass. She stares into the water for a moment before glancing up.

"When I asked you what happened, you mentioned James, but…" Her voice catches, though she recovers quickly and forces a sad smile. "There's no way he did this, is there?"

"Um… Well, he was in the backyard—the same guy I saw

at the mall. I hit my head when I fainted, and I scraped my hands when I jumped out of his car, so…"

"He kidnapped you?" she gasps, hiding her face in her hands.

"I don't really know," I admit. "He wanted the River Sapphire and freaked out when I wouldn't give it to him, but he… He didn't even chase me when I ran away."

"He wanted the River Sapphire?" Her realization gives way to dismay, and, flashing another weak smile, she glances away. "Oh, James, you poor fool…"

"You know why he wanted it?"

She hugs her arms to her chest, gazing out the window. "James is what some call defective. He's never been able to morph. If he found out about you—or learned that Ice sponsored you, and you received a pendant from Human-Immortal Affairs—I'm afraid he may have thought—"

"—it would let him turn into a cat?" The words roll off my tongue with a bitter taste and awful weight.

*I forgot.*

I totally forgot what Ice said when I first asked about James. He's defective. He can't morph. *He's hardly an immortal.*

He only wanted the River Sapphire because he thought—

"But it's linked to the user by DNA." My voice rises. "Even if I gave it to him, it wouldn't do anything. If I knew—if I watched how much I drank last night—maybe I could have…"

*Could have what? Talked to him?*

He was completely out of it. Would he have listened?

"This isn't your fault," she says mildly. "James is…troubled. That much is obvious. But Ice must be furious about the whole thing." She glances toward the den, chewing the tip of her thumb. "I should talk to him."

*What good will that do? He barely talked to me at all.*

I avert my eyes. "He did seem upset."

"I'm sorry—about last night, and if Ice was harsh with you this morning." She stands from the table. "Will you be okay?"

"Some ibuprofen would be nice," I say with a sigh.

"Top right drawer in the bathroom," she says, already inching backward. "Let Smoke know if you need anything else. He can't fix hangovers, though, so, um… Sorry."

I thank her.

Once she's gone, I drop my forehead to the tablecloth.

# thirty-six

Ice has been avoiding me all day.

Whether it's because of what happened last night—whichever unfortunate thing that might be—or our talk after I woke up or maybe something said during the two-hour conversation he had with Night this morning, I have no idea, but it sucks.

At least I feel better physically. My stomach doesn't hurt. My headache is minimal. My shoulder is still rather tender. I must have bruised it, but I'll be fine. It's nothing I won't get over.

Though, I remember the night more clearly now.

The way Ice dismissed me after I kissed him, playing it off like nothing. Climbing the electronic gate to get back into Westbrooke because I couldn't remember the passcode. The horror in James' eyes. I may have hit him. I think he started crying as I took off.

*Ugh.* I almost wish I didn't remember so much.

And Night won't stop hovering. She'll spend several minutes treating Ice with overcautious positivity—talking with a smile like everything is fine—and then cross the room to ask if I'm okay or need anything. I keep drinking water and reading the cheesy chick-lit novel she lent me and trying to take it easy, but she's stressing me out.

Even worse, Ice periodically glances at me from his spot at the dining table—like he has no idea what to do or how to approach me. I get that. I don't know how to approach people all the time, but I never expected him to have a similar problem.

*Considering the circumstances, though...*

Should I say something? Does he feel bad for not stopping me? Does he blame himself for what James did—or that I was hurt?

Either way, we can't sit in the same room and ignore each other all afternoon. It's too awkward. Smoke has said more than Ice has today, and I only saw him for a few minutes after my shower and during lunch.

I glance up from the book as Night stands from the table with her teacup in hand. She ruffles Ice's hair. He swats her hand away, his annoyance passive at best. With a soft laugh, she dips into the kitchen and rinses her cup in the sink.

*There's no perfect time to do this, so...*

I set the book on the coffee table and take another breath to hype myself up before I leave the safety of the couch. Ice doesn't look up from his iPad as I cross the room toward him. He continues typing like I'm not there.

When I clear my throat, standing only a foot away, he finally offers me his reluctant attention.

"Are you okay?" I ask.

"Am I—?" He tips his head, his expression blank. Then he smiles and refocuses on the iPad. "Yes, of course. Are you?"

*Right...*

I run a loose strand of my hair through my hand. "I'm okay. I just wanted to apologize. For how I acted last night. I drank too much, so… I hope you don't blame yourself for what happened."

"I don't."

*Aah— You don't?*

He locks his tablet, sets it on the table, and looks to Night. He asks her to give us a minute—*alone*. She bristles for an instant but quickly recovers and dries her hands on the nearest dish towel.

"It's probably good that you talk," she says.

"That's the idea," he replies, his voice deadpan.

"Be nice." She walks past the table, reacting to Ice's apparent disinterest with a sigh before she smiles at me. "I'll be in my room—in case he gives you any trouble."

*What kind of trouble does she think he'll give me?*

Ice's narrowed eyes track her path out of the great room, and the room fills with an uncomfortable silence as he remains focused on the empty archway she left through.

"I don't think she trusts me," he says with a muted smile.

"Why not?"

"It's hard to say. Perhaps she doesn't believe I've grown up. I'm older than her, but she still treats me like a child." He meets my gaze. "Isn't that funny?"

I frown. "You're upset about what happened last night, right?"

"What is there for me to be upset about?" he asks, distaste creeping into his voice. "You're here, you're fine, and you have the River Sapphire. Yes, last night was…rather unfortunate, but it's nothing of consequence."

*Uh-huh. Right.*

"You can be honest with me, you know?"

He laughs easily. "Oh, Jayde. You do not want me to be honest with you on this one."

I take a deep breath, biting the inside of my cheek before I sit at the table and fold my hands on the cool, glass surface.

So, he's *quite mad* about the whole thing. That's fine. What James did was not okay, but this can't be entirely okay either.

"I am curious, though," he says. "As to exactly what James did last night. You mentioned waking up in his car. Do you remember anything else?"

I hesitate but say, "Yeah. I remember."

He listens intently, his expression fixed, as I explain the gist of what happened after I woke up in the back of James' car. How I jumped out and ran into the creepy, dark building. How he kept asking for the River Sapphire—the necklace he didn't even know the name of. The gun that fell from his pocket and gave me the chance to escape. After that, everything's fuzzy.

"I think, um—" I look up from my hands. "I think he was… pretty drunk too. But I know that's not an excuse."

His eyes narrow. "No, it's not."

"I think…the whole night was a mistake."

"The whole night?"

Our eyes meet, and my face grows hot. "I drank way too much. I wasn't thinking clearly, and I messed up."

"Humans aren't very resilient, are they?" he asks with a soft laugh that quickly fades. "I suppose it shouldn't surprise me if James is similar in that regard. Still, intoxicated or not, what did he think the River Sapphire would do for him even if he did take it from you last night? Is he so desperate he managed to convince himself it would help him morph?"

I glance away pointedly, but I'm not surprised he feels that way. If he didn't care for James before, he certainly likes him even less now.

"There aren't many people in the Human Immortal Program, right?" I mumble, wringing my hands. "I can't imagine the way the gemstones work is common knowledge…"

"Don't tell me you feel bad for him."

I look to him again, but his wry smile only confuses me more.

"It is kind of sad, isn't it?" I ask.

He rolls his eyes as disgust tugs at one side of his mouth. "Oh, I agree, Jayde. It's very sad. But a man like James Reid is hardly deserving of your pity."

"I guess you're right."

"Hm." Frowning, his eyes flick down as his expression levels out. "I've been thinking, considering recent events, that perhaps you should avoid interacting with other immortals as freely as you have the past two weeks."

For some reason, I laugh. "Avoid all immortals? Why? Just because one guy had a psychotic break?"

"No," he says, his voice sharp. "They simply don't understand your situation, and it puts you at risk—as last night so clearly demonstrated."

"That's not fair. I don't even understand my situation, but immortals aren't the issue. James is the only one I've had any problem with. Everyone else has been nice. Or at least ignored me."

His eyes narrow. "You do realize James only knew who you

are and where to find you because of Night and her friends, right? This would never have happened if she didn't get you involved in her social life."

"That's not true."

"You don't think so?"

My hands ball into fists. "No. I don't. And I will hang out with whoever I want, thanks."

"Oh?" He laughs once, his eyes somewhat brighter. "You're not concerned at all?"

"Concerned about what?" I ask, scratching my arm as I lose steam. "Last night, James looked almost as scared as I was. It was a mistake, and, like you said, I'm fine, so maybe we should just…forget it happened?"

Fingers brush my cheek, sliding up my jawline, and Ice cups my face in both hands. Warm. Strong. My breath catches, and a chill runs down my spine as our eyes meet. A foreign electric shock at the sight of blue eyes. Then he tips his head, still smiling that passive, curious smile.

"You want to forget the whole evening?" he asks.

His voice carries a strange lightness, and I stare back at him, my throat suddenly dry. *The whole evening? Everything after I drank too much? The kiss? James? Everything? Is that possible?*

"Maybe I do," I say.

"Done."

He grins, and his hands leave my face. He stands from the table and pushes the chair in. Then, facing me, he crosses his arms. His posture is casual, though. Relaxed. So comfortable, it makes me nervous.

"Now," he says breezily, "about the skyrockets you missed out on; you were looking forward to watching them, right?"

"Oh, um…"

Glancing away, I raise a hand to my warm cheek. *Is it seriously so easy for him to push the feelings down and act like nothing happened?*

"We never set them off," he reasons. "If you still want to see them, we can try again tonight. I'll take you."

I force a smile. "Sure. I'll go."

# thirty-seven

Smoke sighs and leans back into the couch. "Man, if I didn't have a livestream scheduled tonight, I'd tag along to watch those fireworks."

"I'd hate to keep you from your loyal followers," Ice says, his voice dangerously dry.

"When are you planning to leave?" Night asks. She glances from Smoke to me and Ice, where we sit on the other loveseat. "It's getting late."

He laughs. "Are you worried? If it makes you feel any better, we're taking the car, and I doubt Jayde has any intention of running off on her own this time."

*Ha—*

"I'm not worried," she insists. "It's just— Well, it's been a long couple of days, hasn't it? I'm sure Jayde wants to go home."

Everyone looks to me. Skeptical. Expectant. Mildly concerned. My face goes hot, and I scratch my cheek.

*I haven't thought much about going home.*

Things have calmed down since this morning. Everything has been as pleasant as can be considering the circumstances, with no further mention of anything that happened last night, and Ice isn't avoiding me.

So I shrug.

He smiles. "Perhaps we should get to it, then. Ready to go?"

I nod, but I can't match his smile. Even the passing memory of the awful, itchy dread is enough to leave me unsettled.

"Don't keep her out too late," Night says.

"It's only three fireworks," I say, hoping to reassure us both. "I'm sure it won't take long."

Ice stands from the couch. "No, it won't."

I glance at the crack of fading light at the far end of the thick curtain over the sliding glass door. There's nothing to be nervous about, right? I'll be with Ice the whole time. We're taking the car. Everything will be fine. And then I'll go home.

*Right?*

"You coming?"

"Oh—!" I tear my eyes from the door and pop up from the couch too. "Yeah, I'm coming. Just gotta grab my bag."

I grab my backpack from behind the loveseat. Smoke offers me a passive smile and wave, while Night wishes me well. Then I follow Ice down the dark hallway to the garage.

Once we're both inside the car, and I nestle my backpack at my feet, he passes the small cardboard box of fireworks over the center console. I hold it in my lap and study the three thick, cardboard tubes inside. Each is decorated with brightly colored construction paper, contains a golf ball–sized round, and has a long fuse trailing out from a hole near the bottom.

"Where'd you get these?" I ask. "Out of state?"

He snorts, a real laugh. "Try right down the street. Some kid

Night knows in the neighborhood makes them every year, so I had her buy a few off of him. Consolation for not attending his party, I suppose."

"They're homemade?" I suddenly feel like I'm holding a box of bombs. "Are they safe?"

"They're as safe as fireworks can be. I've never heard of any unfortunate mishaps over the years, but you can hide behind me if you want."

"I'm not scared."

He laughs again, more mildly this time. "Nor should you be."

I peer into one of the cardboard tubes. How far up into the sky will they fly? What color will they be? How big will they look, standing so close?

"Maybe we should have gone to the party," I say quietly.

"No." His voice carries an unexpectedly harsh edge. "It's for the best that we avoided it."

"Oh?"

I look up, but his eyes are focused on the road ahead. With both hands on the steering wheel, his expression appears neutral—contemplative, maybe? It doesn't quite match his tone.

The car pulls up to the curb near the front of the cul-de-sac. The engine idles, headlights illuminating the *SOLD* sign in front of the nearest empty lot. With a sigh, he leans against the steering wheel, still watching out the windshield with narrowed eyes.

"You can stay with us for a while," he says. I make a soft noise, and he glances over. "There's not much for you at home right now, is there?"

For a second, I'm relieved—the prospect of my empty house isn't the most appealing right now—but why offer to let me stay? He's still pretending that nothing happened yesterday, right? Is it not as easy for him as he makes it look? Is *he* worried about me?

"Is that okay?"

He shrugs, his expression softening. "I can't imagine it would be much trouble. The twins like you well enough. But I'm your sponsor, Jayde. You're my responsibility now."

*Is that all?*

"Oh, well… I guess I can stay a few days."

"Night may complain, but she'll get over it. We can stop by your place when we're done here." A deep breath. Then he clears his throat and smiles. "Now then, let's set off those fireworks."

We cross to the far side with one of the mortars—leaving the other two on the hood of the car. I listen while he explains the fuse length. Once he lights the fuse, we have about fifteen seconds to make it back to the car before the shell launches. Technically, the car is not a "safe" distance away from the empty lot, but he says it with a laugh like I shouldn't worry. I guess he trusts the guy who made them.

*Still…*

"I'll head back before you light it," I say.

He laughs again. "Go on, then."

I jog back to the car and turn to watch as Ice kneels beside the firework. The tiny, bright flame of a pocket lighter held against the paper fuse. A spark as it catches, and his silhouette glancing over one shoulder. A white cat takes his place and dashes across the blacktop, and he returns to human form a few paces away.

He smooths his shirt, and we watch the fuse burn. A tiny light in the dark that disappears into the cardboard mortar. I hold my breath.

*How loud will it be? How bright?*

A beat of silence.

With a flash of light, a whistling streak shoots out of the tube and flies into the sky. I track it with my eyes—up, up, up, at least a hundred feet in the air—until it goes off with a deafening *BANG!* The burst sheds a globular shower of white sparks and red stars and pale smoke that fills the sky above the cul-de-sac.

A chunk of smoldering cardboard hits the ground with a thud halfway between us and the spent mortar.

"Whoa!"

The sparks fade to black as they drift down from the sky. My heart still racing, I turn to Ice. He watches me with eyes reflecting green in the low light.

"It's that exciting for you?" he asks.

"Mm… I think we're standing too close."

He laughs and excuses himself to set up the second firework. I stay with the car, still unconvinced this is in any way safe. If I lived around here, I'd call the police. Though, dozens of similar fireworks went off in the neighborhood last night, so they might be used to it on holidays.

*Ugh... This is cool, though.*

A feline Ice races back and morphs before reaching the car. He stands a little closer than before. Another inch or two, and his arm would brush mine. But we don't touch, and his eyes zero in on the empty lot across the road.

*Whoosh.*

*Ziiiiiip—*

I catch sight of the flying shell, more prepared for the blast than I was the first time. Like cannon fire resonating within my chest. A shower of white and gold and green. The sparks dim and fall as the smoke drifts higher into the sky. It was so bright, white specks dance around my vision.

For some reason, I want to apologize again. For leaving the group last night. Or for kissing him. Or something. But he hasn't mentioned the kiss once, and he was so eager to pretend like the whole day never happened when I suggested it.

"Last one," he says.

I nod.

He takes the final mortar and crosses to the other side again.

The wind picks up, and I brush my hair out of my face and over my shoulder. A finger swipes the River Sapphire's chain as my hand falls away, shifting the pendant's weight against my skin.

*A chill down the spine. Goosebumps prickle on my arm.*

What's up with that?

I rub my arms, glancing up as Ice sprints from the far side of the cul-de-sac in feline form a third time. Morphing beside me, he runs a hand through his hair and once again turns to watch the fuse burn without speaking.

"The cat thing must be convenient sometimes," I say.

Smiling, his eyes flick down to meet mine. "I suppose it's more comfortable than jogging in denim."

Then he returns his attention to the firework in the distance.

*Whoosh.* My eyes don't leave his face. *Ziiiiip*— Even as the ball shoots into the sky, and his chin lifts as he tracks its upward path, I don't look away.

An instant of silence. A flicker of focused anticipation in his eyes before the earsplitting blast drowns out my question:

*Do you really like me?*

The multicolored sparks in my periphery reflect in his eyes as he turns to face me, and he tips his head.

"What's that?" he asks.

*He didn't hear.*

My face catches fire, but I laugh, shake my head, and wave my hands disarmingly.

"Oh, no. It's nothing."

He watches me with a touch of skepticism before ruffling my hair with his hand, which touches my shoulder for a moment as he looks back toward the empty lot.

"We better collect the debris and get out of here," he says.

Maybe there is a risk of someone calling the police?

I nod, grab the empty cardboard box, and follow at Ice's side.

"Was it everything you hoped it to be?" he asks. "Considering the circumstances?"

"It was neat. And you were right. They were bright. And loud. Um…" My eyes glaze over his empty hand before darting up as I suppress my caught breath. "Well, thanks for taking the time to do this. And for offering to let me stay with you guys."

"Of course."

"It has been a long day, though."

*Unbelievably long.*

"Yeah?" He stops to pick up half of a spent cardboard shell. "You can take my bed tonight if you want."

*HAHAHA—*

"No, that's fine. I'll be okay in the den. Thanks, though!"

He laughs. "Have it your way, Jayde."

* * * * *

It's late.

Everyone already went to bed, and Smoke's music is off, so it's quiet. I've been lying in the dark with my phone screen dimmed for nearly an hour. After I finally manage to collect all fifteen daily bonuses in one of my idle games, I check FaceSpace.

It's almost midnight.

This sucks, but Rose is still online. I could call her.

I want to call her.

With a glance at the curtain over the sliding glass door, I leave the couch. I find the light jacket in my duffel bag and slip it on as I cross the room. Then I pull the curtain aside just enough to unlock the door and step through. The well-lit neighborhood leaves the general details of the backyard clearly visible. Even so, I switch the patio light on, descend the steps, and creep far enough out to peer down the narrow side yard.

It's empty, and the chain-link gate at the end is shut.

*As it should be.*

Somewhat reassured, I sit on the edge of the nearest garden planter and make the call. The phone rings once.

Twice.

Three times.

"Hello?" her voice asks.

*A rush of pure relief.*

"Hey, sorry for calling so late," I say. "I can't sleep."

"It's all good. It's not like I was just about to head to bed or anything." But she laughs, so I laugh too. "Anyway, what's up? You spent the Fourth with Ice, right? How'd that go?"

"Ah—"

"Not good?"

"Well—"

"Oh, boy."

"Shut up," I say through stifled laughter that quickly fades. "Well, um, I drank. Alcohol. And it didn't work out in my favor. I am never drinking again."

Silence. A gasp. "You didn't throw up on him, did you?"

"Thankfully not. But I did kiss him."

"And? Isn't that good? Isn't that what you wanted?"

"It's not good when he calls it nothing and pretends it never happened the next day." With a glance at Ice's bedroom window, I lower my voice. "I have no idea what to think, but he's still being super nice. He even offered to let me stay for a few more days, and I agreed because I've been so bored at home. Is that messed up?"

"Hold up. Slow down. What? Did he reject you?"

"No," I say sharply before clearing my throat. "That's what's so weird. He said he likes me right before I kissed him. But I drank a lot. Maybe he thought I was so wasted I had no idea what I was doing, and that's why he hasn't mentioned it? But it was so embarrassing. I can't look at him without thinking about it. I already apologized for drinking too much, but he obviously didn't want to talk about it. Aah… What do I do?"

"Uh… You guys need to talk about it. Sounds like you're not on the same page at all. Even I'm confused now."

"I don't know how to bring that up. I never would have kissed him if I didn't drink so much."

She groans. "Your relationship is worse than my soap operas. Why are you even with this guy? If it's not because he's hot and rich, I don't get it."

"No, you wouldn't." I sigh and rub my eyes. "Sorry. I feel like I'm just ranting now."

"Ranting is fine. This is something worth ranting about."

"I really like him. I just—"

"Are you okay, Jayde? Do you need help?"

I look up from my lap, but my eyes don't focus on anything in particular in the dimly lit backyard.

Am I okay?

Do I need help?

*After yesterday... Forget kissing Ice, I was—*

But I sigh. "No. Everything's fine. I'm just frustrated. I'm mad at myself for kissing him. And for messing up our plans. I've had a long day—I woke up early with a hangover. Ugh. And then we avoided each other half the day. But everything is fine now."

"Alright," she says slowly. "You'd tell me if something wasn't, right?"

"Of course," I lie.

# thirty-eight

This morning, Night asked if I wanted to get my hair cut. She's taking advantage of Carmen's offer to cut hers, and I— Well, I do not want to cut my hair, but it has been almost a year since I've done anything with it. I'm overdue for a trim.

And I wouldn't mind the distraction.

Things are back to business as usual at the Monroe house, but maybe life shouldn't feel normal so soon after… *Aah…*

Every time I picture the fleeting anticipation in Ice's eyes as the sparks from the final firework faded from the sky, another face flashes through my mind. Another emotion. Another place —dark and hot and dusty.

*I wish I could forget so easily.*

But it might help to get out for a couple hours.

Night looks happy as she bids Ice farewell on her way out of the den. I go to follow, but he stops me. He stands from the couch and asks if I intend to cut my hair.

Laughing, I shake my head. I've kept my hair long since middle school. It's part of my identity at this point.

"You don't have to indulge Night this way, you know," he says.

"I don't mind. It's nice to get out sometimes."

"If getting out is all you want, you only need to ask." For some reason, he seems confused. "I can take you anywhere you might want to go."

"Anywhere?"

He smiles, the playful expression so mischievous it borders on dark—like a dare. Then he reminds me that Night is waiting.

*Oops.*

I excuse myself and meet her out front. As we walk to her car, she no longer looks happy. And my facade falters too.

"Is everything okay?" I ask.

She laughs, the sound more like a choked sigh. "I don't know, Jayde. Is it?"

"Ah, well…"

"Never mind. We do need to talk. About Ice, of course, but—" She forces a smile and opens the passenger door for me. "—it can wait until after we see Carmen."

*She has ulterior motives in going out?*

It's disappointing, but I agree and climb inside.

She glances away. "I'm sure it goes without saying, but we shouldn't mention what happened the other day while we're there either."

"Right."

Night closes the door. I stare at my lap as she walks around the car, unable to look up even as she sits in the driver's seat. The car rumbles to life.

She sighs. "This trip isn't off to a great start, is it? I'm sorry, I just… I want to be careful. The last thing you need is more rumors circulating about you."

"More rumors?"

"Being human and all," she says without taking her eyes off the road.

What are people saying about me? *Nothing too awful, I hope...* Unless Ice had a point in suggesting I avoid other immortals? Did I misinterpret the entire conversation?

"What did he have to say back there, anyway?" she asks.

"Oh." I laugh nervously. "He asked if I was going to cut my hair. He might have been a little relieved when I said no."

Her expression softens, and the awkward atmosphere lifts. As she drives, she tells me more about the salon Carmen interns at. It's downtown, and the clientele consists mostly of immortals.

I'm not familiar with the salon, but it still blows my mind that there's essentially a separate, parallel society most humans don't notice. Anyone could see it if they knew what to look for. It's hidden in plain sight, nestled between a kitschy yarn shop and a Greek restaurant.

Walking inside, the salon is like any other I might have visited in the past, but I'm the only human in the building. The River Sapphire's passive weight on my skin does little to calm my nerves.

I am human, *other*, and everyone here knows it. Two younger girls seated in the lobby sneak curious glances as I approach the reception counter with Night.

She ignores them, so I try to do the same.

Carmen spots us from across the building. Her station is empty, and she basically sprints to meet us at the counter before another stylist has a chance.

"Wow! You managed to drag Jayde here too?" Her lavender eyes flick to me, the excitement within them tangible. "We gonna chop your hair off, or what?"

Night laughs, and I let Carmen down as gently as possible, but she shrugs in return. She knew perfectly well I have no intention of losing more than a couple inches.

"April can do your trim," she says. "She'll be done in a few minutes. Night, you can come back with me."

Night follows Carmen. I return to the waiting area.

Fortunately, there are plenty of chairs, so I can take one and leave two empty seats between me and anyone else. With my nose in my phone to avoid catching a stranger's eye, I scroll down an article about long hairstyles.

I haven't decided what to do with my hair. Should I get bangs? Layers? Right now, my hair is all the same length, so bangs might be nice. If anything, bangs will keep my hair out of my face and make it easier to wear down more often.

When I look up, one of the girls who snuck a glance earlier tears her eyes away. She holds her hand over her mouth and whispers to the girl beside her. I pocket my phone and mess with the River Sapphire, worrying my fingers over the cool stone. But I'm not mad about it.

*After all, I don't belong here.*

"Jayde," a voice calls.

One of the stylists stands by the reception counter, watching me. A smaller woman with brown hair in a neat bun on top of her head. She smiles as our eyes meet. *Blue.*

I stand to join her, and she leads me to the station beside Night and Carmen. The chair is incredibly comfortable for a salon chair.

“Do you know what you want?” she asks, her voice kind.

“Just a trim. And bangs, I guess.”

“We can do that.”

Carmen chuckles off to the side. “Playing it safe, huh?”

“I don’t think I can handle more change right now,” I mutter, pulling my hair out from underneath the salon cape.

“Anyway, April, this is the chick I was talking about,” Carmen says. “The one who knows about immortals and got one of those necklaces.”

“Oh, right.” Her casual tone comes across as only passively interested. “You said Ice Monroe told her?”

“Mm-hm… Seems to me like they’re dating.”

“Oh? You’re dating Ice? Is that true?”

*Why does she sound so surprised?*

I force a smile. “I don’t know if we’re dating, exactly, but he did sponsor me, and we have gone out a few times, so…”

I glance to Night’s reflection in the mirror. She doesn’t look uncomfortable, but her eyes are averted as Carmen works on her damp hair. It’s already significantly shorter.

“How’s that going for you?” April asks.

“It’s alright. I guess I’ve been worried—that I won’t fit in, you know? Everyone I’ve met is fun and cool, and no one’s been mean to me because I’m human or anything, but I’m…”

“Girl, shut up,” Carmen says with a laugh. “You’re cool too. If anyone is ever mean to you for being human, I’ll beat them up. Night will help, I'm sure."

Finally, she laughs a little. "I'm not sure how much help I'd be in a fight."

"I'm still pissed at Taylor for blowing us off last week. Did you know he blocked me after I told him he was a dick for ignoring our messages?"

"Taylor?" April asks. "You mean—? Oh. Right."

Night sighs. "We invited him to meet Jayde, but perhaps it's for the best that he didn't show. I'm not sure they'd get along."

"He's a dick," Carmen insists.

April walks around to the front of the chair to work on my bangs. "From what I remember, he was never accepted in high school. He never fit in. Everyone ignored him."

"That was high school," Night says mildly. "But Taylor didn't care to be accepted by immortals—not even by other social rejects. He didn't even try to reach out. Plenty of kids would have been his friend if he weren't so impossible to get along with."

Because he hates immortals and went to a school full of them?

"Anyway," she continues before Carmen can call Taylor a dick a third time. "I meant to ask earlier—how did Matthew's Fourth of July party turn out?"

Carmen laughs. "Oh, it was a blast. But, to be honest, I only remember the first few hours."

* * * * *

It was good to see Carmen, and April was nice, but it sounds like there are some rumors—about me and Ice and my new status as a human immortal. They didn't say anything negative, but, now that we're alone in the car, I feel weird about the whole thing.

Night, with her new airy pixie cut, seems a little bothered too. She didn't show it when we were inside, though. Her smile and laughter came easily, even when discussing the Fourth of July.

*Are all immortals like this?*

"So… Where's that café you were talking about? Because I think you drove us in a circle."

She grimaces. "I did. The café is right down the block, but I was thinking we could go to a teahouse instead. If that's okay with you."

"That's fine. Are you okay?"

"Me? Oh." She laughs. "I wanted to ask Carmen if she'd heard anything about James recently, but I didn't want to make you uncomfortable, and I was worried she'd ask questions I couldn't answer if I brought him up out of nowhere. I don't want to add fuel to the fire, you know?"

"Do you think she knows anything—about what happened, I mean?"

"Oh, no. If Carmen heard anything, she would have messaged me immediately. Still, I thought she might know something that could help explain why… But she didn't mention him at all."

I frown.

Night holds herself rather apprehensively, her hands tight on the steering wheel. *But what can I say?* She hasn't explained anything about her history with James—let alone how Ice ties into it.

"I want to understand," she says. "Even if James thought your necklace would help him, he isn't the type to— Ah…but I suppose it's been years since we last spoke. I have no idea what he's been up to. He may have changed. I don't know. It's all very…"

"Confusing?" I ask. Her answering smile is forced, and my frown deepens. "Were you friends with James in high school?"

She shakes her head. "It wasn't like that, exactly. It's more… complicated. But I don't want to talk about James. We need to talk about Ice."

"Okay… What about Ice?"

"Let's get a table first."

She falls quiet as she finds a parking spot.

While she fixes her short hair and situates an oversized bow on top of her head with the help of the rear-view mirror, I unbuckle my seatbelt and check myself out in the side mirror through the window. The side-swept bangs are nice. My hair feels lighter, and I don't think I resemble a fifteen-year-old anymore.

I can get used to this.

Once we're done preening, we meet in front of the car. Night offers me a more collected smile than any of the ones she made during the drive.

"Sorry if I worried you," she says. "I'm just frustrated."

I grin. "Oh, me too."

With that, I follow her into The House of Tea. The interior is decorated in pastels and white. Greenery and chandeliers made from glass jars hang from the ceiling. The air is cool and smells of tea and spices. A hostess wearing a dress and frilly apron meets us inside. She has large amber eyes, is all smiles, and carries several small menus in one arm.

"Welcome! How can I help you ladies today?" she asks, her voice bright and refreshing.

"A patio table for two, please," Night says.

The hostess leads us through the sparsely populated tea room, out a door on the far wall, and onto a screened-in patio. We're the only customers outside, seated at a round table overlooking a small garden with a koi pond.

I accept a menu and skim the selection of daily hot teas, iced drinks, snacks, and desserts. I don't know much about tea, so I leave the decision-making up to Night—she orders a pot of milk oolong and a snack sampler.

The hostess smiles again before returning inside.

"We're lucky," Night says. "Business is slow today."

I run my finger over the cloth napkin, folded origami-style into the shape of a heart, on the table in front of me. *This is cute.* And Night fits right in here.

"So, what did you want to talk about?" I ask.

"Right." She laughs, sounding more at ease. "First things first, I wanted to assure you that immortals aren't as complex as you might think. We aren't very different from humans, emotionally speaking."

"I know that." *I'm not dumb.*

"Yes, well, I also wanted to make sure that Ice isn't making you keep…secrets? Or anything like that."

"Secrets?"

She nods, and I hesitate.

*Warm hands cupping my face. A blank smile, asking if I want to forget.* But that's not what she means, is it? She doesn't mean what happened the other day, and she's not referring to immortals. She means...*secrets*. Like something bad—something only the two of us know.

*Right?*

I shake my head. "Not really. The Fourth of July sucked, so we agreed to forget about it, but—" *Wait.* "Well, he did...*suggest* that I avoid other immortals because of what happened with James, but I said I'll hang out with whoever I want."

"Did you?" Her eyelids flutter, but her level expression doesn't change. "And he backed down?"

"Well, yeah."

She glances away. "Hm. I see..."

"Hey, um, it doesn't bother you that I like him, does it?"

"Why would it?" She frowns as she looks to me again. "Before this mess, I honestly thought having you around might be good for him. Even after he told you about immortals."

A small, nervous pit grows in my stomach.

"But?" I ask.

"You said you kissed him." Her thinly veiled grimace only confirms that she pities me. "It didn't go well, did it?"

My face flushes. "I was drunk. He knew that, so he was right to reject me, wasn't he?"

"Ice isn't so much of a gentleman."

A door opens. I bounce my knee, struggling to maintain composure as the hostess sets our table with a porcelain tea set and small, three-tiered serving tray adorned with an assortment of cute finger foods.

Night thanks her, her expression the pinnacle of pleasantry, and the hostess smiles before she leaves. I suck in a deep breath, my hands balling into fists as I refocus on Night.

"You think he doesn't like me?" I ask, though my blank tone makes it come across more like a statement than a question.

Instead of answering right away, she pours steaming, golden tea into two fragile, white cups. She slides one cup on its matching saucer toward me. When she finally meets my gaze again, her eyes tell me nothing.

"I don't know how to say this without upsetting you, Jayde."

*And the sinking feeling returns.*

"He does like you," she says. "If he didn't, he wouldn't bother keeping you so close—that's the type of person Ice is. However, I'm not sure his feelings are exactly what you hope them to be."

I stare into the depths of my teacup. "What does that mean?"

"You really do like him, don't you?" She sighs. "You should tell him yourself. When you're not intoxicated, of course. Don't let him mess with your head like this."

"Is that what he's doing?"

"Intentionally? I can't say."

She takes a careful sip of tea. I drop a sugar cube into mine and watch it dissolve in the hot liquid. When I look up from my cup, she's still frowning.

"You seriously have no idea why he told me about immortals?"

"He doesn't confide in me as often as you think he does," she says, her apologetic tone tinged with disappointment. "Especially now, when it comes to matters involving you."

"But you know him better than anyone else, right?"

She glances down at her cup, neither confirming nor

denying my assessment of their relationship.

"He acts like you know secrets," I say.

"Secrets? Me?" She suppresses a grimace. A flash of surprise. "I mean— Well, I suppose there are things he'd rather me not share with anyone, but—"

"Nothing about me?"

She considers my question, her nails tapping her porcelain cup. Then she sighs. "I may know Ice better than anyone, but you've surely realized he's not exactly an open book. Believe me; I've asked more times than I can count, but he will not tell me why he told you about immortals. Or why he decided to sponsor you. Or why he…wants to be with you."

"Because I'm human?"

"Because a lot of things, Jayde," she says with her teacup at her lip. Resting the cup on its saucer, she sighs *again*. "So, no, I don't have the slightest idea. Perhaps it was because he likes you. Perhaps it was out of spite—because I said he shouldn't. But it's entirely possible he only told you because he was bored. Whatever the reason, the situation changed the moment you learned of immortals—the moment he had that necklace made for you while he was in Seattle—and even he can't ignore that forever."

When I don't say anything, she apologizes and meets my gaze with a certain urgency. "That's why I think you need to talk. You need to— Well, you need to let him know that you're serious. Your emotions aren't a game, and he needs to make a decision. You can't let him do this to you. Teasing you with a relationship? Pretending to forget awful things? How is that fair?"

I blink. *The forgetting was my idea, but—* "It's not fair, is it?"

"No." Pink touches her cheeks, and she slaps them softly. When she refocuses, she's quite serious. "But you should know this, Jayde. Ice has a terrible habit of doing things for absolutely no reason. And, sometimes, he doesn't know when to stop—or how."

I pick up my teacup. The tea smells floral and creamy. Sweet from the sugar. Tasting it, it's smooth. No bitterness. The flavor reflects the scent.

*It's good.*

As I set the cup down, I sigh and meet Night's mild gaze. She looks a little concerned. A little hesitant.

"I think I understand," I say.

Her expression softens. "I hope you get your answers, Jayde. More than anything, I want you both to be happy."

* * * * *

We walk through the great room, still chatting, and find Smoke in the den. His eyes light up when he sees his sister, and he closes the distance between them.

"Aah—" Grinning, he fluffs up her feathery hair. "It's so short. So soft."

"It's different, isn't it?" she asks with a laugh.

"Short hair suits you. You look mature. Mom would like it."

"Mom would say I look like a proper businesswoman," she says, "but that's not quite what I was going for. I want to be elegant and ethereal."

Smoke laughs. "I like it. Yours too, Jayde."

"Ah, thanks!" *I'm surprised he mentioned me.*

"Have any plans for your hair?" Night asks her brother. "It's getting long."

"Hm…" He considers it before gathering the top section of his hair into a ball near the crown of his head. "I've thought about getting an undercut. Would I look good with a topknot?"

As Night laughs, and their conversation continues, I toss my purse onto the loveseat. I walk down the hall, I smooth my hair and fix my bangs, and then I knock on Ice's bedroom door.

A few seconds pass before a voice inside acknowledges me.

I crack the door and peek through. Ice is lying perpendicular on the bed, with his feet hanging over the edge and nearly touching the floor, and his eyes focused on the ceiling. It doesn't look very comfortable, but it doesn't seem to bother him.

*I wasn't expecting this, though.*

"We're back," I say, hesitance slipping into my voice.

"I heard."

Pushing the door open the rest of the way, I step inside. He doesn't move and keeps staring upwards with a most unreadable expression. Thoughtful, maybe? Tired? Annoyed? I can't tell.

"Are you okay?" I ask.

"I'm fine."

*Ugh…*

But he sits up, stretches, and does look fine when he finally meets my gaze. A little pensive. A little curious.

"You said you were out getting a haircut, right?"

"Oh…" My face flushes hot, but I ignore it and mess with my new bangs to make them more obvious. "I did."

He tips his head. A beat of silence. Then footsteps dash down the hall and stop in the doorway behind me. A hand slaps against the doorjamb as I glance over my shoulder to find Night standing there with a flustered fire in her eyes.

"Are you kidding me?" she asks, her frustration only partially feigned. "We both look great, don't we? Smoke said so."

Ice raises one eyebrow. "Smoke is gay, Night."

*Ah.*

"Hmph!"

Then he cracks. He laughs, holding a hand over his mouth, and leaves the bed to join us near the door. He tucks a stray lock of hair behind my ear and pats Night on the head.

"You both look lovely," he says. "There. Happy now?"

She groans, rolling her eyes, and retreats back to the den.

But I don't move. I stare up at him as his eyes return from following Night's path down the hallway.

She's convinced he likes me, but she also thinks he's messing with me somehow. *What does that mean?* Does he not understand my feelings, or is it something else? I could ask, but—

*Do I really want to have that conversation right now?*

"It's not a big change," I admit with a smile, "but…thanks."

# thirty-nine

Night was right. I need to talk to Ice.

I tried last night, while we were hanging out on the patio after dinner. We were alone. It was perfect. All I had to do was break the silence and say, "How do you feel about me?"

*But I couldn't.*

Then he asked how much longer Rose will be out of town, so I talked about her for a while. We talked about his studio apartment in Palo Alto and the book Night let me borrow. The conversation was easy and comfortable. I didn't want to screw it up by talking about my feelings. And—

*Ugh.*

I'm such a baby.

The worst thing he can do is say he lied on the Fourth of July or that he doesn't like me the same way. Or change the subject without addressing my question at all. I'm not expecting a heartfelt confession or an apology or anything, so I don't even know what the best outcome would be.

Recognition? Sympathy? *A less awkward kiss?*

What do I even want?

I agreed to pretend nothing happened too. I hate thinking

about it. How much I drank. The kiss. What James did. Smoke may have healed the wounds, but the memories aren't gone. It still happened.

Is it okay to act like it never did?

*This isn't the real issue.*

I nestle further into the crevice between the plush cushion and arm of the couch, hug the canvas throw pillow tighter, and focus my dagger eyes on the TV screen.

Night put the Netflix-original crime drama series on right after breakfast, but I've been so distracted, I'm not even sure what's going on. Well, I vaguely remember the murder at the start of the episode, but that's it. The lead actor, who plays a rookie homicide detective, is an earth immortal with perfect cheekbones and sharp eyes. And, obviously, there is a lot of sexual tension between him and his equally gorgeous female partner.

It's basically a cop version of Night Hospital.

A door opens and closes in the hallway, and Ice walks into the den looking like he just stepped out of the shower. He pushes back his damp hair with one hand before sitting on the other end of the same loveseat I'm sat at.

Who is more attractive—the crime drama actor or Ice?

*God, I honestly can't decide.*

After briefly acknowledging my existence, he asks Night for the TV remote. She squints at him, but she hands it over without complaint even as he changes the TV input and opens the channel directory.

"You guys have cable?" I ask.

He laughs. "Why are you surprised?"

I shrug, still clinging to the throw pillow.

Night's annoyance over his intrusion is clear—he didn't pause her show before he changed the channel—but she simply watches as he selects a local news and weather station. It's in the middle of a commercial break.

"Something wrong?" she asks.

"Not yet."

She glances at the curtain over the sliding glass door, at me, and then back at the TV. The commercial break ends, and their heightened interest in the program leaves me puzzled. The female news anchor speaks about the success of Music@ThePark's first few events. A brief piece on local election results. Then they cut to the weather. The announcer points to images on the display and predicts a storm.

"I knew it," Ice says. A water droplet falls from his hair and leaves a dark spot on his shirt.

Night sighs in apparent agreement, but I'm lost even as the announcer continues to describe the upcoming "unusual weather event." It's expected to bring high winds, torrential rain, and sporadic lightning with low temperatures ranging from the mid-60s to low 70s.

I leave the couch and pull open the thick blackout curtain over the sliding glass door. The sky is clear and blue. Not a single cloud in sight. Warmth soaks into my skin through the glass.

"You don't believe it?" Ice asks.

I glance over my shoulder. He's watching me with a dry smile and passive eyes. More water drips from his hair.

Frowning, I draw the curtain shut. "But the weather is so

nice."

As I return to the couch, Ice passes the remote to Night. I meet his gaze and bring the throw pillow back into my lap so my hands have somewhere to be.

"I hate the rain," he says, his smile rather fixed.

*Ah.*

Night reminds him that rain is good for the earth, and I parrot something I read in an article a few months ago that said California has experienced drought conditions for several years now, and his expression softens ever so slightly.

"I am aware," he says.

*Five full days of rain, though?* It's not supposed to start for a couple days, but there's a twenty percent chance of rain tomorrow evening. If Ice dislikes rain, maybe…

"Hey," I say.

The overt curiosity in his eyes when he glances over catches me by surprise. My heart races, and my brain forgets how to form coherent thoughts.

"We should go out tonight," I stammer.

"Oh?" He blinks. "Just the two of us?"

Nodding stiffly, I feel the inexplicable need to justify myself. "Before the rain starts, you know? I think…it would be nice?"

Night grimaces from the other loveseat, but I slap a smile on my face for Ice's sake. She tears her gaze away and focuses on the TV instead, where something quite exciting is going down.

"Before the rain?" he asks, laughing slightly longer than I feel he should. Then he smiles with bright eyes. "Of course. Where shall we go?"

*Uh—*

Where should we go?

I didn't pack my new plum cocktail dress because I'm an idiot, and I only have one decently cute outfit in my duffel, so we can't go anywhere fancy. *Unless I borrow something from Night? Aah...* I want to wear that dress out somewhere eventually, but now...

*What have I done?*

"I have an idea," he says. *Thank god one of us isn't completely hopeless.* "How does Aquarius sound?"

"The seafood place? That's fine."

He grins and stands from the couch. "We'll go at six."

I offer a thumbs-up, and he leaves the den. A door closes in the hallway, and I finally draw a full breath. Night is still watching the TV but honestly looks a little embarrassed. I'm not mad.

"I'll talk to him eventually."

"I don't blame you for being nervous," she says, her delicate tone unable to mask the underlying dryness. "He can be... difficult to speak with, but you need to have this conversation. It's getting painful to watch."

*I am aware.*

Rose said something similar when I messaged her last night. Something like, *This is so sad. Rip the damn band-aid off already.*

I know I need to tell Ice how I feel and ask him how he really feels about me. I can't let him ignore my feelings anymore. That technically wasn't part of the *forget what happened* deal.

"Maybe over dinner," I say lamely.

Night pauses her show, leaving the muffled music in Smoke's bedroom behind us the only sound.

"Jayde, listen." When our eyes meet, her expression is level and strangely intimidating. "Ice cares about you in his own way—I know that—but he also turned your life upside down without any regard for your feelings when he told you about immortals, so you deserve to hear that from him directly."

I frown. "It sounds like he's dense when it comes to this sort of thing?"

"Surprisingly so, I'm afraid—either that or he's in denial."

I look away, and my hand reaches for the River Sapphire.

Turns out, I'm not great at dealing with my emotions either. Since I haven't had much luck figuring Ice out, and it took getting drunk for me to say anything to him. I just want to know how he feels about me.

But I guess I can start by telling him how I feel.

* * * * *

Night clips a fluffy silk marigold in my hair. I'm not sure it's the headpiece I would have picked, but she insisted.

I'm just happy she offered to hang out while I got ready. Her advice was constructive, and she let me borrow a pair of ballet flats because they match my outfit better than my new boots.

"You're cute," she says.

"Thanks."

She reassures me that I don't look like a desperate teenager, but I still pause to check my reflection in the dressing table mirror. The cool yellow flower does compliment the various teals in my muslin dress. She obviously knows what she's talking about.

But, honestly, does it matter?

Has Ice ever shown any indication that what I look like matters to him? Sure, he said he prefers my hair down, but I can't recall him mentioning my appearance unless prompted, and he waved it off when I wore a casual dress to a formal restaurant. I don't think he cares about any of this.

Is that good? Is that bad?

*Ugh. You're overthinking it again.*

He obviously likes me. He wouldn't go through all this trouble for me if he didn't, but we need to have this conversation so we can finally be on the same page.

"Don't forget that Ice did this to himself," Night says brightly. "Don't feel bad for him for a second."

"I feel bad for myself."

She laughs, but her eyes are apologetic. "So don't go easy on him either."

"Well… I guess I'll let you know how it goes?"

She pats me on the shoulder, and I convince myself to leave her room. Ice is waiting by the door to the garage, wearing a fitted t-shirt and dark jeans, his hair pushed back and his leather jacket slung over one arm. He looks amazing—a little bored, but amazing as always.

"Ready to go?" he asks.

"Ready."

He opens the door, and I follow him out.

* * * * *

The date is going fantastic. And nothing like I had planned. The drive to the restaurant was pleasant. Ice didn't talk much, but that's typical when he's driving.

When we arrived, he opened the passenger door for me, and he smiled as I climbed out of the car. Then he offered me his arm. I don't know why I laughed, but I did. Though I still placed my hand on his arm, and we walked inside together.

Since then, I've been too nervous to say anything that might ruin the mood, but watching him smile and talk easily as he sits across the table makes me feel pathetic for not speaking up.

*What am I so afraid of?* The worst he can do is reject me, and even that wouldn't be the end of the world.

*Right?*

I sip on my iced tea, still skeptical of his decision to have a rum and coke before dinner. *So much for not drinking much, huh?*

But it's cool.

Ice is an adult, and it seems like immortals don't have to worry about moderation the way I clearly do, but the mere thought of alcohol brings a little queasiness with it—just enough discomfort to set me on edge.

Not that I show it.

My energy is focused on our innocent, safe conversation and not looking like a complete nervous wreck. Maybe that's why it's so hard to ask. My mind really is somewhere else.

But I try to inch closer. I talk about visiting the hair salon with Night. How Carmen joked that I should cut my hair short. He is not impressed, and I can relate. I talk about the teahouse and how I wish my iced tea tasted like the milk oolong I drank there.

Ice listens with a passive interest—a passive amusement—that gives me a rush of determination. Then he smiles, his eyes darting aside for an instant, long enough to catch my full attention.

"I'm curious," he says. "Do you enjoy staying with me?"

"Um…"

What does he mean? *Do I enjoy staying with him?* Like, in general? Or at his parents' house? Or what? This is the first thing he's said all evening that stuck out in any real way. Is he going somewhere with it? How should I answer?

*I don't know.*

"Staying at your house is nice and all, considering, but…"

"You don't like it there?" he asks.

"Oh, no. That's not what I'm saying, I just—" *What are you saying, Jayde?* "—miss my bed. I guess."

His smile quirks up on one side. "Is that all? My previous offer stands: You're free to take mine."

*Ah—!*

I laugh and straighten out the silverware on the table in front of me. "I don't know. I'm alright in the den. I already feel like I'm imposing as things are, so…"

"You're hardly imposing."

"Ha…"

I raise my glass to take a drink, providing an excuse to not speak, but I haven't forgotten why I came here in the first place.

I was supposed to be upfront with him. I was supposed to ask for answers—demand them if I have to. I want to know how he feels. What he thinks. I need to know, but—

"I don't mind sleeping on the couch," he says. He watches the ice cubes swirling in his short glass. Then, with a smile, his eyes flick up to meet mine. "Another convenience of feline form."

*Why push it when I already said I'm fine?*

We stare each other down for a moment. I say nothing while he takes a drink and waits for my answer. But how am I supposed to feel about any of this? He's just trying to be nice. Maybe he understands how anxious I've been and wants to help.

"Fine. I'll stay in your room if it makes you feel better."

"Me?" With a laugh, he sets his glass down and rests his chin in one hand, his elbow on the table. "You're comfortable at the house, then?"

"Yeah? Why wouldn't I be?"

A flicker of recognition. "Right."

*Right.*

Glancing away, I clear my throat. "But I don't think I'll stay much longer. I mean, I'm not supposed to leave the cottage empty. The complex manager will notice and make a fuss."

"Right."

*Right.*

"Honestly, my roommate thinks this whole thing is weird." I sigh and drop my hands into my lap. "She knows I've been staying with you guys, but I can't tell her everything, so… It's probably better if I go back soon. So she doesn't get worried."

"Is she worried?" he asks.

The curiosity in his voice surprises me, and his eyes reflect the same emotion. He's genuinely interested.

But, once again, I'm not sure how to answer.

We're in public. Sure, I've talked about immortals in public before, but this restaurant is busier than the others we've gone to and less chaotic than Riverside Park. I'm still afraid of breaking the Secrecy Agreement by mistake.

"I don't know if she's worried, exactly," I say. "But everything is more complicated now, you know? I don't know what to tell her sometimes."

"I suppose. Friends can be a pain."

At least he seems to understand.

I brush my bangs out of my eyes and smile.

*Maybe it's fine if I wait until after dinner. Maybe I should enjoy this moment of normalcy.*

# forty

When we get back to the house, Ice shuts himself in his room to do…*something* while I continue into the den to pack my bag.

Night stands from the loveseat and hits me with a *so, how'd it go?* look. All I can do is shrug. Dinner was lovely. But I failed to ask Ice anything of importance.

And now I'm moving into his bedroom.

*Ha!*

"I know I just need to get it over with," I mutter, shoving my phone charger into my duffel bag. "But that's easier said than done. You get it, right?"

Smoke snorts from his spot on the far loveseat. "Oh, yeah. We all know that guy's impossible to talk to."

*Difficult. Impossible.*

The adjectives keep getting worse.

I heft my bag over one shoulder. The joint twinges—a strange reminder that I hit the floor a bit too hard a few days ago. *Maybe I packed too much.*

Night turns away from her twin and sighs as she approaches me. "He owes you an explanation, Jayde."

"I know."

I grip the strap of my duffel tightly, avoiding her gaze. She adjusts the silk marigold in my hair before planting her hands on my shoulders.

"I'm serious," she says. "I'm at a complete loss here, but you deserve to know why he dragged you into this. Dating. The secret. The Human Immortal Program. You need to talk. You deserve to know what he really thinks about you."

"Ha… You're freaking me out a little."

She averts her eyes, and her hands fall away. "Sorry. I just— Ugh. He makes me so…angry sometimes. Please talk to him. Now. Whatever he says, I'm sure it'll be fine."

*It'll be fine? Whatever he says?*

"Calm down." Smoke laughs. "Y'all are making me nervous."

I cough. And Night sighs, peering down the empty hallway.

"Well, as I said before, I hope you get what you want out of this conversation." With another glance at me, she flashes a smile. "Tell me if you need someone to beat him up for you. Perhaps we could call Carmen over."

I laugh, and some of the tension leaves my shoulders. "Alright, thanks. For everything."

She nods, and I take the first step. Another step. Then I'm standing in front of Ice's bedroom door—soon to be the room I'll stay in—and I knock.

No answer, but he knew I was coming, so I let myself in.

He's standing in front of the desk with his back to me. Messing with his phone. His other hand on the desktop. With the way he focuses on the screen without looking up to acknowledge me, I worry he's in the middle of something important.

*Though, it doesn't really matter.*

I close the door and drop my duffel bag at the foot of the bed. Another moment of quiet watching, and he still doesn't glance up from his phone. So I clear my throat.

"Yes, Jayde?"

He pockets his phone and moves a few sheets of paper from the top of the desk to a drawer. He looks busy, but I ask, and he says he isn't, so I go for it.

"Can I talk to you for a minute?"

*We've been talking all evening, so asking sounds weird, but here I am.*

"Of course," he says, still tidying his desk. "What is it?"

*Just ask. Don't think.*

I take a deep breath and force my hands to relax. "I want to know exactly why you told me about immortals."

He turns to face me. Golden evening light streams through the window and accentuates both his unreasonable good looks and his mild confusion.

"Does it make any difference why I told you?" he asks.

"Well—" I hesitate, caught off guard by his response. "I don't know. I guess I've just been wondering."

"Do you regret your decision?"

"No—"

My eyes dart up from the floor to find him watching me, his head tipped slightly, and his expression calm but expectant. My fleeting panic fades, but…

*Ugh.*

"That's not it." I step closer and mess with my bracelet to keep my hands busy. "I don't regret getting involved with immortals—not at all—but I can't stop wondering why you want me around. I'm human, and you're not, and it doesn't seem like immortals do this sort of thing, so I guess I don't understand…"

My voice trails off, and he takes a deep, thoughtful breath. After studying my face a moment longer, he shrugs. *Shrugs!*

I fold my arms over my chest. "Well, there is a reason, right?"

His continued passive silence and unreadable face only serve to frustrate me more. *Is this what Night meant?*

"Why did you tell me about immortals?" I ask again, my voice rising. "Why did you talk to me in the grocery store? Or offer to be my sponsor? Why did you do any of it? If you want me to stick around, you can't keep doing this."

"Doing what?"

"This," I say, gesturing vaguely. "I just want to know why you want me around. That's all."

Irritation flashes in his bright eyes. "There is no mysterious reason, Jayde, and looking for one is a waste of time. Why are my intentions so important to you in the first place?"

*Are you kidding me?*

"I just—"

I glance out the window to my left. The curtains are partially drawn. My eyes focus on the strawberries on the far side of the backyard. Tiny white flowers and red dots in a lush planter.

Please don't cry, Jayde. Calm down.

"I want answers," I say. "Because I feel like… Well, I feel like I don't know why I'm here anymore."

He frowns. I stand my ground as he shifts his weight from

one foot to the other. Then he sighs, his expression muted.

"You're interesting," he says—the same thing he said on the Fourth of July *right before I kissed him.* "But I fail to understand what you hope to get out of interrogating me."

My face flushes hot.

*Interrogating him?* Is that what he thinks I'm doing?

What am I supposed to say to that?

I'm just so…frustrated. So upset. And I'm not even sure who to be mad at anymore. Him, for acting like this? Me, for letting it go on so long without saying anything?

"Ice, I—"

The room falls silent. We stare at each other for some time. Five seconds. Ten seconds. He searches my face, and the words are on the tip of my tongue, but I…*can't.*

Then his eyes widen, but only for an instant.

"Oh, is this about—?" As he cuts himself off, his posture relaxes. His face softens, and he smiles. "You're in love with me, right?"

*Love?*

Am I—?

The warmth drains from my cheeks as my chest fills with an uncomfortable tightness. I can't tear my eyes away from his—that expression of discordant patience. I've been struggling to verbalize my feelings for weeks, but he said it so casually? Just like that?

*Why?*

"Ah… I don't know if I—" I bite my lip, finally averting my eyes. "But, um, I guess it was something like that."

*Ugh!* That's as vague an answer as he usually gives me. *Why is this so hard?*

He sighs. "Yes, I am well aware of your feelings for me, Jayde. You're rather easy to read."

Even now, he won't mention the kiss?

Does he seriously think I was too drunk to remember?

*Never mind.*

The conversation is headed more or less in the right direction now—for better or worse—so I may as well spit it out. He clearly understands how I feel. There's no point in beating around the bush anymore.

*Get to the point.*

*Don't let him mess with you.*

*Don't go easy on him.*

Okay.

Our eyes meet, and I don't look away.

"What I really wanted to know is—" I pause to take a breath between words. "—how you feel about me. I guess."

He takes a deep breath too, but he remains quiet and glances around like he needs time to think. Like it's something he hasn't considered or isn't sure how to answer. But my question is simple enough, isn't it? He either has feelings for me or he doesn't. That's how it works, right? So why can't he give me a straight answer?

*Is this bad?*

What will I do if he turns me down? After everything he's done? Sponsoring me? Giving me the River Sapphire? Letting me stay here for days on end?

*Ugh... I might cry. I seriously might cry.*

Surely, I can't stay here if he rejects me outright. It would be too hard. Too awkward. I don't want to make him uncomfortable, but I don't want to force myself to hang around him if we feel so differently about each other. I don't know if I *love* him, but I'm not sure Ice is someone I can be *just friends* with.

*So, if that's how it's gonna be, what will I…?*

A fleeting frown as he glances away. A few tense seconds pass. Then he offers me a small, tight smile, his eyes betraying unease as they meet mine again.

"Do you want an honest answer?" he asks.

The last thread of hope I was clinging to snaps, and, for an instant, I want to say no. If saying no meant I'd hear what I want to hear—what I wish Ice would say more than anything…

*But I can't say no.*

What's the point if I let him lie to me?

"Of course," I say. My voice wavers, but I power through. "Of course, I want the truth."

He nods, and his expression shifts. His overall posture remains relaxed, but his mouth forms a soft and uncomfortable frown. Eyes cast ever so slightly downward. He seems… disappointed, almost.

*Oh, no…*

"Well, ah—" He clears his throat, and his face softens further as our eyes meet again. "I'm sorry, Jayde. I do like you, but I don't feel the same way."

*No?*

"I've never thought of you—or what I'm doing with you—in terms of love or romance or anything like that."

*Never?*

I grit my teeth. “What about what you said to Carmen?”

“What about it?”

“You were messing with me this whole time?” My voice rises as my panic swells. “Is this a game to you?”

“No.”

“No?”

He blinks, his frown more pronounced. “Are you—?”

But I stop listening.

The moment he acknowledged my feelings for him, I knew he would say he doesn’t feel the same, but that doesn’t make it hurt any less. My face is on fire. My heart pounds in my chest, which feels so tight it’s hard to breathe normally, and my head fills with nervous static.

If I’m gonna cry, if it’s inevitable, maybe I should leave before I start. He doesn’t need to watch me break down. Rocking back on my heels, standing in front of the person I hoped—

*Ugh.*

My duffel bag is right behind me. Everything is already packed inside. I could have Night drive me home right now.

*Damn it… My eyes are already watering.*

I turn my head, only a little, to glance back at the door. But Ice stops me with a sharp motion. One hand lands on my shoulder. The other touches my chin, sliding through my hair to rest at the base of my neck.

And he pulls me into a kiss.

*He kissed me.*

Is he close enough to hear my racing heart?

Can he tell I stopped breathing?

But, even with the roles reversed, it's the same as the Fourth of July. Our lips pressed together. His body tense. His eyes wide and bewildered. Like he doesn't know what he did or why he did it. Like he has no idea what's happening at all.

And I don't either.

But I can't move.

*He rejected me, and now this?*

Then his eyes close, and the kiss ends.

His hand lingers in my hair. Our eyes meet as his open, and he takes a deep breath while I still can't breathe at all. His fingers brush my jaw, soft against my skin, as his warm hand slowly leaves my face.

His eyes remain wide. I'm sure mine do too.

*What just happened?*

*And why the hell do I want to kiss him again?*

His other hand falls from my shoulder, brushing against my arm on its way down. His expression softens, and he glances away.

"Don't get the wrong idea, Jayde." His voice is mild, bordering on indifferent. "This changes nothing about what I said."

*I don't understand.*

His expression reveals very little. All hints of prior confusion and alarm are gone. He doesn't look embarrassed or ashamed. No. He's perfectly composed after rejecting me, kissing me, and rejecting me a second time in quick succession.

"But—"

I don't know what to say. *What can I say?*

As I glance aside, my focus drifts beyond Ice, past his clean desk, and out the window. But, this time, my view of the backyard is obstructed. Someone stands on the patio just outside.

Round, amber eyes. Short, orange hair.

*James Reid.*

Our eyes meet by accident, and his already wide eyes grow even wider. The blood drains from his cheeks. Sweat drips down his brow. He's frozen in place—unable to move.

But, this time, I can move.

I tear my gaze away, tripping over words. I raise a finger and spit out half of James' name, and Ice glances over his shoulder.

He reacts immediately.

Fire burns in his eyes and both hands grip the edge of the desk as he growls something positively vulgar. For an instant, it looks as though he's ready to fling himself through the window to get at the terrified man on the other side, but he changes his mind at the last second and speeds out the bedroom door instead.

Drywall cracks, chipping the sage green paint, as the doorknob hits the wall on his way out.

*Holy shit.*

Outside, James tries to make a break for it. He jumps off the patio and bolts toward the far side of the house just as Ice arrives at the sliding glass door. Fighting the morbid temptation to continue watching, I turn away from the window.

*Ice's wild eyes. Bared teeth. Pure anger.*

I shake my head.

What should I do?

*Aah...*

I look toward the door, half-closed after bouncing off the wall, and slowly—very slowly—creep out of the room. Night stops me in the hall before I reach the den by placing a hand on my shoulder.

As I jump at her touch, time returns to normal speed.

"What happened?" She's visibly agitated, but her voice is calm and level. "Is everything okay?"

I shake my head and glance toward the den.

"No. I talked to Ice, but James—"

When I look back, her face is pale. And she shakes *her* head.

"James?" she asks.

She stares down the hallway. At the curtain fluttering in the breeze let in through the open sliding glass door. At Smoke standing in the den. He shakes his head too, his expression rather grim.

Her eyes flick to my face. "James is here? Right now?"

When I nod, a cold darkness overtakes her, and she ushers me back into Ice's bedroom. I glance between her and the window a couple times.

"I'll take care of it," she says, her hands held at chest level. She forces a smile, her eyes still wide. "James will be fine. Everything will be fine. Just— Stay here."

"Wait—"

But she shuts me inside the room. I blink at the closed door before wandering to the desk, where I stand and keep an eye on the backyard through the window. *What else can I do?*

For several seconds, there's nothing.

Then Night steps out onto the patio. She stands motionless

at the top of the steps for a long moment, staring into the empty yard. *Where did Ice and James go?*

Quiet. Nothing.

Then her posture stiffens.

She rocks on her heels once before darting down the steps and across the yard. She stops at the corner of the house, looking down the narrow side yard. A sidelong glance toward the house—toward me.

*The look…on her face…*

My stomach twists.

I draw the curtains over the window to block my view of the backyard. Then I pace the room. I twirl my hair around my finger. I gnaw the inside of my cheek.

Ice kissed me. James probably saw. *And now…*

What did Night see out there?

*James will be fine?*

*Ice wouldn't… I don't want to think…*

But, no matter how I try to block them out, vivid images of a beaten and bloodied James Reid flash through my mind. *Thick, red blood dripping from my hands—*

*What? Ugh.*

I sit on the edge of Ice's bed and hold my head in my hands.

There's no way. He doesn't like James, and that's fine, but Ice wouldn't hurt him, would he? Not so badly, right? Not like—

*Oh, god…*

James is in the wrong here. He's absolutely in the wrong. He shouldn't have come. Not today, and not on the Fourth of July. He shouldn't have snuck into the backyard. He shouldn't have been watching us through the window.

But—

*Stop, Jayde. Stop.*

*Stop, stop, stop.*

*You're fine.*

I open my eyes.

Tears fall into my lap, leaving wet spots on the teal muslin. I run my fingers through my hair. I remove the marigold hair clip, but I have nowhere to put it. I just hold it in my cupped hands. A tear lands on the flower and disappears in the tight, silk ruffles.

*Everything will be fine.*

I jump as a door slams in the hallway—*Night's bedroom.* When I recover, I scramble to stand and stare at the closed door.

Quiet. Quiet. Quiet.

*Why is the house so quiet?*

Then the door opens, and Ice strides through.

At first glance, he appears to be his usual, unruffled self, but his bright, blue eyes smolder with muted rage, and his knuckles are bloody and raw. *He hit something. Hard.* Past that, he appears unscathed by whatever confrontation occurred outside.

Was James on the receiving end of those fists? If so, there's no way he came out unharmed. *Why am I worried about him?*

"Are you okay?" I ask, my voice weak.

He sighs, waving a hand through the air, and takes a seat at his desk. It's an unexpectedly nonchalant gesture and seriously throws me off, but his anger has faded more completely.

*Well, at least I know he's fine.*

But there's no ignoring this. I don't care what Night said

about mentioning James or Ice's past. This time, I have to address it.

"So, that's him, huh? James?"

He stares at me without answering, but the meaning behind the look is clear. The awkward man I ran into at the mall—the guy who basically kidnapped me on the Fourth of July—is the same person Ice and Night apparently knew during high school.

"Right," I say slowly. "Do you know why he was here?"

He shrugs. "He didn't say much."

"Did you…hurt him?"

*Is asking rude?* Ice clearly hates him—more than I realized, it seems—but I need to know. Otherwise, the multitude of horrifying possibilities will haunt me for eternity.

"Not terribly," he says. "Despite my overwhelming desire to."

*Am I supposed to take comfort in that?*

I acknowledge his answer in as few words as possible.

He studies me a moment longer. Then he spins the desk chair around. Once facing the desk, he puts out a hand to stop himself.

"Don't worry. James Reid left the property walking."

He opens a desk drawer and raises his right hand to show off the damage. Red blood oozes from his split knuckles. The wounds are raw and angry, and the gore turns my stomach a little, so I step back and sit on the bed.

"I have the wall to thank for this." His voice is breezy and less detached than before. "Brick does a number on the hands. But I know my limits."

*Okay... But did you hit James or not?*

*I can't ask that!*

So I keep quiet and wipe my eyes to remove any extraneous moisture.

With a sigh, Ice takes a roll of gauze from the drawer he was digging through. I watch him wrap his right hand for a moment before I look away. My idle thumbs pass over the petals of the silk marigold in my lap. I can still make out a few tiny, damp splotches where tears landed on my dress.

The desk chair swivels again after a few minutes. When I look up, both of his hands are neatly bandaged with white gauze. He offers me a smile, but there's something off about it. Or maybe it's my perception that's off.

"James will not bother us again," he says.

I nod but can't return the smile—not even a forced one—and his smile grows even more strained.

"Perhaps…" He sighs, a deeper, more explicit disappointment in his averted eyes. "Perhaps we could forget about this too?"

"Um…"

My eyes dart down to my lap.

*God, I wish I could.* I so desperately wish I could forget the past half hour. Or the past week.

"Jayde?"

*Why did I see so much blood? Today wasn't the first time, either. Why do I keep picturing it?*

I shake my head. Then I take a deep breath and look up again. He watches me with a quiet discomfort—like he truly wants the entire evening swept under the rug. This sucks, but I'm not in the mood for more drama.

"If you think that's best," I agree mildly.

His smile fades, not that it was much of a smile to begin with. Then he turns to the window, pulls the curtain aside, and gazes out.

"The storm will be here soon," he says.

*And that's it?*

"You think so?" I ask. "The weather's still so nice."

"Not for long."

I have no intention of arguing about the weather, but I seriously dropped the ball on this one. I misread the situation—our entire relationship, it seems—from the very beginning.

How the hell did I manage that?

*And what does it mean moving forward?*

After a long, quiet moment, Ice turns away from the window.

"Perhaps I should stay in here with you," he says.

"What?"

*After everything—*

He rolls his eyes, the disinterest clear on his face. "I'll take feline form, of course, and sleep at the foot of the bed. No need to panic."

*Oh.*

My face grows warm anyway.

"I suggest it as a precaution only," he says. Our eyes meet. A mild, uneasy expression. "James Reid is an idiot. A coward. He clearly can't be trusted to do the sensible thing."

I frown.

Based on what I saw, James is afraid of Ice. He would be

crazy to come back after whatever happened out there. But, if that's true, what's the point of sleeping in the same room?

*Whatever.*

I can't handle any more conflict today. None. I'm over it.

"Fine," I say.

"Good."

*But, right now, I can't stay in here another second.*

I leave the bed. I leave the room. I close the door, and, as I stand in the empty hallway and wipe my damp eyes, the Monroe house suddenly feels so big. I feel like I don't belong here. I'm starting to wonder if I ever did.

*But I guess I can't go home now.*

# forty-one

I sat alone in the den for at least half an hour. The house was quiet. Then a door opened in the hallway, and the twins walked out of Night's bedroom. She was laughing, her voice a bit too light, but Smoke's annoyance was obvious.

I don't know why it made me feel so guilty.

Still smiling, she asked if I was okay.

I shrugged.

She asked if Ice was okay.

I said he was fine.

She never asked me to elaborate, and I couldn't bring myself to ask what she saw in the backyard. Then the three of us moved into the great room. I sat on the couch and Smoke set himself up at the breakfast nook while Night made tea.

Ice came out not long after.

He looked at me, his expression downright indecipherable, but he said nothing. Night gave him a glass of water before she joined Smoke in the bay window, and Ice stationed himself at the glass dining table.

Since then, I've been trying to pretend I don't exist. It's the only way I can act like what Ice did earlier didn't happen.

I can't unhear what he said. I can't unfeel the sinking dread as I realized the conversation wasn't going the way I'd hoped. I can't unexperience being kissed. I can't unsee the fear in James' eyes or the blood on Ice's knuckles.

I can't.

But I also can't unsign the Secrecy Agreement or drop out of the Human Immortal Program. I can't forget about immortals. Ice is my sponsor. Whether we're dating or not, this is my reality. And I understood that when I signed the paperwork, didn't I?

*Do I regret it?*

I don't know.

I'm upset, I guess? But I panicked and agreed to forget about it again—which is exactly what Night told me not to do—so how am I supposed to approach the subject with anyone?

Now, I'm running out of ways to distract myself with my phone. I scrolled down my FaceSpace newsfeed for ages. I checked Snapgram. I even redownloaded a lame bubble pop game I haven't played in months.

*This seriously sucks.*

It's dark outside. After 10PM.

But no one has moved, and I don't want to be the first.

Night glances at me from time to time. She'll look up from her book to check on me. Or Ice. Or the window.

It's so quiet.

Then a chair shifts. I look up—with my eyes, without moving my head.

Ice, who is now standing, pushes the chair back into place. Dark blood peeks through the gauze over his knuckles. His hand falls away from the back of the chair, and he crosses the room. He doesn't say anything as he leaves through the den.

A door closes softly further inside the house, and Smoke snickers from the breakfast nook. Maybe it was a coincidence. I wasn't looking, but he seems focused on his phone screen. Night, who sits across from him, watches me with a rather terse frown. She sets her book on the table beside her tea saucer and beckons me over.

*Ugh.*

Still, she has always been the easiest of the siblings to talk to, and we absolutely need to talk, so I leave the nest I formed against the arm of the couch.

"Here," she says, scooting over to make room.

I sit on the edge of the bench seat. Our eyes meet, and I force a smile. She doesn't bother mirroring it.

"What happened?" she asks under her breath.

Two pairs of identical blue eyes watch me with interest, hers more nervous than her brother's. But I don't know where to begin or what she wants to know. Does she want to know how my talk with Ice went? Because it was a disaster. Or does she want to know how James got involved? Which is more important?

*My feelings are one thing, but...*

"I saw him outside the window," I say.

"James?" When I nod, she sighs. "Okay, but what happened before that—in the bedroom? You spoke with Ice, right? What did he say?"

I avert my eyes. "He, uh— Well, I asked for answers. Why he did any of it—sponsoring me and hanging out with me, you know? And he said there isn't a reason. He said it's not important. But, if that's how he sees it, it's probably better if I don't know."

"Wow." She seems surprised. Disappointed and more frustrated than she was at the teahouse. "Did you at least manage to tell him how you feel?"

"He already knew."

She frowns, her eyes darting down. "I see. That…makes sense. What did he have to say for himself?"

"He asked—" I stare at my hands. "He asked if I wanted an honest answer. I almost said no. Maybe I should have said no."

Glancing over, I laugh, but Night, who watches me carefully, doesn't find it funny at all. And Smoke is wearing headphones, his full attention once again on the phone in his hand.

My smile fades, and I pick at the gel polish still firmly attached to my nails. "Anyway, he's not interested in me like that. But it's fine, I guess."

"Is it?" she asks. "Is that okay with you?"

I shrug.

Her frown deepens. "It's okay if it's not."

"Are you sure?" I ask, growing frustrated—more with myself than with anything else. "Does it matter if I'm okay with it or not? Knowing he doesn't love me doesn't change anything, does it? I still like him, and he's still my sponsor, so do my feelings about it really matter?"

Her eyes search mine, a soft pain etched into the lines of her face. Then she looks away, into her teacup.

"I'm sorry."

"I thought about asking you to take me home. After he said

that, I almost walked out on him, but he—" I touch my lips and shake my head before dropping my hand back to the table. "He just had to go and kiss me."

Her expression blanks.

For an instant, I'm not sure she believes me. Then she holds a curled hand over her mouth. Her eyes dart toward the den for an instant. Then her brows furrow, and her jaw strains like she wants to speak but isn't sure what to say.

Smoke glances up from his phone, his attention on his sister.

"I need to go," she says, standing abruptly. "Excuse me."

I step out of the breakfast nook, and she hurries past me, but she pauses mid-step, already halfway across the room. When she looks back, her frown is more severe.

"Did James see?"

My breath catches. "I— I don't know. I didn't notice him until after. But he could have. I mean, we were standing right in front of the window the whole time."

"I see." Her voice carries a hint of tension. "Well, after what happened today—not with you, exactly, but, you know… I need to talk to Ice. If you want, I can take you home when I'm done."

"It's fine. I already agreed to stay a few more days."

Her smile doesn't touch her eyes. "Alright. If that's the case, we can talk later."

I nod, and she's gone fast.

Suddenly uncomfortable, I turn to Smoke. He's still watching the wide, empty arch his sister disappeared through. Then his eyes meet mine.

"Sit," he says, having dropped the headphones to his neck.

As I comply, he takes a long drink from his porcelain teacup. He seems calm and unperturbed. It's strange considering Night's reaction.

"Is she okay?" I ask.

He shrugs. "Sure. She always finds a way to be okay. Someone has to be an adult around here, you know?"

"Ha…" I avert my eyes and scratch the inside of my wrist.

"So, Ice kissed you?" he asks. "Right before he beat the shit out of James Reid, huh? What a guy."

My pleasant facade falters, but he watches me with a passive smile and muted interest that only confuses me further. *Night ran outside after Ice, and I know she saw something. Maybe—*

"Do you know what happened out there?"

"Nah." He sighs—more of a huff, really—and his smile fades. "She hasn't said a word about it, but we all saw the bandages, so I can imagine."

"You think James is hurt?"

"Does that bother you?" he asks, his head tipped. "James hurt you on the Fourth of July, right? Your injuries weren't too bad—easy to fix, but it didn't look fun. Decent gash on your head."

"That doesn't mean I want—"

He stifles a laugh. "You seem like a bright girl and all, but you don't know the first thing about the mess you've found yourself in. With immortals. Our family. Ice. I bet a million bucks he didn't hesitate before breaking James' nose."

"He said he hit the wall," I stammer.

"And you believe that?"

I bite my cheek, but I don't respond.

He sighs again and pushes himself out of the bench seat like it takes serious effort. “Anyway, I should check on them. Night can get real emotional when it comes to these things.”

“Oh. Okay.”

“Mind cleaning up for us?” he asks, cracking a small smile. “The china goes above the sink. Step stool’s by the fridge.”

I agree, relieved to have something productive to do, even if it’s washing cups and saucers. So I stand and collect the dishes. The porcelain feels so fragile in my hands.

Smoke wishes me luck on his way out.

“Thanks.”

*As always, I need it.*

* * * * *

It’s almost midnight.

A few doors opened and closed in the hall earlier, but I haven’t moved from the breakfast nook, and no one has come out to join me or check up on me or anything. The entire household, myself excluded, may have gone to sleep. Who knows?

I’m nervous to find out, I guess.

With a sigh, I look out the window. Up from the houses and the streetlights. The sky is dark. Navy, dotted with stars. Clouds.

*Clouds?*

Ugh. Maybe the weather forecast is right. The clouds are wispy things, gathering in the sky behind the houses, but there’s no telling if they’ll turn into something else later. Like storm clouds.

It's late. I'm tired.

*But...*

No, I need to get over myself. I'm fine. Everything is fine.

It's time for bed. It's time to stop avoiding Ice. If it's anything like the Fourth of July, he'll at least pretend he's over it—or that it never happened.

I meant what I told Night, though.

What does anything that Ice said change? *Nothing.* It merely reframes his actions. Now, it seems like he only wanted someone to talk to or get out and do things with. A friend, maybe?

Maybe Rose was right. *Maybe I am a platonic sugar baby.*

But he kissed me.

Maybe he needs more time. Maybe he doesn't know exactly how he feels yet. He still hasn't said anything about what we're supposed to do when summer ends, so it's possible, right? Sponsorship isn't a casual summer thing—or I can't imagine it is, anyway.

I leave the breakfast nook. I turn off the lights on my way through the house, and I creep down the hallway. I raise a hand to knock on Ice's bedroom door. But I hesitate.

*Do I need to knock?*

*Is he alone in there? Is he awake?*

Shaking my head, I knock. Twice. Softly.

The door opens, and we stand face-to-face. He looks tired—like visibly tired. More tired than he did after his concurrent trips to Seattle. Maybe it shouldn't surprise me after today. It was a rough one.

"It's late," he says.

I force a laugh. "I've been thinking that for the past hour."

"Yes, well…" He glances over his shoulder, and his uneasy expression softens. "Come in."

He opens the door the rest of the way. As I step inside, he retreats further into the room. He morphs and jumps onto the bed. Ice, as a white cat, glances from the mirror on the closet door to the window behind the desk and finally to me.

"Do I…make you uncomfortable?" he asks.

"Ah—"

With another laugh, I drop to my knees at the foot of the bed, both to hide my face and to dig through my duffel bag.

"No," I say, though the word sounds more like a question.

*What else can I say?*

Today was uncomfortable for everyone, and we both know it.

It's not him entirely, or even what he told me or whatever he may or may not have done to James after he caught him in the side yard. It's everything. Dinner. His confession. The kiss. The blood.

*Everything.*

So, yeah, I'm a little uncomfortable, but I don't want to think about what happened today either. Maybe I should be happy he bothered asking.

"I'll be fine," I say, standing up with my pajama shorts in hand.

He continues watching from his spot on the far side of the bed. His ears are angled forward, and his eyes are round and attentive.

"You're tired?" he asks, his head cocked at a perfect ninety-degree angle.

I nod, hold up my pajamas, and smile. "Yeah, but, um… Can you turn around for a minute?"

With a dry laugh, he burrows underneath the comforter. *I guess that works.* I change clothes the fastest I've probably ever changed. Then I turn the light off and sit on the edge of the bed.

The patio light filters in through the sheer curtains, so it's not too dark. The blankets shift behind me.

"I'll sleep against the wall," he says. "Don't worry. I'll stay in feline form the whole time. I won't touch you."

"Thanks." *I guess.*

I glance over my shoulder as he curls up near the middle of the bed, inches from the wall. There's plenty of space, and his feline form is small, but I…

*Why is this so weird?*

"Goodnight, Jayde," he says, his eyes reflecting green in the low light.

I lie down, facing the room with the comforter pulled up to my chin. Ignoring the urge to watch the window, I close my eyes. I listen to the sound of air blowing through the ducts in the ceiling.

But I can't fall asleep.

Knowing Ice is so close. Knowing our feelings aren't the same. Wondering what he did to James. *The shock on Night's face as she rounded the corner of the house.*

*The blood on his hands.*

And what Smoke said earlier.

Ice told me he hit the wall—that James left the property walking. But Smoke is right. *That doesn't mean he was okay when he left.*

# forty-two

Standing in front of Ice's desk, I pull the curtains aside. The backyard is empty, but the sky is overcast. Grey. Unfriendly, thunderstorm-type clouds peek above the neighboring house.

"I feel it," Ice mumbles behind me. "The rain in the air."

He's half-asleep, his feline form sprawled near the foot of the bed. Eyes closed, he seems rather listless. I doubt he woke up early to jog like he usually does.

"It's not raining yet," I say.

A soft laugh. "Oh, it will."

By mid-afternoon, if the forecast is correct. But I don't want to accept it. A rainstorm is the last thing I need.

Ice stretches, his jaw unhinging in a yawn. Then he curls into a tight ball, and I resist the urge to pet him.

"Give it two hours." His voice is muffled by fur. "It will rain."

"You getting up?" I ask, collecting an outfit from my bag.

"No. You're free to leave."

His face is too buried in fluff to receive my dramatic glare, but I don't say anything else. I get dressed and leave.

The den is empty and dark. I open the heavy curtain over the sliding glass door on my way through. The great room is empty too. It's almost 10AM. Night would usually have cooked breakfast by now, but I'm alone, so I browse the kitchen cabinets and find something to eat.

The house is quiet. It leaves me feeling a little itchy, but I'm not surprised. Yesterday was chaotic at best, and I stayed up late. It's a miracle I woke up this early, considering…

*God, the look on James' face before he bolted.*

The hatred in Ice's eyes. The blood. Night's suppressed panic, and Smoke's deadpan certainty. How am I supposed to feel about any of this?

*Ugh. Stop thinking about it.*

"Oh. Jayde."

I turn toward the voice as Night walks into the great room. She's wearing a silky, cream nightdress, and her hair is a mess.

"You're eating," she says through a yawn. "Good."

She continues into the kitchen, where she picks out a mug and turns on the electric kettle. She asks if I want tea, but I shake my head.

"Excuse us if we're out of it until the storm blows over," she says. "Some immortals don't do well in dreary weather—especially when it comes on so suddenly during the summer."

"Weird."

She laughs. "Ice is the worst with these things."

*I believe it.*

Her warm expression falters as our eyes meet. She turns away and busies herself with picking out a tea bag from the impressively large tea collection she keeps out on the counter.

I glance at my hands—at the nails that are growing out and no longer look amazing. I ask Night if she can help me strip the polish later. She agrees, her voice soft, but I decline her offer to paint them again.

By the time she joins me at the table, I'm done with my cereal. I don't move, though, and she doesn't speak. I glance outside. It's not raining, but the sky looks like it wants to start.

*Say something, Jayde.*

"Can we—"

"—talk about yesterday?" she asks with a sigh.

I meet her careful gaze and nod.

"You talked to Ice last night, right?" I ask. "What did he say? Because, ah…I'm still confused."

Another sigh. Frowning, she stares down into her steaming mug. "He didn't want to talk about it, of course. He said it didn't mean anything."

"The kiss?" I ask, my face flushing uncomfortably.

"Mm-hm." She props her chin in her hand. "He laughed at me. Accused me of being jealous. I was so mad, I thought it best to let it go."

"Jealous of what?"

She rolls her eyes. "God knows what that man is ever thinking. Granted, he wasn't expecting to see James here, but— Ugh."

"Surely a kiss can't mean nothing," I protest.

"This is Ice we're talking about." She meets my gaze, a hint of frustration seeping into her otherwise level expression. "But you're right. It doesn't mean nothing. He's deflecting because *emotions are scary*."

"But he doesn't like me the same way."

*That was his honest answer.*

"No," she agrees. "That's what bothers me. But, for him to go so far, he must be awfully afraid of losing you."

"You're saying he kissed me so I wouldn't leave?"

She frowns. "I don't know, Jayde. You're obviously important to him, but, to be honest, I have a theory that Ice is asexual—or at least aromantic. I've known him since he was eleven, and he's never shown much interest in intimate relationships, so I wouldn't take it personally."

*Why do I feel like I should cut my losses and go home?*

"I really like him," I say lamely.

"I know."

She takes a drink, and the table falls quiet. I have absolutely no idea what to say. All I know is that I don't want to discuss *feelings* anymore.

"What happened outside?" I ask.

Her expression shifts. A fleeting grimace. Then she coughs, her attention darting to her hands as they grip the mug more tightly. *Not a good sign.*

"Outside?" she echoes. "With James, you mean?"

"Ice came in with his hands bleeding," I say through my teeth. "He didn't deny hurting him when I asked."

"James will be okay," she says slowly. "He—"

"—left the property walking?"

Her jaw tenses, eyes still averted, and she brushes a hand down her cheek. "Ice may have hit James a couple times, sure. But he broke his knuckles on the wall."

*Broke them?*

Grimacing again, she shakes her head. “Broke is not the right word. Ice is fine, and his hands are fine. He just— You know? He hit the brick on the side of the house. It’s… Well, this isn’t the first time he’s done something like that.”

We stare at each other. She looks guilty, ashamed, as though there were anything she could have done to stop him.

Once again, I don’t know what to say.

“James shouldn’t have been here,” she says, her shoulders falling as she shakes her head. “I can’t believe he’d risk it. After the Fourth…”

*Me either.*

I couldn’t believe it either.

She takes a slow drink from her mug, staring into the liquid. “Ice said that he—that James, I mean—asked about you. He was worried about you. But he knows your necklace won’t do anything for him now. So, there’s that.”

“He was worried?”

That’s why he came here? As misguided as it is—ever thinking it was a good idea… If Ice hurt him, I feel kind of bad. *But he should not have been here.*

“I don’t think he meant to hurt you,” she says, her voice low.

“I’m pretty sure he was drunk,” I mumble into my hands.

She sighs. “Drunk, desperate, or both, there is no excuse for what he did. He kidnapped you, Jayde. You were injured, and you had to walk back here in the middle of the night by yourself.”

“Yes, well—” *I did knock myself out on a table leg in front of him.* “I guess I’m lucky that Smoke could fix me up.”

Forcing a smile, she takes another drink.

"I'm just glad it wasn't anything serious," she says. "And I do believe Ice is doing his best considering the less-than-ideal circumstances. Yesterday was rather trying. But enough about all that. How are you holding up?"

"Me? I'm okay."

She regards me with overt skepticism. "As I said before, Jayde, immortals and humans are the same this way. We're not perfect. None of us are. We all make mistakes and bad decisions. We all suffer and hurt others and have things we don't want to talk about. You get what I'm saying, right?"

I nod, but I realize what I'm asking is another one of the things no one wants to talk about.

"I can take you home if you don't want to stay here anymore," she offers, her nails clicking against the side of her mug. "Ice will get over it, but you need to take care of yourself above all else."

"I—"

Would being alone at home be any better than staying here? Ice can be confusing—and *intense* at times, it seems. I have no idea what I'm doing when it comes to anything anymore, but would I feel any differently at home?

"No, I'm okay."

"Hm. Alright." She glances out the window. "Let me know if you change your mind."

# forty-three

The first raindrops fell around noon.

Ice didn't come out of his bedroom until after 1PM. Only then, with both him and Smoke in the great room, did Night start lunch.

She made sandwiches, and the four of us ate in relative silence. I finished first, and Smoke dipped out when he was done, so only Night, Ice, and I remain at the table.

Ice, who ate so slowly he still has a plate in front of him, is quiet. He sits across from me at the breakfast nook, staring out the window and watching small streaks of water flow down the glass. He's obviously displeased with the state of the world.

The rain is a soft drizzle, but it'll pick up later today. The storm is serious business, I guess. A tropical cyclone. There are flood warnings on the coast and everything.

As Night cleans the kitchen, her movements are more sluggish than usual. A plate clatters in the sink, and she gasps softly. *Less precise than usual.* She wasn't kidding when she said bad weather messes them up.

Across from me, Ice yawns. He drops his fork onto his plate, which still has half a sandwich and some fruit salad on it, and my attention settles on his hands—his knuckles. They're scraped, the skin visibly damaged, but only the deepest split on his right hand looks fresh.

I hesitate, but I ask, "How are your hands?"

"My hands?" He raises one to examine it and flexes his fingers, closing and opening his fist a few times. "They're fine."

"Can I see?"

He laughs easily, but he slides his hand across the table. Then he watches my face with such careful focus that I pause before I finally look down.

The cracked knuckles are scabbed over after only one night. Some redness, but no swelling. My finger brushes against the worst split. His skin is warm, but the touch is like an electric shock seizing my heart. A series of images flash in my mind—something that can't be real. For half an instant.

*A jolt of pain. Blood. Wide, yellow eyes. Pleading.*

*Ah—* My eyes dart up as I retract my hands and fold them in my lap. Ice is still watching me, but I don't think he noticed my breath catch.

"Why don't you have Smoke heal it?" I ask.

He blinks and pulls his hand back. "Why should I?"

"I don't know. I just thought—"

Night sighs from the kitchen. "Ice won't let Smoke use his healing ability on him. He's never liked it for some reason."

"Perhaps I don't mind waiting for a wound to heal on its own," he says. His expression is mild, but his voice carries an unfamiliar edge. "Injury doesn't bother me, and it won't scar, so there's no point in healing it artificially. Besides, this is nothing.

It'll be gone in a few days."

"Nothing? Doesn't it hurt?"

He rubs his knuckles and studies the injured hand with a soft frown. Then, after looking up to meet my gaze, he shakes his head.

"It doesn't hurt at all?" I ask again, surprised.

He glances out the window. "My hand does not hurt at all."

*How?* Even considering that immortals apparently heal faster than humans, his hands were a mess yesterday. Broken skin, oozing blood from several splits. But, now, the wounds look days old and don't bother him?

Maybe Smoke was right.

Maybe I don't understand anything about immortals.

*Whatever.*

"Night and I were talking earlier," I say, trying to sound as casual as possible. "About how much longer I should stay."

His focus darts to me. A bit uneasy. Then his eyes narrow, and he turns toward the kitchen, where Night was minding her own business and drying her hands on a dishtowel.

"There's no need to look at me like that." She drops the towel on the counter and joins us at the breakfast nook with a smile. "Of course, I said she's welcome to stay as long as she wants."

*Yet she leaves out her offer to drive me home...*

Ice runs a hand through his rather unkempt hair before meeting my gaze with a most unreadable expression.

"You want to leave in this weather?" he asks.

"Oh, no." I laugh, gesturing with my hands as I shake my head. "It's not that. I already told you Rose is getting worried. I can't tell her what's really going on, obviously, but it's not, um… I guess it's not like me to do something like this."

"Your roommate?" With a sigh, he rests his chin in his hands. "Right. You did mention that. Well, at least stay until the hurricane blows over."

*Calling it a hurricane is a little dramatic.*

"That's fair," I agree. "It'll only be a few days, and that's what I was thinking anyway."

"Thanks." He suddenly looks very tired.

* * * * *

Ice turned in for the night immediately after dinner, and Night left the den an hour later. Since then, I've been reading the book she let me borrow. I turn the page, I find *The End*, and I sniffle.

The last few chapters nearly made me cry.

Hoping to distract myself from *feelings*, I set the book down and check my phone. It's almost 10PM. There's rarely anything interesting on FaceSpace, but I scroll down my newsfeed anyway.

A notification pops up—the soft ding of an incoming message.

**Rose:** Hey! Sorry we haven't talked in a few days, I've been pretty busy. How are things in Riverview?

She knows I drank too much and kissed Ice, but she has no idea that James exists. And, after yesterday…

**Me:** Things are okay. It's raining.

*Nice.* Is that the best I could come up with?

> **Rose:** Rain? In July??
>
> **Me:** Yep. It's a tropical storm, I guess.
>
> **Rose:** A whole storm? Wow. Are you still at Ice's house?
>
> **Me:** Yep…
>
> **Rose:** LMAO
>
> **Rose:** Are you moving in?
>
> **Me:** Absolutely not.

I say no, but I honestly can't blame her for thinking I am. The ringing that cuts through the silence startles me, though. Stifling a groan, I drag myself off the couch and answer the phone.

"Hello?" I whisper.

"Jayde. What the fuck are you still doing there?"

"Um…"

I glance down the quiet hallway. Then at the sliding glass door.

"You've been sleeping at this dude's house for a week now, right?" I can't tell whether she's impressed or concerned. "You've seriously been there this whole time? Since the Fourth?"

Rain falls steadily in the backyard, but a canopy covers half the patio. I don't know if anyone is still awake, but—

*I'm not scared of the rain.*

"Yep," I say, stepping outside.

The air is surprisingly warm. The sound of rain pattering on the glass above fills my ears. It's comforting, but it doesn't give me any ideas. I still don't know what to say.

Immortal topics are off limits. James, and the full extent of what happened on the Fourth of July, is definitely off limits. I don't want to worry her. I don't want her to think I was hurt, or…

I sit on the ground just outside the closed door.

"It's weird being home alone," I say. "And I'm good friends with Ice's sister, so I guess it's easier to stay here."

Rose laughs. "Aww, Jay… It almost sounds like you miss me."

I do. *I really do.* But part of me dreads her inevitable return.

"How's it going with Ice, anyway?" she asks. "Things sounded sketch as hell the last time we talked, so I cannot believe you're still there."

I grimace. "For one, he is not my boyfriend."

"No?"

"Um…" *She wants gossip?* Where do I start? "You remember how I kissed him on the Fourth of July, right?"

"Uh-huh?" she agrees, her interest growing.

"Well, I finally asked him how he feels about me—while I was sober, obviously."

"Aaaand?"

"He rejected me."

"Oh," she says. There's a long pause during which I chew on my lip and stare out into the rain. "And you're still staying there?"

Now that I've said it out loud, it does sound ridiculous.

Ice is my sponsor, though. He's legally responsible for me

and wants to make sure I'm safe. I mean, James has popped up out of nowhere twice already. He's clearly unstable. And the whole tropical storm thing does bother me a little.

"It's fine. I'm only staying here until the storm blows over."

"Okay. You'd tell me if anything…bad was going on, right?"

I wince. She doesn't believe me. She has every right to be concerned—and she might be catching onto something—but I can't let her worry more than she already has.

"Of course," I say. "Everything is fine. No one's forcing me to stay, but it sounds like the weather is gonna be rough for a few days, and I'd rather be here than alone at home."

She laughs, the sound light. "You're seriously that worked up over a little rain? So worried you'd stay at this guy's house even after he rejected you?"

"First off, it's not *a little rain*. It's a tropical storm." I pause to groan. "But I don't know if I was rejected…technically. He said he likes me, but not the same way, since he thinks I'm in love with him or whatever—"

"In love?" she asks.

"Yeah…"

She lets out an exaggerated sigh. "Didn't I specifically tell you *not* to get too attached?"

I stare into the darkest corner of the backyard, where the light from the den can't reach. "I don't know if I'm in love with him," I say under my breath. "And I don't get what he meant, exactly. He doesn't like me the same way, but he also kissed me, so—"

"Okay, wait. He kissed you *after* he rejected you?"

"It wasn't great. I have a feeling we won't do it again."

"And you still agreed to stay there?" she asks.

I laugh. "Trust me, Rose, I am going home as soon as the rain lets up."

"Alright," she agrees, her suspicion only feigned in part.

"I swear," I say with another laugh. "Hanging out with Night is fun, anyway. It's not like I'm miserable here."

*At least that much is true.*

# forty-four

When I wake up to my quiet alarm, the rain is audible on the roof, and I can just make out the shadow of fat droplets through the sheer curtains. The soothing drumbeat almost convinces me to close my eyes again.

*But I shouldn't.*

Ice is in a dead sleep, curled up near the foot of the bed. I don't bother talking to him. I just grab a change of clothes and leave to shower. Then I throw my damp hair up in a messy bun and wander out to the great room. It's empty, but Night made it clear yesterday that breakfast will likely be fend-for-yourself for early risers until the storm ends.

That's fine.

I make toast and a bowl of instant oatmeal and watch out the bay window from the breakfast nook. The rain is impressive. It's not too windy yet, and there's no sign of lightning, but the water comes down steadily, leaving the street outside slick.

When I'm done eating, I clean up after myself and move into the den, where I nestle myself on one of the loveseats and pick out a nature documentary on Netflix.

A half-hour in, a noise from the great room startles me. The front door opening. But I don't move. An itch of concern tickles the back of my neck, and I stare at the arch and listen to the door close—to the rustling in the other room.

Then Night walks through, wearing an oversized hoodie and cotton shorts. She lights up when she sees me. My muscles relax, and I pause the TV.

"Good morning," she says brightly. "Did I surprise you?"

I scratch my cheek. "I guess I figured you were still asleep."

"That's fair." She flashes a smile that borders on embarrassed. "But I had some shopping to do and thought I'd get it out of the way early. All sense goes out the window here when it rains."

"Need help putting anything away?" I ask.

With a glance down the empty hallway, she agrees. I follow her into the great room, where three grocery bags sit on the floor beside the dining table.

"I have something for you," she says.

"Oh?"

The hesitance in her voice confuses me, but I ignore it. I heft one of the shopping bags onto the counter and start sorting the groceries. By now, I know where just about everything goes.

"Ice is your legal sponsor, right?" she asks. When I nod, she smiles. "Honestly, I feel responsible too, so I want you to see this house as a safe place. You will always be welcome here."

"What about your parents? It's their house…"

"Don't worry," she says with a mild laugh. "They won't mind. My parents support the Human Immortal Program—anything that aims to improve human-immortal relations. So, that's why—"

She reaches into the pocket of her hoodie and pulls out a key.

"It goes to the front door. I took it upon myself to have one made for you since Ice hasn't bothered to do so himself."

I tip my head, having never once considered I might need one. But she grins and tosses it in my direction, and I surprise myself by catching the candy-striped house key.

*Now it really feels like I've moved in.*

I tuck the key in my pocket. "Thanks?"

"Of course! I picked up an extra umbrella too. I assume you didn't pack one?"

"No, but I doubt I'll get much use out of it," I say, glancing out the window over the counter.

"I suppose, but you never know. The weather doesn't affect you the same way, so you might get bored and change your mind."

She removes a small, blue travel umbrella from one of the bags and hangs it on a hook near the front door. Then she returns to help put away the groceries—which mainly consists of snacks and other marginally healthy convenience foods.

Why do I have a feeling this will be a long few days?

* * * * *

Ice doesn't come out until lunch. The same as yesterday, he's dressed in day clothes, but his hair is a mess. He eats slowly and quietly, and then, while I'm helping Night tidy up the kitchen, he snags an unopened bag of trail mix from the cabinet beside the fridge.

"Goodnight," he says on his way out of the room.

I pass Night another rinsed plate. She accepts the dish and sets it in the dishwasher without speaking. When she looks to me again, her expression warms.

"Is he gonna be okay?" I ask.

She laughs. "Ice is fine. He's more affected by the weather than most immortals, but he's perfectly fine. You don't need to worry about him."

Smoke snickers from his spot at the breakfast nook, but he also looks quite tired. I'm fairly certain he spent most of yesterday in bed too.

When we finish loading the dishwasher, the three of us move into the den. The twins take one loveseat while I take the other, and I watch the historical drama Night put on in between snippets of conversation and checking my phone.

I manage to have an uncontroversial exchange with Rose over messenger for the first time in days. We talk about her pregnant cousin. Her mom. Kyle. The Grand Canyon—she already bought a few souvenirs.

Then she asks about the weather.

I leave the couch and send a picture of the view outside the sliding glass door.

Riverview is dreary. Grey. Wind disturbs the trees, bending their branches, and the rain comes down in sheets. It hasn't stopped since it picked up last night. The north side of town is under a flood watch, but Westbrooke's drainage system is modern. It shouldn't be so bad here.

It's loud, though. A constant buzz in the background.

When I turn back, Smoke is leaned on Night's shoulder,

with his half-lidded attention on his phone rather than the TV. I catch Night's gaze, and she smiles softly.

Ten minutes later, Smoke is asleep in feline form—a slender, black cat—with his head resting on his sister's leg.

*Honestly, it's kind of cute.*

* * * * *

Night asks me to check on Ice while she's cooking dinner—he ignored a text earlier, I guess—so I do, though I hesitate outside his bedroom door. I listen to the sound of the rain for a moment. Then I let myself in.

The lights are off. He's passed out on top of the comforter, in human form and wearing only sweatpants. Eyes closed, bare chest slowly rising and falling.

*Aaaaa—*

Well, he's asleep. I'm not about to wake him up.

I return to the kitchen alone. Night shrugs and continues cooking, so I join Smoke at the dining table. He doesn't glance up from his phone—busy playing a mobile game or something.

Not sure what else to do, I check my phone too. FaceSpace is boring. A handful of people who are still in town have posted about the rain. A local news page wrote an article about a neighborhood uptown that experienced flooding along the riverbank. I delete a few spam emails.

Night finishes cooking and sets aside a plastic-wrapped plate in the fridge before joining me and Smoke at the dining table. Dinner is calm. Uneventful.

No one has plans to do anything until after the rain ends.

As we finish eating, I offer to clean up.

Night, who had just stood from the table before I spoke up, agrees. She drops back into her chair and rests her head on crossed arms. Smoke pats her on the shoulder before leaving the room, off to sleep again.

"You've been a great help," she mumbles.

"It's no trouble, honestly." I return my attention to the dishes in the sink. There's not much to do. A few plates and forks. A couple pans to rinse. "I have to ask, though: Does half the town end up like this when it rains?"

She laughs. "No. We just happen to be especially vulnerable—ironic considering we're *water* immortals. Most don't have such a hard time."

"It's supposed to get worse tomorrow, isn't it?"

"Can you feel the storm coming?"

I glance over my shoulder, catching her curious gaze. Only one blue eye is visible through her fluffy, unstyled hair. And I wonder, *is my human life half as mysterious to her as her immortal life is to me?*

"No," I admit. "If it weren't for the internet, I'd have no idea what the weather was up to. But you can tell?"

"We can sense when the weather's about to shift. It has something to do with the scent of the air. The humidity. Static electricity, perhaps? To be honest, I'm not sure exactly how it works. Instinct, I suppose."

"Well, I guess humans lost that ability somewhere along the evolutionary line."

She laughs again, the sound muffled as she must have buried her face in her arms. I focus on the dishes. On the sponge in my hand. The warmth of the water. The sound of the sink running.

I sigh. “You don’t have to stay up with me.”

She sighs too. “What’s the point in being here if you never see any of us? Ice convinced you to stay, but he’s hopeless in the rain, so keeping you company is the least I can do.”

I start the dishwasher and turn toward the dining table. Night is sat up straight, hugging her arms as she watches the rain through the bay window.

“You’re a good person,” I say.

“You think so?” Her eyes are a little wide, like I surprised her. Then her expression softens. “Well… Thanks, I suppose.”

I manage to talk her into going to bed, assuring her that I’ll be fine on my own. Then I snuggle into the corner of a loveseat in the den. A nature documentary and the pattering of rain outside makes for soothing background noise while I kill time on my phone.

The documentary ends, and I decide to turn in for the night too. But, when I step into the bedroom, Ice is still sprawled out in the middle of the bed in human form.

I call his name, my voice quiet. He doesn’t react, so I carefully change into pajamas before inching closer.

His face is still. Neutral. Wavy, blonde hair falls over his eyes. His chest rises and falls, muscles shifting beneath smooth skin with each deep breath.

*Now it just sucks that he’s so attractive.*

Even if he’s taking feline form, this is the person I’ve been sharing a bed with. *It hurts…* But I suppress my disappointment, take a deep breath, and tap him on the arm.

"Hey. Ice."

He makes a soft noise before opening one eye. "Do you need something?"

"Just, um—" I avert my gaze. "Can you scoot over a little?"

His other eye opens. He glances at the alarm clock. With a tired laugh, he sits up and runs a hand through his hair, pushing it out of his face.

"Of course," he says.

I catch a brief flash of a smile before he morphs. His paws sink into the comforter as he retreats to the far side of the bed, where he lies down again, facing the wall.

"Better?" he asks.

I stare at the queen-sized bed. At the fluffy white cat curled on top of the comforter. At the wide spot left for me.

*He moved so far away.*

Why does that bother me?

# forty-five

The low rumble of thunder rouses me from sleep.

I don't open my eyes, having noticed a small, gentle weight pressed against my back through the comforter. I can just make out Ice's soft breathing over the rain thrumming on the roof. There's something nice about it—the sound and the rhythm and the warmth transferred through the blanket.

*Can he purr like a normal cat?*

A second roll of thunder—a louder, crackling boom—finally snaps my eyes open. The red numbers on the alarm clock blink. The power must have gone out at some point overnight, so I check my phone. It's 8:34AM.

I could probably get another hour or two of sleep, but waking up at a decent time feels like the one aspect of my life I can still control.

I am not ready to give that up yet.

Careful and slow, I crawl out of bed. The movement didn't bother Ice. His feline form remains lying on its side in the middle of the bed, dead asleep.

I grab my phone and a change of clothes.

The room lights up for an instant—a flash of lightning through the window. More thunder as I step into the hallway. The house is quiet. I check, but neither of the twins are up, so I shower, pull my hair into a messy bun, and wander into the great room.

The house smells like peaches, and I'm no longer alone.

A small cat with short, black fur is seated in the bay window's deep sill, staring out at the rain. A tall, orange candle burns on the table. The cat turns to me with large, blue eyes as I approach.

"Good morning," Night's clear voice says.

"You're up early."

She laughs. "Am I? What about you?"

"I'm fine. Bored, I guess."

"Considering the weather, I imagine most of Riverview is bored," she says, turning back to the window.

Her tail curls over her dainty paws, and she gazes up into the grey clouds. The rain is heavy and unrelenting, falling at an angle. A bolt of lightning illuminates the sky, far in the distance. Thunder rumbles through the house a moment later.

I step away to get a glass of water. When I return to the table, it seems she hasn't moved at all. She's just…staring. I look through the window, but I don't see anything noteworthy.

I slide into the bench seat. "Is something wrong?"

"Wrong?" She glances over her shoulder. Then she shrugs and turns away again. "I can't say if anything's wrong. I suppose I'm just thinking. Or…listening?"

A chill runs down my spine, but I shake it off.

"Listening for what?"

"I had a strange dream this morning. It could be nothing—as many dreams are—but today does feel off somehow. It's difficult to explain."

"The storm, maybe?"

She sighs. "Perhaps. Even so, a troubling dream and lingering sense of unease don't automatically mean tragedy will strike."

"You're sure?"

"Well… Yes. And no."

*Are you psychic or not? Should I be concerned?*

She morphs. Her human form, dressed in pajamas, sits in the sill of the bay window with crossed legs hanging over the edge. She watches the rain. Then she faces me, her expression careful —guarded.

The constant drumming on the roof shifts, growing tinnier and more pelting as the wind picks up and the rain turns to hail. Pellets of ice bounce in the street as they fall. More thunder.

Our eyes meet again, and she offers me a warm but tired smile.

"Life is a mess, Jayde. An uninterrupted series of events and decisions. Actions and reactions. Even with my ability, the future is impossible to predict with much accuracy. There are simply too many variables. A single impulsive move on the part of one person can change everything. Not to mention how easily a dream can be misinterpreted—"

Chin held in her hand, she cuts herself off with another sigh.

"I guess what I'm trying to say is that surprising things happen often—things you never would have seen coming. But change isn't always bad. We shouldn't be afraid of something simply because it's different."

*Is she talking in riddles?*

"What does this have to do with your dream?"

She hesitates, then laughs and shakes her head. "It doesn't... exactly. I can't explain the dream well. It was mostly emotions. Abstract thoughts. Nothing specific. What I said is just something to consider."

I frown. *For some reason, this reminds me...*

"After what happened with James, do you think Ice is right? Do you think I shouldn't talk to other immortals?"

"Of course not." She rolls her eyes and folds her arms over her chest. "Ice may act like it, and he may even sound convincing at times, but I assure you he does not know everything."

"I know that."

She gazes out into the rain, her expression growing pensive. "Don't worry about Ice. Do what you think is right."

What I think is right?

*Is staying here right?*

* * * * *

Ice didn't come out for lunch. I ate with Night and Smoke at the breakfast nook. Neither of them mentioned him, so I didn't either.

We talked about the weather. The rain is still heavy, the street outside slick as water streams into the storm drains. There might be another bout of thunder tonight, but the worst of it should be over by morning. The rain will only last a couple more days.

My phone's weather app agrees.

It's almost dinnertime now. The twins are in the great room, preparing to cook, but I haven't heard a peep from Ice's bedroom all day. *Should I check on him?* Night and Smoke aren't concerned, but it's weird to sleep all day without coming out to eat or do literally anything else.

Isn't it?

*I don't know.*

Moving into the great room, I sit at the table and watch the twins work in the kitchen. They chat between themselves, laughing at things the other never said out loud. They're having fun, and I don't mind watching.

But I keep thinking about what Night said this morning.

She never clearly explained what she meant or what abstract emotions her dream conveyed, but I feel something now too. The energy isn't overwhelming like it was on the Fourth of July. It's not scary. It's just…off. A little itchy. A little *strange*.

Maybe it is the storm. The static electricity in the air. Maybe it's nothing. She doesn't seem uncomfortable anymore, and she hasn't mentioned it in hours.

When she finishes cooking, Night takes a plate to Ice before she returns to the dining table.

"Did he wake up?" Smoke asks.

She tips her head as though confused. "He wasn't asleep."

"He wasn't?" we both ask in surprise.

"No," she says with a mild laugh. "He was staring up at the ceiling with this blank look on his face. Like he was thinking about something. Anyway, he thanked me for the food and told me to leave."

*Kind of rude, but that sounds about right.*

He's had a few moments when he'll talk and smile normally, but the storm-induced lethargy has made him moody. He doesn't want anyone to bother him. Our presence is an inconvenience that interferes with him sleeping all day.

Night says he hates people seeing him like that, but he can't control the way his body reacts to the weather. Either way, hiding in his bedroom 24/7 is a little dramatic.

She laughs when I say that.

"Ice? Dramatic?" Smoke's eyes flick in my direction, and he flashes a well-humored but crooked smile. "Impossible."

*Well, they know him better than I do.*

* * * * *

The credits roll, and Night sighs from her spot on the other end of the loveseat. She looks tired, and she leans against the arm of the couch with her head propped up by her hand.

Smoke went to bed before the movie began, and it's starting to get late—by storm standards, anyway. I'm surprised she stayed up this long considering how early she woke up this morning.

"Everything okay? Are you still worried about your dream?"

She cracks an uneasy smile. "My dream? I still can't say it meant anything, but it reminded me of things I wish it hadn't."

*Oh?*

Before I say anything, her expression shifts. She frowns. Then she picks up the remote and turns the TV off.

"Do you ever wish you could forget something?" she asks, not looking at me or the dark TV screen or anything in particular.

"And I mean truly forget it forever—to have the memories wiped from your mind with no trace?"

"Um..." A handful of unpleasant events come to mind—some recent, others not. "I don't know. Maybe."

She looks at me then, her expression unreadable. "Would you still want to forget it if it wasn't always bad? If parts were good?"

"I don't know." *How am I supposed to answer this question?* "Your experiences make you who you are as a person, right? Good or bad."

"What if the bad parts were unspeakably awful?" she asks, her jaw strained as she watches me with a more careful, nervous intent.

I frown. "What is this about? Are you sure you're okay?"

The tension leaves her shoulders as she glances away. With another sigh, she stands from the loveseat and smooths the front of her muslin dress.

"Yes, I'm okay," she says, her voice level. "Never mind what I said. I'm glad you haven't gone through anything like that. You're lucky."

I'm not convinced I haven't experienced things I wish I could forget, but something leads me to believe I haven't gone through anything quite as traumatic as whatever she has in mind. But, even being so terrible, it wasn't all bad? Parts were good?

*Ugh.* It's more confusing than our conversation this morning.

"You sure you don't want to talk about it?" I ask, both because I'm concerned and because I'm dying to know what she's talking about.

But she shakes her head, one arm drawn across her body to hold the other. "One day, perhaps." She glances over her shoulder to offer an apologetic smile. "But it's a long story, and it's pretty boring."

*Uh-huh...*

I give up and ask if she's heading to bed. Her smile brightens.

"I think so," she says. "I'll see you in the morning?"

"I don't have anywhere else to be."

She laughs, looking more like her usual self, before she retreats to her bedroom and leaves me alone in the dimly lit den.

*You know...* I think I'll sleep out here tonight.

Before I left Ice's bedroom, I found myself lingering beside the bed. He didn't wake up when I opened the door or walked inside. He didn't wake up when I unzipped my duffel bag to find pajamas.

So I stood at the foot of the bed, and I watched him sleep for a minute, fighting the urge to pet his fluffy feline form.

His small body shifted with each steady breath, and I just... watched him, and I let myself wonder. *Is he as soft as he looks?* He looks like a normal house cat. How would it feel to run my fingers through his fur?

*How would it feel to run my fingers through his hair?*

I doubt I'll ever find out.

Because he doesn't like me.

I tried to convince myself I was fine, but a small pinprick of hurt followed me. As I stepped out of the room. As I took a shower. As I dried my hair with a towel to avoid waking anyone with the blow-dryer. It bothered me as I watched the rain through the sliding glass door before I closed the curtain.

I stared at my dark silhouette in the mirror on the wall behind the loveseats. Then I took the River Sapphire off and set it on the edge of the TV stand beside my phone. I lay down, and I pulled the blanket up to my chin, and I shut my eyes.

At least an hour has passed, but the thought is still there.

*Ice will never like me as much as I liked him in June.*

The thunder's supposed to start soon.

Will I fall asleep before it does?

# forty-six

It's late.

I don't know how late, or what woke me, but it's still raining, and only a dim light filters into the den through an uncovered sliver of sliding glass door.

With a quick stretch and yawn, and without leaving the warm comfort of the oversized throw blanket, I reach, reach, *reach* for my phone on the TV stand. The screen is too bright, but I manage to catch the time before locking the phone and dropping it to the floor.

1:48AM.

Thunder rolls through the house—a loud, crackling rumble that startles me. Is that what woke me? The storm?

I sit up and listen to the rain. The heavy patter on the roof I've grown so comfortable with over the past few days. It's familiar and strangely…*nostalgic?*

Then something intersects it. Another series of sounds.

This new sound is just audible over the rain and, like the rain, comes from outside. *Slow footsteps on the wooden patio.* They stop somewhere in front of the sliding glass door, which is still obscured by the thick blackout curtain.

A pang of anxiety.

Could it be Ice? *No. There's no way.* I haven't seen him step outside once since the rain began.

Night? *Why would she be up so late? And outside?*

Smoke? *I seriously doubt it.*

I freeze momentarily as the door engages with a soft click and creeps open. Slow. Quiet. The light shifts, the curtain disturbed by a hand.

And I recover. I drop from the couch and duck behind the TV on its low stand. My heart races, but I reach for the remote.

Someone pokes their head into the house. I hold my breath as the intruder glances around the den. Then they step through the door. They wear dark clothes with a hood pulled over their head. I can't make out any details in the low light, but I don't dare move from behind the TV stand.

They haven't noticed me yet.

The door slides shut but doesn't latch, and the intruder takes another careful step inside. They move slowly, glancing around, their posture stiff and hunched.

I position my thumb over the power button on the TV remote.

*Whoever it is, it's definitely not one of the Monroes.*

After a deep breath to steel myself, I pop up from the floor and jam the button with unnecessary force. The TV menu's blue light reflects off the large mirror behind me, illuminating the room and the intruder, who turns to figure out where the light came from.

A man with wide, shadowed eyes.

*No way—*

The remote falls from my hand. It lands on the carpet with a soft thud as I draw my arms close to my chest.

*James.*

He stares at me like a deer in the headlights, silent and unmoving.

I glance down the hallway, but both bedroom doors are closed. All is quiet. *For now.*

*He shouldn't be here. I can't believe he'd come back.*

Stepping past the corner of the TV stand, I open my mouth to yell at him, but I freeze again. A second look at his pale face brings with it a sinking realization that steals the air from my lungs and shuts me up.

*Even from this distance with only the blue light reflected by the mirror…*

Thin, dark lines hatch the right side of his face. Another scab stretches across the bridge of his nose. A split lip, only partially healed. Altogether, the obvious remnants of a beating.

*Smoke was right.* Ice punched more than brick that day, and his fists weren't the only thing to hit the wall.

Injuries aside, both his dark, hooded jacket and beanie cap are soaked. Water drips from strands of short, orange hair poking out from beneath the hat. He must have been in the rain a long time to end up this wet.

*Miserable. He looks miserable.*

He absolutely should not be here, but I can't risk alerting the rest of the house now. What would Ice do if he found James here again—*and inside?*

"It's you," he says, his voice blank.

*Me?*

"What do you want?" I ask, careful to keep my voice low.

I inch a bit closer, positioning myself between him and the River Sapphire on the TV stand. *Just in case.*

"I don't know." His wide eyes turn downcast as he scratches the short stubble on his jaw. "I think… Maybe I hoped to find you here. To see you. One last time, I guess."

"What? Why?"

"Ah…"

He glances at the door, clearly uncomfortable. Then he looks to me again. He takes a step forward, but he freezes in place with his hands held at chest level as I adopt a more defensive posture.

For a long moment, neither of us move.

I listen to the storm outside—to another rumble of distant thunder. As I watch the anxiety playing about on his face, the tension in my muscles slowly dissipates.

He lowers his hands and sighs disparagingly. "Calm down. I'm not here to hurt you or anything. I swear."

Strangely, I don't *not* believe him. There's no way he's looking for a fight in this condition, but I certainly don't trust him, and he *should not be here.*

"You need to leave."

He shakes his head. "Not yet."

"Shh," I hiss, holding a finger to my lips as I peer down the dark hallway behind him. "You can't be here. What if—"

"Give me a minute," he says, desperation twisting his features.

"A minute?" *Ugh…* I move closer, desperate to speak even quieter than I already have been. "Well, what do you want?"

He nods, but he looks nervous and fidgety, and he glances over his shoulder again. Then he meets my gaze with a pronounced frown. A dark, purple bruise circles his left eye, the white of which is stained by pooling blood.

*This is worse than I imagined.* How awful did James look as Ice bandaged his bleeding hands and acted like he'd done nothing but scare him off?

A pang of sympathy worsens the pit in my stomach.

*I cannot let Ice catch him here.*

"I wanted…to apologize," he says. "For what happened."

*What?* He broke into the house of someone who hates his guts and just beat his ass a few days ago, not knowing if I would even be here? *Just to offer me an apology?*

"You shouldn't be here," I say. "You should—"

He shakes his head and takes another step forward, leaving only a couple feet between us. His eyes are wide with fear and despair. His expression holds no obvious malice, but I'm scared to move.

"It was a mistake," he insists, the words spilling out, frantic and staggered. "I didn't mean to hurt you, but you hit your head. You were bleeding. I didn't know what to do. I just— I panicked. I'm sorry."

I gesture with my hands, trying to shush him as my eyes wander toward the hallway again.

*Does he not realize how stupid this is?*

"Shut up," I say through my teeth, my attention trained not on the distressed man in front of me but on the door I know Ice is sleeping behind.

"I know," he groans, ignoring me. "I fucked up, but I want

to make things right before I—"

I look back to James, and my concern of Ice stepping out of his bedroom suddenly feels unimportant.

His quivering lips form the ghost of a smile, but his jaw is set, and tears prick his wide, bloodshot eyes. It's the face of someone struggling to hold it together. The face of someone desperately trying not to cry.

*With those injuries... Knowing what Ice did...*

My chest tightens, I ball the hem of my shirt in my hands, and I break eye contact. I can't bear to look directly at him. I stare at the floor between us instead.

"Please forgive me." His voice cracks. "I don't even care if you don't mean it. Lie to me. Keep hating me if you want. That's fine. I just—"

He shouldn't be here. He shouldn't be asking for forgiveness at 2AM after breaking into the house. How am I meant to respond? I don't want to deal with this right now. *I don't even understand why he's here.*

What difference does it make if he apologizes?

Why does it matter if I acknowledge it?

He flashes a pained smile, but his glassy eyes remain empty. "Please," he begs, his voice rising. "After tonight, you will never have to see me again."

"Shh!"

He visibly startles. His uneasy, about-to-cry smile falls, and I sigh.

"Fine." I hug my arms, trying to quash all emotion within me. "I accept your apology. Now, can you just leave before you wake someone up?"

He lets out a shaky breath, and, as he wipes his nose with the sleeve of his damp jacket, he suddenly looks more exhausted than before. There's something incredibly painful about it.

"Thank you," he says.

"Okay, now *go*."

He doesn't respond, and the room falls quiet.

Watching my feet again, I shift my weight. I relax my arms and scratch an itch on my wrist. Rain patters on the glass canopy outside. James' breathing is uneven.

I wait without moving, but he doesn't leave.

Instead, he takes a step closer. He reaches for his back pocket. I look up and raise a hand to stop him—we're too close—but I freeze as my fingertips brush cool, damp fabric.

*I hear thunder.*

James leans closer. His chest meets the resistance of my raised hand, but I can't bring myself to push him away. I can't speak or breathe. I can't *think* as trembling lips brush the top of my head.

*What—?*

We're so close. Far too close—my nose almost touching his jacket zipper. I smell the rain. Dirt and sweat and a hint of tobacco smoke. He touches my hand, pressing something into it. He closes my fingers around the thin, plastic object before he lets go and takes a step back.

"I don't understand…" My voice is so soft, I don't know if he heard me, so I raise it a little and ask again, "Why are you here?"

Shadowed eyes meet mine for an instant, and the room plunges into darkness. The TV shut itself off before I could make out his expression. Now, I can only watch his silhouette.

He shakes his head.

James turns away without answering my question. He walks to the sliding glass door. The door slides open, and the room fills with the sound of rain, but he doesn't step out.

He glances at me again, darkness obscuring his face.

"Bye," he says. "Sorry for everything."

Then he steps out onto the patio. The door slides shut, the click carrying an uncomfortable finality, and I'm standing alone with the lingering scent of rain in the air and a plastic card in my hand.

I tear my eyes from the door and turn around. The faintest hint of light reflecting off the River Sapphire's polished gemstone catches my eye.

*He didn't even mention it.*

But he left...*something*. It's too dark to see, so I turn on the nearest lamp and hold the card under the light.

A vertical California driver's license.

*James Nathaniel Reid*

He left his ID?

*Why do I have this?*

Heart racing, card in hand, I spin toward the sliding glass door—the place he disappeared through. The thin edge of the card digs into my palm and fingers.

A familiar sensation. A jolt of anxiety. A slow, sinking dread.

*A flash of red. Dripping blood. A puddle forming on a dark, wood floor. A hand—*

My stomach twists, and I move without thinking. One hand

hits the edge of the door, and the other drags it open. I stumble outside and flip the nearest light switch. The fairy lights illuminate the backyard, but it's empty.

James is gone.

My eyes wander down to the card again.

I barely recognize the guy in the photo as the one who just left. He's not smiling—not really—but he looks like a normal person. He turns twenty-one next month.

A flash of lightning startles me. I gasp and look around, unable to ignore the nagging discomfort as it settles in my chest. I rub my arms to flatten the goosebumps, and I turn the lights off before I step back inside.

I lock the doors. I pick the remote up off the floor and return it to the TV stand. Then I sit on the loveseat.

And I realize I'm still holding James' driver's license.

Using my phone as a flashlight, I stare at the amber eyes and neutral expression in the photo and can't help but compare it to the wreck of a person I just spoke with.

Why would he leave this with me?

*What am I supposed to do about it?*

# forty-seven

~ ∞ ~

*It's dark and so, so quiet.*

*I see nothing. Hear nothing.*

*After a long moment of surreal desolation, impossibly dark shapes materialize out of the shadow and drift about within the murky depths like deep sea creatures.*

*When I try to move, my body doesn't respond. It's as though I'm floating in a vast ocean of nothingness—and I am part of that nothingness—but that can't be right. I must be somewhere. This can't be nowhere. I can't be nothing.*

*So where am I?*

*From the dark, flashes of stark white shock me. The light is blinding compared to the darkness around it. Images and short scenes that play out like old film clips join the jarring lights, the images so brief and blurry I can't begin to identify them.*

*The light is painful, but I can't look away or close my eyes. I'm forced to watch—to experience it all.*

*A flash of white teeth.*

*An open door. A dark silhouette runs through.*

*Several faces pass by in such quick succession their features muddle together.*

*Nervous laughter. A hand held over the mouth.*

*Hardwood floors. Clean, white walls. A reflection in a mirror.*

*The glint of polished steel.*

*I have no physical body in this strange place, but that doesn't stop the emotions and sensations that accompany the images from washing over me. A sinking horror. A wave of nausea. A sharp, hot pain. One after the other.*

*Heavy sobs echo around me, growing louder and louder until they're deafening and threaten to drive me mad. I finally reach my breaking point, but, just as I do, the sounds and lights and foreign emotions vanish as quickly as they came.*

*Once again, I'm plunged into a silent dark.*

*The sound of breathing rises around me. Soft. Quiet. I can't sense the emotion behind it, and it soon fades.*

*A scene replaces it, exploding from a single point in space before me. A sunset sky awash with oranges and fiery reds. The tangy scent of saltwater. The gentle breaking of ocean waves upon a distant, unseen shore.*

*The beautiful scene envelops me, comforting me. It's peaceful, like everything in the world is perfect in this one, fleeting moment.*

*There's no concern. No fear. No pain.*

*But a flash of light erases the sunset all too soon, and my surroundings fade to black. It's painfully quiet for so long. Like sitting in a room without so much as a ticking clock. I worry I'll be trapped in this lonely place forever.*

BANG!

*An anguished scream breaks the silence as a blinding, white light obliterates the impossible darkness. While someone laughs coldly, another person weeps. Pain. Grief. Loss.*

*It's too bright.*

*The light hurts. Burns.*

*I fight to squeeze my eyes shut in a desperate attempt to block out the awful light. To my surprise, I finally can, and I relish the natural darkness that closing my eyes brings.*

*The laughter and crying fade until the only noise remaining is a quiet dripping. Drip, drip, drip. Like a leaking tap. Something about the sound—some quality I can't quite explain—makes me deeply uncomfortable.*

*I open my eyes and find I'm neither in the bright light nor the pitch black.*

*Instead, I'm standing in the middle of a dimly lit hallway lined with wooden doors. Illuminated by only a yellowed light fixture on the dark ceiling, the hallway seems to stretch on forever in both directions before eventually fading out of sight.*

*Weird.*

*I glance down.*

*Hands.*

*They don't quite look like my hands, but they're drenched in blood. I stare at my palms as the warm, red liquid drips in thin ribbons from my skin to the floor, where a puddle forms on the dark hardwood.*

*What—?*

*What happened here?*

*The hands disappear. The hallway does too, and the darkness around me morphs into a deep, crimson red. It's hot and sticky, and I am drowning—suspended in an ocean of blood. The salty, metallic tang overwhelms my senses as the thick, warm liquid chokes me.*

*Unable to breathe, I desperately wish to claw at my throat. I would do anything to make the pain stop. Though, if I have a body anymore, it refuses to respond.*

*The space goes black once more, and I fall to the ground.*

*As I cough and wheeze, I hear myself for the first time since the nightmare began. I open my eyes. I have legs. I'm sitting on my knees. I have hands too.*

*My hands.*

*I touch my face. My hair. My arms. My chest.*

*I am here, and I am myself. Jayde Palmer. In the middle of the suffocating darkness. It's strange, but my body is somehow fully illuminated against the void.*

*Once I catch my breath and recover my strength, I stand up to better survey my surroundings. But there's nothing. No walls, structures, or details off in the distance. There aren't any visible lights in the area, nor do I cast a shadow on the smooth, black ground.*

*Seriously... What is this place?*

*When I turn, someone is there.*

*How? I was alone. When did someone else show up?*

*The person—a man—stands several yards away, his back lit up the same unnatural way I am. His form sticks out against the darkness like a shining beacon. Messy, orange hair and dark clothes.*

*It's James.*

*I call out to him, but no sound leaves my throat. Confused, I try again with the same result. It's no use. For some reason, my voice doesn't carry through the air.*

*Despite my apparent inability to speak, James turns to face me. Bile rises in my throat as he does—and I catch his expression. His eyes are wide and pleading. His mouth twists in horror as he calls back, but the dark void absorbs the words the same as mine.*

*Then he raises an arm to point in my direction, and I freeze.*

Behind me?

*I turn around to find Ice standing inches away.*

*When did he get here?*

*His bright, blue eyes seem to glow in the low light as he smiles, but something isn't right.*

*Something...*

*Before I can figure it out, his smile hitches up on one side.*

*The floor drops out from underneath me with a sharp, musical sound reminiscent of thin glass shattering. My body is missing, as before, but I somehow still register the sensation of falling through space.*

*I fall down, down, down through the dark expanse.*

*An electronic beeping wells up around me. A slow and steady sound with a deep, unsettling emotion following it.*

*I want to cover my ears, but I don't have hands.*

*I want it to stop, but I have no control here.*

*The further I fall, the darker and colder the air becomes. An impossible color, darker than black. An uncomfortable chill. Then, slowly—so slowly—everything fades into the cold, inky darkness.*

*Even the beeping ceases.*

*Dark. Quiet.*

Finally, I hit the bottom.

~ ∞ ~

# forty-eight

*Blood—*

I sit up with a start, my heart pounding. My hands trembling. My cheeks warm and wet with tears. I hug my knees to my chest until my breathing calms, but I…

This isn't the first time I've had a dream like this.

*The Fourth of July.* The two dreams were related, if not identical. I don't know why or how I know, but *the flashes of blood... The dread. Paranoia. Itchiness.*

This is similar, but it's different too.

Instead of a haunting discomfort and the prickly sensation of being watched, I'm suddenly filled with determination. Drive. A rush of energy. The inexplicable but overwhelming desire to *find James Reid.*

I don't care about the storm—the wind or the rain still falling. We need to talk. What was he thinking? Why show up to apologize like that? Why—

*Lips brushing my hair.*

Something was wrong.

*Something was very wrong.*

I need to find him, but I can't tell Ice. He wouldn't understand.

The two have history—serious bad blood by the sound of it. They knew each other in high school, but Night won't elaborate beyond that. She doesn't want to talk about it either.

If I find James, can he explain more?

Maybe I should know exactly what happened when Ice caught him outside. Or what he did to earn Ice's hatred in the first place. Maybe it isn't important in the grand scheme of things, but…

*Something is wrong, and I can't sit here and do nothing.*

I wipe my eyes with the back of my hand and glance around the den. I'm alone. My phone is on the floor beside the couch—it's just after 7AM. James' driver's license is still under the pillow. I slip the card beneath my phone and set both on the TV stand as I leave the couch.

I pull the curtain over the sliding glass door open. Light floods the den. The backyard is empty, the world grey and miserably wet.

*Am I seriously about to walk through that?*

With a sigh, I leave the den and creep down the hallway.

I press my ear to Ice's bedroom door, but I don't hear anything. Slow and quiet, I turn the knob, crack the door, and peek inside. Ice's human form appears to be fast asleep with his back to the room, half covered by the grey comforter.

He doesn't shift, so I let myself in.

As I dig through my duffel bag, the most suitable clothes I find are skinny jeans, a light jacket, and my new leather fashion boots. Not ideal—or warm—but I didn't pack any rain gear, and the boots will work better than my old Converse.

Once dressed, I grab my wallet. The candy-striped house key is still inside. *I'm not moving in, but maybe this will come in handy.*

When I stand again, Ice hasn't moved. His shoulders rise and fall gently as he breathes.

For a moment, I second-guess heading out. But I recall the fear on James' face—both in that stupid dream and during his apology last night—and I know what I have to do. I slip my wallet into my pocket, sling my jacket over one arm, and leave the room.

I catch a glimpse of myself in the mirror. My reflection reveals a soft frown and green eyes shadowed by concern.

Concern for what? For whom? Myself? James?

*Ugh.*

I put my jacket on and comb my fingers through my hair before pulling it back into a long ponytail. As I fix my bangs, my eyes land on the empty space where the River Sapphire normally rests below my collarbone. I turn to the TV, where my phone and the necklace sit on the low stand. The light shining through the sliding glass door reflects off the polished, blue gemstone and leaves a spattering of bright white on the ceiling.

*The River Sapphire hasn't done much good so far, has it?*

Instead of wearing it, the necklace goes into my jacket pocket with my phone and James' license. Then I head to the great room, where I make a bowl of cereal and brainstorm a note to leave behind on a pad of sticky notes I found on the counter.

I assume Night will see the note first, but I don't dare mention James. *Something about going out for a walk. Something about being back later.* Vague. Ultimately meaningless. I sign the note with my name and a smiley face and leave it on the dining table.

*Well, I'm as ready as I'll ever be.*

I zip up my jacket, grab my purse and new travel umbrella from their hooks—thanks, Night—and open the front door.

*Oh.* It is very wet.

I stand on the landing, weighing the pros and cons of going anywhere now that I'm face-to-face with a literal curtain of water two feet in front of me.

The nearest bus stop is a block and a half from Westbrooke's east gate, which means I'll have to walk for at least half an hour through this downpour. Even if I do hop on a bus, where will I go? How am I supposed to find James? He could be anywhere.

I almost change my mind.

I almost give up and turn around.

I almost do, but the sickening unease and desperate longing for answers overpower my doubts. I can't ignore either. Not anymore.

*Okay, let's do this.*

My umbrella pops open at the click of a button, and I abandon the shelter of the covered landing. I descend the steps and make my way down the half-flooded path to the sidewalk.

The umbrella does its job, so I reach into my pocket and move onto the next hurdle: checking the address on James' license. I type it into my phone and recognize the general location. It's on the northeast side of town. The bus could get me within a few blocks.

*But…*

The more I focus on the location marker on my map—the more times my eyes follow the red line tracing the bus route—the more I feel like I won't find him there. Eventually, I delete the marker and stop walking to study the map again.

The only other place with any connection to James is the creepy house he drove me out to on the Fourth of July. The thought sends a shiver down my spine—but it might just be the wind.

*Where was that, again?*

The route I walked to get back to Ice's house on the Fourth is a total blur, but I might be able to piece it together using my phone. *I don't have any better ideas.*

With a sigh, I put my phone away. I tuck my ponytail into the back of my jacket, pull the hood up, and zip it up to my chin. Then I continue down the sidewalk.

Choosing the decrepit mansion in the middle of the woods over the address on his license means I can only take the bus so far. No matter how close it can get me to the turn-off, I'll still have to walk down that long gravel road. There's no guarantee I'll even find him there, but my gut tells me it's right, so…

I step in a shallow puddle, splashing water past the top of my boots. Cool moisture wicks up the exposed denim, and I glare down the manicured street as the determination I felt this morning slowly wanes.

*James had better be there when I show up.*

# forty-nine

By the time I round the final bend on the empty, tree-lined road and catch sight of the finish line, my boots squish and squelch as I walk. The umbrella helped, but water has been leaking through the seams for a while, so I'm both freezing cold and near soaking wet.

In daylight, the three-story building is far less creepy, though it's still imposingly large—like a cross between a giant, wooden crate and a Victorian mansion. A brick arch borders the large front doors and more brick forms decorative columns on the corners of the first floor. The rest of the exterior is wood coated with peeling paint of indeterminate color.

*What I remember of the interior isn't much better.*

I think it was once a house, but I can't imagine anyone actually lives there now. It's beyond wrecked. Several windows are broken. A few are boarded up with aging plywood. There's no way it's safe for human habitation.

Though, a dinged-up white sedan is parked off to one side of the building. James or no James, I should be able to escape the infernal rain as long as *someone* is inside.

I break into a jog and head for the large front doors. I splash through all sorts of mud puddles in the uneven gravel, but my jeans were already wet up to the knee. What difference does a little more water make?

When I reach the sheltered porch, I stand around, shifting my weight and collecting myself, until I finally muster the courage to knock on one of the heavy doors.

*Ow.*

I rub my sore knuckles before turning my attention back to the door. There's no immediate answer or sound from inside—not that I hear much over the rain drumming on the corrugated metal above my head.

Unsure what to do next, I shake my umbrella, dislodging as much water as possible, and fold it up. With the umbrella hanging around my wrist, I try to shake some of the water off my body too, but the results are far from spectacular.

I'm quite damp.

After another minute spent waiting, I press an ear to the door. I still don't hear anything on the other side.

*Please,* please, *be here... James. Anyone.*

Maybe whoever is inside didn't hear my first knock. I hadn't managed to knock very loud, anyway, so I give it another try—this time using my umbrella's plastic handle rather than one of my cold, numb hands.

I waste more time by pouring the water out of my boots, and then I get back to standing and waiting. I wait and wait, staring at my muddy boots and uncomfortably wet jeans, and I listen to the rain as the last remnants of hope and energy slowly drain from my cold, tired body.

*What if I just—*

My hand reaches for the door handle.

And then I hear someone shuffling around on the other side.

*Yes!*

I pat the door with the palm of my outstretched hand to let the person inside know that someone is standing out here. *Trust me; you weren't hearing things.*

"James Reid?" I call hopefully.

There's a pause. I hold my breath.

"Yeah?" a muffled voice responds.

*Oh, thank god.*

"Can I come in?" I ask, hoping my voice is loud enough. "I'm not sure how much more rain I can take."

Another pause, and the left door creaks open. James peeks half of his face out from behind the cracked door.

I wave and offer him an anxious, yet wholly relieved, smile.

He does not return the smile and instead looks horrified. "Why you?" he asks. "What are you doing here?"

When I shrug, his mouth closes tightly. He pokes his head further out and looks past me to scan the gravel lot. His eyes are wide and alert, as though he expects danger to pop out from behind me at any moment.

His concern is so contagious, I glance over my shoulder, but the lot is empty. Wet, but empty—save for what I assume is James' own vehicle.

"Is he here?" he asks.

"Who?" He doesn't answer my question, but I quickly realize what he means and shake my head. "No. It's just me."

He exhales deeply before opening the door the rest of the way. With the exception of the missing knit cap, he's wearing the same clothes as last night. Exhaustion dulls his eyes, but his frown grows more pronounced as he looks me over.

"You're soaked," he says, glancing around the empty lot again. "You…walked here? Through the rain?"

I nod, my smile fixed.

He grimaces and steps aside. "Maybe you should come in."

"Thanks." *That was the plan.*

James closes the heavy door behind me, muffling the sound of the rain. As we stand in the dusty, dimly lit vestibule, I think only of the last time I was here. It's different somehow—just as dingy and cluttered, but less dark, I guess. Is it the time of day or because I'm here under different circumstances?

The window closest to the door is broken. The frame is patched with plywood, but several large shards of yellowed glass still litter the floor.

*Definitely not fit for human habitation.*

I turn to James, but he looks just about as lost and confused as I feel. Avoiding eye contact, his attention darts around the room. He scratches his arm, tugging at the material of his coat.

He's obviously uncomfortable, but he eventually clears his throat and gestures further into the house.

"Here," he says. "Follow me."

*Jeez…* I'm starting to regret coming here.

I peel my jacket off as I trail after him, through the vestibule and into the next room. He flicks a light switch that activates a surprisingly bright lamp and livens up the room. A little.

As I look around, the room appears to be a trashed parlor or some kind of sitting room. There's a stairwell to the left. A small wicker couch against the opposite wall. An armchair. A cushioned chaise. A short table. A bookcase, knocked over and empty. The wallpaper is peeling, and there's more broken glass on the floor, along with a few sheets of plywood piled at the far end of the room near an empty door frame.

*Which board tripped me up before? If I looked, would I find a smear of blood somewhere?*

James stops near the couch, which is terribly dusty—as damn-near everything is. On second glance, though, it's dry and free of broken glass, so it's good enough. I unceremoniously dump my purse, umbrella, and damp jacket onto a nearby table before taking a seat at one end of the couch. It's not very comfortable, but sitting at all is a nice change.

James remains standing a few feet away. He doesn't face me, his shoulders slumped.

"Why are you here?" he asks.

His words are tinged with insecurity and annoyance, and both things bother me. Something about his hesitation now and the desperation in his voice last night. I don't understand—I'm not sure I want to—and I don't know how to answer.

Why did I come here? What dug its way into my subconscious and convinced me to leave Ice's house to find him? Was it only the dream that set me on edge?

*Or was it…? Something…*

"Hey, um…" I look up from my lap. "Are you okay?"

He flinches like my innocent question shocked him. Then he

turns to face me, his head tipped to one side, appearing confused and…disappointed, almost. His injuries are even more upsetting in daylight, and I have to force my expression to remain unchanged.

"I just wanted to apologize," he says, averting his gaze and adopting a more uneasy posture. "I didn't expect to see you again. You weren't supposed to come here. This is all wrong."

He didn't answer my question. He's obviously upset—about what he did or what Ice did or something else—but he's avoiding it? He doesn't want to talk about it?

"Apologize for the Fourth of July?" I ask.

"I mean, yeah…" He scratches a scab on his cheek. "But I'm mostly sorry you met me at all."

*Wow. Um. Where do I start?*

I clear my throat. "Anyway, I came here to talk to you."

"Why?" he asks, prickling uncomfortably.

*That's a great question.*

"Well," I say, thinking as I speak, "life has changed a lot for me since I learned about immortals, and it's all been very strange, you know? Between Ice and the Human Immortal Program, Night, and now you… I don't understand how any of this works. I don't know why anything happened the way it did, or who you even are, and no one wants to explain it to me, so—"

Wary amber eyes search my face. "What do you mean?"

"For one: Who are you?"

"Me?" he asks, surprised *for some reason*. "Oh, I'm nobody."

"I'm serious. No one will tell me anything about you."

"I'm not surprised," he says with a short laugh that cuts off as he meets my gaze. "But you've asked?"

"Of course I have."

As he stares at me, and I stare back, the hand held to his face slowly falls to his side. But neither of us say anything. So, with a sigh, I slip his driver's license out of my pocket.

"Why did you leave this with me?"

His eyes are wide, locked onto the card in my hand. A sinking, anxious dread builds in his expression—an air of guilt, like a child caught doing something naughty. Then he sits at the other end of the wicker couch. Shoulders slumped, he avoids my gaze and angles himself to better hide his face, but I don't take my eyes off him.

"You didn't want me to come looking for you?" I ask.

"No," he says.

"Then why leave your ID behind?"

He clasps his hands in his lap and takes a deep breath. "Okay, ah… Well, you remember what happened on the Fourth, right? When the gun fell out of my pocket? I knew I messed up. Anyway, you screamed at me—and, um, you hit me—right before you took off…"

*Ah. Is that what happened?*

"This is gonna sound so stupid," he continues with a weak and bitter laugh, "but it got stuck in my head somehow. Your voice, I mean."

"My voice?"

He scratches the back of his neck.

"I kept hearing it over and over, '*What is wrong with you? You freak! I hate you!*' Like that." He sighs, pausing as his shoulders droop further. "It really does sound pathetic, but I couldn't get your voice out of my head. I heard it all the time. Ice's voice too. Constantly. Saying terrible things. It kept me awake at night. I thought I'd go crazy."

*You were...literally hearing voices?*

I frown, but I hold my tongue.

"Anyway, I was sure I hated you because it was your voice in my head, but... What I did was terrible. You seem like a decent girl, and I just..."

He trails off and stares at his open hands, held up as though covered in blood only he can see. Then he sighs and returns them to his lap.

"I knew it was a waste of time," he says. "Surely, you hate me more than anything for what I did. I mean, you have every right to. But I couldn't take it anymore, so I went to apologize, anyway. Nothing changed, really, but I didn't know what to do once I got back here—"

Finally, I raise a hand, and he stops to watch me.

"What are you trying to get at?" I ask.

He meets my gaze with shadowed eyes and an empty smile. "Oh. It's not important."

"What isn't important?"

His mouth opens like he's about to answer, but he quickly glances away and goes quiet instead. He scratches the stubble on his jaw. And then he nods.

"At first, I thought it was just the necklace," he says, his voice low. "I was jealous. But that's not important either. When I bumped into you at the mall, before I even realized who you were, I noticed it. You didn't know who I was, but you smiled at me, and you looked at me like I exist. And again last night. And now. Even after what I did."

*Like...you exist...?*

"So, yeah, I don't hate you." Bitterness creeps into his voice as he glances over. Our eyes meet, and his frown becomes something far more painful. "Actually, I think I'm in love with you."

*Huh?*

*What?*

The thin edges of the driver's license dig into my palm, my grip too tight on the card. But what can I say? I know how hard it is to tell someone how you feel when you have no idea what they think of you.

It sucks. It's the worst.

So, if he is serious… *I feel sorry for him.*

"I don't know what to say," I admit.

"Say whatever you want." He cracks another sad smile. "It doesn't really matter, you know? None of this matters anymore."

*What does that even mean?*

At a complete loss, I say the only thing I can with any honesty. I say, "I don't know."

"I don't know either."

A minute of tense silence passes. At least a minute. Probably a few minutes. I set the license on the arm of the couch and zone out, listening to the rain. I'm trying to process—to understand anything James has said. To piece it all together and figure out why he won't answer my question.

*What do I know about him?*

He's defective. Troubled. Unstable. Ice and Night knew him in high school, but their respective opinions of him are strangely incompatible. Ice led with him being harmless—a pathetic idiot—before calling him *bad news*. Night said he was never unkind to her, and his recent behavior surprised everyone.

*Ugh.* I guess there's nothing to do but ask him directly.

"Ice told me—"

"Bet he lied."

"Excuse me?"

"What did he tell you?" he snaps, golden eyes blazing. "That you guys are friends? That he would protect you from me because, to him, I'm the goddamn Antichrist?"

"Ice is my friend, and he never told me anything stupid or crazy about you other than that you are stupid and crazy."

*But that isn't true, and I know it.*

Ice said some downright nasty things about James even before the mess that went down on the Fourth of July. He hates James, and, from what I can tell, everything he's done recently is only the tip of the iceberg.

Dark pieces of my nightmare flash before my eyes, overtaking the dusty parlor. *Broken glass sparkling on the floor. A white, tile ceiling. Ice's narrowed blue eyes. James. Blood.*

*Too much blood, dripping from trembling fingers.*

I force the images from my mind, but a nagging discomfort remains.

"You weren't there when he caught me." His voice shakes, and his hands ball into fists in his lap. "Do you have any idea what your *friend* said to me?"

I grit my teeth, catching the inside of my cheek.

He laughs once. "You know, Ice loves hearing himself talk so much. You think I'm crazy—and that's fine, and maybe you'd be right—but he said some downright insane shit while he bashed my face into the side of his house."

*Oh?*

"Like what?" I ask, my voice loud but surprisingly calm.

James freezes. The resentment fades from his eyes as he stares at nothing in particular. Then his hands relax, and he sighs.

"Forget it," he mutters. "He would kill me if he knew you were here. You should go."

He moves to stand from the couch.

"James, wait—"

I grab his arm, my fingers closing around the fabric of his dark jacket. He stiffens at my touch and glances over his shoulder, his eyes wide. I don't free him until he sits back down.

"You only went there because you were worried about me, right?" I ask. He immediately averts his gaze. "You have to tell me what he said. I need to know."

He groans. "Honestly, I, uh— I wasn't paying much attention to what he said. He likes to spout a lot of shit when he's pissed, and he has it out for me anyway, so…"

Our eyes meet. He frowns, clearly struggling to maintain eye contact. Brows furrowed. Jaw set. A bead of nervous sweat glistens on his temple.

*Is he…lying? Why?*

"What did Ice say?" I ask again, growing frustrated.

"He was probably just trying to get a rise out of me—like I

said—but…" After a brief pause to gauge my expression, he looks away. "Well, he first made a point to clear up the deal with your necklace. So, ah… Sorry about that."

I look away too.

"Anyway, I asked why he was with you, since you're human and all, you know? And he said—"

He hesitates once more, causing a beat of tense quiet while I stare at a cobweb on the ceiling across the room. *Is it that bad? Just spit it out.*

"He basically said he was screwing with you for fun," he mumbles. "Called you stupid. Maybe some other stuff— I dunno."

*Wait, that can't be right.*

"I asked if he cared about you at all because, um—"

*Because he kissed me?*

Our eyes meet for an instant before his dart away. His ears turn red, and he flashes an uncomfortable smile as he wrings his hands.

"I was freaking out, scared he might kill me right there, and he'd already slammed my head into the wall a couple times, so…" He scratches his cheek, still crosshatched by scabs. "But he said he's your sponsor, or something, so he can do whatever he wants. Ugh. Yeah, I really don't know. It wasn't great, but—"

"He said all that?" I ask, my voice taut.

"You think you guys are close, and I probably mean less than nothing to you." With a nervous laugh, he shrugs, leaning further away. "I can't blame you if you don't believe me, but he made it pretty damn clear he doesn't care what happens to you—as long as it doesn't involve me, anyway."

"But—" As I stare at James' battered profile, my mind reels. "Even if he said that—"

He meets my gaze and shakes his head, mirroring my concern in a way that makes me falter. "Ice is only with you because he's bored. He'll toss you aside like trash when you're not fun anymore. You asked me to tell you what he said, and that's what he said. I'm only trying to help."

"But—"

"Trust me." His eyes flick to his lap as he deflates. "That's the kind of guy he is. Didn't you ever wonder why someone like Ice would want to hang out with someone like you?"

*Someone like me?*

I stand from the couch. "What is that supposed to mean?"

He watches in alarm.

I sound offended—and I am a little offended—but he's right. I have wondered, and I've never gotten a real answer. When I asked, he…*called me interesting.*

Night said the same thing. *Perhaps he was bored.*

But why take it so far? Why bind himself to me as my sponsor if he was just bored?

*None of this makes any sense.*

James frowns and tips his head, his brows furrowed. "I mean, you have thought about it, right?"

My chest tightens, and my stomach twists itself into knots. The insecurity I've been suppressing for weeks… The aside glances Night made whenever we talked about Ice… The conversations I wished I could have with Rose…

But I shake my head. "I— I don't know."

*If what James says is true…*

If even part of it is true, was Ice ever honest with me?

*Well…* Maybe he was.

He never *lied*, did he? By omission, maybe, but not outright. He admitted to stalking me when I recognized his feline form. He never claimed to *care* about me. He never said we were *friends*. He said he likes me, but…

Does he seriously only want me around because he finds me interesting? Because spending time with me somehow alleviates his boredom? Does he seriously not care beyond that?

*Maybe I should have gone home after he rejected me.*

*God…*

My fists relax, my eyes lose focus, and I let out a breath.

"Am I stupid?"

"No—" James jumps up from the couch and reaches out to touch my arm, but he drops his hand at the last second. "Ice knows what he's doing, and he only lets people see what he wants them to see. Literally anyone would fall for it."

"How do you know what he's like?" I ask.

He prickles. "Guys like Ice don't change."

They have history, yes, but I'm now certain that James watched Ice kiss me through the window. If Ice said those things to him right after—

My hand comes away dry when I wipe my eyes. "I know Ice doesn't like me the same way. He admitted it, but…"

"Are you gonna go back there?"

"I don't know what to do." My feet start to ache, so I sit again. "Ice has never been…mean to me, you know? And I have done some stupid, horribly embarrassing things since we met, but he's always been so nice."

"Yeah, he's good at that," he agrees dryly.

The vague comments are annoying, but I'm more curious than ever. *What is their history, exactly?* I could ask—he might even tell me—but am I ready to hear that on top of everything else?

Still standing, he shifts his weight from leg to leg, holding one arm and watching my face. Uneasy. Apprehensive.

*Ah, right.*

He did confess to potentially being in love with me.

I clear my throat. "What you said before…about me… Are you serious? I mean—"

"Oh, *that*, um…" He laughs nervously, scratching the back of his neck as his face flushes. "I'm not… Uh…"

It threw me off when he first said it, but I chose not to take it seriously. I figured it was some ploy to distract me and change the subject. Even if I was right, it doesn't necessarily mean what he said isn't true. It simply means it surprised me enough to work.

"Hey, it's, um—Jayde, right?"

I nod.

"You mind if we go somewhere else for a bit?" He glances toward the front of the building. "I can't be here right now."

"I guess that's fine," I agree despite my confusion.

As I leave the wicker couch, James studies me as though he didn't really look at me before, and he frowns.

"You want a dry coat or something?" he asks.

"I'm fine," I mutter. "You want your license back?"

He hesitates. A darkness flashes through his eyes as he stares at the card in my outstretched hand, but he eventually nods, takes it, and slips it into his pocket.

"Let's get out of here," he says.

*Right...*

I grab my things and follow him outside.

The rain is still coming down hard.

He half-jogs for his car, which is parked a good thirty feet from the doors, but I dawdle on the covered porch. I wring the excess water out of my light jacket, but it's still too damp to wear. After draping it over my arm, I pop the umbrella open and step out into the rain.

The car is idling with James inside as I approach. While I close my umbrella, he leans across the seat to open the door for me. Then he makes a soft noise. I watch wordlessly as he swipes an open pack of cigarettes off the dashboard, stuffs it between the driver's seat and center console, and stares out the windshield with both hands firmly planted on the wheel.

His face is red again.

*Alright...*

I set a hand on the edge of the car door, but I hesitate. He looks up at me, and, for a moment, I stand in the rain and stare into his amber eyes—one still bruised and tinged red by blood.

He tips his head.

James is a mess, injured and nervous and sleep-deprived, but he seems more comfortable now that we're outside. There's less darkness. Less...whatever that empty energy is.

*This place bothers him? What about it?*

I glance back at the building, with its peeling paint and

broken windows. It does give off a creepy vibe, so I wonder…

*Wait.* This guy basically kidnapped me a couple weeks ago.

Why am I here?

Why should I listen to anything he says?

Why do I want to hear him out?

*Why do I want to trust him?*

"You coming?" he asks, blinking.

I nod and, with a mumbled apology, brush a few crumpled sheets of lined paper from the passenger seat onto the floor before I step into the car. I close the door and buckle my seatbelt. Water drips from my bangs and lands in my lap.

*I don't get it.*

Why do I care about James at all?

# fifty

We stop at the first fast food restaurant we pass in town.

James opts for the drive-thru over eating inside, but I can't blame him for not wanting to hang around in public looking the way he does. Then he parks the car in the corner of the parking lot.

"So, why'd you walk all the way out there yourself, anyway?" he asks, fishing something out of the paper bag.

He hands me a small carton of curly fries I never asked for, but I accept it and thank him all the same. *Arby's fries* are *very good.* After eating one, I regret not ordering anything.

"I needed to talk to you," I remind him. "Didn't I say that?"

He pauses, probably remembering I had.

"Okay, fine. But how'd you know where to find me?"

I shrug. "I didn't. I guessed."

"You walked out to that run-down manor house in the middle of nowhere, through the pouring rain, without knowing if I'd even be there?" he asks, his expression rather blank.

"I took the bus halfway. But, yeah, I guess I did."

"How'd you even remember where it was?"

"I wasn't that out of it on the Fourth of July," I mutter. "And I did have to walk back to Ice's house with a sprained ankle."

He averts his gaze and takes a bite of his sandwich.

*Oops.*

I listen to the rain pattering on the roof of the car and watch a line of vehicles stopped at the red light while I slowly eat fries. It's lunch rush hour. Traffic is slow.

As I shift my weight, a crumpled paper bag crunches beneath my foot. I glance down, unimpressed by the assortment of paper trash and empty soda cans on the floor. The air is stale too, tainted by the faint scent of smoke despite the dusty, yellow pine tree air freshener hanging from the rear-view mirror. But the intricately carved wooden bookmark ornament that accompanies it is neat, I guess.

*Mm... There's something incredibly sad about all this.*

"Anyway, what were you saying before we left?" he asks.

I cough, but I remind him.

"Oh. Right. That. Ah—" He scratches the back of his neck as a warm flush and uneasy smile spread across his face. "It's stupid, isn't it? I'm not in love with you—I mean, I don't know anything about you, and you're human anyway, so…"

*Ouch.* My humanity is why he can't possibly be in love with me? Well, there's my confirmation that relationships between humans and immortals are taboo.

*Annoying,* but I understand.

I was a mess over Ice as soon as we met. I didn't know him —who he was; *what he was*. I just…saw him, and that was it. Then I heard his voice, and he smiled at me, and I—

*Isn't that basically what James said about me?*

I sigh. "It happens. Feelings are stupid."

"You think so?" His eyes brighten for an instant, but he quickly looks away. "It sucks, though. Before Ice told me it was a waste of time, I was dead convinced your necklace could help me. But, by then, it was too late. I feel like I caused all this trouble for nothing, you know?"

"You're defective, right? Ice mentioned it."

I'm kind enough to not mention any of the other things Ice said about him, but he still grimaces. *Was the question too personal? Should I have said that Night told me instead?*

Tearing my eyes away, I stuff more fries into my mouth to keep from saying anything horribly insensitive.

He sighs. "That's right. I'm defective."

Is that why the storm doesn't bother him?

James obviously has his own issues, but he's more energetic than the Monroes have been. He was awake before noon, walked in the rain without hesitation, and hasn't complained about the weather once. Not to mention how he ventured out during an active thunderstorm for an indeterminate period of time in the dead of night less than twelve hours ago.

*Did he sleep at all?*

"Can I ask about that?" He doesn't answer or look over, but I accept his silence as an invitation. "What does it really mean to be defective?"

His fleeting glance is skeptical at best. "There's no need to spare my feelings. I'm sure Ice told you all about it—he loves to rag on me—but…"

After trailing off, he meets my gaze in surprise, as though he legitimately thought I asked only to spite him. But I force an apologetic smile, and the guarded edge to his jaw softens.

"You really want to know?" he asks.

"I am curious—if it's alright."

"Oh. Well." He looks away again. "I have no idea what Ice told you, but it's not just him. There's this whole stigma that comes with being defective. I can't morph, you know, and I don't have any cool powers, so I'm weird and different. My night vision only works when it wants to, which is literally never, small injuries like this take twice as long to heal, and I can't do anything right in the first place, so—"

*Wow...*

Staring at his half-eaten sandwich like it's some unachievable goal, his voice carries a wistful sadness. "I'm a lousy immortal. To the others, I'm…less than human."

"There's nothing wrong with being human."

Recognition replaces his mellow confusion, and he laughs. "Well, that's easy for you to say. You are human."

Seeing a real smile is a strange relief, even if it was made after a self-deprecating comment. But I can't be bothered to do anything but sit and wait.

"So, anyway…" His smile fades, but his expression remains less upsetting than before. "When I bumped into you at the mall —which was a total coincidence, I swear—and you mentioned Night, that's when I noticed the necklace. You being in with immortals and all made me wonder. I knew a human guy with a special immortal necklace in middle school, but I don't know shit about that sort of thing, honestly, and it was more of an afterthought."

He pauses to sigh.

"You know, I kind of forgot about it until Ice popped out of nowhere a couple hours later to threaten me."

"What?" I choke on a curly fry. "He threatened you?"

He grimaces, averting his gaze. "Okay, I mean— No, yeah, he basically told me not to talk to you *or else*. You're here now, so I fucked that one up real good."

*Wow, um... This is a lot.*

"Anyway," he says with a cough, "I saw pictures of you with a couple of Night's friends and heard that your necklace is one of those special ones, and I…resented you. Thinking dumb shit like, '*Why does some human girl get to have this thing when I was born an immortal and can't morph?*' I don't know why or how I came to the conclusion that it might work for me, but I did, and I couldn't stop thinking about it."

*That's what started it? A photo?*

*Maybe Ice had a point.*

I stuff my empty french fry container into a paper sack on the floor and dig the River Sapphire out of my damp jacket pocket.

James lets out a dry, tired chuckle. "Of course, I'll never be so lucky. I can't believe I was surprised to hear it doesn't even work for you."

I don't speak. I just stare at the polished, blue gemstone.

"I'll never fit in with immortals or humans, you know?" he says, his voice low. "All I do—all I've ever done—is screw things up. No one likes me, and, honestly, why should they? Just look at me. I'm a fucking mess. A disaster-prone loser. Besides, I bet you hate me for what I did to you. I'd hate me for it if I were you.

Hell, I do hate me."

I glance up. James is done eating and has since leaned forward with his arms folded on top of the steering wheel. He stares through the windshield and continues talking, his voice soft and sad, but my mind wanders.

Night wanted to know if Ice asked me to keep any secrets. Besides the secret of immortals, he never did, but why did she feel the need to ask? What secrets did she think he wanted me to keep?

*What secrets is she keeping?*

What is the shadow that falls over her face before she changes the subject? Why doesn't she want to talk about their history with James?

She knows Ice better than anyone, but he doesn't tell her everything. She loves him, but her trust in him is tenuous—to the point he's aware of her suspicion. Yet she encouraged me when it came to dating him. She told me things she knew he wouldn't want me to know, but there were other details she wasn't willing to discuss.

*How does James tie into it all?*

If Ice were as manipulative as James claims, he could have easily used my anxiety after the Fourth of July to his advantage by exaggerating the danger or twisting facts to keep me closer.

*Well…* He suggested that hanging out with other immortals was dangerous, but he didn't fight me on it, and he was quick to agree we should pretend that everything involving James never happened. He hasn't held it over my head, but Night also thinks he only kissed me because he thought it would keep me from leaving. Because he realized how upset I was, and he was scared to lose me.

That's manipulative, isn't it? Isn't asking me to act like bad things never happened manipulative too? *Even if it was my idea at first?*

*Ugh...*

James thinks Ice is only using me to alleviate boredom. Night says he can be hard to read but cares for me in his own way. Ice said he likes me even if the feeling is not romantic.

*They can't all be telling the truth, can they?*

*Fine.* I'm willing to accept that Ice has used my emotions against me several times. I can't argue otherwise—not after the kiss—but why would he go this far if our entire relationship were nothing more than a game to him?

Why tell me about immortals or confess to having stalked me? Why sponsor me or sign me up for the Human Immortal Program? Why suggest to Night's friends that we're dating? Why be honest and rebuff my confession? Why admit to hurting James? He didn't have to do anything that might create more tension between us, so I don't think he's been lying to me exactly.

*It still doesn't make sense, but I...*

I believe James' story too. He's telling the truth—or at least the truth as he perceives it—but I doubt Ice meant what he said to him. I don't think James completely believes it either.

"Hey," I say. "It's alright. I don't hate you."

He blinks, eyes wide. "What? Why not? After what I did—"

"You messed up. You shouldn't have done what you did—obviously, that was crazy—but I know you didn't mean to hurt me. And I'm fine, so…"

His expression softens, but he doesn't look relieved.

I offer to let him see the River Sapphire.

He hesitates, staring at the necklace for a long moment before he finally takes it. He holds the gemstone up to the light. His eyes narrow as his frown grows more pronounced.

"It's pretty," he says. "Too bad I can't use it."

"Hasn't done much for me yet either, but, um… Did Ice say anything about why he told me about immortals in the first place?"

"No. I don't think he mentioned it."

*Dang.* I was hoping to get a straight answer for once, but that's alright. Maybe Ice was telling the truth when he said he just felt like telling me, and so he did. A whim. Maybe there isn't any other reason.

*Maybe asking was a waste of time.*

Rain pummels the windshield. The fat water droplets merge and run down the glass in wide streams. A few streams catch in a thin crack in the glass, merging to follow the crack to the edge of the windshield. There's nothing comforting about the sound of the rain now.

Finding James left me with more questions than answers. I'm more confused—more conflicted—but this was a conversation I've needed to have for a while. I needed the outside perspective from someone who could understand what I've been going through.

James returns the River Sapphire, and I put it away.

"You plan on going back to their house?" he asks. "He'll be pissed if he finds out I talked to you."

"Well, obviously. I don't plan to tell him where I've been."

He gauges my expression carefully before speaking, "If you need more time to think about it, you could—I dunno… Stay here for a while?"

"At that abandoned house?"

"Well, yeah, I guess." He averts his eyes and scratches his cheek. "I mean, if you're not comfortable at Ice's place right now, I can look out for you until—"

I laugh. "Whoa. Slow down. I don't hate you, but that doesn't mean I want to stay with you. The Fourth of July was a complete disaster—fine, we both had way too much to drink, I guess—but let's not forget you literally kidnapped me and threatened me with a gun."

He grits his teeth, pointedly avoiding eye contact.

*I guess he knows perfectly well what he did. He felt bad before I said anything.*

I sigh. "Anyway, I'm supposed to go home once the storm blows over. It should only be a couple more days, but I have to go back to Ice's house first. I have a lot of stuff there."

"You could be in danger," he says quietly. "I don't want you to get hurt."

"I can accept that Ice is only with me because he's bored. I can even accept that maybe he's not the person I convinced myself he was—that I saw a lot of things that just weren't there—but I am telling you right now that I am not in any danger. He wouldn't hurt me."

His expression grows strained. "Sure, fine, you're safe, but we both know he's more than willing to hurt me. Whether you like it or not, Ice is dangerous."

*Ugh...*

He's right. I can't argue—not with him looking like that—and I don't really feel like crawling back to Ice right now, anyway. James gave me a lot to think about, and I need a minute before I can face him again.

But Ice will be upset if he finds out why I left, and I don't want James to get hurt because of me a second time.

*Somehow, I'll keep his name out of it.*

"Please, you have to trust me on this," he says, though his nerve falters as he glances away. "If it helps at all, we can swing by his house tomorrow. You can pick up your stuff, and then I'll take you home—or wherever you need to go."

"Tomorrow?"

*I don't know...*

A moment of tense silence passes before he looks up again. His expression is muddled and strange, and it doesn't quite match what he's said. He made it sound like he's worried about me—like he feels I need protecting—but his wide eyes and set jaw reveal a far deeper anxiety. It's more like…now that I'm here, he doesn't want to be left alone.

Is he honestly that afraid of Ice? Or is it something else?

*Maybe I don't want to know.*

"Fine," I say. "If it makes you feel better, I'll let you help me."

# fifty-one

I watch the trees pass by through the passenger window as we drive down the gravel road on our way back to the dilapidated house. James pulls into the lot and parks his car off to one side of the porch.

We run the short distance to avoid getting wet, and, as he opens the heavy front doors, he laughs about a raindrop that fell into his eye. *It's weird.* Even as we walk inside, he seems like a different person—like he's not the hopelessly miserable man I found when I arrived this morning.

*This place…*

I ask how old the building is, and he shrugs. Late Victorian is his best guess. Though, he does offer to show me around, so I follow him into the next room: the parlor we sat in before, where the tour begins.

The house is massive, and he navigates it easily, but I'm not convinced he knows what he's talking about as he leads me around on the so-called tour.

*The kitchen is in the back, but I don't use it.*

*This is a bedroom—I think.*

*Whatever you do, do not use the rear staircase. It's dangerous.*

*Dunno why, but the sink in this bathroom doesn't work.*

*This looks like some sort of...storage room?*

He keeps saying things like that.

The first floor has a fair amount of wood debris and broken glass strewn about. It's the worst by far—the least livable—but only half of the rooms above it have anything noteworthy inside them. A chair or chest of drawers. An old TV. A broken bed frame. A collection of furniture covered by off-white sheets.

The air smells of mildew, and most every surface is coated in a thick layer of dust. Half of the doorknobs are dusty—some with hand imprints indicating the door has only recently been opened. Many of the light bulbs flicker or stay dark when James flicks the light switch upon entering a new room.

*I can hardly believe the place even has electricity.*

It's not until we reach the third floor that he finally admits to not living here. I'm not at all surprised, but he goes on to explain that he was recently kicked out of his father's house—*again*—and couldn't think of anywhere else to go.

But it's fine.

We're not trespassing. *Technically.* The building, aptly named Reid Manor, is owned by his family, though it's been left uninhabited and neglected for decades.

"Anyway," he says, opening another door, "I've been crashing in this room. It's not much, but there's less dust."

I scan the room, and I have to agree. It's not much, but it is the least dusty room he's showed me thus far. The square bedroom is as stuffy and sad as the rest of the house—the green wallpaper peeling at the top edge—and it smells faintly of smoke, but…

*No, it is significantly better than the others.*

James enters the room ahead of me. The first thing he does is grab a pack of cigarettes off the top of a small, black mini-fridge, crumple the box, and stuff it into a nearby backpack.

*Okay...*

Ignoring him, the room is plain and sparsely furnished like many of the others, but it feels more…lived-in. The bed's original, aged bedding is piled in one corner of the room, having been replaced by a single throw blanket and flat pillow. There's also a chest of drawers with chipped white paint and a worn reclining chair.

James stands around, holding a cell phone he grabbed from the top of the mini-fridge—next to where the now-sacrificed cigarettes used to be.

Imagining him holed up here, alone during the storm with nowhere better to go, is kind of depressing, but I appreciate the lack of dust motes in the air, and the room is brighter than the others. A large window with no curtains—the source of the light —faces the forest outside.

The boards creak beneath my feet as I cross the room to stand in front of the window. Past James' car and the large, gravel lot, a sea of trees stretches into the distance. The weather is cool, leaving the indoor temperature comfortable, but I bet this place turns into an oven during the summer. There's no way it has central air.

"You expect me to sleep in here?" I ask, turning around.

James slowly looks up from his phone. He unplugs it, stands up straight, and scratches the back of his head with his free hand.

"I guess," he says. I assume he's also wondering if asking

me to stay was a good idea. "You can take the bed if you want. I'm fine with the chair."

"Right. Thanks."

I'm certain he needs a night of quality rest more than I do, but I'm not about to argue over a single night's sleeping arrangements. If he'd rather sleep in that ancient recliner, it's his loss.

Sitting on the edge of the bed, I check the time—it's just after 2PM. I set my phone to silent this morning, so a text from Rose has gone unnoticed for over an hour.

**Rose:** Sooo… how are things? Is it still raining?

*Great... Should I talk to her?*

I glance across the room at James, who is still standing around awkwardly and messing with his own phone. He soon meets my gaze, and I flash an apologetic smile.

"Can I have a few minutes?" I ask. "I need to call someone."

Detecting a flicker of concern, I laugh nervously.

"Don't worry; she's a human friend—my roommate. I am not calling Ice."

He hesitates but nods. Then he digs a set of over-the-ear headphones out of his backpack and leaves the room. The door latches shut, and I try to get as comfortable as possible considering the circumstances before I make the call.

Rose answers promptly. Her cheery voice is a breath of fresh air, and my muscles relax ever so slightly as we exchange normal pleasantries.

"Any news?" she asks.

"I don't even know where to start."

"Uh-oh. Things not going good with Ice?"

"No," I admit. "I don't think they are. As if everything else wasn't enough, I kind of, um…took off this morning without telling anyone where I went."

"Took off? Are you okay?"

*It sounds worse than it really is when I say it out loud.*

"Of course I'm okay," I assure her. "Sorry if it seems weird. It's just that… I don't think things are working out between us after all, you know? I needed some time to think."

"Oh. Well, it's about time you've come to your senses," she says with a mild laugh. "Are you at home, then?"

"No, um…"

"No? Where are you?"

*How much can I get away with telling her?*

"I found out that Ice…hurt someone last week," I say carefully. "I talked with the guy today, and he told me that Ice said some…things about me, so—"

"Hold up. Ice hurt someone? Like, *hurt* hurt someone? Why? What happened?"

I groan. "It's hard to explain. The guy's fine…mostly, but Ice did not want me to talk to him, and, after coming here, I think I understand why. He knows things about Ice, and getting away has given me time to think—"

"You're freaking me out, Jay," she says, her voice noticeably uneasy. "You said you're not at home?"

"No."

"What—"

*Maybe I should have lied.*

With a sidelong glance at the closed door, I lower my voice further. "He lied to me, Rose. Ice lied to me about this guy and how he feels about me and who knows what else. I have no idea what to do now."

"Okay, hold up. You're seriously telling me that you're with a different guy right now?"

"Ugh. Yes."

"A guy your last boyfriend…beat up?"

"Ice was never my boyfriend. But yes. Essentially."

"Just for wanting to talk to you?" she asks, her voice thick with confusion.

"It's a little more complicated than that. They have some kind of history. I don't really know what happened between them, but I think I accidentally got caught up in the middle of it."

She makes a slow, uncertain noise. "This is too much drama even for me. What the heck is going on in your life right now?"

I stare out the window, holding the phone against my ear. The storm is starting to ease up. The wind isn't as strong. The rain is lighter.

"Honestly, I have no idea."

"But you swear you're safe?"

*Eh…* "Ninety-five percent positive."

"Alright," she says slowly. "So, what's the deal with this guy you're talking to now?"

*I give up*. I'm done hiding things that don't matter.

"His name is James. He's weird, but he's alright, I guess."

"Is *he* cute?"

"Oh, shut up," I mutter, ignoring her laughter. "It's not like that at all. I came here to talk—to figure out what happened. But I'm not going back to Ice's house today. I need more time to work things out. Then I think I'll just pick up my bag and head home."

"Good. Is James a friend, then?"

I pause. "Not…really? He seems alright, like I said, but I hardly know him. It's complicated. I have a lot on my mind right now."

"I get it. I'm confused for you, to be honest. I thought a little stupid summer romance would be good for you, but I guess you attract shitty guys."

"Or something," I agree.

"But I do wish you'd actually talk to me about it."

*Oh, god. Why now?*

"What do you mean?" I ask, feigning naivety.

"You know what I mean." Her voice is low and serious, almost uncharacteristically so. "I may be a blonde, but I am not dumb. I know you've been hiding shit from me. I don't understand what's going on with you and your boy trouble, but I keep telling myself you must have a good reason for not explaining it to me."

*Rose…*

The line goes quiet for a moment, and then she sighs. "I want to trust you, Jayde, but you have to swear to me that you're safe. If you need help—even if you think it's stupid—tell me. I will pack my car and be home tomorrow."

"No, it's fine." I laugh, but it feels forced. "I think I can handle it myself."

I wasn't expecting relief, but it's a weight off my chest and sheds a sliver of the guilt I've carried for weeks. At least I don't have to hide the fact that I'm hiding things anymore.

"I wish I could explain more, but it's a real mess."

"I won't bother asking."

*That's fine.*

We talk about her vacation instead. She hasn't seen a drop of rain in Arizona, and she just bought another souvenir for me —though she still won't tell me what any of them are. She's having a great time. I'm glad.

Then she asks if I'm sure I'm fine, and all I can do is say yes. All I can do is tell her that she shouldn't worry about me.

"Call me as soon as you're home," she says.

"Of course."

"Good luck with everything. Talk to you later. Love youuu."

"Yeah. Thanks."

I end the call, and all I hear is the rain on the roof.

What do I do now?

My hand falls into my lap. I switch my phone off silent and scroll down my FaceSpace newsfeed, but there's nothing important, so I glance out the window and watch the steady rain falling from the grey sky instead.

I turn toward the closed door.

Should I find James?

*Should I tell anyone else where I am?*

I scroll down my list of friends. *Robbie?* No way. We haven't talked in months. He has no idea what I've been up to. *Carmen?* That would be weird. I flick past Night's name and, once I hit the end of the list, scroll up again.

*Should I message her?*

I could tell her where I've been. What James told me. That I plan on picking up my stuff and going home tomorrow morning.

My finger hovers over the text input box.

*What if she tells Ice that I met with James?*

*What if she tells him where we are?*

I don't message anyone. I lock my phone and leave the room.

* * * * *

I sit on the bed while James sits in the recliner across the room. We don't talk, for lack of anything meaningful to say to each other, so we just…stew in a terribly awkward silence.

When staring at my phone gets too boring, I look out the window. It's still raining. I look up at the ceiling, at the wooden boards. Then I look around the room.

James, who, I think, is listening to music, does the same. Mess around on his phone. Scan the room. Glance at me. Frown. Back to his phone. He looks more functional than before, though. He took a shower during my call with Rose. His face is cleaner, shaved, and his hair is still damp.

He notices me watching and drops his headphones to his neck. I resist the urge to look away.

"I know I said I'd take you to get your stuff tomorrow…"

"You don't want to?"

"No." He grimaces, his eyes darting away. "Showing my face around there again is probably the worst idea I've ever had. But

I don't have much of a choice, do I? Since I said I'd do it?"

"You don't have to help me, you know."

"But, I—"

Catching himself, he meets my gaze. His jaw is tense, his previous anxiety having returned. I get it. He's scared of Ice, and Ice will almost certainly be home when we drop by.

I could reassure him that everything will be fine or offer to take the bus if he can drive me to the nearest bus stop—like a normal person—but I don't want to worry about it right now. I'll get there with or without James' help, but dealing with Ice is a problem for tomorrow.

*Instead...*

"Hey, um... Why'd you bother telling me all that stuff earlier? About how you feel about me or whatever?"

He grimaces again. "I don't— How I feel doesn't matter, does it? It's not important."

"It matters to me," I say, my voice sharper than intended. "No one has ever said that to me before. Not like that."

"Really?"

For whatever reason, he's surprised that I've never been the victim of an unsolicited love confession before today. I nod, but I can't decide whether to take offense or consider it a compliment.

"Well, I dunno," he mumbles. "I mean, you probably wouldn't have listened to me at all if I didn't say it, so..."

*So it was both a distraction and a trap?*

"Did you mean it, though?"

"I told you; I don't know." He shifts his weight and scratches his arm before glancing aside. "To be honest, I haven't been doing so great lately. I've been…tired, I guess."

*Tired? Hm…*

After a moment of silent hesitation, his eyes flick up from his phone. "Were you—?" But he cuts himself off, runs a hand over his short hair, and tears his eyes away again.

"What?"

He forces a smile. "Nothing. It was a stupid question. Sorry."

The room falls quiet, but I don't press the matter.

A few minutes pass. I watch the rain through the large window. Falling, falling, and collecting in muddy puddles in the gravel lot below.

Then my phone rings.

I jump at the sound, and I hate the way my surprise turns to dread when I recognize the ringtone.

*This is it.*

It was inevitable, right? I've been gone all day. I left a note, but it was probably the least helpful note ever written. And Ice is awake now, so I have to face that.

After telling James to *keep quiet*, I answer the call, careful to keep my voice light and casual.

Of course, Ice immediately asks where I am.

He doesn't sound *angry*, but he does sound slightly irritated —though, he's been in a near-constant state of mild annoyance since the storm began. I can only hope his current problem is with the rain and not my unexpected absence.

"I left a note," I say. "It's on the table."

"I saw the note, but you neglected to specify where you went or when you'd return."

I wince. His tone is so dry, it's hard to believe he's not annoyed with me.

"Oh. Sorry." I glance at James, but his silent, wide-eyed stare isn't helpful, so I run with the first story that comes to mind. "I'm in town. With a friend from school who wanted to hang out. We haven't been doing much at your house because of the storm, so I thought it wouldn't be a problem if I spent the night."

A beat of silence. I chew on the inside of my cheek.

"You walked there?" he asks. "Through the rain?"

*That is exactly how James reacted when I first arrived.*

"What? No." I laugh, having successfully suppressed my sigh. "I took the bus. Anyway, it's not a big deal. I'll drop by first thing tomorrow, okay?"

As we continue to talk about absolutely nothing, James listens with piqued interest, leaning forward in his seat in an apparent attempt to make out both sides of the empty conversation. I frown, and he offers me an encouraging yet uncomfortable smile that does nothing to instill confidence.

"Anyway, I'm sorry if I worried you or Night or anything."

"We weren't worried," Ice says. "In any case, the storm should pass overnight. I will see you in the morning, correct?"

"Yeah, of course."

"Goodbye, Jayde."

He hangs up before I have a chance to respond.

*Ugh...*

I set my phone down and look to James, who frowns.

The conversation was brief but relatively painless—almost too painless considering recent events. His irritation faded as we spoke, and he seemed understanding enough, but he was quite brisk…

*Does he not believe me?*

Was my explanation too vague? Is it too hard to believe someone might invite me to hang out? Or was leaving a note without coming up with an excuse in advance a mistake?

"I can't tell if he believed me," I say.

James shrugs. "As long as he doesn't find out you're with me, I'm sure it'll be fine."

# fifty-two

When I wake up, the sky is just growing light.

The only sounds are the gentle pitter-patter of rain on the roof and the soft hum of the mini-fridge across the room. I'm warm, but the mattress is as lumpy and musty and sad as it was when I first laid down in it. The blanket, while soft, smells like sweat and rain and smoke, and the pillow is terribly flat.

James is in the same state as I last saw him too—asleep in the recliner. He is out cold, but he can't be comfortable. His neck is at a bit of an odd angle, and his arms are folded over his chest.

I'm sure he'll feel it when he wakes up.

Knowing he's still asleep, I fall back on the bed and stare at the dark ceiling. I'm frustrated. Falling asleep took hours, but I slept light and woke up early, and my feet still ache from walking.

I hope my socks are dry. I doubt my boots are.

*This sucks. My life is such a mess.*

No matter what happens today, and no matter what I choose to do moving forward, I'm stuck with the secret of immortals for the rest of my life. Even if Ice was lying or playing me for a fool, he's still my sponsor, so I'm probably stuck with him too.

But I haven't had nearly enough time to myself to process the information I learned yesterday or over the past few weeks. I don't know what to do. Or what I want. Or anything.

Ice was quick to forget everything messy, but he was more protective of me after the Fourth of July. Even when I no longer saw the danger or felt the lingering anxiety myself. Even though he's the one who freaked me out the last time, and had reason to believe he made me uncomfortable, he still asked me to stay with him.

Did he think James would show up a third time despite being threatened and knowing the River Sapphire can't help him? Was he worried about that?

*I mean, he was right. James did show up, but—*

Why didn't anyone lock the doors?

*Well...* Maybe it's better they didn't.

Maybe it's better that James was able to get inside if it led to me coming here. There are obviously things he still doesn't want to tell me—things I imagine are too personal to share with a complete stranger—but I could sense his vulnerability yesterday.

*And seeing firsthand what Ice did to him?*

He's afraid of Ice, and that fear is both genuine and warranted. I hate thinking he would say those things about me, whether he meant it or not, but I should take James' fear into consideration either way.

*And I hate that.*

I wish I could go back in time.

Maybe I could rewind just far enough to change my mind

about looking for James. I would never hear what Ice said to him, and I wouldn't be here, stuck in this awkward, tense situation. I wouldn't be so conflicted or confused.

*No.*

Coming here was the right thing. After seeing him the other night, I needed to hear what he had to say.

Well, what about my stupid love confession? If I hadn't put it off so long, I wouldn't have caught James watching us through the window. He wouldn't have been hurt, and Ice wouldn't have said anything to him in the first place.

*Or…I could have asked him to lie to me.*

No.

I should have left the moment he rejected me instead of falling for that stupid kiss. I could have spent the rainstorm at home, heartbroken but cuddled up in a blanket and drinking hot chocolate.

*Sounds nice, but—*

A better idea: *Fix the Fourth of July.*

I could stop after one glass of Night's spiked lemonade. I never would have kissed Ice if I hadn't been drunk. Even if I forgot my phone at the house, I wouldn't have been upset, so I wouldn't have used it as an excuse to go back alone. If I could change that one decision, I wouldn't have run into James in the backyard, and none of this would have happened.

*But that's not how life works.*

Time flows in one direction, so, for better or worse, I'm stuck with what I did. All I can do now is move forward.

Besides, Ice's motives have bothered me for a long time. As

much as I hate to admit it, everyone seems to think he's only with me out of boredom. I still don't know what he was thinking—when he asked me out, when he told me about immortals, or when he said those nasty things to James—but I guess that much is true.

He was just bored.

*But...*

Does he seriously see me as nothing more than a stupid human girl? Does he not care what happens to me? Or think he can do whatever he wants? James says he likes to talk shit, but what if he meant it?

*Seriously? What if he meant any of it?*

He has some level of legal standing over me as my sponsor, but what does that even mean? I didn't read his portion of the paperwork. I hardly even glanced at the pages he asked me to sign. For all I know, he really can do whatever he wants with me, regardless of his intentions.

*This is ridiculous.*

We may not feel the same way about each other, but Ice is still my friend. He likes me and finds me interesting enough to hang out with, and after everything he's done for me—the dates, the money, the River Sapphire, and letting me stay over so long—I seriously can't imagine he would hurt me.

I can't imagine it, but—

*If he tried, could James stop him?*

Ice is fast and powerful. I saw it with my own eyes. James' heart may be in the right place, but I can't imagine he stands a chance against Ice. He obviously didn't last week.

*These are not healthy thoughts, Jayde.*

Calm down. Think rationally. I'm crossing into horror movie territory. Things like that don't happen in real life, right?

*Though, shapeshifters shouldn't exist in real life either.*

Forget it.

Ice was bluffing. He was pissed to find James outside. Maybe it was something he said in the heat of the moment, knowing it would freak James out and scare him off. *Assuming he said any of those things in the first place.* James could be lying.

*Eh...*

James isn't the most eloquent, but he tried. He admitted to screwing up. He apologized—several times. He feels awful about what he did, and he was scared to tell me what Ice said. But he was at least willing to talk.

That's not quite the experience I've had with Ice, who, while generally chatty and charismatic, managed to turn side-stepping questions into an art. *What is he hiding from me?*

*Ugh...*

It is way too early for this kind of stress. I sit up and roll the throw blanket into a ball in my lap.

James is still passed out. I don't think he's shifted since I last checked. At least he got some sleep out of this deal. It seemed like he needed it.

*I wonder...* How does he really feel?

Does it not matter? Is it not important?

With a sigh, I set the blanket aside and check my phone. *Of course, it won't turn on.* The battery must have died overnight.

I leave the bed. I stand in front of the window and look out over the gravel lot. Grey clouds fill the sky. Rain falls, constant but slow and gentle with little wind shifting the tops of the trees.

The storm is passing.

*Great.*

I turn away.

Should I wake James up now? If we leave early enough, Ice might still be asleep when I get there. I could stay and have him drive me home when he wakes up.

*Or I could just grab my bag and go.*

I cross the room. Standing in front of the recliner, I reach out to touch James' arm, but I hesitate. My hand falls back to my side.

Despite his awkward, dead sleep and the dark circles beneath his eyes. Despite the myriad of partially healed injuries across the right half of his face, the faint bruise on his jaw, and his black eye and slightly crooked nose, James is very much an immortal, and still blessed with the gift of conventional attractiveness.

I thought he was cute when I first saw him at the mall too.

But he's somehow different from the other immortals I've met. His features are softer. His cheeks hold a touch of roundness. He's more down-to-earth, less refined, and lacks an immortal's signature heightened focus and deliberate ease.

Is it because he's defective? Because he didn't grow up with the privilege "normal" immortals have? Is it his low opinion of himself? The fact he views himself as an outsider?

*Or because he simply doesn't take care of himself?*

Whatever it is, something about James strikes me as more human—more approachable and relatable. There's something less performative and more…authentic about him.

*Ah—*

My breath catches as I notice my heart beating faster than it should. *You are not supposed to be checking him out, Jayde!* At this rate, the existence of immortals will turn me into Rose.

*Stop being so weird.*

"James." He doesn't react, so I tap him on the shoulder. "Hey, wake up."

With a small start, he opens his uninjured eye. "Oh, good," he breathes. "You're still here."

I cross my arms. "Where else would I be?"

"Yesterday could have been a fever dream," he says, still blinking away the sleep as he sits up straight.

"Right… Anyway, can we go now?"

"Yeah, sure." He yawns and stretches his arms over his head, popping a few vertebrae in the process. "What time is it?"

I shrug and mention that my phone died, so he retrieves his phone from the depths of the recliner. His expression blanks as he stares at the screen with some level of disappointment.

"Ah…" He glances up with a pained smile. "The first time I sleep for more than a couple hours in days, and you wake me up at 6AM? Can't you wait?"

It's that early? *Oops.*

"I've been up for at least an hour," I say.

"Whatever. It's fine."

He leaves the chair to stretch more. He surely needs it, especially if his head was at that angle the entire night.

I walk back to the bed, where I sit and scrape partially dried mud off the sides of my boots. I can try to scrub them properly when I get home, but it's not good. They might be a lost cause.

*And I just bought them...*

"It's better if we go early," I say with a sigh. "If Ice is asleep, there's no chance of him seeing you."

"That's fair."

If Ice is asleep, all I have to do is grab my bag and walk out.

But the storm is over. The rain is easing up.

*Will he be asleep?*

I give up on cleaning my boots and put them on as they are, looking up as James casts a nervous glance from across the room.

"What will you do after?" he asks.

"Go home, I guess."

He shrugs on his dark jacket while I gather my things from beside the bed. My own jacket is still a little damp. It's not cold today, though, so I ball it up and tuck it under one arm.

*The River Sapphire.*

I put the necklace on. I don't turn into a cat, but I haven't been expecting to in a while.

After pulling my hair up into a messy bun, I join James near the door, and we walk downstairs in silence. I grab my umbrella from the coat rack in the vestibule, and we're ready to go.

I still have no idea what I'll do once I get to Ice's house, though.

Do I want to grab my bag without waking Ice up and have James drive me home? Do I want James to drop me off and leave, so I can talk to Ice without worrying about him getting caught?

Should I confront Ice at all? Could I without bringing James into it?

"Can we stop somewhere to eat?" I ask. "I'm hungry."

"Of course. Whatever you want."

*Good.* My empty stomach surely isn't helping my nerves.

I suggest we stop by a convenience store on the way. Something quick and easy, so we don't waste time.

James agrees. As the car rattles to life, he mutters, "God knows I could use some caffeine."

# fifty-three

We've been in Westbrooke for a while. At least fifteen minutes. We're procrastinating—sitting in James' car, idled on the curb a block down from the house. I finished my biscuits and gravy a few minutes ago. James is on his second energy drink.

He's clearly…*stressed.*

But there's nothing to worry about, right? It's fine if I leave. I already told them I planned to go home after the storm, and the storm is over, so…

I tear my eyes from the window to watch James again. He takes a drink, nests the can in the center console's broken cup holder, and returns one hand to the steering wheel.

After a long, quiet moment, he sighs and turns to me.

"You won't have trouble grabbing your stuff and coming right back out, will you? You know I can't afford to get caught around here again."

*Oh, jeez.*

"My duffel bag is in Ice's bedroom," I say slowly. "Everything is already packed up, but— What should I do if he's awake?"

He frowns and folds his arms over the steering wheel. "You told him you were staying at a friend's house, right? Just say your friend will drive you home. He won't want to come out in the rain, anyway."

"Maybe…"

*Will that work?*

Glancing down, I bite my lip.

Ice didn't seem to mind when I first mentioned wanting to head home after the storm blew over, but he did kiss me to keep me from leaving the last time I considered it. What if he gets suspicious? What if I say the wrong thing? What if he doesn't want me to leave right away for some reason?

Night said he's scared of losing me.

*What does that even mean?*

James sighs. "Just… Whatever you do, you better not tell him I'm the *friend* parked out here."

"Well, obviously."

"I'm serious," he says. "Don't even let him leave the hallway. If he sees me, or my car, it's over. I will take off without you."

*That's fine. I wouldn't expect anything else.*

"Are you sure you don't want to just drop me off and go?"

He stares at me with a strange murkiness. "I'm already here, aren't I? I can take you home."

*Fine.*

James pulls forward until we're stopped in front of the Monroe family home. I fumble with the manual crank to roll the window down, and I stare out into the light rain.

The house is so normal—just a normal house on a quiet street in an expensive gated community.

Night's blue sedan isn't parked out front, and the awareness of being in James' car where hers usually sits bothers me. I hope it's in the garage.

*No.* Stop thinking like that.

I shouldn't be nervous. I have nothing to worry about. Night told me I'd always be welcome here, and Ice is my friend. I trust him. But a voice echoes in the back of my head:

*What if he's home alone?*

*What if it's just the two of you?*

A shiver runs down my spine.

The image of blood dripping from my fingers. The sharp crack of shattering glass. I can't escape the barrage of awful images from my nightmare. And, suddenly, *I do not want to step foot inside that house.*

This is ridiculous.

I spent a lot of time with Ice this summer, just the two of us. It never mattered whether we were in public or at his house or my cottage, I never once felt unsafe while I was with him.

*But now...* After sitting in James' car for so long, watching the house through the window, my apprehension only grows.

I'm second-guessing myself. I'm overthinking it.

I hate feeling this way, but I'm not convinced he trusts me anymore—assuming he trusted me to begin with. The cool undertones in his voice when we spoke last night shook my faith a little.

*Did he realize I was lying?*

Is he inside, waiting for me to show up? Is he planning to call me out? Ask where I went sneaking off to yesterday? Is he upset? Angry?

*Stop.*

Ice couldn't possibly know where I've been or that it had anything to do with James. *Though, if he did…*

*Ugh. Calm down.*

"Don't worry," James says, failing to sound at all reassuring. "I'll be right out here, ready to take off when you are."

I nod. *Okay, I can do this.* I unbuckle my seatbelt, give myself no choice but to return by shoving my purse and damp jacket underneath the passenger seat, and open the door.

"Thanks for the ride. I'll be as quick as I can."

My hand pushes the door shut, but I don't move from the curb. The soft, cool rain raises goosebumps on my arms. James watches me through the open window. He still looks wildly nervous, but he offers me a thumbs-up.

I force a smile. Then I turn away and steel myself for the walk up to the front door. Water splashes beneath my boots. The house looms before me. My hand touches the doorknob.

It's locked.

*Huh.*

If Ice is expecting me, why would he lock the front door? I mean, they rarely lock the doors even at night, but it's almost 8AM. There's no reason for the door to be locked. Unless—

*Is anyone home?*

I raise a hand to knock but drop it before my knuckles contact the door. *No. Wait—* I take the candy-striped house key out of my wallet's coin pocket.

*Night's timing was a coincidence, right?*

Shaking my head, I unlock the ornate front door. I return the key to my wallet, step through the door, and scan the great room.

I'm alone.

The lights are off. I hear no voices. No TV sounds from the den. No muffled music emanating from Smoke's bedroom. There's only the soft hum of the central AC and the gentle rain falling on the pavement behind me.

I close the door and glance out the bay window.

James' conspicuously dirty, off-white car idles on the curb outside. He's leaned against the steering wheel and watching the house through the rolled-down passenger window.

*Alright. Here I go.*

I turn away and venture further into the house. The air smells faintly of lemon as I cross into the den. Without the thick blackout curtain covering it, the sliding glass door floods the empty room with light.

I catch my reflection in the mirror. *Ugh.* I let my hair down and run my fingers through it to work out the worst of the tangles.

Then I glance at Smoke's bedroom door. *Is he asleep?* I hate to think he might be gone. If he is, Night's probably out too. He's never left the house without his sister in all the time I stayed here.

*Great.*

It's early, though, and it's still raining.

As I peer down the dimly lit hallway, I find myself hoping that Ice is out with the twins. Maybe they went somewhere for breakfast. If he felt more energetic this morning, Night could have talked him into it. It's possible.

*Unlikely, but possible.*

I flip the hall light on to lift the darkness, but I still pause in front of the bedroom door. *Sharp, blue eyes on a placid face.* My breath catches, my hand hovering over the doorknob.

*Are you here? Are you awake?*

Why am I so nervous?

He can't be nearly as bad as James thinks. I don't believe it.

Sure, Ice hurt him, but it was an overreaction. He was pissed. He got carried away, took it too far, and said some stupid things to someone he was desperate to hurt. James told me that Ice likes to talk shit. That's all it was. James shouldn't have been here in the first place.

But Ice was so calm after, with cool hatred smoldering in his eyes, and he asked me to pretend it never happened. *He wants to ignore everything that makes him look bad.*

Am I imagining things in hindsight? Misremembering details?

Considering how flustered I was after he kissed me, and the shock of seeing James, maybe I… Maybe talking to James only made things worse? Maybe I'm confused.

*Just open the door.*

My fingers brush the doorknob, and a familiar anxiety crashes over me. The sensation of being watched. A weight pressing on my chest. The feeling that something isn't quite right.

*A pulse of searing pain, and a flash of white light. Drowning in hot, sticky blood as it fills my lungs. Wide, amber eyes. James' pale face, silently calling out.*

*Ice behind me.*

No. *Stop—* I hold my head with my free hand, desperate to banish the unwelcome images.

Ice is my friend. I'm only leaving because I told Rose I would go home after the storm ended. Well, the storm is over. The rain will clear soon. And I know now that James is more pathetic than dangerous, so it's time to leave. I have no more excuses to stay here and keep worrying Rose.

That's it.

*Isn't that it?*

Ugh. I'm such a child.

Thoroughly fed up with myself, I turn the knob and push the door open. But I freeze in the doorway.

"Hey. Where were you last night?"

"Uh—"

From where he sits at the desk, Ice's posture appears casual, but his expression is unreadable. Maybe a little cold. Maybe a little guarded. The ceiling light is off, but the curtains are drawn open, and bright blue eyes bore into me from halfway across the room, full of questions.

You're imagining things, Jayde.

He's irritated because of the rain and annoyed that I up and vanished for a day. That's understandable, right? Anything else is James' anxiety rubbing off on me. I'm jumping to conclusions and seeing things that aren't there because of what he told me. *Because I can't stop wondering what face Ice made when he hurt James and said those things about me.*

*Right?*

Not that it matters. I'm too nervous to say much of anything, let alone come up with a convincing lie on the spot. I can barely meet his gaze for more than an instant.

"Where were you?" he asks again.

"Oh, um, I was at a friend's house. Like I said on the phone?"

"A friend's house," he says. "Right."

*My duffel bag is right there—*

Ice studies me carefully. Curious. Alert. No longer under the spell of storm-induced lethargy. His focus pauses near my feet, and my heart stops.

My boots, and the ankles of my jeans, are still stained by mud.

*How could I forget something so obvious?*

I told him I took the bus into town—which is partially true—but anyone with functional eyeballs and any sense could tell I spent more than a reasonable length of time trekking through the rain.

*Shit.*

This was stupid. This whole plan was stupid. But I already lied. I set myself up for this. I walked right into it. And James is outside, sitting in his car. *With my purse!* I should have brought my stuff in and told him to leave without me. I shouldn't have stayed the night at the manor. I—

*What should I do?*

Forcing my panic down, I expand upon my original story. A friend I met at RCC. We went to a few parties with Rose during the school year. Someone who just got back into town a couple days ago and was looking for someone to hang out with. I was bored, I saw her post on FaceSpace, and I thought it would be fun. *Blah, blah, blah.*

Ice listens for a minute before he raises a hand to stop me.

"Jayde, please."

He stands from his chair, sending my nervous heart into a

frenzy. My eyes dart around the room, keeping track of him. And the exact location of my bag. And the empty den at the end of the hallway.

"I, uh—"

Forget my stuff. Forget the truth.

I want to get the hell out of here *now*, but I can't seem to move anymore. My feet are glued to the floor. My body suddenly weighs a million pounds. And Ice closes the distance between us.

He looks down on me, standing only a foot away.

*Why am I so afraid?*

I need to stop thinking about what James said. I need to stop thinking about the fear in his eyes or the scabs and bruises on his face or the dried blood on the underside of his pillow.

*You're freaking yourself out.*

*Stop. Thinking.*

Ice flashes an easy smile—one I've seen many times. "What do you say we forget yesterday, and you come inside?"

*Forget? No.*

I shake my head. The pit in my stomach grows, and bitter bile rises in my throat, but I can't ignore it.

I can't ignore any of this anymore.

The thin, uncomfortable smile that doesn't quite touch his cold, sharp eyes. The weight of James' guilt when he told me what Ice said. Knuckles oozing fresh blood. A cool voice betraying anger. The blank look in his eyes the first time he asked me to forget.

Even if I wanted to—even though part of me still wishes I

could—I cannot forget what I've seen and heard. I cannot pretend that none of it happened. I'm done pretending.

So, what should I do now?

Who should I believe?

*Who can I trust?*

"I—" I take a step back, laughing nervously. "Can I just… grab my bag real fast?"

"You want to leave now?"

Surprise flashes across his face. Then, like the flip of a switch, his expression chills. Narrowed eyes glance away, and he frowns. Smiling again, not even a half a second later, his eyes flick up to meet mine.

He laughs—the sound soft and low. "Goddamn it, Jayde. Why would you do this to me?"

"Do what?" I ask, my mouth dry.

I take another step, but he keeps pace.

"What did he say to you?"

"Who?" I squeak.

My chest tightens again. *A flash of unexpected panic in wide, blue eyes. A strong hand grabbing me by the wrist. Something that really happened. Something that wasn't a dream.*

But how does he know?

*Doesn't matter.* I need to get out of here.

I tear my eyes from his stifling gaze. I look down the hall, into the den. *Could I make it?* If I ran, could I make it outside? To the front door? To the bay window?

*If James saw me before he saw Ice, maybe—*

"Don't mess with me," he says, a hard edge to his otherwise

level voice. "I know you met with James behind my back, but I'm willing to overlook it and give you another chance."

I look back at him by mistake, and I don't like what I see. Head tipped. A soft smile. Vacant eyes. It's upsetting and familiar, but…*worse, somehow.*

"You trust me, right?" he asks.

*I did. I really did, but—*

I take another step back. He matches it.

"You fell in love with me, right?"

*What should I do?*

*What can I do?*

*I should have realized—*

*I should have never come back here.*

Ice holds out a hand, offering it to me, his mild expression a mockery of kindness. "So, Jayde, what do you say? I can pretend you never saw James if you can forget everything he told you."

*What James…told me?*

What does he think James told me? What did he think James told me before—on the Fourth of July when he asked the same question with even more alarm in his eyes?

*What the hell does James know about Ice?*

A heavy chill washes over me. A sense of tragic understanding. A deep, gnawing anxiety. *Fear.* And I know I need to find a way out of here. I can't stay with Ice another second.

I shake my head, drawing my hands close to my chest.

"No," I say. The words waver. "I told Rose I would go home. I just want to go home."

His smile vanishes. Frustration replaces it. His eyes burn with a desperate savagery. He plants his hands on my shoulders, and I freeze under the weight of them.

"Why would you go to him now?" he asks, his voice rising. "What did that pathetic little shit say about me?"

My heart pounds in my aching chest.

Surely, he's close enough to hear it.

I want to turn away—*to run away*—but I can't. I'm frozen in place and locked into eye contact, painfully aware of our proximity. His firm touch. Short nails digging into my shoulders through my thin sleeves.

"You're scaring me," I say.

"I scare you? Oh."

His expression is wiped blank. The anger fades from his eyes, and the line of his mouth softens. He looks…tired. Then his hands slide down my arms, his warm fingers brushing my elbows before they finally fall away.

I bite the inside of my cheek, fighting the moisture that collects in my eyes.

"You don't have to answer," he says. "There's no point. You're just like James. He can't lie when he's scared either, and I don't particularly care to hear you try again. It was depressing."

"Can I go now?"

*Stop talking. Please stop talking.*

"Go now? Wait— No way. Did he come with you?" A wicked grin splits his face, crinkling the corners of his wide eyes. "Don't you dare tell me that James Reid is outside my house right now."

I say nothing, but I finally manage to avert my gaze.

"Holy shit, Jayde." He laughs, a bitter sound, and massages

the pale, pink scars on his knuckles. "How stupid can he be—coming here now? Do you know what I said to him? Do you have any idea what he looked like when I let him run away?"

*That's enough. I don't care what you have to say anymore. I don't want to hear another word. I can't...*

I glance over my shoulder. A single backward step will leave me trapped between Ice and the wall.

*So, how can I escape?*

He sneers down at me as he speaks, but he's not distracted. I can tell he's watching me like a hawk, taking in my every movement. Following my aside glances. What my hand is doing. The subtle shifting of my weight. Everything.

Even so, I look toward the den again.

*I don't think I can make it.*

How could I outrun him when James didn't stand a chance with a decent head start? But my body begs me to try. My pounding heart. Panicked lungs. Tense muscles. With every ounce of my being, I want to run, and *this is my last chance.*

One more step, and my back will touch the wall. *Only one step.*

But I can't.

*He's too fast.*

"It's sad," he says, and it sounds like he means it. "I gave you a choice. I didn't have to do that, you know, and you still chose wrong. After everything I've done for you—"

The slightest movement in the corner of my eye sets me off, and I lose it. My body leaps into action, turning. I try to push past him and run for the den.

He stops me as I take my first step.

A hand catches me by the arm. A momentary crushing pain, his grip far too tight. He drags me back, and my shoulder hits the wall. *Hard.*

I cry out. He leans in close to shush me.

“You’re fine,” he says with an easy laugh. “We don’t want your new *friend* to think you’re in trouble, do we?”

*Am I not in trouble right now?*

I bite my cheek, my hands balled into fists.

But I can’t do anything.

With one hand wrapped around my wrist and the other planted on the wall, Ice has me pinned. I can’t get away. If I tried, I’d only hurt myself. I’m trapped, locked in tense eye contact with the most dangerous person I’ve ever met.

Mischievous eyes. A wide smirk. Relaxed posture.

He’s in control, and he knows it.

*I could call for help, but—*

He glances aside. “Considering this most recent development, I am certainly not bored with you, Jayde. Yes, you’ve turned out to be more of a nuisance than I anticipated—what with James’ unexpected involvement and all—but it’s interesting all the same. And, you see…” He pauses, and his expression softens as his eyes meet mine again. “I rather like you.”

*Why? Why say that now?*

I stare into the fabric of his grey button-up.

For the first time since I met Ice, I wish he would shut up. The familiar, honeyed sweetness of his voice isn’t nearly enough to mask this new condescension or the clear indifference behind his words. It's like scaring the shit out of me doesn't bother him at all.

*I feel sick.*

"As for James, I was thinking I may kill him."

My eyes dart up to his face. "*What?*"

"Don't tell me you care." He laughs before releasing my arm. "I'd be doing us all a favor, really."

I rub my roughed-up skin. "Why are you doing this?"

"Why?"

He frowns and glances around the otherwise empty hallway. Then he refocuses on me with lazy eyes and a crooked grin that makes my skin crawl.

"Well, why not?" he asks. "You listened to him, didn't you? You sought him out behind my back and dragged him here, *to my house*. James is an idiot, but you aren't innocent in this either. Don't forget that you got yourself into this mess. You signed that paperwork."

*Boy am I regretting that decision.*

"I'm in too deep, Jayde. I'm too invested in you." His voice is level, conveying both sincerity and contempt. *But for whom? For what?* "As your sponsor, relinquishing you to another man without consequence doesn't sit right with me. I don't want you to suffer, but, ah…"

*But what? What does that mean?*

"You want to go home so badly. Very well."

My back presses against the wall as he leers at me. His eyes glint, fierce and cold, and he smiles.

"One last thing, before you go—"

# fifty-four

Ice takes a single step back.

A knife appears out of nowhere.

One moment, it didn't exist—his raised hand was open and empty. The next, something was grasped in that same hand, and time slowed to a crawl as I recognized it as a folded pocketknife.

A mottled, silvery blade flicks out of the handle at the press of a button. My arms shoot up as if by instinct. The knife completes its downward arc, and time returns to normal as a sharp pain scores my forearm. I slam a hand over it, but the burning doesn't stop, and a thin trail of warm red oozes toward my elbow.

*What?*

I look up.

A weak smile. Glazed, blue eyes watch the clean blade but quickly sharpen, and I recoil as our eyes meet. All muscles tense. I can't move.

He laughs. Then he swings the knife a second time.

My other arm deflects the blade, and I scream—at least, I think I do. Several drops of bright red blood splatter the cream carpet. *My blood. On the floor.*

Another flash of movement.

Without thinking, I shield my face with my hands. A thread of fire turns into a dull throb, and my eyes snap open. Dark blood pools in my palm. More drips onto the floor from both elbows.

*This can't be real.*

*Am I dreaming? Is this another nightmare?*

"I pictured this differently in my mind," Ice says. His clear, level voice cuts through the static buzz, but it still doesn't feel real.

*This isn't possible.*

*The blood dripping from my hand.*

*The blood staining the carpet.*

"Oh, well."

*No.*

I turn to run. The den at the end of a tunnel. The light from the sliding glass door. The scent of blood overtaking the faint citrus.

A hand catches my shirt and slams me against the wall again. The back of my head connects. My vision goes black. My arms flail uselessly.

*I'm gonna throw up.*

Something hits my chest, snapping me back to awareness. The blade sliced clean through my shirt and the camisole underneath. The River Sapphire is fine, but my bra is exposed, and blood blooms along the knife's diagonal path.

Eyes watering furiously, I bring my bleeding arms over my chest. I say, "Stop," but my voice is so weak and soft I hardly recognize it.

And Ice does not stop.

Instead, seemingly unimpressed, he grabs ahold of my arm. He squeezes. *Squeezing. Squeezing.* Fingernails dig into raw flesh, the pressure like hot metal forced beneath broken skin.

*No—*

Desperate. Frantic. I try prying his hand away, but my right hand is unsteady and slick with blood. I can't gain any traction. Touching his hand only makes the pain worse. Only makes his grip tighter.

*This is impossible.*

I search his face. For an explanation. For help. For mercy. But he flashes a crooked smile and meets my gaze with passive eyes before he glances down the hallway.

*James.*

Is he still out there? Waiting for me? Is he wondering where I am? *If I called for help... Would he come? Or would he run?*

Ice's hand makes a mess of my injured arm. Tearing pain. Red blood on my hands. My chest. My arms. It drips from my elbow and soaks into the cuff of Ice's shirt.

*How did it come to this?*

*I just wanted to go home.*

Hot, bitter tears fill my eyes. I squeeze them shut, forcing the beads of moisture out.

*This has to stop. I'm sorry.*

Drawing my arms as close as I can, I cry out for help. I scream as loud as possible. I beg Ice to stop, and I call James by name, hoping he can hear me from his car on the curb. Hoping he won't drive away at the first sign that something went wrong.

Ice chuckles, so soft it's almost a sigh, and I fall quiet.

"Good," he says, finally releasing my arm.

*I'm free.*

A dull, aching throb and a strange sense of relief replace the sharp pain. I slide down the wall until I'm sat on the carpet, and I look at nothing in particular. The blood on the floor. The space between Ice's legs. Through the bedroom door behind him. The corner of my duffel bag, on the floor at the foot of his bed.

Then down the hallway.

*If he wants to hurt you, I'm sorry. There wasn't anything else I could do. There's no one else here, and I need help. So... Please.*

My hands—

*Oh, god.*

Warm, wet crimson coats my arms and chest, leaking from wounds I can't make out through the blood. Staining my shirt. Dripping onto my jeans. So much. *Too much.* The metallic tang assaults my nose, sticking in the back of my throat. A bleeding hand presses against a bleeding arm. Pain flares in both.

*In the awful darkness as hot, sticky blood fills my lungs. Choking me. The compulsion to claw at my throat.*

My lungs are clear, but I gasp for each breath.

*The dream—*

My vision goes dark for a second.

Then Ice kneels in front of me. I remember where I am, and remember what he's done, and I blink to clear my vision. Our eyes lock. Hands cup my cheeks, but I can't move.

*He's still holding the knife.*

I feel the cool metal near my eye. Light glints off the blade in my periphery. *And I still can't breathe.*

"I never wanted to hurt you, Jayde. Not like this. Truly, I'm as surprised as you must be." His voice is strange, gentle and pitying, but his overall expression is mild and neutral.

*I don't understand.*

"Please," I gasp between breaths. "Stop."

"Haven't I?" he asks.

His frown grows more pronounced. Vacant eyes look past me, as though he can see straight through to the wall behind my head. He looks at me like I don't exist—like I never have.

And the sharp edge of a blade brushes against my cheekbone.

"It's remarkable." His voice is so soft and breathy, it's almost a whisper. "I thought I would feel something, but I don't. I don't feel a damn thing."

With a sigh, his eyes refocus on me, cool and indifferent. The blade presses into my cheek, pushed by his thumb. Threatening to break skin. I hold my breath.

*I can't—*

Finally, a noise breaks the tension. *The front door.* The crack of a doorknob hitting drywall.

The slow increase of pressure on the knife pauses, but the blade doesn't leave my cheek. I open my eyes to find Ice staring down the hall with wide, expectant eyes.

When he looks to me again, I burst into tears. But he smiles and leans back. As he moves away, his hands—and the knife—leave my face unharmed.

James calls my name from the great room.

Ice chuckles, his eyes narrowing, and he stands as James

skids to a stop at the end of the hallway. I can't make out his expression through my tears and the hair falling into my eyes, but his voice and guarded posture is telling.

*He's afraid.*

"James Reid." Ice's voice is conversational as he wipes his bloodied hand off on his jeans. "I seem to recall I promised to kill you if I caught you sneaking around here again."

James doesn't respond. Then I hear a sharp inhale. He takes an awkward step back. A physical recoil. I can't see, but I imagine his face twisting in horror, the same as in my dream.

"Oh, god— What did you do?"

What do I look like to him? *On the floor. Slumped against the wall. Covered in blood. Can he even tell I'm still alive?*

Murmuring reassurance, I lift my head and brush the hair out of my face with the back of my hand. Ice looks down on me with a grimace—a mask of disgust. I ignore him.

I need to go. I'm ready to go home.

*Can I stand in this condition? Can I still walk?*

I press both hands to the wall. They slip down the smooth surface as I drag myself to my feet. My legs tremble. Standing takes more concentration than it should, but I…

*I think I can do this.*

Then James says my name again—a weak, despondent sound that I hate more than anything.

I wipe the tears blurring my eyes. Warm liquid tracks across my face—whether it's blood or tears, who really cares? At least I'm steady enough to look up from the smears of red my hands left on the wall.

James' attention flicks between me and Ice. Eyes wide. Face pale. He still hasn't moved from the far end of the hallway.

*This is my fault.*

I should have listened to him. I should have been more careful. I should have said, "Screw my duffel bag," and gone home without bothering.

"I'm fine." I force a smile. "Honestly. It doesn't…even hurt."

My hand falls away from the wall. I take my first step, but I glance at Ice as I pass by. Our eyes meet. *A mistake.* His glare is hostile. Animalistic.

He says something, his voice rising.

And the knife hits hard, slicing through my shirt and into my side. *This is bad.* I cry out, but I don't fall back to the floor. Somehow, I'm still standing.

I lean against the wall and struggle to catch my breath.

*Wow. It stings.*

My shirt grows damp and heavy. The warm, wet fabric sticks to my skin. *This is very bad.* But I don't look. I don't have time. I need to get out of here, so I can get help.

Forcing each movement, I continue down the hallway.

Ice doesn't stop me, but James doesn't do anything either. He merely watches in mute horror, tracking me with wide eyes. Frozen in place as I stumble closer.

I can't believe he came inside to find me. Even if he heard me scream, I'm not sure I could have done the same if I were half as afraid as I was a moment ago. And, after what he said in the car…

I stand in front of him for a second, unsteady and wavering.

*Well... Is Ice done? Are we okay? Can I go home now?*

I open my mouth to speak without knowing what question to ask, but my legs buckle under my weight before I figure it out.

*Oh.*

James drops to his knees to catch me before I hit the floor. A hand brushes my injured side, but he quickly retracts it and pales further, his eyes locked on the blood staining his fingers.

"Why?" he asks blankly.

I cough. "So much for…taking off without me."

He says nothing, but he bares his teeth and turns his attention on Ice, who is still standing outside the open bedroom door. After adjusting his grip on me—careful not to touch my side again—he stands up.

My head spins at the altitude change. I close my eyes.

*I feel warm. And...strangely light.*

"Why would you do this?" he asks, his voice shaking. "Why go this far? Why hurt her?"

"It's nothing," Ice replies with a short laugh. "I simply felt damaged goods would better suit someone like yourself. Consider it a favor, James."

"You're sick! What the hell did she do to deserve this?"

Jostled by James' movement, I open my eyes.

He's still yelling at Ice, who calmly counters everything he says. I don't hear the exact words, but James is clearly upset. *I'm upset.* Angry tears form in his eyes as he bares his teeth in response to whatever was just said.

"She trusted you!"

Ice's cold voice comes clearly: "Get out of my house."

James steps back, some of the tension leaving his shoulders. He glances down at me, frowning as our eyes meet. His brows furrow, and he looks up and away.

Then he turns to leave.

*Wait—*

I crane my neck to see down the hallway. Ice is still standing there, watching quietly. But I look past him.

"My stuff?" my voice asks.

James shakes his head. "We have to go."

*Why did I say that?* I'm bleeding to death, and I asked about my stuff? *Ugh... What is wrong with me?*

My neck threatens to stop supporting my head. I hold onto James' dark jacket and rest my cheek against his chest. He's warm. His heart races through the fabric. I stare at my hand, mere inches from my face.

*Why is there so much blood?*

My weight shifts in James' arms, and I open my eyes again. A drop of cold water lands on my face. When did we get outside? *I don't remember passing through the great room,* but we're beside the car now. His hand trembles as he tries to open the back door without dropping me.

"Can you stand?" he asks.

My vision tracks over the car slowly to meet his concerned gaze. He wasn't able to open the door. I mumble something in agreement, and he carefully sets me on my feet.

I lean against the side of the car and glance back to the house. Ice stands in the doorway across the small front yard. I can't make out his expression. Only the dark red blood staining the sleeve of his grey shirt. Then he turns away and closes the door, and he's gone.

*Will this be the last time I see him?*

"Here," James says, resting a hand on my shoulder.

With his help, I crawl into the backseat, tracking red on everything I touch. I don't bother with the seatbelt. I situate my legs and hold my hands over the wound on my side. My shirt is saturated near the tear. A red stain on the pale fabric seat where I touched it. My body aches, pulsing with an uncomfortable warmth.

James shuts the door.

Footsteps race around the car, and he hops into the driver's seat. He curses under his breath. Punches something. My attention leaves my side, wandering toward the front seat, where the bottom of his fist is still in contact with the top of the steering wheel.

"We're going to the ER," he says, his voice low.

I echo half of what he said as a question.

If he answers, I don't hear.

The last time I went to the ER, I was young. I had pneumonia. I collapsed in the cafeteria at school. I barely remember it.

*Smoke could heal this, couldn't he?*

Where are the twins? Why weren't they here?

The car sputters to life. Everything grows fuzzy—or… *fuzzier.* The sounds. The sights. The artificial lemon from the air freshener mixing with the coppery blood.

My hands tremble from the effort of maintaining pressure on my side. But I think it looks worse than it is. Somehow, I know I'll be okay. *Somehow.*

Even so, time passes slowly. Too slowly.

I feel like I'll wake up any moment—like it was all a dream. Another crazy nightmare. I'll touch the tears on my cheeks and run my hands over smooth, undamaged skin. I'll breathe and drink some water and—

If I woke up, where would I be?

*The manor house? Ice's bed? Home?*

Maybe I died when I hit my head on the Fourth of July. Maybe I've been in a coma, imagining everything that could have played out since then.

*Oh, good god.*

I stare out the window and watch the blurry world outside. My eyes don't register the buildings or streets. I feel like I'm here—covered in blood in the back of James' car—but I don't feel like I'm anywhere. It feels like I don't exist. Like I'm not real.

*Like none of this is real.*

A sound startles me to alertness.

I open my eyes as James says something I can't quite make out. Our surroundings seem greyer than when I last looked. Are we downtown?

*Did I lose more time?*

James continues speaking as he drives with one hand on the steering wheel, but I can't hear clearly. I make out one word. Half a word. A single syllable. But I don't understand. I don't think he's talking to me, anyway.

Is he on the phone?

*I can't tell.*

Suddenly, I'm outside, hobbling along with James' help. A

raindrop lands on my nose. My legs feel like jelly. Then I'm standing inside a brightly lit room—well, partially standing.

*And I still have no idea what's going on.*

We've stopped moving, so I lean on James for support. I look around, trying to soak in my new surroundings. Plastic chairs and pale counters. Several people sitting or otherwise wandering about. There are a few posters on the walls. It's familiar, somehow.

I look to James again.

*Oh.*

He's talking with someone. The woman, her brown eyes on me, glances away before replying, an urgent worry etched into her soft features.

What were we doing?

*Wait, is this the hospital?*

"I don't know her last name, okay?" James says, his voice taut. "Just look at her! What does any of that matter right now?"

*Oh. My name. Right.*

My hand falls from where it held onto James' jacket and reaches for my pocket. I feel for my wallet, but it slips from my fingers and lands on the tile floor at my feet. A few droplets of red follow the wallet, joining several others on the tile.

*The contrast of bright red on stark white—*

I gasp as tears spill from my eyes.

James tenses beside me. Someone kneels to pick up my wallet. I don't see their face, but their voice is kind. They tell me to calm down and take deep breaths.

My chest heaves, and I cry harder.

James makes a sound, takes the wallet from whoever picked

it up, and continues his conversation with the person behind the counter.

"Palmer, I guess," he says. "Jayde Palmer. Here's her ID."

A woman in green rests her hand on my shoulder. She asks if I'd like to sit. She has a chair—a wheelchair—but I swat her hand away and turn to James. I grab ahold of his jacket. The scent of dust and rain and blood lingers on the fabric as my cheek brushes against it.

I feel his hand on my back. *Warm.* When I can no longer stand on my own, he picks me up.

Still crying, my vision blurry, I cling to James' arm. He carries me down a hallway. We stop in a bright, square room with no windows. We're not alone, and I listen to a conversation I can't seem to comprehend.

Two people I don't know ask me to lie down. When I don't respond or comply, they try to pry me away from James.

He says it's alright. I need to stay. I should go with them.

I protest vehemently, but no amount of shrieking or thrashing about stops the three of them from ushering me onto a crinkly bed.

"Sorry," James says.

*This is unacceptable.*

Someone holds me down. I sob while my shirt is cut away with a pair of scissors. The three or four people in the room talk to each other in clear voices I still can't make out.

*Are they asking questions?*

*Why can't I understand them?*

*Is James still here?*

Something sticks into my arm—like a bee sting—and I stop struggling. I don't know how long I lie there. People continue messing with me, but I stop fighting. Then the room falls quiet and dark, and time fades away.

# fifty-five

A noise. An unnatural beeping.

It's not loud, but it is annoying. I try to will the sound away, but nothing changes. The steady *beep…beep…beeping* continues.

*It's familiar somehow…*

Have I heard it somewhere before?

On TV, maybe?

I feel weird too. Almost like…*nothing.*

*Am I floating?*

No, but I can't feel my body.

*No.* That's not it either.

I can feel my body. I can even move it. My fingers flex. My foot shifts. I'm numb and tired, and my head feels like it's stuffed with cotton balls.

*That beeping isn't helping.*

I open my eyes only to be blinded by bright overhead lights. I shield my face with my hands, sensing a strange resistance as I move. After what feels like a full minute of blinking, my vision finally clears.

*My hands*— One is bandaged, covered in bright green medical wrap, with a plastic bracelet around the wrist. The other has a clip on the index finger. Past my hands, still partially shielding my eyes from the light—is a white, tiled ceiling.

*Beep…beep…beep…beep…beep…*

Oh.

I'm in the hospital.

*Right.*

Lowering my hands, I sit up. The bed's papery sheet crinkles loudly with my every movement. I look around. The room is small and clean and smells of sanitizer—definitely a hospital room. The analog clock above the door reads 12:48, but I can't tell whether it's day or night. There are no windows leading outside.

And I'm alone.

Though, I quickly locate the source of the beeping: a portable heart monitor set up beside the bed. Thin cords snake from beneath the collar of my hospital gown and connect the silver stickers on my chest to the machine, where my heart rate is displayed on a screen.

My right hand and both forearms are neatly bandaged. One arm is hooked up to an IV. The liquid inside the bag is clear, but I can't tell whether it's saline or pain medication. Maybe both?

What did they give me? Is that why I feel so strange?

My fingers brush the collar of the cotton hospital gown. A line of raised skin on my chest beneath the thin fabric. Thick gauze on my right side.

I push the pale, blue blanket that covered me from the waist down onto the floor. My jeans and boots are missing, along with my shirt and bra. Some kind of dark grit forms a crust beneath my fingernails, and reddish-brown flakes fall from my hair when

I run a trembling hand through it.

*Is this blood? Why is there so much?*

How did I get to the hospital, again?

*Why am I even in the hospital?* Where did these injuries come from? Why did seeing them not surprise me?

A mess of vague memories swirl in the deepest recesses of my mind, but what little I glean from them feels distant and muddled and unreal—like something out of a movie.

Did I stop by Ice's house? I've been staying there for a while. Since the Fourth of July, but… Where was I this morning?

*Wait—* I *was* at Ice's house. Was that yesterday? *I went out in the morning…and then…* I remember James—

*James.*

It comes back to me in a torrent of dark memories. A series of seemingly impossible images and snippets of scenes straight out of a nightmare. Flashes of pain. Hot blood soaking my shirt, dripping from my fingers and the marbled blade of a knife. Cold blue eyes. Someone else's racing heart.

*That wasn't a dream.*

Is James here? If I find him, I need to tell him I'm okay. I need to apologize for getting him involved.

*Please be one in the afternoon and not one in the morning…*

I glance around the room again, and my focus eventually lands on an observation window looking out into a hallway.

The window was previously empty, but someone stands outside now. *James.* He's with a doctor wearing a white coat. His face in profile is serious and anxious. He nods slowly as the doctor speaks to him. Then he nods with slightly more vigor, and they walk out of view toward the door.

A moment later, the door swings open.

James walks in after the doctor, and his eyes brighten when he sees me awake. He lets out a breath but says nothing and averts his eyes while the doctor acknowledges my consciousness with a short greeting. After a glance at the thick clipboard in his hand, he meets my gaze with a smile.

I manage to mirror it for a second—also relieved to be alive.

"Good news, Miss Palmer. You were a sight to behold when you arrived. We had to sedate you before we could clean your wounds and stitch you up, but all five lacerations were relatively superficial, and the blood loss wasn't extreme. I'm confident you'll make a full recovery, save for some minor scarring."

*Good news, right?*

James watches him intently and quietly, so I try my best to do the same—though I'm sure I'd be more upset if his voice weren't so disarmingly kind.

"Let's see…" He flips through a few pages on his clipboard. "You can take any over-the-counter NSAID for pain management. We gave you a sedative and IV morphine upon arrival, so you should be good to go until we get you discharged."

I make a soft noise in agreement.

"Though—" His eyes flick up to meet mine. "I do wonder how the two of you happened to meet."

*What?* I search his face for answers, and—

*Oh. Of course.*

The ER doctor is an immortal. A handsome, middle-aged man with dark blond hair, a neat beard, kind lavender eyes, and thick-rimmed glasses.

I look to James without answering, but he merely averts his eyes and stammers something unintelligible.

"You know better, James," he says with a sigh. "Of course, I'm aware this isn't your fault—let alone your doing. I know very well who Miss Palmer is."

*Does he, really?*

At this point, even I'm not entirely sure who I am anymore.

James' frown deepens, his eyes shadowed.

The doctor looks like he has more questions, but he leaves James alone and addresses me again, "As I said, none of your wounds were especially concerning, so you're free to leave today if you feel up to it."

When I nod, he removes a packet from his clipboard and goes over the discharge paperwork with me. A summary of my hospital visit. A page detailing proper wound care. A couple things I have to sign before I can go home.

It's a lot of words.

"A nurse will be in soon to remove the IV catheter and electrodes," he continues. "Let them know if you're ready to leave, and, please, give us a call if you have any issues using your hand. The cut wasn't deep, but there is some risk of lasting nerve damage."

I nod again despite having blanked on half of what he said the moment he mentioned nerve damage. He wishes me a good day, pats James on the shoulder, and steps out of the room.

James stares at the closed door for a moment. Then he turns and, after hesitating, scrambles to my bedside, where he plants himself in a wireframe chair. The dark jacket he wore this morning is missing, and dark stains blot the hem of his t-shirt and the front of his jeans.

*It was pretty bad, wasn't it?*

As his eyes soak in my current, less-than-ideal physical state, I can only hope I look better than I did when we first came in.

"How do you feel?" he asks. "Are you really okay?"

"I guess, but…I'm confused."

His brows furrow, concern flashing in his amber eyes. "Do you remember what happened? Ice pulled a knife on you."

"Yeah, um…" I massage my temple with my bandaged hand. "And you…saved me?"

"If you can call what I did saving you."

*What happened, exactly?*

James drove me to Ice's house. I drank chocolate milk. I was supposed to pick up my duffel bag and go home. I went inside the house. *But I can't remember what Ice said.* He attacked me —that much is obvious, and I vaguely remember it—but we talked for a while first.

*He pulled a knife on me. He…tried to kill me?*

That doesn't sound right.

*What did he say? I can't remember.*

When I glance up from my lap, James is still looking away. His clenched fists rest on the edge of the tall hospital bed. A fire burns in his eyes.

"I will never forgive him for this," he says.

*Oh—* I tap him on the arm. "Hey, I'll be fine. You heard the doctor, right? My injuries weren't serious."

"I know, but—"

He meets my gaze with tired, glassy eyes.

"I am so sorry," he says. "I never should've let you go in there alone. I should have realized something was wrong. I should have sucked it up and gone in with you. Or something. I can't believe—I just—"

Without thinking, I place my bandaged hand over his fist. "No. I'm fine. Really. You couldn't have possibly known he would do this."

"Still… I should've…"

He glances away, his jaw set.

"It's not your fault." But my voice falters, and I return my hand to my lap. "I know you were scared, so… Thanks for trying to help. And thanks for bringing me here."

"Yeah…"

The room falls relatively quiet. I listen to the electronic *beep...beep...beeping...* of the heart monitor, wishing a nurse would show up and free me from the sound already.

James' eyes track the path of the thin electrode wires from the collar of my hospital gown to the digital display on the machine.

"Hey," he says. "Something…bad might happen."

"What do you mean?"

I try to meet his eyes, but he doesn't look away from the heart monitor. The lines and numbers and symbols on the screen. After a beat of silence, unbroken only by the steady, electronic beeping, he looks back to me.

*Nervous. Uncomfortable.*

"What do you mean?" I ask again.

He takes a deep breath. "Okay. Dr. Corel told me earlier—"

Before he has the chance to finish, the door swings open across the room. He falls silent but doesn't turn to look as three men enter, accompanied by a member of hospital staff. The men wear dark blue uniforms with silver badges pinned to their collared shirts.

"James Reid," one says. "You need to come with us. We have a warrant for your arrest."

He flinches and lowers his head. "Damn it…"

*What?*

One officer says they need to bring him to the police station for questioning. Someone takes a step into the room—a heavy boot against tile—but my eyes remain fixed on James.

He glances over his shoulder. "Give me a second."

They don't come any further, even as James turns away from the door and leans closer to my bed with a grave expression. One eye is still bruised and bloodshot.

"Listen to me," he says.

I glance between him and the officers near the door.

"Hey," he breathes. "Don't tell anyone what happened this morning. Nothing about Ice. Nothing about *cats*. Don't tell these people anything. I know they're cops, but—"

He grimaces, stealing another glance at the men, who appear to be growing impatient.

"They're from RPD. *Human police.* Do you understand?"

I hear what he's saying, sure, but I don't understand what he means. Human police or not, what do they think he did? Why do they have a warrant for his arrest?

"Please," he stresses, his voice still low. "Forget about me. Go home. But, for your own sake, don't tell them anything."

With that, he stands from the chair, the metal feet squeaking against the tile. I grab the hem of his shirt in a feeble attempt to stop him, and he hesitates.

Guilt flashes in his eyes as he looks down at me.

"What's going on?" I ask.

"Sorry." He turns away with a strained smile. "I should have warned you, but I— I have to go. It'll be fine."

*Fine?*

My eyes water, but I force my fingers to release his shirt, and he crosses the room to meet up with the police officers at the door. They talk for a moment. I don't listen. Then the men escort James out.

The young orderly who led them here offers me a bleak, apologetic smile before she closes the door on her way out. And I'm alone. Again. Staring at the door and listening to the heart monitor's relentless beeping.

*Do the police think James did this? Why?*

No one asked me what happened. I was sedated. Asleep. No one talked to me about it at all. *This is crazy.* If anything, James is the reason I'm not still bleeding on the carpet in the hallway at Ice's house.

*So…how could this happen?*

**To be Continued in Borderline**

# Content Warning

This list includes potentially sensitive or upsetting topics and themes present, mentioned, or otherwise alluded to in Sidetracked (covering all four parts), so readers can make an informed decision prior to reading. Specific context is not included here, but be aware that this information may still be considered spoilers.

Mental illness (including anxiety, depression, and PTSD)
Suicidal ideation and references to suicide and self-harm
Trauma and abuse (mental, physical, and emotional)
Toxic relationships and toxic behaviors
Injury, blood, and physical violence
Guns and knives (including their use as weapons)
Hospitalization (including references to major surgery)
Prescription drug use (as directed by a physician)
Alcohol use and references to alcoholism
Sexually suggestive content (nothing too spicy)
Swearing and offensive language
Nausea and vomiting

Sidetracked contains **NO** sexual violence

As the author, I acknowledge that characters in Sidetracked display harmful and problematic behaviors. However, Sidetracked is a work of fiction, and is in no way meant to condone, promote, or glorify such problematic and toxic behaviors. My characters are heavily flawed and were not written to be viewed as role models.

www.ingramcontent.com/pod-product-compliance
Lightning Source LLC
Chambersburg PA
CBHW022234020726
47496CB00004B/892

*9781955240017*